A

DARK

FALL

SCARLETT DRAKE

For Milo, who was my real-life Fred.

A
DARK
FALL

PROLOGUE

I WANT TO FUCKING KILL HIM.

It's moments like this where I drift off and wonder what the fuck I did in a past life to deserve this shit. Where I drift off and wonder if, really, I'm supposed to be living some respectable life somewhere miles away from lying cunts like Eddie fucking Cartwright.

It may not be a respectable life, but I do maintain a certain level of respect. People respect me because the consequences of not respecting me are painful, loud, and very fucking bloody. So being respected is a consolation I'll live with for now. Until my real life comes walking through the door wondering where the fuck I've been for the past thirty years.

"I told you, Jay, I don't know where he is. I haven't seen him for weeks," Eddie says, not meeting my eye.

I take another deep breath. He's pale and sweating, which is down to the coke partly, but also down to the fact he's lying through his teeth.

"Yeah, yeah, I heard that, Ed, but it smells like bullshit to be honest." I glance over at Kev. He has a smirk on his face that would make your blood run cold. Not mine—I've seen it too many times for it to have any effect—but Eddie looks as if he's about to piss himself.

Kev has that effect on people. Built like a tank with hands that could bash in your skull without breaking a sweat. His typical expression is the kind that tells you everything you're afraid might happen is, in fact, about to happen. He's a violent fucking psychopath to be honest. But he's my best mate.

"Two weeks ago, he sent a text, said he was going to Spain. That's the last I heard from him."

I close my eyes on a sigh. I'm fucking tired. I hear Kev's knuckles crack, and I look back at Eddie who pales a bit more. Spain. Spain sounds perfect. I really need a vacation. And a new life. Yeah, a new life would be better.

Get on with it then. Why the fuck are you still taking Freddie's trash out for him?

"So, you *do* know where he is then. He's in Spain." I rub at my forehead, feeling totally knackered all of a sudden.

Eddie's shoulders drop, and he looks at the floor.

"Tell me something, Ed. Why would Tony go to Spain when he knows I'm looking for him? That Freddie's looking for him? When he owes Freddie fifty large? Why would he do that?"

I know why he'd do that. Eddie knows too. We're playing a game here. A game Eddie's shit at. I squeeze the bridge of my nose as the headache starts to creep in.

"Why don't you ask him that?" Eddie's voice is louder, braver. He thinks he's more in control of this situation than he actually is. Freddie wanted a bullet in him. Kev offered to do it. I talked them both down. Mainly because I don't find that kind of solution benefits anybody. It's a mess that needs cleaning up, and no one is any better off financially.

Kev moves forward to speak, his huge, muscular shoulders pulled back in a fighting stance. "And how do you suppose we ask him, Ed? You got a number for him over there? An address?" Kev barks, crossing the room to where Eddie's sitting on the dining chair. I can tell Kev wants to throttle him, and to be honest, I don't think I have the energy to stop him.

I pull a chair over and sit down facing Eddie, leaning forward on my knees. I rub my hands over my face a few times. I feel like slapping it a few times too, but it wouldn't look right in front of other people.

"Ed. Is Tony in Spain or not? It's getting late, and I got places I need to be, so let's stop fucking about, yeah? Try telling us the truth now, would you? Because if I have to come back here after I find out you've been bull-shitting me, you won't like how we sort that," I say, trying for my reasonable voice. It takes less effort than the other one.

"I'd never bullshit you, Jay. Fred neither. I swear. All I know is, he told me he was heading out to a mate's place near Malaga. Never told me where, exactly." Eddie looks from me to Kev who's now standing behind him.

I look around the tired kitchen as I think. I hate this fucking house. It reminds me of terrible parties that went on until the next afternoon and desperate girls I'd fuck over the sink upstairs. Countless, nameless faces that all blur into one.

Kevin cracks his knuckles again. Not because he needs the release, but because he knows it makes people nervous. Eddie looks nervous.

"Okay, okay. A place near Malaga. The Costa del Sol. Nice. We're getting closer. Good. I'll tell you what, assuming you're telling me the truth—which, to be honest, I doubt, because when have you ever told the truth about anything, Eddie?—I'm gonna give you forty-eight hours to get your cousin's share of what he owes. If you don't, then you and I are going to have a problem." I bite the longer nail of my index finger. Technically, Eddie will have the problem; I'll have to help clean up the fucking mess. Which is going to piss me off because I have a lot on this week.

Fuck, I need to stop biting my nails if I ever want to learn that fucking guitar.

I drop my hand from my mouth and fix Eddie with a hard stare. "Am I lying, Ed?" I ask.

Eddie says nothing, just looks around for a means of escape. He looks behind me, out the back door, through the hole in the laminate floor.

"Am I fucking lying, Ed?" I repeat.

Finally, Eddie shakes his head. Not good enough.

"Gonna need you to say it, mate."

"No, Jay. You ain't lying."

As I stare at him, I wonder why the hell I bothered my arse talking Freddie and Kevin out of getting rid of him. I hate this pasty-faced fuck. He's a snake. A coke-headed waster with a violent streak—mainly against women—and he contributes nothing to society as far as I can see.

I clap my hands together and stand up. "Good. Glad we cleared that up," I say.

Eddie goes to stand up too, but Kev plants his hands on his shoulders, stopping his ascent.

"I'll call you later and tell you where you'll bring Freddie's cash. And I'm gonna add five grand onto it 'cause we've been here"—I check my watch—"forty-five minutes longer than we needed to be, and it's cut into my personal time." I stand up and tuck the cheap dining chair back under the table. No point making a mess.

"Come on, Jay. This is fucking bullshit, mate. I don't have Tony's money," Eddie whines.

My head turns sharply to him. "You think I'm your fucking mate?" I look at Kev and laugh. He snickers. "And it's not Tony's money, Ed, is it? It's Fred's. You vouched for him. This is on you." I sound reasonable. Too reasonable, because this little shit doesn't know how close he came to being dead.

Eddie shakes his head and puts his head in his hands. Probably the best place for it.

"Now, we're going to head off, let you get that flight booked." I give a nod to Kev who looks as if someone just stole his Lego. He's not happy unless his knuckles are bruised and an ambulance has been called.

"What's going on?" a familiar voice says behind me.

I sigh. Sharon, Eddie's less than monogamous wife. Blonde with a tan as fake as her chest. She's the kind of woman I can't seem to get away from no matter how hard I try. As I turn, she looks me up and down, a flicker of something in her eye I don't particularly like. I say nothing to her and turn back around to her husband.

"Shaz, wait in there, will you?" Eddie says. He's trying to sound as if he's got everything under control—which, I think we've already established, he hasn't.

"No. What's going on, Eddie?" she says, her voice like a fork scraping a patterned plate. High-pitched and sickening. It makes me wonder, though not for the first time, what the fuck I was thinking with her. I could have gone somewhere else—anywhere else.

In my defense, I was out of it. Plus, Eddie's been screwing a nineteen-year-old lap dancer for the past year and a half, and Sharon looks all right on a good day. I'm having trouble seeing it right now though. But then I always have trouble seeing it after.

"Are you thick? Go into the other fucking room, Sharon," Eddie snaps. It makes my nostrils flare. Why do guys always talk to their wives like shit? Like they can't stand the sight of them. I've never understood it. Yeah, okay, Sharon isn't exactly the kind of woman who inspires worship, I get that, but why marry them if you can't stand them? One night is more than enough to get what you need and walk away with everybody's pride still intact. Marriage? Fuck that.

I mean, don't get me wrong, it's not as if I've no desire to ever settle down with a woman. It's just the kind of woman I want to settle down with isn't hanging around places like the Cartwrights' kitchen.

Eddie's exasperated expression when Sharon clicks back into the living room is almost conspiratorial. It says, "Women, eh? What are they like?" Fucking tosser. I feel like telling him I fucked his wife from behind in his bed upstairs—which I did—and that she came screaming my name—which she did—just to see the look drop from his pasty, lying face. But I won't. Because I don't tell people my business.

"Okay. Well then, I guess we're done here. I'll call you later, Ed. Keep your phone on, yeah?" I say with a nod. "And we'll meet in a public place, don't worry. I'll let you pick where."

I'm pretty sure Freddie will still put a bullet in Tony once he finds him, but Eddie, if he does what he's told, might just survive this. He looks about three shades whiter than he did when we came in. Maybe he should go join Tony in the Costa del Sol. A tan would do him the world of good. Fuck, if I thought Tony was actually there, I would volunteer to find him myself. Anything for some peace away from this shit.

But then I remember I can't fuck off to Spain right now because I really do have a lot on this week.

I give Kev a look to tell him the party's over, and he lets go of Eddie who stands and shakes off his shoulders immediately. When I walk through to the living room, Sharon is leaning against the fireplace, arms folded, face like a bulldog chewing a wasp. She has the kind of face I imagine used to have men chasing her up and down Bromley High Street ten years ago. She was a dancer, and you can still see it. Tall and slender and blonde. She's older now, but she still has something. I give her a cursory glance as I pass, and for some reason, she decides it's enough encouragement to follow me to the front door.

"You didn't tell him, did you?" She looks worried—scared even. That's because Eddie Cartwright is a wife-beating scumbag who'd put her in hospital if he knew.

I look around at her. "Why the fuck would I do that?" I shake my head as I glance toward the kitchen, wondering why the fuck Kev is still in there.

"Oh, okay," she says. She fluffs her hair in a way that's definitely flirtatious. "So . . . you wanna do it again sometime then?" The hope in her eyes is painful for me to look at. I rarely "do it again" with anyone. I can count on one hand how many times I've done "it" again.

"I don't think so, babe," I say. Seriously, where the fuck is he? Kevin really can't be trusted not to break something. But as I go toward the kitchen again, he comes out shoveling crisps into his mouth from a large red bag. He's fucking unbelievable.

"You said it was nice," she mutters under her breath, but loud enough that I'm supposed to hear it. I have to resist the urge to roll my eyes. Brilliant. As if I needed this right now.

"I'm sure it was," I say. "Nice" sounds like exactly the kind of thing I would say. I never say I'll call them, and I never say, "Let's do this again." Because my experience with women ensures I never want to. That's why I steer clear of any sort of relationship shit. I don't want to be an Eddie. I don't want a Sharon.

Eddie comes out behind Kevin, alive, and he doesn't seem to have broken anything either, which is a bonus. Way to go, Kev. I'll need to buy him a milkshake on the way back.

"Hey, Jay, I know where we could meet. Somewhere public," Eddie says, narrowing his eyes.

"Yeah? Where's that, Ed?" I ask. The pounding behind my eyes is worse now. I need to get out of this house. Then I need a session on the bag or the weights, some loud music. I don't need to hit someone. Not that.

"How about that play park on Fosters Road? That's pretty public, especially around 3:00 p.m." His voice is bravado, amused. It's totally fucking misjudged.

"Fosters Road is a bit out of your way, Ed." It's a warning while I count to ten.

Eddie shrugs. "Yeah, but I know it. I could go out of my way." He pulls his shoulders back, and his mouth lifts into a smirk. I've no fucking clue what he's trying to do, but it doesn't fucking matter. He's already lost.

"What the fuck did you say to me?" I feel my face contort, my breathing quicken, my blood begin to boil. My question makes out as if I didn't hear him properly, but I did. That's why my feet carry me across the room toward his pasty, lying fucking face. It's why he backs into the kitchen, arms spread out in a fighting stance. His misplaced smirk is still there, but it's fading. He thinks he has something on me, that he's taken back a bit of control. He hasn't. Not even fucking close.

I watch as Eddie reaches into the knife stand and pulls out a black-handled blade, thrusting it out toward me. He's not quick enough though. I stamp on the side of his right calf hard, and he goes down on it, the sound of bone crushing beneath my feet a comfort to my ears. The knife stand topples uselessly out of reach on the vinyl floor, spilling knives everywhere, but nowhere near him. He shouts something, but I can't hear him because the pounding rage in my ears and behind my eyes is way too loud. I can't see anything except his cowering body as my feet pound into it again and again.

He's not that small, but he looks tiny as he cowers under my feet now, holding his leg while he shouts in agony. What the fuck did he think was going to happen? Did the piece of shit actually think he had an inkling of leverage over me?

Kevin is somewhere to my right, no doubt watching, waiting for his chance to jump in, but he knows not to come near this now. Now, he'll need to stand there and enjoy the show. The kind of show I know he enjoys.

I hear Sharon's high-pitched scream, but it's faraway, and there are a lot of louder noises now. My foot cracking Eddie's ribs and face, for example. His groans of pain at each thrust of my boot on his body.

Then I feel something pinch at my neck. I ignore it initially. My red rage isn't even partly penetrated by it. But then it gets really quiet all of a sudden. Sharon stops screaming. Eddie stops shouting—and moving. I look around at Kev who stares at me wide-eyed as he holds Sharon tight against his chest, one arm around her throat, the other around her body to restrain her arms. She looks terrified, but she's not looking at Eddie who's silent and still on the floor; she's looking at me.

Suddenly, I feel heat and warm wetness begin to spread down my back and chest. Then I feel a draft on my neck as if someone's blowing on it. When I look down and see a dark stain growing wider and brighter on the front of my top, I bring my hand up to my neck. The drafty sting there is hot and wet.

"I . . . didn't . . . You were going to kill him. You wouldn't stop . . ." Her voice is panicked, barely-there. I snap my eyes up to find her looking very pale and very, very sorry.

The next ten minutes happen in a haze, as though I'm drunk, which I'm not. I'm losing blood though—fast. Because a woman I slept with and didn't call afterward just stabbed me in the neck. I've also most likely kicked her husband into a coma. It's probably fair to say I'm off the Cartwrights' Christmas card list.

This is not how the night was supposed to turn out. I'm normally the calm one—in comparison to Kev anyway. I'm the yin to Kevin's yang.

Paul gets called in from the car. He drives Eddie to the hospital before he dies and I make even more of a mess. Then Kevin and I stumble the short distance to the doctors' surgery two streets over from Eddie's place. I can't go to the same hospital as Eddie and explain why I've got a hole in my neck, and the next closest is too far away. Sharon assures us the surgery runs a late drop-in, and by the sound of her terrified voice, I'm inclined to believe her.

She stabbed me. Unbelievable. I almost respect her for it. She protected her man. A woman prepared to kill for her man . . . or maim at least. From her perspective, I guess I deserved it.

I feel a bit sick and cold too, my legs shaky as though I've done a few hours on the weights, but the adrenaline still pumps as Kevin helps me up the front steps of a converted townhouse that has a sign reading "Eastwoode Surgery" on the window. There's a light on inside, but the door is locked when we try the handle. Great. Though, I guess the hole in my neck can't be too bad. She couldn't have nicked an artery, otherwise I'd be dead by now.

Kev bangs on the door as I hold my hand to my neck to stop any more blood from escaping. It's not flooding out, but it's a slow, consistent pour.

"We'll get them to fix you up, and then we'll fuck off before they get a chance to call anyone," he says. He sounds relaxed, not in the slightest bit concerned by the hole in my neck. It can't be that bad then. But Kev has a habit of looking relaxed in the face of utter destruction, so I can't exactly use it as a measure.

Vaguely, I wonder how the fuck Sharon managed to stab me in the neck while he was standing there eating his fucking crisps. That's a conversation for later though.

"And what if there's only a cleaner inside?" I choke out.

This was a bad idea. I should have gone to the fucking hospital. I should have called Sharon after I fucked her.

"We'll see if she has superglue and masking tape." He barks out a laugh, relaxed as ever. It's comforting. He bangs again before I finally hear the lock turn from inside.

When it opens, I decide not to risk looking up and having anyone see my face. I need to get fixed and out of here before this shit gets any messier. It's already far too messy. I shouldn't have lost it like that. I've normally got way more control. I need to have more control.

Then she speaks. My body relaxes instantly, a weird calmness settling over me.

She confirms she's a doctor before ushering us both inside. Her voice is calm and low and sort of husky, and it reminds me of the soft, contented purr of a cat. She sounds young from what I can tell, and well-spoken. Her tone is professional but somehow still manages to be sexy. From money, I reckon. I want to look up and see the face that goes with the voice, but I don't want to risk her seeing me or at least being able to identify me with any certainty later on. Safer for everyone that way. Instead, I look down at my hands, which are covered in blood, the knuckles aching and throbbing. They'll be worse later once the adrenaline fades away. Everything will be worse later. Fred is not going to be happy about how this went down. I still don't regret kicking the lying shit's head in though.

I keep my eyes down and see creamy, smooth bare legs leading into what look like designer purple heels. They're suede, I think. I seriously must be half-dead because I'm not thinking straight—what the fuck do I know about women's shoes? Though, the legs make me wonder if the face is as fit as the body. She says something about an ambulance, and I shake my head and say no, and Kev clarifies it in his distinct growl. Ambulances lead to police, especially in this kind of circumstance. The knife wound to the flesh circumstance.

Plus, for some reason, I want her to fix me.

She sits me on the table and presses something soft, a scarf maybe, into my neck. It smells of flowers and soap powder, and it feels soothing and warm against the draft at my shoulder. She orders Kev to hold it tight against me and goes off toward another room.

"No calling anybody. No cops, no ambulance, no one. You fucking hear me?" Kev says harshly. Way too harshly. Not fucking on.

When I hear her walking away, I glance up and see the back of a tall, dark-haired woman with an amazing arse walk into an office across from us.

"Watch the tone, Kev, yeah?" I choke out. "She's helping. No need to fucking terrify her to death."

"Making sure she doesn't call the pigs, Jay," he grunts.

"She won't," I tell him. I honestly have no idea why I'm so sure of this, but I am. "So, calm down, yeah?" I fix Kev with a hard stare until he gets me.

When I hear the door open a second later, I look back down even though everything in me strains to look at her. The thing she pressed at my neck is cream-colored—or was—and has purple flowers on it.

She comes back and sits next to me on the table, putting a leather bag on the floor between us. It's a proper doctor's bag. Brown, well-worn leather. As she leans down to open it, I look at her left hand. No wedding ring. She has a silver band with a green stone on her left forefinger, but that's it. Her nails aren't painted, just neat and manicured, and her fingers are long and slender.

What the fuck am I doing? Is this what happens when you can't see a chick's face—you get turned on by her hands? Am I turned on? No, I'm fucking light-headed from blood loss.

Then her hand goes to my neck, and she speaks again. Closer to my ear this time. *Fuck.* Is she doing that on purpose? Talking like that?

"When did this happen?" she asks me in a soft almost-whisper.

I look up at Kev, keeping my head turned away from her.

"Why the fuck does it matter? About fifteen minutes ago," he grunts, taking his phone out. I really don't like the way he's speaking to her. She deserves more respect than that. More respect than the women he's used to speaking to.

"With what?" she asks in the same soft tone, apparently undisturbed by him.

He says nothing and looks at me. I nod. She digs around in her bag, pulling out a small case, a packet of something, and some gloves.

"A kitchen knife," he says.

She opens the small black case, which holds a syringe. "Was it clean?"

"How the fuck should I know?" he snaps.

I feel and hear her take a deep breath. "Okay. Well, I think the bleeding is slowing, but I need to inject you with this." This, she says to me. "It's an antibiotic. It'll help stop any infection."

Her tone continues to comfort me. She certainly doesn't seem to think I'll drop dead at any minute.

"Do you have any other injuries?" she asks me quietly.

I keep focused on my hands and shake my head.

"Well, that's good, I suppose. Only this scratch to deal with then." It's light and reassuring, and I know then she must be a fucking amazing doctor.

I notice why her voice sounds like nothing I've ever heard before. It's because she says her words properly, tongue curling around each syllable, pronouncing every letter exactly how it's supposed to be pronounced. I let my mind linger on thoughts of her tongue for a moment.

Okay, I'm definitely turned on. I imagine her screaming my name in that accent as I fuck her, and I have to shift my legs together and away in case she notices what's going on between them.

What the fuck is wrong with me? I haven't seen her face, I'm bleeding, and I'm semi-hard from the sound of her voice alone. Does that even happen? Maybe after you get stabbed in the neck it does.

She slides on a pair of white latex gloves, and a second later, I feel the sharp point of the needle pierce the crook of my shoulder.

"Are you able to hold this for a moment?" she asks me. This time, it has authority in it.

I do as I'm told and slide my hand up to take the scarf, grazing her hand as I do.

"I'm going to cut away your top now," she tells me, and I nod. It's so fucking difficult not to look at her then. I wonder where she's from. Berkshire? Surrey? A fair distance from the Bow Bells anyway, that's for sure.

A fair distance out of your league too.

Kev hisses some shit down the phone in a hushed tone, presumably at Paul, and so I focus on that instead. Instead of her. Instead of the increasing throb between my legs and the proximity of her and the faint floral scent lingering on her skin. But then her hand grazes my thigh accidentally, and I almost groan out loud. *Fucking hell, doctor.* I flinch reflexively away, the total fucking opposite of what I want to do.

"Do you need something for the pain?" she asks. I imagine it's the tone she would use to tell you she loved you. I imagine the kind of wanker she says that to. I fucking hate that wanker.

I look back down at her legs, which are silky smooth and pale like cream. I really am a piece of shit. She's helping me. She's selflessly caring for me, and I'm ogling her as if she's a fucking lap dancer. *Classy, Jay. Really fucking classy.* Only, how can I be ogling her when I haven't even seen her face?

Okay, enough of this shit. Who gives a fuck if she sees me? I'm never gonna see her again anyway, nor her me. I need to see her face.

I lift my head, but she's turned away from me, focused on the hole in my neck—the one inflicted by some violent, irrational bitch who is way more within my league. I wonder if it's fitting that Sharon fucks me up and I get to be fixed by this pristine, classy, elegant wet dream.

The first look I get of her is the side of her neck and face and its smooth, flawless, cared-for pale skin. It makes me wonder if her whole body is like that. I picture her sprawled naked on my bed, and then I picture fucking her from behind, hard.

I wonder what she smells like right there, in the crook of her neck. I want to smooth her hair back before touching my mouth to it. It's reddish, I notice, her hair. A rich, deep red, not brown, and it's redder where the light hits it. It's tied up at the sides, but it's long and thick and falls way past her shoulders. I wonder how that smells too. Her nose is small and turned in at the end. Her fucking nose? *Seriously?* When have I ever looked at a chick's nose? When have I ever looked at a chick's hands either? Her mouth is pink and set in a straight line as she concentrates. I picture it wrapped around my cock.

Now, that image I don't feel bad about, because I could die at any moment, and having that as my final image is only fair. Her sucking my cock with that mouth. Jesus fucking Christ. I'll think about that later, in the shower, assuming I live through this.

Then, because I'm staring at her like a tool and not answering, she looks around at me.

And it's over.

Something flashes across her eyes, and they widen for a split second before relaxing again. They're smart and warm and a bright pale green color I've never seen before. She has a small beauty mole under her right eye as well as a sprinkling of pale freckles on her nose and forehead. Perfection. She's fucking majestic. I want her.

More than that, I want her to want me back. I want her to look at me as if she needs me. The way I normally wish women wouldn't. Fuck, I'd do anything to get her to look at me like that.

My heart feels as if it's going to beat out of my chest, and I am hard for her. Fully fucking hard. I'm staring at a fully clothed woman who's sewing my neck back together, and I have a fucking hard-on. I laugh inwardly at how pathetic it is. How pathetic I am.

The longer I stare at her, the clearer it becomes that I have no fucking clue how to go about getting a girl like her. It's not as if I mind a bit of hard work, but what would make a woman like her even look at me? Unless I'm bleeding all over her in her place of work, of course.

Getting what I want has never been much of an issue for me though. And if I don't get it, then normally, I take it.

Yeah, I'll get her. Fuck it—I might even keep her for a bit.

I need a fucking plan.

ONE

FOR THE ENTIRE DRIVE HOME, MY MIND RELIVES THE EVENTS IN HD. What if I weren't around? Would he have bled to death on the street? Do I care? Why the hell didn't he go to a hospital? The reasons I come up with make me feel uneasy and out of my depth, as though I've been involved in something unwholesome.

At some point between getting off the A23 and reaching Shere, I decide not to mention it to the other doctors in the morning. Whether it's the threat from the aggressive one or something else, I'm not sure, but since I don't know who they are or what happened, there isn't a whole lot to tell anyway. If anyone asks whether I happened to treat a bleeding man at my drop-in, then of course I won't lie, but I also won't be sending out a group email either.

As my mind flits back to the memory of the attractive one I sewed back together and how he looked at me, I start to feel warmer. I reach out and turn the blower down to the coldest end. Try to think about a glass of wine instead.

It's just before 10:00 p.m. when I get home, and Fred starts meowing hungrily at me as soon as I walk through the front door.

"I'm sorry I'm so late, baby. Are you the hungriest cat in the world? Aw, I bet you are. Mummy is sorry." I pick him up to kiss him on the nose as I stroke his tortoiseshell fur.

The moment I put him down, he bounds enthusiastically into the kitchen to purr against the cupboard that stores his food.

I feed Fred too much before going to the fridge to see what I can salvage for myself. There are a few slices of leftover chicken on a covered plate from yesterday, which I uncover and start to nibble on before pouring myself a cold glass of chardonnay. Then I stick the empty plate in the dishwasher before going upstairs to run a bubble bath. There's little chance of me sleeping tonight without the aid of wet heat and wine, and by the time I climb out of the bath an hour later, my eyes are heavy and my bones languid and soft.

Boiled, pink, and too hot, I crawl under the duvet as Fred jumps up, stretches out, and curls himself into a tight little furball at my feet. My eyes close almost instantly after I switch out the light, but before my conscious-ness fades, an image of a hard, tattooed body, green eyes, and full, kissable lips floats across my mind.

The rest of the week is truly remarkable in its banality. So banal it begins to feel as if I imagined the whole episode on Tuesday night. Maybe it never actually happened, and I invented it purely to add some excitement into my life. Which wouldn't be unreasonable since excitement is something my life distinctly lacks at the moment. No one mentions a local knife attack, and no policemen turn up at the surgery asking any questions about it either, which makes it far easier to stick to my decision not to mention it to anyone.

I say "easier" when, actually, I feel heavy from it, guilty even, as though I've committed some terrible crime and I'm going back to the scene of it over and over again.

Exactly a week after my run-in with my dangerously attractive patient, Sam asks me out. I get the sense it's something he's been working up to. It has the feel of something practiced about it. Sam's adorable—one of those genuinely nice guys. As well as being cute, smart, and a doctor, he also has a lot in common with me. We're a perfect fit. So I wonder why I'm not more excited by the prospect of going out with him. Maybe it's the fact we work together. It's never a good idea to mix the two, but how else do you meet pro-spective partners if not at work? Certainly not in nightclubs or bars, where everything is a line or a come-on for the sole purpose of getting you into bed.

At the end of another monotonous week, the weekend finally arrives, and with it, the first night out with the girls in a while. I'm mainly a hermit homebody these days, but this is a chance to catch up with Robyn's hen-night girls before her wedding. We've also managed to swag invites to the opening night of a new "nameless" club in town via my brother.

During the week, the invites came by special delivery to the surgery with no return address or sender details. But since they're addressed to Dr.

Marlowe, with a VIP booth and access to a free bar, we are most certainly going.

Nick's job in PR comes with a wealth of freebies, which he often passes my way. Three months ago, it was movie premiere tickets where Rob and I sat next to the members of a boy band we'd never heard of. The film was based on a comic book and terrible, but the after-party was fun.

I still haven't decided whether to tell Robyn about what happened with the hot tattooed guy last week. I'm also not sure why I'm still thinking about him, or at what point he went from probable criminal to "dangerously attractive" to "hot tattooed guy" either. Probably around the time the whole incident began to seem like a dream and I started to fantasize about him.

Last night, I had the briefest, most fleeting sex dream about him. It was gone before it began, but I woke up thinking about him. Then I spent the rest of the day falling into daydreams about what might happen if I were to come out of the surgery and see him standing there one night. He'd tell me he hadn't been able to stop thinking about me and demand I go somewhere private with him. The blush that hits my cheeks as I imagine myself on top of him in the back seat of his car somewhere causes my stomach to clench almost painfully, a soft moan escaping my lips.

I'm sure Robyn would champion my daydreaming over a hot and dangerous stranger; she's desperate for me to get over Ben and move on. And since it's completely safe, as this is a man I'm never going to see again, I decide at some point tonight—after several glasses of champagne—I'll tell her all about it.

"You know, there are times when I think I might not mind your brother." Robyn sighs as she turns the black embossed invite over in her perfectly manicured hand.

Robyn is blonde and gorgeous, and for about six months six years ago, she and my brother were an item. It didn't end well for Rob when Nick brought another girl to her birthday party as his less-than-subtle way of breaking it off. Though, now, of course, I know had he not done the shittiest thing imaginable, it still wouldn't have worked out between them.

I say it didn't end well for Rob, but it did, because after my brother broke her heart she met Daniel, and as far as I can see, they're the most perfect couple on the planet. It's almost sickening how perfect they are. If I didn't love them so much, I'd hate them.

As she stands to fill our glasses with the freshly popped Veuve Clicquot, I stare longingly at her tanned, lithe legs. Where I'm pale and freckled in places, Robyn is the opposite. She goes golden-brown at the first hint of sunlight, while I need SPF 100 so I don't go lobster-red.

We've been friends since our second day at Holly Lodge Primary School in Surrey, when she picked me up after a boy whose name escapes me now knocked me over into a puddle in the middle of the playground. She knows me inside out and with such accuracy it should freak me out. It doesn't. I love her for it.

I give her a skeptical look. "Tell me when the moment passes."

Robyn laughs and takes a sip of her champagne while I study the invite.

"I'm surprised Nick gave these to me though. Sounds totally like his kind of thing," I muse as I sip the cool, fizzy goodness. Champagne is always my going-out drink because it makes me feel perky, sexy, and spoiled. I love the way it fizzes on my tongue and down the back of my throat in that almost ticklish way. It makes going out with the girls feel like a celebration—which I firmly believe it should be.

"Well, cheers to Nick the prick!" Robyn says, raising her glass to clink it with mine.

I bite back a smile.

"So, do you promise not to brush off every single man who looks at you tonight, or . . .?" Robyn asks. Robyn who, in her wisdom, thinks everyone's perfect soul mate is only a few awkward conversations away.

"You say that as though it's possible to even strike up a serious conversation in a nightclub. All that loud music and small talk. Nightmare."

"Um, I wasn't talking about serious conversation, Al . . ." Robyn widens her eyes. "You seriously need to get sha—"

"Don't bloody say it!" I laugh.

"You do though!"

"I'm fine, thank you very much. Anyway . . ." I say as I nudge the conversation in another direction. "The eligible Dr. Sam Wardley asked me out the other day, so you never know . . ." I giggle.

Robyn halts mid-sip. "What! So, he finally asked you out? Ugh! I said he wanted you when I saw him swoon over you at his birthday drinks you took me along to. But of course, you were still with 'the cunt' then. Never thought it would take him so bloody long!"

It goes on like this for another hour, with Rob convincing me Sam, with his floppy hair, boyish face, and glasses, is exactly what I need right now, that he's practically perfect for me, blah blah blah. All the things I've been telling myself all week. Except while she's speaking, all I can think is that perhaps what I *actually* need right now is a pair of green-blue eyes, a muscular, tattooed body, and a night of wild, no-strings-attached sex in the back seat of a probable criminal's car.

TWO

THE TAXI DROPS US OFF ACROSS THE STREET FROM THE CLUB IN THE trendy part of Brick Lane.

The nameless club is a black stone building—a sort of neogothic affair with blacked-out windows. It looks as if it's been involved in a fire, but as I get closer, I see it's that the stone has been painted a dark charcoal color. It must have been here for years, yet I can't remember ever seeing it before. Though, it's not as if I frequent Brick Lane a lot these days. Or London for that matter. I try to avoid the city unless absolutely necessary. And for the past six months, I've had an ex and his new girlfriend I want to be at least fifty miles away from at all times.

Of course, the venue is ridiculously crowded. Normally, this sort of queue would put us off and we'd totter along to the next place, but these VIP passes get us to the left-hand side of the doorway, which has a much smaller line moving down at a faster pace. As we walk to stand in line, the heavy thump of the music from inside gets louder.

Rob's hen group are waiting outside the gated entrance for us and wave excitedly as we approach before pulling us into fragrant hugs. I met some of them at the hen weekend a few weeks back—a weekend spa break to Barcelona, which was divine—and some I've known for a while through Rob. They're all lovely, genuine girls. Becca is the first to thank me for the invites. She's a gorgeous, petite brunette with an infectious laugh and a saucy wit who often makes me cry with laughter whenever I'm in her company.

"Oh, you're welcome. They'd only be going to waste."

"Is your brother single . . .?" Lucy asks.

"He's a priest," Rob says with an eye roll.

"He is?" Tamsin asks, intrigued. She's a solicitor from Bath and has the largest eyes I've ever seen.

"She's joking." I shake my head.

"Well, let's hope it's a good night. I've *soooo* needed this." Saskia beams excitedly.

"We don't even need to wait in the muggle queue. Another point to Nick the Prick . . ." Robyn says, craning her neck down the line and back up with wide, impressed eyes. "Oh my god, is that Adam Smith?" She nudges me.

Adam is a stand-up comedian I vaguely remember seeing on one of those panel shows I hardly ever watch. As I glance ahead of us in the direction she indicates, I nod. It is. I think. He's one of those new young comedians who looks like a student, so I guess it could be him, or it could just be a student. From looking around at the people queuing, it appears the clientele is mixed. Those in the "muggle queue" definitely look more like trendy student types, whereas ours seems to be for yuppie city boys who could also be footballers, their WAGs, and stand-up comedians.

Our queue moves fast, and a few minutes later, we're ushered into a dark, moody foyer where several gorgeous maître d's are taking coats and signing VIPs in.

"Good evening, doctor," a six feet tall, black-haired glamazon says to me after I hand over my invite. "So, six of you tonight?"

"Yes, six." I nod.

"Fab. If I could get you to sign in here, please, and if we could have an address and contact telephone number for you . . . I assure you, it won't be passed on to any third parties. It's to maintain our VIP guest list," she tells me professionally.

I hesitate briefly. I never give out my details, but since I don't want to appear rude or snooty by refusing, I scribble down my mobile number and email address and hand the pen back to her.

"Thank you, Dr. Marlowe. Okay, so we have you at one of our best tables this evening on the mezzanine level. It has a great view of the stage. Our main guest DJ is onstage at midnight, and there is champagne chilling on the table for you right now. Please help yourselves. There will be hosts on each floor should you need anything, and Kyle here will show you to your table," she says and indicates an incredibly attractive young guy who's smiling at us eagerly.

Kyle is pretty.

"Oh, and before I forget: There are cards on the table inviting you to pick a name for the club. Why not submit a few? You never know. The person with the winning name gets a magnum of champagne and a VIP table for a year. Worth a shot. I hope you have a great night. Kyle?"

Kyle beckons us forward, and we follow him up an elegant staircase to the mezzanine.

The inside of the club looks more like a swanky hotel than a nightclub, with elegant features such as gilded banisters and intricate paneling on the ceiling, polished wood floors, and gold embossed mirrors. As we're led down a carpeted high-ceilinged hallway, the music starts to get louder. Kyle stops at a door that reads "Number 3" in gold lettering and slides a hotel-style key card into the lock before pushing the door open.

Inside the main part of the club it's dark, with lots of exposed brick and warm but moody lighting. Kyle leads us along the mezzanine to a circular table with dark velvet seats and a contemporary black chandelier hanging low. Three ice buckets, each holding a chilled bottle of champagne, and another bucket to chill the glasses await. The girls beam at me in appreciation as we move to sit down.

"Ladies, this is your table for the night. The ladies' toilets are across the walkway to the right." Kyle gestures beyond us to a set of lit glass bridges that crisscross over the dance floor, already crowded with dancers. "If you need any drinks, you only need to press this button, and someone will come and take care of you. There's a bar in the VIP section though, which is down to the left there, and there's another across the walkway. There's also one at ground level. At the end of the night, this door will unlock, and you can leave the way you came in. Or, if you are down on the main dance floor, you can exit via the main entrance. That okay?" he asks, and we nod, somewhat awed by his pretty face and professional tone. "Great. Now, can I open this champagne for you?" he says, reaching to lift the bucket from its ice bed.

God, he's good.

"Yes, please," we answer together before breaking into stupid unified laughter.

Kyle pours our drinks with a perfect smile and wishes us a good night, though when he turns to leave, he throws a strange look in my direction.

"God, this place is amazing!" Rob exclaims. "I'm definitely coming back. Dan would love it."

"Seriously though, to think I almost binned these invites. Who do you think the guest DJ is? Anyone famous?" I take a large sip of the cool champers and lift the bottle out of the ice bucket to see it's Lanson Le Black Label

Brut. "God, they must be spending a fortune on this launch night. This is not cheap."

"Well, I'm glad they've spent a fortune. Okay, I'm going to the ladies and to have a look around."

"I'll join you," Becca says, standing.

"Robyn, please don't spend hours chatting with random strangers in the toilet again. Becca, don't let her!" I shout as she steps out of our booth. Robyn is notorious for striking up deep and meaningful conversations with complete strangers in bathrooms . . . or supermarkets . . . or DIY stores. She's one of those approachable, known-you-forever types of people.

Becca gives me a smiley thumbs-up before they both teeter off across the bridge. While they're gone, Tamsin and Saskia tell me about their futuristic hotel in Shoreditch, and more specifically about the hot concierge who was one hundred percent angling for Saskia's number, according to Tamsin.

When Rob and Becca return, it's with the declaration that this is the best club since Pacha and they're convinced they saw two Chelsea footballers coming out of the men's toilet.

"Okay. My turn to pee," I say after draining my second glass of free champagne. My trip to the loo gives me a better look at the place, and though I'm not really a nightclub-goer—hot, sweaty people pressed together tend to make me think "germ transfer" rather than "good time"—the club is impressive and high-end but somehow manages to feel cool.

I'm coming out of the ladies and heading back across the bridge when pretty young Kyle comes striding toward me, beaming. He looks pleased to see me, as if he was looking for me, though that's probably wishful thinking on my part. Too young anyway.

"Dr. Marlowe, there you are! Hi! Kyle—do you remember?" he says, pointing at himself.

"Of course, Kyle. Hi." I smile.

"Eh, listen, I'm really sorry to do this, but one of our guys is feeling a bit under the weather." He rubs the back of his neck and looks at the floor. "We were going to call for an ambulance, but then we remembered from the attendee list we have a doctor here." He gives me that beaming smile again—the one that makes me feel like a cradle snatcher because he must be about twenty, if a day. "Any chance you could give him a quick once-over, make sure he's not about to keel over on us?" He laughs nervously.

I resist the urge to sigh. It really is a twenty-four-hour job. Well, at least they didn't stop the music and call out, "Is there a doctor in the house?" over the sound system.

"Oh, I think he's probably fine," Kyle tells me. "He just took a bit of a . . . um . . . dizzy turn. Our manager was a bit worried." He doesn't wait for my response before he starts to walk toward a set of stairs across from the toilets. He turns and gestures for me to follow him. Which I do.

"Okay, but I have been drinking, and so you know, I would never do a consultation after drinking, but I suppose I can look him over," I say as I catch up to him.

"Of course. You're honestly a superstar. Sorry to interrupt your night like this. But the boss will be delighted," Kyle mutters.

I follow him up a flight of stairs and along another carpeted hallway exactly like the one on the first floor. At the end of the hallway, there's a door marked "Private," which he knocks on twice. He doesn't wait for a response before punching in a code and holding it open for me to follow him through.

It's a large, stylish office with more exposed brick, dark gray walls, and a few leather couches arranged to form a seating area in one corner. In the center of the room, a solid oak desk dominates the space. On the wall nearest the door, several monitors show various parts of the club: the foyer, the bar, the stage, some hallways, and two showing outside—front and back.

Behind the desk is a large flat-screen TV showing the main stage downstairs, though the sound is muted. The wall on my right is almost entirely made of glass, and through it, I can see the whole of the VIP mezzanine and down onto the dance floor below. This must be the other side of one of the large gilded mirrors I spotted on the inner walls. What a view. I immediately begin looking for Rob and the girls across the way.

"Erm, I'll go let him know you're here," Kyle says before crossing the office to leave via a different door.

As soon as he leaves, I look around the room for some water but see only champagne in an ice bucket on the desk, two glasses beside it. There's a fridge over in one corner, but I think it may be rude to go over and start rummaging through it. While I wait, I count the number of drinks I've had. Four glasses of champagne at home, and half a glass here. Okay, definitely too much to practice medicine. I'll make a brief assessment as to whether this guy needs the hospital or not and then go back to the girls.

Walking closer to the large, wall-sized window, I gaze out and across the now extremely busy club. I find our table immediately. In fact, it's almost directly across from where I am now. I see Rob and Becca dancing near the balcony while the other girls chat animatedly to a group of guys in the next booth along. Behind me, I hear the door open, and I turn around to get a look at my dizzy barman.

My heart stops dead in my chest.

Oh, god. It can't be. I can't breathe. I'm not breathing. My hot, tattooed probable criminal is walking toward me looking as if he's about to devour me whole.

THREE

I'T'S TOO HOT. *I'M* TOO HOT. MORE IMMEDIATE THOUGH IS THE WARM, tight clenching that's begun low down in my belly—or lower. Yes, definitely lower. Nearer to my thighs and in between them. Instinctively, I move toward the desk for something solid to lean on as he comes to a stop not far from me. I swallow as I take in the full sight of him, slowly savoring the image, tasting it on my tongue.

Absent of blood, he's dressed in a perfectly tailored black shirt, sleeves rolled up to show off an expensive watch, and immaculately cut gray trousers. He looks exactly like the dangerous, fierce, edgy male model I remember.

It's comforting to know my memory didn't exaggerate his face or his body or the deep intensity of his eyes. It's his mouth I can't stop staring at though. Full lips curled up into a sexy, knowing smile as his eyes glitter deliciously in the dim light.

I'm aware my mouth is open too wide, so I close it. I can't do anything about the unbelievable heat flooding my body. I'll just need to deal with it.

As we continue to stare at one another, it occurs to me that he looks as though he's enjoying himself; enjoying watching me disintegrate in front of him. Oh, god, is that what I'm doing—disintegrating? Oh, please let me look more in control than I feel. I could try speaking, saying something—anything.

Before I get the chance to think, he speaks.

"Doctor." He grins playfully. His voice is low and sexy like I remember it. Do I remember it being sexy? Am I admitting that now? I mean, he's still not my type. He's still the sort of man I'm sure I've been warned to stay away from.

"You?" I manage. Christ, it's pathetic. My parents paid a lot of money for an expensive education, and that's all I have. Three whole letters.

His mouth twitches mischievously. "Me," he says.

I nod once, unable still to find words. I really want to act like the

Cambridge Medical School-educated woman I am, but he's having a strange effect on my head . . . and my ability to form sentences and breathe.

"I don't . . . understand. How are you here?" I ask. What I really mean is, how am I here with him, but that's a more complicated thought than my mouth is able to verbalize.

He smiles a full smile before flicking his tongue over his lower lip. I feel a quiver over my entire body. Christ, what a smile. I knew it would be special. With a mouth like that, it had to be. It's gorgeous, sexy, and a little wicked. His teeth are a straight white line with two sharp pointed canines at each side. They make me wonder if he bites. I feel a tingling on my neck as the image gains momentum.

"I own this place," he says, sounding faintly embarrassed.

I frown, confused. "You're not the dizzy barman?"

He looks marginally confused before smiling again. "Nah. Sorry to disappoint you."

Finally, my brain gets it. *Finally.*

"Wait—you sent the invites? To my surgery? It was you?"

He nods, watching me closely.

"Why?"

When he speaks again, his voice is lower, less playful. "I wanted to see you," he tells me. "To thank you for what you did."

His manner is a strange mix of forced politeness, as though he isn't used to it, as if the words and even the tone are unnatural to him. I like it though. It's rough around the edges, and it tickles my ears and skin.

I glance at his neck. His shirt, open at the collar, reveals the flash of a white bandage covering the knife wound I stitched together exactly eleven days ago. He shifts slightly on his feet, and his scent washes over me: that same heady mix of manliness I can almost taste on my tongue. It's more intense than I remember. Everything about this feels intense. Jesus Christ, what even is this? This isn't *me*. I don't have pathetic, girly reactions to good-looking men, no matter how good-looking. It doesn't happen. It has never happened.

"You did thank me," I say in what I hope is a casual tone. "You were bleeding. I just did my job." I shrug, finally managing to glance away from him. I look past him, over his shoulder, and then down at the floor before bringing my eyes back up.

So, I managed not to look at him for all of five seconds. Great work, Alex.

"No," he says with a shake of his head. "The way I see it, you didn't have to open the door." His eyes narrow as though he's trying to work me out. Figure out why I opened the door, perhaps?

"Of course I did." I frown. "You were bleeding, and I'm a doctor."

He bites his lip thoughtfully. Those lips. That mouth. It's so kissable. I lick my lips involuntarily.

"Well, you were kind about it. You didn't have to be. We weren't exactly gentlemen."

He sounds guilty. I think about that for a moment and decide maybe he's being unfair to himself. He was gentlemanly. Polite and grateful. His creep of a friend wasn't. Instead of mentioning this, I simply press my lips together and shrug again.

"It's not really kindness. It's more like . . . bedside manner. It's part of the training," I say.

His mouth quirks, and he draws his eyes slowly down my body, a hungry look creeping into them again. I think he's going to say something about my dress that might make my insides explode, so I decide to speak instead.

"So, this is really yours?" I ask, turning away from him. I look back through the large one-way window toward Robyn and the girls. Like an anchor, seeing them there reminds me that this in fact reality and not a sex dream. "I'm impressed."

He chuckles, and it's a soft, sexy sound. "Well, that means a lot. Coming from you."

From me? When I turn back around, I find him still looking at me, his eyes narrowed as he runs his teeth along his bottom lip. I wonder—and not for the first time—what those lips would feel like; whether they'd be hard and demanding or soft and tempting.

I swallow. "Well, we're having a great night. Thank you."

He doesn't respond but looks pleased by my comment, his chest puffing out a fraction. He's staring into my eyes, but I feel the heat of them everywhere on my body. They're deep and intense, and the closest color I can think of to describe them is a light emerald turquoise that seems to be aflame.

"You look really beautiful tonight, by the way," he says after a moment, stealing the breath out of me. And as he draws his hungry gaze down my body once more, I'm pretty sure I want to be eaten by him. I want him to devour me whole. I've never wanted anything as much as I want that. He seems to shake himself out of a partial trance and locks onto my eyes again. "I'm really glad you came. I wasn't sure if you would. If it would be your kind of thing. But I'm really glad you did."

I take a moment to enjoy the warm vibration still lingering from his compliment. He's glad I came, and he thinks I look beautiful. The knowledge does things to me. Hot, dangerous things.

"Thank you for inviting us. It's been a great night so far." I realize I've already said this, but as I sound remarkably calm despite feeling anything but, I'm going to ignore that.

"I'm glad, Alexandra," he says.

My mouth almost falls open. He knows my name. How does he know my name? My full name; my Sunday name. The name my parents use when they need to tell me serious things.

"How . . . how do you know my name?" I whisper, no longer sounding calm.

He shrugs. "I know where you work. Wasn't hard to find out which doctor was on that night. Lot of men at your surgery, a fifty-year-old woman, and you," he explains.

I honestly don't know if I should be frightened or flattered by his efforts. Naïvely, I decide I'm a little of both.

"You could have sent a thank-you card." I smile. I'm flirting, definitely, for some reason only the champagne knows.

He watches me closely. "Yeah, maybe. But then I wouldn't have gotten to see you in that dress." His voice is low and quiet as he runs a hand over his perfect mouth then turns toward the desk.

I can't breathe again.

"Have a drink with me, Alexandra, yeah?" he says, lifting the champagne out of the bucket.

I really want to tell him to stop calling me Alexandra. Only people who don't know me call me that. And my Aunt Audrey. But he doesn't know me, and I don't know him, and so maybe he should be calling me Alexandra.

"It's a big night for me," he adds, fixing me with another of those intense stares. He pops the cork on the champagne with little effort, and for some reason, I don't jump the way I normally do when people pop champagne corks. I'm too entranced watching the easy motion of his hands as he lifts one glass then the other, filling them both halfway.

I've always had a particular thing about men's hands. Rob teases me about it incessantly. His hands are beautiful. Long, tanned fingers. Smooth skin with raised veins across the back, topped off with clean, short fingernails. I watch transfixed as he holds out a glass of the chilled, fizzing champagne to me. As I take it from him, my hand grazes his, and I note he feels warm to the touch. My own are cold and clammy. The only part of my body that is cold.

As I look back up at his eyes, I decide it feels surreal being here, in this place, with him. People say that all the time. It's a completely overused term. But this *is* surreal. Not only seeing him but knowing that he wants me here. That he thinks I look beautiful. That he orchestrated this so he could see me. Did I not daydream about this exact thing?

It all makes me feel slightly giddy and light-headed, and it's only partially from the champagne. I try to focus on something real, fixed, to anchor myself back to reality: the TV on the wall, the champagne bucket, the desk. It's pointless though, because as soon as I glance at him, I'm dizzy again. Distracted by his eyes and his smell and the way his mouth moves when he says my name. In contrast, he appears totally calm and utterly at ease. I'm normally an at-ease person. Calm, analytical, thoughtful. I've been called these things often enough, and I believe them.

"Did you visit a hospital?" I ask in the most professional tone I can muster.

He gives me a guilty look as he sips his drink. "I told you, I really don't like doctors." When he smiles, he shows me a flash of sharp tooth, and my womb clenches anew. "How do I look to you? Good, or . . .?" He smirks.

I swallow. "You should have visited the hospital. They're far better equipped to deal with a stab wound . . ." I say, ignoring his question. I lift my glass to take a sip of the cold, fizzy champagne. It's sweet, wet, and welcome on my dry, nervous tongue.

"Well, I'll keep that in mind, Doctor." His eyes continue to assess me, glittering serious pools of blue-green. He looks as if he's in a focused kind of trance, as though wherever he is I'm with him, and it's only us there.

Suddenly, something occurs to me. "I don't even know your name," I say as I take another sip of champagne. "Though, you know mine and where I work. Seems a touch unfair, don't you think?" Okay, so I'll admit, I may potentially be flirting with him—but in my defense, I'm giddy and perky, and he thinks I look beautiful in this dress. While he isn't my type, he is extremely attractive, and I'm very, very single.

He blinks as though until I mentioned it, it didn't even occur to him. He takes another sip of his champagne and sets his glass down on the desk, then he stretches his hand out toward me. It hovers mid-air for a second before I reach out to take it. It's hot, soft, and large.

"Jake Lawrence," he says. There's an authority to it. *Jake Lawrence.* I repeat it over internally a few times as I decide whether it suits him. It does. It's a name for an extremely attractive, slightly dangerous man. I have a feeling it's not a name I'm likely to forget anytime soon.

He doesn't shake my hand; he just holds it in his. Then, softly, he grazes his thumb slowly over it. It sends a shiver down my spine. It feels almost sensual somehow. I realize if I consider the way he is holding my hand to be sensual, I'm even more single than I think.

It's not oral sex, Alex.

Oh, dear god, why did I have to think that? Now I'm thinking about oral sex, and his mouth, and oh my god . . .

When I glance at his mouth, I worry he can read my mind because he gives a slow, measured smile before licking his delectable bottom lip and biting it softly. Teasingly.

"Alex Marlowe," I answer, barely recognizing my own voice. It sounds girlish and breathless. It sounds ridiculous. "But then you knew that already, didn't you, Jake Lawrence?" I raise an eyebrow. Better. Stronger. Faintly sarcastic too. Well done, me.

He takes another step toward me, into the space between our bodies— so close now that I have to tilt my head back to look up at him. When he looks down at my mouth, I know he's going to kiss me. He's going to kiss me, and I've never been so nervous about being kissed before.

"I like hearing you say my name, Alex," he says as he licks his lips again. "I could get used to hearing my name come out of your mouth." His accent sounds more pronounced now, rougher in its lower decibels. As I wonder where he grew up, he moves forward and kisses me, swiping every other thought from my head.

His mouth is gentle at first, teasing mine open, but when I begin to respond he becomes more forceful, hungry. His hot mouth and tongue become increasingly possessive as he begins to stroke, suck, lick, and taste. I taste spice and heat. Mingled with the expensive champagne, it's delicious.

Oh, god, he can kiss.

I knew he'd be able to kiss. To not be able to kiss with that mouth would be a travesty.

He moves his whole warm, muscular body into me, causing me to stumble backward. He follows, keeping me pressed tightly into him, a firm arm around my waist. When I hear him moan softly against my mouth, it releases something inside. An unleashing . . . unraveling. I let myself go completely then, melting into him. The champagne glass in my hand threatens to crash to the floor, but I manage to keep a hold of it.

He moves his hand up my thigh, under the hem of my dress, grazing my underwear. He tastes amazing, raw and hot, and with my eyes closed and his smell invading my senses I definitely feel as though I'm in a dream. Jake slides his hand under my dress and grabs my butt to pull me into him. His erection, loud and thick against me, causes a rush of something sudden and damp between my legs. Because my body is well aware of how single I am, it works as an alarm call to stop. I need to stop this now.

God, I don't want to stop this.

When I push at him, I hear a low, frustrated noise akin to a growl escape his mouth before he finally steps back. I stare up at him, panting. His mouth is wet and red, and he's breathing hard too. He looks aroused, fierce, almost annoyed.

I swallow. "I need to get back . . . to my friends," I say, breathless, embarrassment flooding my entire body. Who on earth was I just there? What on earth was I thinking, letting him kiss me like that and touch me like that? I don't do things like that. Like this. But god help me, I'm so turned on.

I bring my hand to my mouth and smooth down my dress before walking on unsteady legs to set the champagne glass on his desk. When I look back at him, he seems satisfied with himself, a proud, arrogant smile arching his pretty mouth. I wonder why he looks so pleased with himself since what happened there wasn't even nearly enough.

He licks his lips again, and then, to his shame—or perhaps mine, because he doesn't seem ashamed in the slightest—he adjusts the erection straining against the front of his expensive trousers. It's obvious and disgraceful, and it makes me even more embarrassed.

So, he's hard. This ferociously attractive man is hard from kissing me.

I feel a surge of power at that notion. At the sheer idea of it. In fact, the thought dispels something from my psyche entirely, and for a split second,

I think I might let him have me right here against the glass window like a wanton woman. Or on the sofa. Or on his desk.

Clearly, I'm not thinking straight. Clearly, I'm drunk.

Okay, I really need to get away from him. Now. If only I could detach my feet from the floor . . .

Then, when I think he's going to move forward and kiss me again, there's a loud knock at the office door. I nearly jump out my skin at the interruption, but Jake doesn't flinch. Neither does he move to get the door. He continues to stare at me until there's another knock, louder this time, accompanied by the sound of a girl calling his name from the other side. He curses under his breath, spins on his heel, and stalks over to open it, revealing a tanned pretty thing with dark hair and big blue eyes who beams up at him.

"Hey, Jake, sorry," she says, waiting for him to forgive the interruption. He doesn't. She glances behind Jake and then at me, and I see something harden her pretty features. "So, um . . . so, they called to say Aleska is caught in traffic—Knightsbridge, they said—but he should be here in the next thirty minutes. I've stocked the dressing room, but the bar needs you to sign this off." She hands him a tablet, which he grabs, signs quickly with his finger, and hands back to her.

While Jake's head is down, she throws another stare in my direction, and it's the same look: resentment. The fact I'm clearly stepping on someone's toes being in his office makes me feel like even more of a hussy.

As he goes to close the door, she steps forward and says quietly, though not quietly enough, "See you later then?" There's a hopeful lilt to her voice.

I tense, looking away. So, he sleeps with his staff. What a gentleman.

"Just get back to work, Gemma, yeah?" he says brusquely and closes the door in her face.

I feel sorry for her. Whatever they had going clearly meant more to her than it did to him. I glance toward the leather sofa and desk, and a myriad of sleazy thoughts go through my head. Namely: I wonder how many girls he's had in here. I was nearly another one. Though, I suppose, since it's the opening night . . .

How depressing. Great. Now I feel cheap. Drunk and cheap.

I really have to get out of here.

"Well, thank you, Jake," I say, moving toward the door. "Again, thanks for inviting us. The hospitality really has been lovely." Too late, I realize that sounds like an innuendo. As though him kissing and groping me is part of the hospitality. Christ. *Go, Alex. Now. Leave.* "It's a really great place, and I'm sure it'll do really well. Good luck with . . . everything." I'm jabbering now, which must be really sexy. I get to the door, but suddenly, he's beside me, close and hot. He puts his foot against it to stop me from opening it.

"I want to see you again," he says. It sounds like a demand, his whole persona that of someone who isn't defied often.

See him again. Of course, my sensible head knows it's a bad idea. Warning after warning flashes loud and bloody clear. He's dangerous and seductive, and he sleeps with his staff. However, my body thinks it's a fabulous idea, especially the part between my legs. It's pretty much screaming, "Yes!" and asking when.

"I don't think that's a good idea," I say, hoping my body gets the picture too. But when I look up into his eyes, I can't think straight. Again. All the warnings would be so much easier to heed if not for his eyes and his mouth and his smell . . .

Christ, what are the warnings again? I shake my head to clear it. If I can just get out of this room and away from him, it'll be fine. He's distracting me from the obvious, and I'm too hot. It's so hot in here. Why doesn't he have air-conditioning in his bloody office?

His head tilts to the side, studying me, a lazy half-smile on his lips. "That's not a no, Alex," he points out, reaching up to brush a strand of hair away from my face.

Was it not a no? God, that's not even proper English.

"I've thought about you a lot since that night, Doctor," he continues in the low, soft, rough-edged tone, reaching out to skim his finger softly across my jaw. "I thought about what I'd do if you came here tonight and I saw you again."

His eyes are piercing. So piercing. He thought about me a lot?

"And what was that?' I ask in a soft voice I don't even recognize. God only knows how I'm able to speak because I'm barely breathing.

He grins again, slow and lazy. "First, I told myself I'd kiss you." He leans in, and I think he's going to kiss me on the mouth again, but he doesn't. Instead, he brings his head to my neck and takes a deep breath of me there. "Then I told myself I'd find out how you smelled right here . . ." His voice is barely audible, so low and gravelly my nipples harden and I have to bite back the moan that catches in my throat. I can't breathe. "I also thought about fucking you."

I gasp. An image of his strong, tattooed body thrusting into me without any tenderness or care explodes into my mind, and I feel another surge of something hot and damp rush between my legs. He makes an almost pained noise. Soft, growling. It vibrates over my entire body.

"Are you thinking about it now? Wondering how good I'd feel inside you?" His voice tickles my tender skin, hot and deep. "I'd feel good, Alex. You can trust me on that."

I turn my head slightly to meet his eye, our lips so close I feel the heat of his breath on mine. He looks confident. He *would* feel good inside me. How on earth is it that he's so confident? Sexual arrogance. Is that even a thing? Because there's only one way a person would know they're good at being inside someone, and that's from experience.

His sexual experience is another warning I should heed.

"I really have to go," I plead in my unsteady voice, which I realize still isn't saying no. I need to get away from him and back to the safety of Rob and the girls, where I can think straight. Where it isn't so warm and intoxicating.

When I pull on the handle, he shifts his foot, and though his stare never leaves me, he lets me pull open the door. Squeezing myself through the gap into the cool air of the hallway, I scurry away from him like the coward I am.

I look back only when I reach the top of the stairs, and it's mainly to check he isn't following me. He's not. He's standing in the doorway, arm stretched up against the frame, watching me retreat with a small, sexy smile on his face. He nods once, sort of like he's accepted a challenge. A challenge he knows he'll win hands bloody down.

FOUR

I SCUTTLE BACK ALONG THE BRIDGE TO OUR TABLE WITH ALL THE GRACE of a criminal fleeing the scene of a crime, checking behind me now and then to make sure he hasn't decided to follow me after all. Our table now seems to have merged with the one next door—a small crowd of good-looking guys dressed in smart shirts and smelling of too much cologne. I say "good-looking," but my barometer of good-looking has gone up a notch or ten, and so, really, they all look pretty average to me.

"God, Alex, where the hell have you been!" Robyn exclaims.

"Sorry. I got a bit lost," I explain. I'm still lost. What day is it?

"The DJ is on soon. We were waiting for you as the girls want to go down and find a good spot on the dance floor!"

I wonder what's wrong with our current spot. Surely it's called VIP for a reason. I have little power to resist though, because I'm far too hot, and my brain is all soft. I can still smell him and feel his hands and mouth on me.

"Sure, let's go down." I shrug. Maybe a dance and a shot will clear my head of him.

The dance floor is heaving, the sheer number of people making it hard to move, let alone dance. Somehow, we squeeze our way to the bar, the guys from our neighboring VIP booth pushing their way through the crowd with little care or manners, ignoring the looks other dancers throw at them. I, however, smile politely and mouth, "Sorry," to them as I slip into the path they've made.

Rob refuses to let the guys pay—a rule we stick to on every night out no matter where we are—and turns to hand me a glass of champagne and a shot of "mercury." Of course, I know better than to knock back shots for the sole purpose of getting drunk, but my nerves are frayed and my decision-making questionable, so I tip it back into my mouth.

The stuff is vile. It's warm and thick, and it crawls its way down my throat. With my face screwed up in disgust, I turn to place the small glass back on the bar and take a long gulp of champagne to drown out the taste.

As Rob passes the drinks to the other girls, I turn slightly to see I've been positioned next to one of the guys from the neighboring table. He beams at me wide. Dark, almost black hair, tall, with delicate skin and kind eyes—the sort of guy I would normally find attractive. Normally.

"So, your friend says you're a doctor," he bends to shout in my ear.

I plaster on a smile and nod. "Yes. What about you?" I ask, my eyes drifting up toward Jake's office. I wonder if he can see me from here. Do I want that?

"I'm in the financial sector," he tells me, showing me his perfect white teeth again. No sharp ones, just straight and even and white. Probably a little too big if I have to nitpick.

Big teeth? Seriously, Alex?

"Sounds interesting," I lie.

"It's not. But the money's great, you know?" He laughs.

"I imagine it is." God, I am so truly awful at this. Truly. Small talk. I hate it more than most things on earth.

I sip my champagne again so I don't have to speak.

"I'm Matt, by the way."

I gulp down my champagne. "Alex—hi," I shout back. The beat of the music changes, deepening into something more euphoric, and presumably because the mercury has done its job, I begin to sway slightly in time with it.

"Want to dance?" he asks close to my ear. When I look at him, he nods behind me toward the dance floor.

I think about Jake watching me dance with this guy, and it makes me feel odd. I'm almost sure he isn't watching. A "pretty big night" for him, he said. I'm sure he has a million and one other matters to take care of. Young, pretty bar staff for example.

"Actually, yes, I do," I tell him, and he grins. I place my glass on the bar and reach out to grab Matt's hand as he moves us onto the dance floor. Rob gives me an open-mouthed stare as I pass, then a bright thumbs-up.

We find a less densely populated spot by a large stone pillar, and I'm grateful for the gust of air that rushes at me as we leave the busier part of the club. While I dance, Matt moves in closer so he's pressed against my back, hips grinding into mine. When his mouth immediately makes for my neck, I shift to move out of his reach, making it look as if I'm swaying to the music.

As the beat slows, I close my eyes and sway, the music beating away at my body, the image of Jake making love to me shaping itself once more behind my eyes. I feel Matt lean into me again, mouth against my ear. He smells sweet and overpowering. There's an underlying maleness too, but it's not as affecting as Jake's.

Seriously? His scent? What is my deal with scenting men tonight?

"You're absolutely stunning, by the way," he says, his voice low.

I groan inwardly. The dreaded clichéd come-on. I hate this, the attempt to chat you up with lines they think you want to hear.

Opening my eyes, I turn to look up at him, and he gives what I presume is his knee-trembling smile—the one he uses on girls all the time. I'll bet it rarely fails him too. I smile back, not really knowing what else to do or say. I'm already regretting asking him to dance because, essentially, I've encouraged the come-on. I've made him think I'm interested in more than dancing, clearly.

Matt misreads my look, and suddenly, he's far too close, and then his mouth is on mine, his arms wrapping around me. I move back until I feel the pillar against my spine. God, no, I don't want this. I start to push at him, but he doesn't shift immediately, and then, just as the panic kicks in, I feel his entire weight disappear. When I look around, I see Matt being dragged away from me by a large man in a dark suit who looks like security. As I shift my gaze around to see if anyone saw us, I see him. Jake. Staring at me with a dark look on his face, his mouth in a hard line. His eyes hold mine for a few long seconds before he gestures to his security guard, a small flick of his head.

As Matt is pushed roughly through the crowd by the large security guard, I turn back to Jake, frowning. His expression doesn't change; he still looks angry, but he also looks as if he might come toward me, maybe even kiss me again. God, I want him to kiss me again. But for some reason, I feel worried for Matt and as if I'm responsible for what's happening now.

Turning away from Jake's glare, I push forward, squeezing through the thickening crowd toward where they took Matt-who-works-in-finance. By a fire exit, I see the violent creep who accompanied Jake to the surgery that night, and he gives a look that turns my stomach before pushing open the fire exit for the security guard to practically throw Matt out of. I speed up, slipping through it before it closes into a brick hallway filled with kegs and boxes and a cold, damp smell.

"What exactly is going on?" I shout, trying for my reasonable, professional voice. I walk toward Matt, the creep and the security guard both turning to me. When the creep's eyes flick over my shoulder, I turn to see Jake entering the hallway, the door closing hard behind him.

"You want him outside, Jay?" the creep asks.

What? I turn to Jake, incredulous. He still looks angry—a glare that only intensifies when he turns his stare on Matt.

"Did you come with him?" Jake asks. I don't realize immediately he's talking to me because he's glaring past me, but then his eyes catch mine. Piercing. "You and him, together?" he asks me, quieter.

I shake my head. "No. I just met him." Does he seriously think I'd have allowed what happened upstairs to happen if I came with Matt?

Jake's face softens a fraction before he goes toward Matt, brushing past me, all coiled strength and sexual arrogance. Yes, I decide, it's definitely a thing.

"Come on, mate. What's this all about? This is crap." Matt sounds indignant, but there's panic there below the surface.

Despite being a few inches shorter, Jake's demeanor makes him look the more powerful of the two. He holds himself completely differently from any other man I know, as if he's trying to contain something destructive. Power reined in tight. He looks dangerous suddenly. Matt seems to come to the same conclusion because he takes a step back and swallows, expensive vacation tan fading before my eyes.

"First off, I am not your fucking mate," Jake growls.

I stiffen. His voice is an unwholesome mixture of calm and malice, and it puts me completely on edge. Matt looks at me as though sending out a visual SOS. I wonder whether to step in.

"Hey, hey—you don't look at her, yeah?" Jake snaps, quiet. "You hear me? Eyes back here, pretty boy."

Matt looks back at Jake for only a moment before dropping his eyes to his feet. My mind catches on the term "pretty boy," because there's an irony in the fact that compared to Jake, Matt looks like Quasimodo.

"I'm just here with my mates having a good time," Matt mutters quietly.

"Yeah, I fucking bet you were," Jake's friend snickers, shooting a glance at me.

I see Jake's jaw clench hard, a tremble of rage moving over him. Something propels me forward.

"This is ridiculous, Jake. What is this about?"

His head snaps around to me, his eyes harsh and cold still. "What this is about, Alex, is that this prick here was trying to mount you on my fucking dance floor," he says coldly.

I jerk back as though he's slapped me. *Mount* me? I feel indignant, defensive, embarrassed. My cheeks flare. As I stare at Jake open-mouthed, he studies my face—every inch of it, it seems—for a bloody eternity.

"What, wait—she's your girlfriend? Oh, fuck. I had no idea, mate," Matt says, breaking the silence. "Sorry."

Jake and I speak together:

"I'm not his girlfriend," I snap.

"I am not your fucking mate," Jake hisses. Something flickers behind his eyes, something less cold, and he licks his lips in that slow, deliberate way. As though he deliberately wants me to think about kissing him. As though he deliberately wants to remind me of him kissing me.

Suddenly, his face softens, and he nods once, the suggestion of a smile tugging at the corner of his petal-pink mouth. He turns away from me to address Matt again, his shoulders more relaxed this time, his body less murderous.

"Well, it looks like it's your lucky night, mate," Jake tells him. "There happens to be someone here I'm trying to show my nice side to. Also, I don't really fancy getting your blood on my shirt. So, take this as a warning, yeah? I see you back here anytime soon, it ain't going to end like this. Your friends can stay, but I want you the fuck out of here. Now."

I can't believe he sounds so reasonable considering what he's saying. For a second, Matt looks as if he might say something back, maybe try to argue the point, but he doesn't. Instead, he nods once and shakes his head.

"Smart move," Jake says. "Kev, get him the fuck out of here."

The security guard, aided by the creep, immediately starts hauling Matt down the hallway away from us.

"You can't throw him out for absolutely no reason, Jake. That's ridiculous." I use my professional voice again, and it stops Kev and the security guard in their tracks, amused. Matt looks annoyed, which is ungrateful to say the least.

Jake takes a step toward me—so close I can feel his heat and smell his smell again. "See, that's where you're wrong, Alex," he breathes. "'Cause I can do whatever the fuck I want in here. And we both know it's not for no reason." He darkens.

"Oh, that's right. It was for trying to mount me." I nod. "Well, since I was also a part of that, maybe you should throw me out too." I raise my eyebrows.

Jake's eyes darken. "From where I was standing, you didn't seem to be enjoying it. But maybe I was wrong." His voice is quiet, his breathing fast. "Were you?"

I wasn't enjoying it. In fact, I distinctly remember wishing to be rescued at the exact moment he came along and, well, rescued me. I'd feel like a weak, drunk idiot telling him that though, so I bite my lip instead, glancing briefly behind him at Matt.

"I still think it's an overreaction," I mumble. "I'm sure there are far worse things going on out there."

Jake stares at me, mind ticking over, a measure of indecision or confusion on his face. Finally, he turns and strides toward Matt, leaning in to whisper something in his ear. Something I can't hear from where I am. Matt's eyes close for a moment before he nods, opens them again, and looks at me.

"Listen, Alex, it's fine. I've had too much to drink anyway. I should go. But you stay with your friends, please. And I'm really sorry if I was too forward—really sorry. If you could mention to my mates I've gone home, that'd be great," he says. It's as if he's reading from a script.

Jake turns to me with a look on his face that says, "Your move, Doctor."

Since I don't really fancy following Matt out into the street for some bizarre show of solidarity, I say nothing. Jake motions to Kev who once again begins pulling Matt off down the hallway away from us. As soon as they turn a corner at the end and leave him and me alone, the freezing hole in the wall begins to heat up. He's moved so he's leaning against the opposite wall, hands in his pockets, staring at me hard again. I feel a lot of things under that stare.

"Well, that was all a bit unnecessary, don't you think? Not the best PR for your opening night."

"Do I look as if I give a fuck about my PR?" he asks, his voice low. It occurs to me it's the kind of tone he might use in bed, and my face flushes with heat.

No, I suppose he doesn't look as if he cares about his PR.

"Well, it was still unnecessary," I say.

He doesn't respond right away, and for something to do, I skim my hand down over my dress then fiddle with a strand of my hair. He leans up off the wall and stalks toward me, coming too far into my personal space. As though I mean to stop him, I place my hands on his chest, but I don't put any strength into the movement. His chest is hard and warm under my palms, and I feel it rise and fall quickly with his breath, his heartbeat powerful and fast. He inclines his head, and his stare intensifies. I can't tell if he's still angry, turned on, or both.

"I disagree. It was totally necessary," he says. "And totally your own fucking fault."

He swears a lot, I've noticed. That's two "fucks" in a brief space of time. Wait a minute—*my* fault?

"Excuse me? How was any of that my fault?"

"You wanted me to see you with him, didn't you?" His eyes are narrow and dark again.

I look at him, outraged. He's unbelievable. He really thinks I was thinking about him when I took Matt to the dance floor. Oh, wait . . . I was, wasn't I?

"Why on earth would I want that?"

"You tell me, Doctor."

"We were dancing. This is an establishment where people dance, is it not?" I sound like a brat.

"He had his fucking hands all over you, Alex," he growls.

"Dancing," I repeat, indignant. Though, he's right: Matt had his hands all over me. Hands I wished were his instead. It's not the point though. The point is that Jake has no right to decide who can and can't have their hands all over me.

"So that's how you let every guy you've *just met* touch you then?" he asks, the accusation clear in his eye. My cheeks burn from it.

I narrow my eyes on him and go to push past him, away. He stops me by putting one leg between mine and his hand on my waist, pressing me back against the wall. His other hand comes up to rest on the wall above my head as he leans in closer.

"Oh, we're not done here, Doctor," he says in that low voice, thick with warning and something else.

I wonder then if this should scare me. Dangerous (sexy) stranger trapping a drunk woman against a wall in the hallway of a noisy nightclub certainly sounds like a government-sponsored video. One about the dangers of drinking and getting separated from your friends while out partying. But I'm not afraid. Perhaps the alcohol has numbed my fear receptors.

"How dare you? And tell me, what on earth has it got to do with you if some guy had his hands all over me? I have literally just met you. These may be your premises, Jake, but I am not your bloody property."

"Yeah, these are my premises, and you're lucky that prick left unharmed," he says. "I watched for a bit before stepping in. It didn't look to me like you were enjoying it. Not like you were enjoying it with me for example." There's a quiet smirk hovering behind his words, and the memory of his hands pulling me into his erection as his wet, fiery mouth explored mine makes my stomach clench tightly.

"You know nothing about me. Or what I enjoy," I lie, looking away from his stare.

"Okay. So, I got it wrong then, yeah? You were planning on taking him home and fucking him then, were you? Did I mess up your plan?" he snaps.

God, I really could get lost in his eyes. Green pools of heat that seem to burrow straight into my core, warming and softening it. Wait—what did he just say?

"Who I take home or don't take home is really none of your business, Jake. Like I said, I am not your property."

He smiles, and it's that wickedly sexy, sharp-toothed smile that makes me think illicit thoughts. It makes me think he's thinking illicit thoughts too.

"Well, if you had,"—he leans in to whisper close to my ear—"I'm willing to bet everything I have that you would have wished it were me the entire time." He inhales deeply at my neck, breathing me in. "As he fucked you, you'd have closed your eyes and imagined it were me." When he brings his head back up, he looks arrogant, and for the first time, I find the quality so bloody sexy. He doesn't need to know that though.

"Your arrogance is astounding. Do you know that?" I shake my head and look at the wall behind him, the beer kegs on the floor—anywhere but at that arrogant mouth I want so badly to wipe the smirk from. Preferably with my mouth.

He sighs, and even that sounds arrogant. "Again, not a no, Alex. So, like I said, upstairs. I want to see you again."

Again, I try to think of all the reasons it's a bad idea. But I can't think, because his mouth is wet, and I can see his tongue, and the heat radiating from him makes it hard to concentrate.

"No," I say. *Finally.*

To my surprise, he smiles again. Then he lets out an exaggerated sigh. "People don't tend to say no to me, Alex."

"Oh, really? Well, I do like to be unique," I retort. My heart thunders so loud in my ears. Even I don't understand why I'm saying no. Except it seems like the sensible thing to do, and I'm nothing if not sensible.

He nods. "You're unique all right, Doctor Marlowe. Why don't you want to see me again?"

"Because it's not a good idea." It's not. Because he makes me far too weak, and too hot, and I enjoy maintaining a normal body temperature. "You were my patient. I can't see patients like that. It's not . . . ethical."

"Okay. Well, first off, how about I promise never to turn up at your surgery again? Ever. And second, how about I remind you of why it's a good idea?" He lowers his gaze to my mouth. He's going to kiss me again. To remind me. I can't think of anything I've ever wanted or needed reminding of more in my life.

A small sound escapes my mouth, something between a moan and a plea, but he still doesn't move his mouth to mine; he just stares at it. As I stand there willing him to kiss me, to remind me, minutes pass, maybe even an hour. When he doesn't move, I take the initiative, impatient and needy, leaning forward to press my lips to his. I'm sure before our mouths touch he smirks again, but the thought goes out of my head as soon as his taste floods onto my tongue.

I slide my hands up his chest, curling them behind his neck into his hair to pull his head down to mine. He moans as I do this, and the sound does something to my insides, making them thrum and vibrate. Need.

My god, he tastes divine. Like danger and sex and heat. Masculinity and intoxication. Sin and desire. I'm pretty sure I could kiss him forever. Who needs to breathe anyway? Or eat. I'm in no rush to pull away this time. It's good here—I want to stay. His mouth milks my own, tongue lapping at mine, skin against skin, breaths dancing together. The sound and feel of his hot, quick breath against my face is arousing beyond belief.

From somewhere far, far off, I hear a throat clearing, but Jake continues his assault on my mouth. Or is it my assault on his? I'm not sure. I've utterly lost track. Lost once more.

"Jay," a voice says.

Slowly, reluctantly, Jake peels himself from my mouth, staring longingly into my eyes. He places a last lick of his tongue on my upper lip before raising his head, allowing me to look away and find the voice.

Kev looks between Jake and me, leering, knowing, as though he's just watched us do more than kiss. It makes me feel exposed and spied on.

I glance down. Jake turns to him.

"You're needed upstairs, mate," Kev tells him.

Jake mutters a curse, which must be about being needed upstairs rather than being called "mate" again. Kev the creep is apparently one of those allowed to call him that.

"Yeah, okay. I'll follow you up," he says, and Kev nods before heading off, back the way he came.

As Kev's footsteps die away, Jake turns to me. Slowly, he brings his hand up to trace his fingertips over my collarbone before gently moving my hair back behind my shoulder to expose my neck. *I wondered how you would smell here . . .* His face is softer now. Softer than I've ever seen it.

"So . . . still think it's a bad idea to see me again?" he asks with an almost boyish grin.

How does he do that? Sexy and arrogant one moment, adorable and boyishness the next. In any case, I do in fact still think it's a bad idea to see him again. He has heartbreak written all over him. Plus, he is absolutely not my type. I can't date someone like him. He probably doesn't date anyway. He probably has sex—a lot. And probably not with the same girl twice.

God, I want to see him again though. I want to do more than see him. I want him. I want to know what he looks like undressed, and what he sounds like while having sex, and how he takes his coffee.

If I were at home, out of his reach, I'd feel far more confident that seeing him again is a terrible idea. But I'm not at home. I'm here, and he's looking at me like a hungry animal looks at meat, and that should be enough of a warning. I shake my head no, but he grabs my chin gently, forcing me to meet his eye.

"You know, I knew getting you wasn't going to be easy, Alex. I knew that." He strokes his thumb over my bottom lip, soft, tender. "So, if you want me to chase you, then I'm prepared to do that. First time for everything, I suppose. Might even be fun." He grins.

He knew "getting me" wouldn't be easy? He wants to chase me?

What the hell happens when he catches me?

"I . . . do really have to get back." My voice is quiet, uncertain, not saying no.

"To your friends, yeah, I know." He takes a step back and adjusts himself, fixing his collar and running a hand through his perfectly styled hair. He needn't bother adjusting anything because he still looks immaculate. Sexy, immaculate, and dangerous. Not my type.

Yet when I glance down and see a definite bulge in his crotch area, I feel like purring.

I've managed a few steps away from him when I hear him call my name. I turn back.

"Just so you know, when I want something, I normally get it," he states. "And in case it wasn't clear, though fuck knows how it couldn't be, I want you." He studies me for a long moment before giving me a smile that almost makes me orgasm on the spot.

I say nothing because I honestly have no words. He wants me. The knowledge does something to me. Something powerful. I feel warm and weightless and drunk, but it's not from the alcohol.

When Jake turns on his heel and strides off down the hallway with all the grace of a tiger, I notice he has an amazing backside. Of course he bloody does.

He's still not my type though.

With a tremulous sigh, I pull open the door, the heavy bass assaulting my senses anew. I need to get out of this place.

FIVE

"Leaving so soon, ladies?" A male maître d' asks as we get to the front door.

"Just me," I tell him.

"Aw, that's a shame. Can I call you a taxi?" he offers.

Slightly stunned, I accept. Jake certainly doesn't do things by halves.

After giving the maître d' my name and table number, he goes into his booth to lift the phone. Rob thinks I'm leaving because I have a headache. Which isn't a complete lie. I do feel as though I've been whacked over the head with a Jake-sized sledgehammer.

As we wait for the taxi to arrive, Rob says I do in fact "look a bit peaky," telling me to drink a pint of water and take two ibuprofen before going straight to bed. As though she's the medical practitioner, not me.

"Yes, Mum." I sigh, distracted. My head keeps going back to the feel of him and the smell of him and everything he said. He thought about me a lot. He wants to see me again. I'm something he wants. These things excite me far too much. It feels like the sort of rush you get as you climb to the top of a roller coaster, that moment right before the fall.

Also, he used a ruse to get me here. Guys don't orchestrate meetings aimed at seducing me. I have never been seduced. Do I want him to seduce me? With that mouth, taste, smell? All these things are seductive by themselves, but as a package deal? On him? Jesus. I'm too hot again.

Dangerous. Player. Possible violent streak. Not my type. Repeat.

"Alex? Did you hear what I said?"

"What?" I shake my head. "Sorry, babe, I was thinking about something else." *Someone* else.

"I was saying, Becca is definitely onto a sure thing with the footballer. Did you see them?" She gives me a look as if to say, "That could have been you, babe."

Vaguely, I wonder what Rob would make of Jake and how far he would be from her idea of a sure thing.

"Your car's here, Dr. Marlowe," I hear from behind me.

My head whips around. I only gave him my surname. Does everyone in this place know my name, age, and occupation? I give him a nod and look back at Rob.

"Okay, well, you have fun, lady," I order lightly. "I'll text you when I get home. Enjoy the rest of the night and call me tomorrow, okay?" I hug her tight before following the maître d' out to the still bustling street where a shiny, expensive silver car awaits. I assume Jake's club has a contract with an upmarket taxi company to take his VIP guests home. Another pleasant touch.

The host opens the door for me, and I thank him and get into the back seat, which is all cream-colored leather and smells brand-new.

"18 Pilgrims Way, Shere, please," I tell the driver, waiting for the sigh they normally give when they find out I'm a forty-minute drive out of the city. He doesn't sigh though, only nods politely, and I settle in for the drive back home.

"Would you like the radio on, love?" he asks through the rearview. He's an older man, about late fifties, with a friendly, mustached face.

"Sure, why not?"

He nods, flicking through a few stations before settling on one playing something slow and haunting. It calms my busy, fevered mind immediately, and I settle farther into the seat, resting my head against the window, watching as London and its suburbs pass me in a trance-inducing blur.

I always love leaving the city to go home. I love that I live far enough out to feel separate from its heaving oppressiveness, but close enough to enjoy it whenever I want. Which, to be honest, is rare—even rarer since Ben moved back. Selling his flat in Islington to make the big sacrificial move to the country for me was the best thing he ever did for us. He called it huge and sacrificial; I called it a simple lifestyle change. "Emigrating to the country" was something he did for me because he always put me first. Other demonstrations, he said, were allowing me to adopt a cat and proposing.

It was ironic then that the commute from London was the perfect cover for his affair during the six months before I found out. The affair, adversely, wasn't one of the things he did to demonstrate his love for me. Fucking a blonde sales executive in his car, hotel rooms, and at her flat was something he did to feel like a man.

Christ, I hate dwelling on Ben. It wasn't a wasted eight years, I know that deep down, but right now, it still feels like it. I resent any moment my thoughts go to him, and so I change their direction immediately and think instead about the man who demonstrated tonight how much he wants me.

Right on cue, my stomach does another of its involuntary lurches at the memory of him and both of tonight's episodes.

I wonder what his story is. A fortnight ago, he turned up at my surgery covered in blood and looking like a hooligan. Tonight, he's immaculately dressed and opening an expensive nightclub in Brick Lane. It makes no sense. Neither does his effect on me. He's attractive, obviously, but when has that ever been enough to turn my mind and body to something sludgy and not solid? Good-looking men have never intimidated me. I have a brain and enough self-esteem to ensure I'm comfortable around attractive men.

But Jake Lawrence seems to trample all over that. His effect on me has the same swagger as he does. Sexual, arrogant, dangerous. And then there's the kiss. *His* kiss. I run my fingers across my lips, remembering how he felt on them. I must have kissed Ben a million times, and not once did it feel like that. As necessary as breathing.

If that was what kissing him felt like, I couldn't even begin to imagine what sex with him would feel like. Okay, I could partially imagine what sex with him would feel like. Hard, hot, and all-consuming. Like he is. I wonder if it is the danger. If that's the reason my brain leaves my head around him. The forbidden, risky vibe that hangs over him like an aura. God, if that's it, then I'm a cliché. I'm a girl who likes bad boys after all. How bloody unoriginal. I almost groan in disgust.

Except there's this: If I didn't meet him like I did, under that veil of danger and threat, he would still have that mouth and those eyes and that smell, and he'd still have kissed me like that. This time, I do groan aloud.

"Where's 18, love?" the driver asks, startling me.

I look out the window to see we're driving up the narrow road toward my house. Did I just spend the entire forty-minute drive home fantasizing about this man? Ugh. Ridiculous behavior.

"Oh, I'm up at the end there, on the right-hand side." I sit up, unbuckling my seat belt to lean between the two front seats and point at my house. "That road up there's a private one, so you'll need to turn around and go back down the way you came."

"No problem, love." He stops the car in front of my cottage, engine idling.

"Perfect. Thank you so much. How much do I owe you?" I open my bag to get my purse.

"Oh, no charge, love," he says. "Jake's orders."

My heart skips a beat at the mention of his name. His name spoken like *that*. "Wh—what do you mean? No, I have to pay you. How much?" I rummage through my purse for the money, shoving three twenties at him.

"Honestly, love, it'd be more than my job's worth if you gave me any money. Our boy was pretty clear: drive you straight home, carefully, and make sure I see you're in the front door safe," he explains.

Our boy? Did Jake order this man to drive me home? This man calls him "our boy."

"This . . . isn't a taxi, is it?"

He chuckles softly. "No, love. I work for Jake." A nod. Jake's name is said with a reverence I don't entirely understand, as if he's talking about his son or a family member. I clearly have no choice in the matter of paying this man.

"Okay, well, thank you then. And give my thanks to your . . . boss," I say, shimmying across the seat to get out. I'm annoyed but not entirely sure why.

"Will do, love. I'm just going to watch until you get in the door, and then I'll be off," he tells me.

I stop, my mouth dropping open. Watch until I get in my front door? Of the house I've lived in for three years in the sleepy village of Shere?

"Oh, gosh, that's not necessary, honestly. It's perfectly safe here. I'll be fine." I can't believe Jake thinks I need a chaperone to get to own my front door.

"Orders." He shrugs easily. I clearly don't have a choice in this matter either.

"Good night then," I say, annoyed with this man though it's not even his fault. It's Jake's fault. Jake gives orders, and people follow them, which apparently includes this man and me.

I exit the car and walk the short distance up the pebbled driveway to my front door. My house sits back from the road, almost secluded, but the doorway is still visible from where my chaperone sits, watching. The security porch light pops on as I get to the door, helping me find my front door key in my bag. I glance down at the car and nod, but he continues to wait.

It's only when I'm inside and the door's closed I hear him head off down the road. I lock the front door as Fred comes toward me, purring against my leg before flopping down on his back for his obligatory greeting.

"Well, hello, baby." I slip off my heels and bend down to rub his stomach. "Did you have a fun night? You won't believe what happened. Mummy met a ridiculously sexy man who has trouble written all over him . . ." I pick him up and nuzzle his face as I head through to the kitchen. After feeding him, I fill the kettle and flick it on to boil. Then, following Rob's orders, I gulp down a pint of ice-cold water and take two ibuprofen and take a seat at the kitchen table.

What a bloody night.

Rob calls after lunch. "I could kill you!" she starts. "All night, I was checking my phone, and then, when I tried to call you, your phone was off."

"It must have died through the night. Sorry, babe."

"Well, as long as you're fine, I forgive you."

"So, how was the rest of the night? Do you have a hangover?"

"Ugh, marginally. But Alekso was fab—the place went nuts when they announced him. He played for about an hour then went off and came back on to announce the name of the club. *Annnnnd* . . . Becca went home with the footballer." Robyn says the last part with a measure of judgment, I think.

"So, he was a footballer," I say absently, licking a blob of marmalade from the side of my hand. My croissants are going to be freezing. Hard and freezing.

"Yeah. He said what team—a lower division, I think. Can't remember. So, no doubt that'll be her in love again . . ." She sighs.

Oh, Rob, let her have her fun. Someone should at least get to sleep with whoever they want regardless of whether it's sensible. I try to change the subject. "What was the name?" I ask.

"Oh, I can't remember. It had a city at the end. I'd remember if I heard it again, though I'll ask Dan," she says, missing my meaning.

"No—the club's name. What did they call it?" I have to change my direction of thought quickly so as not to ask what *he* called it. What name would Jake Lawrence choose for his club, I wonder? Jake's Den of Sin?

"Oh. Yeah, they called it Surgery. Or *The* Surgery. No—just Surgery, I think. Quite cool, I guess. Was that your suggestion?" She snorts.

I can't hear anything after that because my head is spinning. Why the hell would he name it that? Really? Out of all the possibilities and suggestions he would have had last night, that's what he chose? Or perhaps I'm reading too much into it. Yes, it's probably that. A coincidence. A bizarre one. That's all.

"So, what are your plans today, babe?" she asks before I hear her cover the phone to speak to Dan. "What? Oh, yeah, she's fine. Dan and I are going for a picnic if you fancy joining us?"

"Oh, that sounds lovely, but I'm going to Mum's for dinner in a bit. Nick's coming," I say cautiously. I try to avoid talking about Nick around Rob as much as possible. It was years ago, and she's completely moved on, but she also has an amazing memory and holds a grudge like no one else I know.

"Well, that'll be fun. Say hello to him from me," she drawls sarcastically.

"I won't." I smile.

"Oh, and when is your date with the eligible Dr. Wardley?" she asks excitedly.

God, I completely forgot about that.

"Um, not sure. Next week sometime, I guess."

"Good. It's been far too long since Voldemort, and you need to get some." Rob's nicknames for Ben switch frequently between "The Prick," "Voldemort," and "He Who Must Not Be Named." She's right though: I need to "get some." The problem is that the person I want to get some from is not Dr. Sam Wardley.

"Yeah, you're right, and he's a lovely guy. But I really don't want the complications at work if this goes badly, that's all."

"Well, if you go in with that attitude, as if it's going to go badly, then it doesn't give it a great shot, does it?"

Another good point. Thanks, Rob.

"Yes! Okay, I'm coming! Okay, Dan is rushing me. Call you later?"

After I hang up, I go back to my cool coffee and cooler croissant. When I call Mum to check on the plans for dinner, she's excitable and talking a pitch or two higher than normal. Whenever Nick comes home, it's as if the prodigal son returned. She's probably polishing the china while we talk. No, I don't know if he's bringing a girl or whether he's seeing anyone seriously yet. I tell her I'll see her later and hang up, wondering vaguely how she would react to me bringing Jake to Sunday dinner.

I spend the rest of the day pottering around the house doing laundry, light cleaning, and some reading in the garden. These are things I do, but mentally, I'm somewhere else. Mentally, I'm pressed against a glass window in a dim office. Against the cool brick wall of a nightclub hallway.

As I walk into the house I grew up in, the smell of roasting meat overcomes me, and my mouth waters. A good, homely roast dinner and a hug from Dad will re-center my scattered brain, I'm sure. Also, it was "The Chopin Sessions" on Classic FM on the drive over, which helped relax my jostling thoughts a bit too.

"Hey, guys, it's me," I shout as I drop my bag by the front door.

Mum and Dad's house still feels like home to me. Even after Tash, Nick, and I moved out, they never even considered downsizing. I think Mum believes the place will be heaving with grandchildren soon and so she'll need all the spare bedrooms she can get. Besides, it's not as if they can't afford it. My parents have always been comfortable as far as money is concerned, like both their parents were before them. Financial stability in our family is passed down like freckles.

"Oh, hi, sweetheart," Mum says as I come into the kitchen. She sounds harassed. As I cross toward her, she puts an arm around me, warm, smelling of roses and familiarity.

"How are you?" I ask. "Smells delicious. Where's Dad?" I pinch a piece of buttered bread as I pass.

"Fine, darling. I'm fine. He's in the garden. How are you? How's work? Nick is still coming, isn't he?" She looks up at me from the pot of boiling potatoes.

"Yes, he's coming, Mum." I nod.

I leave her watching the mash and head into the garden to see my father. He's spraying the border plants with the hose just off the patio. Since he retired, the garden has been his surgery, the flora and fauna his patients, and so my parents' garden is a thing of beauty.

"Hey, you," I shout over the sound of the hose.

He turns, beaming at me. Dad's face never fails to put me at ease no matter what's going on. It's the doctor in him. The reassuring manner once learned is never forgotten, it seems. He turns off the hose and comes to hug me, squeezing tight.

"There's my girl. You're early. Or is your brother late?" he asks gently. "She's been fussing about all day." Sighing, he inclines his head toward the house.

"No surprise there." I smile. "How are you doing, Dad?"

"Great, love. How are you doing? How's the practice?"

"Slow, mainly." *Unless sexually arrogant, tattooed hard men barge in demanding you stitch them up.* "I should have gone to A&E for some excitement." I sigh.

Dad laughs, and we walk together into the conservatory/dining room, his arm still around my shoulders. "Well, you can still switch sides, sweetheart. It's never too late. You've only started out. You don't want to be stuck with something that makes you unhappy," he says, eyes wide and sincere. Somewhere behind his familiar green eyes, I think this might be about Ben. I don't know.

"Oh, I know. And I'm probably being silly, but it's like I have this feeling constantly as if something's missing, you know?" I shake my head. "God, that's bad, isn't it?"

"Perhaps what you're missing out on isn't work-related," Dad says, sounding startlingly accurate. He's always had this uncanny ability to pinpoint my exact thoughts before I've even thought of them myself. It's as if sometimes, he can see into my bloody soul. "Perhaps if you had something else to focus on . . ."

Yes, okay, this is definitely about Ben.

"I have plenty of things to focus on. Plus, I have a cat. And a piano," I say lightly.

"That's not really what I mean, sweetheart."

"Oh, I know, Dad . . ." I roll my eyes.

"I'm sorry, darling. I worry about you, that's all."

"You do? Or Mum does?" I raise an eyebrow.

"Both. Okay, well, mainly her. But there, that's the talk out of the way. Now we can have a nice dinner, can't we?" he says with a wink.

"Sounds great."

He makes a clicking noise. "She worries too much about you all, you know that. But especially you now." Meaning she used to worry about Nick the most, but now, since my fiancé cheated on me and moved in with another woman, it's me she worries about. "I don't. I tell her you're the most sensible one of the lot, and you'll be absolutely fine." His face is still completely sincere as he says this, and it softens me.

The sensible one. That is me, isn't it?

Just before 7:00 p.m., almost thirty minutes late, Nick arrives. He bounds into the conservatory buzzing with energy. I haven't seen him in close to a month, and he looks good, his recent trip to South America ensuring he's tanned and healthy. My older brother is dark-haired—far darker than I am—and tall, with a perfect white smile he uses to devastating effect. Nick's looks made me very popular at school with smitten girls. If only they knew.

"Little sis, you look bloody great. Come here," he says, leaning down to pull me into a citrusy hug and kissing me on the cheek. He moves to hug Dad in the same fashion. "Old man Marlowe, how's it going?"

"Fine son, fine. You look well. Maybe we'll get fed now the guest of honor is here." Dad winks at me.

Nick beams and rubs his hands together before drumming his fingers on the table as Mum comes scurrying in with the first of the plates. Nick's is put down first, of course.

Throughout dinner, Nick chats excitedly and enthusiastically while the rest of us listen. As ever, I wonder where he gets his energy from, since his job in the city has him working, like, seventy-two-hour weeks. He talks about his recent trip to Colombia and Peru, his new car, and how he's looking at buying a new flat south of the river as an investment. We have another lighthearted argument about London again because unlike me, Nick loves living there and still can't understand why I chose to live miles away in a village with a community of OAPs.

It doesn't take long before Mum steers the conversation toward Nick's inability to settle down and find a nice girl. It was only a matter of time. I'm off the hook tonight, thank god, but Nick and I still meet eyes across the table as soon as she starts.

"Oh, Nicholas, really. I mean, you're thirty-three years old now. All this, you know, messing about"—she waves her hands dramatically—"won't satisfy you forever, you know?"

She's wrong. Nick could easily mess around forever and be more than satisfied. Well, for another two years anyway, until he is actually thirty-three. I cover my mouth with my hand to stifle a laugh before dropping my fork to stab a bit of sweetcorn.

"Eh? I'm thirty-one, Mother," he states, outraged.

Mum waves her hand absently as though Nick's age is unimportant.

"But thanks for adding a few years onto my already sensitive age insecurities."

When I look up, he's giving me a different kind of stare.

"Well, I suppose my dream of a house full of grandchildren rests firmly on Natasha's shoulders then," she says huffily, looking between Nick and me. I take this as my opportunity to excuse myself for the bathroom.

Haranguing us about our personal lives is only going to make us less likely to introduce her to anyone important to us. Nick more than most. Her interference in mine and Ben's dying days was almost impossible. I always got the feeling she wanted to blame me for his infidelity somehow, as though I must have caused him to look elsewhere. To her, Ben and I were the love of the century, and Ben was perfect for her youngest daughter. I really couldn't have done any better in her eyes. Handsome, older, talented surgeon. Even now, I think she still believes that. Despite the fact he's now living with the woman he cheated on me with.

She couldn't understand why we never set a wedding date. But then, neither could Ben. I put it off with the explanation I wanted to concentrate on my career, but really, it was because whenever I pictured our wedding day or our marriage thereafter, a ball of anxiety would flare up so strongly it would choke me into inertia.

My anxiety is something that has always been there, living inside me like some stray pet I don't exactly care for but can't seem to get rid of. Doctors aren't supposed to have mental health issues, but this one has followed me around for years, manifesting when I least want or need it. Maybe this was part of the reason Ben looked elsewhere.

In the time we've been apart, I've had plenty of time to drag every single one of my shortcomings as well as every aspect of our relationship under the microscope, and it does not make for an enjoyable study.

On the way back from the bathroom, I check my phone. There's a missed call from a number I don't recognize and texts from Tamsin and Becca, both thanking me for the VIP freebie. As I reenter the conservatory, I hear Nick speaking quietly but sternly. It's not a tone I usually hear from my brother, so it has my attention.

". . . thought the sun shined out of his effing backside, but he was sneaking around long before we all knew about it, so he was hardly the catch of the century if you ask me, Mother. So, stop it. What on earth would Al care if he—?"

He stops talking immediately as I enter, the next words dying on his tongue. Mum looks into her wineglass awkwardly while Dad, who was reading his paper, looks up at me sadly.

"Oh, don't mind me. Please continue," I say, trying to be nonchalant.

Nick looks guiltily at me. "Sorry, sis. Not my choice of subject." He looks at Mum, grimacing.

"Don't tell me, he won the Nobel Prize?" I joke dryly.

Nick makes a grunt of disapproval, anger clouding his features.

"Sorry, darling. It was a silly thing, not important. Let's change the subject. Pudding, anyone?" Mum says, standing.

"Sorry about that, sis. You know what she's like," Nick says while we load the dishwasher. "And she wonders why we don't visit more often." He shakes his head.

"It's fine. I'm fine. But please don't pretend that's the reason you never come around, Nick." I look at him askance.

"Yeah, fine. But it's one of them." His mood has turned sour, heavier too.

"You are going to have to talk to them at some point though." I turn to him. "And as soon as you do, this will—"

"Al, please. Not tonight." His voice isn't hard, just tired. Pleading.

I nod, making a motion as if I'm zipping my mouth closed.

He groans. "Can't she be happy Tash is halfway there already?"

"Yes, but Tash is in California. We're all she has. She feels redundant, I guess. She wants lots of Marlowes running about screaming in Russian," I say as I wipe down the worktop.

"She's not redundant. She has Dad. Who clearly wouldn't be able to tie his shoelaces without her." He rolls his eyes. "Anyway, it could be worse. We could all be in California."

Yeah, we could. Since Tash left, we've discussed it often. It would break Mum and Dad's hearts, of course. Losing one daughter to the States was bad enough. It's the reason she never warmed to our older sister's American husband.

"Nick, shh . . ." I say, glancing behind to make sure they haven't heard.

We finish up in the kitchen and sit down with Mum and Dad, drinking tea and eating biscuits for a while longer. We chat about our semi-planned summer in France this year to my parents' farmhouse, the earlier atmosphere from the talk of Ben long dissipated.

As we're saying our goodbyes, Dad pulls me close, leaning in to whisper, "You're doing fine, sweetheart. I'm so proud of you, you know?" His voice is quiet and warm.

I pull back to smile lovingly at him, the depth of his words almost bringing tears to my eyes. My dad is my rock, somehow always knowing exactly the right thing to say at exactly the right time, no matter the circumstance. His reassuring bedside manner has always translated so well to parenting.

At the car, Nick hugs me, telling me to come to him for dinner soon, which makes me laugh out loud. He has never cooked more than toast in his life, I'm certain of it. He corrects himself quickly, offering to take me out for dinner instead.

I stifle a yawn as I flash the lights of my Mini at my brother's Lexus to say goodbye before turning in the opposite direction.

The moment I'm tucked up in bed, I think about Jake again. With a sigh of resignation, I reach into the drawer of my nightstand and take out the gold-and-purple toy, looking at it rather hopelessly.

"Jake bloody Lawrence . . ." I sigh as I lower my hand beneath the quilt.

SIX

THE MUSIC VIBRATES THROUGH MY ENTIRE BODY, EACH POUND OF THE bass matching the beat of my heart as I make my way through the heaving mass of dancers. When the crowd parts slightly, I see him, his eyes trained on me with lust and desire. So fierce it makes my insides tighten, warmth pooling between my legs. Slowly, he walks toward me, the crowd parting for him easily. The dark T-shirt he wears shows off his tattooed arms and hard chest, making him look fierce and dangerous and beautiful.

He comes to a stop in front of me, so close I have to tilt my head up to meet his eye. His hand comes up to graze my cheek, the seam of my jaw, his fingers tracing my lips before he slides his hand around the back of my neck to pull me into him. As our bodies collide, he kisses me slowly, hungrily, forcing my mouth to submit to his.

Gradually, the people fall away, only the music remains, and I feel something solid at my back. He pushes his hips into me, moving them obscenely as he moans fiery breaths against my lips. His arm wrapped around me feels strong and possessive, and I'm totally at his mercy. Pliable to his will.

His mouth kisses a wet trail across my cheek to my neck below my ear, sending a delicious shiver up my spine. I hear his voice then, low but forceful, a half-uttered growl: "Fucking hell, Alex, I want to fuck you right here. Feel myself inside you. Feel you come for me . . ."

I grip his shirt tight as he slides his hand up my thighs, parting them. When his fingers stroke at the dampness between my legs, he moans a rough sound against my ear. Unable to contain it, I move against his hand, against his hot, needy fingers that circle torturously.

"I want it too . . ." I hear myself whisper against him, desperate. "Fuck me . . . please . . ." I hardly recognize my voice as I reach for his belt, for the buckle, pulling at it.

The music changes pace then, speeding up as my need for him increases. He's hard, steellike, and hot, and the instant I have him free, I pull him toward my *entrance. His breathing is hard and loud against my ear as the music gets high-er-pitched, more urgent—distractingly so. It sounds familiar somehow, more of a screeching than a dance beat now. It's awful. I hate it. I've never hated a noise so much; never needed anything as much as I need to feel him push into me. The moment I feel his cock push against my entrance, weeping wet and hot and hard, my eyes blink open.*

His weight disappears immediately, and I awaken in my bed with my alarm screaming in my ear and the sunlight blinding my eyes. I feel groggy and sleepy, but worse than that, I feel insanely turned on and damp between the thighs.

Perfect. Bloody fabulous.

With a groan that's more of a whine, I lie back down and beg sleep to take me back so I can return to there and finish. Return to where he's touch-ing and kissing me, and where it's okay that he is. When I close my eyes, I swear I can still feel and taste him, and it's enough to make me slide my hand between my legs and into my knickers.

I stop after a few seconds because it's not the same. It's not him.

I groan and kick out my legs, which wakes up Fred, who stands and stretches before immediately mewling at me for his breakfast.

Monday is my on-call day, and on every drive to every appointment—and sometimes during every appointment—I think about the sex dream.

I'm always thankful for sex dreams when they happen. I have them fre-quently, and they're almost always vivid and memorable for hours after I wake up. And since it's the only sex I'm having right now, I'll take what I can get.

They don't normally happen with people I've had close calls with in real life. I have sex dreams about random strangers I saw on the train, or ac-tors I didn't realize I found attractive. Sex dreams about dangerous men who want to chase me and fuck me are another thing altogether. Though, perhaps sex dreams are the only realistic option with Jake Lawrence. Sex dreams are manageable and safe. Something real-life Jake isn't.

In the end, I decide that although I'm thankful for the sex dream about Jake, I'm not thankful that my stupid alarm woke me up before I got to feel dream-Jake inside me.

My first visit of the morning is Mrs. Matthews, who lives closest to the surgery but has been bedbound for the past few months after a nasty fall. She also suffers from Alzheimer's, so on some days when I visit her, we don't talk about how she's feeling at all and talk instead about the weather and the large oak tree at the foot of her garden and whether she should have it preened.

Lucy Dawkins, who I visit after Mrs. Matthews, is a thirty-two-year-old expectant first-time mother who looks after an elderly father-in-law at home. We get on well, and after her checkup, she makes me a nice cup of Earl Grey, and I spend too long chatting with her about how we don't get out much anymore since we became old and boring. Lucy seems totally content and excited about her upcoming arrival, and it makes someplace deep inside me flare with something like envy and regret. Not regret that I didn't marry Ben and have his children; regret over spending eight years with the cheating, arrogant prick. Years I could have spent with someone else. Lucy knows I'm single with a cat, and so, to be nice, she offers to set me up with her thirty-four-year-old also single brother-in-law. I politely decline.

The next couple of appointments drag, and Mr. Harris, my twelve o'clock, doesn't even answer when I arrive. I make a call to his next of kin who apologizes and tells me he's visiting family in Bath this week and must have forgotten to cancel his monthly appointment. It's actually a minor triumph because it gives me an extra-long lunch.

I'm reading the paper in my favorite deli and sipping my cappuccino when I see a feature on the opening of Jake's nightclub in the up-and-coming section of *Time Out London*. It makes me freeze mid-sip, goose bumps raising over my arms.

Under much secrecy and with a cleverly executed viral marketing campaign, Saturday night saw the opening of Brick Lane's newest and—at the risk of sounding uncool—coolest nightclub. Until its opening night, no one had a clue what was being done under the tarpaulin-covered monolith structure at the junction of Parker St. and Bond. Then the covers came off, the world's highest-paid DJ played a set that almost blew the roof off the neo-gothic space, and all of those questions were answered.

"Surgery" (a name picked by a guest, apparently—another genius marketing ploy by the owners) has been touted as the next Ministry of Sound, and if last weekend was anything to go by, then they may well have hit the nail right on the head. Decadent, atmospheric, and ridiculously stylish, it is the place to be for all

dance fans. (Or pseudo-cool journalists who want to be as cool as the people who were there on Saturday night.)
—*Ed Smith*

I breathe out. So, Jake's club got a five-star review. I feel proud of him even though I know I have absolutely no right to feel anything on his behalf. I wonder if he's seen it. He must have. An image of his boyish smile as he reads the review flashes before my eyes, and I smile too. I'm thrilled for him. I'd tell him that if I could. How would I even contact him? Didn't he say something about chasing me? No doubt he has my number since I gave it to his maître d'. He also knows where I work and had his driver take me home . . .

Do I feel disappointed he hasn't contacted me? Maybe. Do I want him to? Absolutely not.

I'm typing up today's notes back at the surgery when I hear a small knock on the door, and then Anna pops her head around.

"Hey, Alex. Sorry to interrupt, but these arrived for you." She comes into the room carrying a gorgeous bunch of white roses framed with green leaves. I frown, confused, as she brings them toward me. "They're so beautiful I gasped. Special occasion?" she asks, setting them down on my desk.

"Um, no, not at all." I shake my head. Dad, maybe? He sends me a bouquet every year on my birthday, but that isn't for months. Maybe he wants to cheer me up. God, I must have looked miserable yesterday.

"I think there's a spare vase in the kitchen. I'll get it for you," Anna says and disappears out of my office.

From my angle, I notice a flash of white in the green and reach in to fish the creamy white card out of the bouquet and tear it open. It's handwritten in a neat, boyish scrawl, and it causes my heart to flip over.

~ *Like I said, I want to see you again.* ~

His mobile number is scrawled beneath the message.

Holy Christ, he sent me flowers. Jake Lawrence sent me flowers. How gentlemanly of him. I bite back a stupid, girlish grin. My face feels hot and my mind giddy before I hear another soft knock on my office door. I think it's Anna with the vase, but Sam pops his head in, a weird expression flitting across his face when he spots the roses.

"Wow. Secret admirer?" he asks as he comes into the room, the door closing softly behind him.

"Um, no . . ." I smile as I slip the card into my desk drawer. "They're from my dad." I see something like relief in his eyes as he nods. "Is that you off then?" I ask. "You caught up okay?" He was harassed when I arrived back after lunch, four appointments behind after having to arrange an ambulance for a patient. I told him to buzz me if he needed a hand. "Did St. John's call you back?"

"Yeah, she's fine. A mild stroke, but she's doing okay," he says, but it's clear he never came to talk about this. He's opening his mouth to say something else when Anna knocks and enters with the vase.

"Thanks, Anna. I'll decant them."

When the door closes again, he looks back to me and begins shifting on his feet. I know exactly what he's going to say.

"Eh, so, I was wondering if you were free this week, or at the weekend, for that drink?"

And so just like that, months and months with no male attention, and now I have two to choose from. Well, one is less of a choice and more of a steamroller to the senses. A steamroller that just sent me the most gorgeous bouquet of white roses I've ever seen.

"Oh, right, yes, sure. Saturday night?" I suggest. I'm surprised at how enthusiastic I sound because I don't feel it.

His face brightens. "Yeah, great. Saturday is great." He sounds pleased, which makes one of us. "Pick you up at seven?"

"Yeah, seven is good. Though, we could go to the Pig and Hen in my village. They do great craft beer and cider." Which I know he likes. Also, it would be far less formal than dinner, and much more like two friends going out for a few drinks. Which is most definitely what I want it to be now that Jake Lawrence has sent me flowers.

"I do like beer—and cider." Sam grins.

The first thing I do after Sam leaves my office is open my drawer to retrieve the card from Jake. After storing his number in my phone, I turn the card over in my hand and trace my fingers across his words. Seeing his handwriting has a weird effect on me I can't explain. Then I feel foolish, because maybe he didn't even write it himself and got the woman in the shop to write it. Yes, that's probably what he did.

I'd guess that when Jake sends a woman flowers, he expects a lot in return. Thoughts about what I would be willing to give him keep me entertained for the entire drive home. Perhaps I could do one night of passion with him and move on from this madness. A night of Jake Lawrence being inside me isn't the worst thing I could imagine doing with an evening. He would be magnificent in bed, I have no doubt about it.

One night with Jake.

Does it matter if he's the kind of guy people want to cut open with a knife on a Tuesday night if all I'm going to do is sleep with him once and walk away?

Christ, what on earth am I doing even considering this?

I decide that at the very least, I should thank him for the flowers. But that would involve having to think about the wording of a message I'm not sure I want to be ambiguous or not. So, I'll do it tomorrow when my head is clearer.

Tuesday is the longest day of the week because it's another late drop-in. Each week, the six of us alternate in pairs to do it, and this week, Sam and I are it. Technically, it's supposed to be James and Sam, but James has his daughter's play or ballet recital or something, so I swapped with him. Late surgery days mean I'm on a twelve-hour shift, so I always try to make sure I get a decent hour and a half lunch.

I leave the surgery at noon on the button and head along to the deli the next street over to grab my favorite guilty treat of a smoked salmon and cream cheese bagel, followed by a white chocolate-chip muffin. I've been dreaming about it since 10:00 a.m. It's fatty and unhealthy, but it keeps me going until I get home at 9:00 p.m. I justify it by only having it every other Tuesday.

As usual, the deli is busy with housewives and their pushchairs. Or, as I like to refer to them, their weapons of choice. Miraculously, I manage to find an empty table by the window, and I'm halfway through my bagel, Americano, and the deli's copy of *The Guardian* when I feel someone standing over me. I glance up and blink a few times, the air leaving my lungs instantly.

Oh, dear god. Why is he here? *How* is he here? What is he doing here?

I literally have no idea how long he's been standing there, but surely, I would have felt his presence were it an interminable amount of time. He's smiling a closed-mouthed smile as he stares at every part of my face all at once. He looks casually stunning in a gray shirt buttoned down with a white T-shirt underneath, dark sunglasses tucked into the low V-neck. So, he does daywear equally as well as tailored formal wear. Of course he does.

The way he stares at my mouth so intently makes me think I have cream cheese on my face. I touch my fingers to my lips to check, and he smiles deeper.

"Mind if I join you?" he says, taking a seat before I can answer.

I stare at him dumbly before picking up my napkin to dab my lips. I really can't be sure my fingers got it all, and he's still staring hard at my mouth.

"What on earth are you doing here?" I ask, sounding ruder than intended.

He lets out a sigh. "Would you believe me if I told you I was in the neighborhood?"

I shake my head. "No, I wouldn't." Nothing with him is by chance. Such as me meeting him in the manager's office of a nightclub I didn't know he owned. Such as the way his hair looks accidentally messy when it's not. It's deliberate, to make women like me want to grab it and run their fingers through it. It's no accident he's here.

At that moment, a barista comes over with a brown take-out cup and places it in front of Jake. It has his name written on it in big, girlish black letters. He thanks her without taking his eyes off me.

"Did you get the flowers?" he asks when we're alone.

"I got them."

There's a challenge in his eyes as he nods. "So then, you don't like roses. That why you never called?"

"What? No. I mean, yes, I like roses." I look away from him. I sound like a babbling idiot again. Great. Christ, what is it about his eyes that makes me feel so exposed and uncertain? "I was going to text you and thank you . . . Today has just been really busy." I drag a hand through my hair.

He raises an eyebrow skeptically before nodding again. I don't know if it's the setting, the fact it's daytime and perhaps he becomes a completely different person in the dark, but he doesn't seem as cocky as he usually does. He seems a bit tense and out of sorts, his sexual arrogance dimmed somewhat, and I'm glad for it.

I lift my cup to take a sip of coffee, which is cold now, but I keep drinking anyway because I want to keep my dry mouth and nervous hands busy. As I put my cup back down into the saucer I miss the landing pad, and the cup tips over, spilling my cold Americano across the table toward him. He slides back slightly to avoid getting wet, and I curse, grabbing my napkin to try to mop up the mess.

I glance at him as I wipe, and he hands me another napkin with an amused look on his face.

"Do I make you nervous, Alex?" He grins, confident again.

"What? No, of course not," I lie. I do my best to clean the mess before sitting back down, Jake's turquoise eyes watching my every move.

Just then, the same barista comes over, having spotted my accident, and leans to wipe down the table with a damp cloth, picking up the sodden napkins. As she leaves, she smiles sympathetically at me as though she gets it. As though she feels sorry for me for making an idiot of myself in front of the sexy, edgy model guy.

When she's gone, I turn my eyes back to find him still staring at me. Great, he looks cocky and relaxed again. He takes a deep breath before speaking.

"All right, Doctor, I'm gonna try something here, so bear with me, yeah?" He runs a hand over his mouth and licks his full, luscious lips. "I think you're amazingly beautiful, classy, smart, and completely out of my league. You're a woman I do not stand a fucking chance with. But I think you've been fighting with yourself since you met me. Fighting against all the reasons you should stay away from me, all the good-girl reasons you've probably lived your entire life with—which, to be fair, are extremely fucking valid here." He looks at me as if he wants me to confirm or deny this, which, of course, I don't. He leans forward, and when he speaks, his voice is quieter. "But I think you want me anyway. I'm pretty fucking certain you do. I'm certain you want me almost as much as I want you."

It's stated so confidently, so completely without doubt, it takes my breath away. I wonder what my giveaway is. Can he hear my breathing from over there? See my heart beating far too fast? Or maybe my face is red. It feels red. I swallow. Then I realize swallowing is probably a giveaway too.

Wait a minute—he thinks I'm amazingly beautiful and out of his league?

"How many times have you thought about me since Friday night?" he goes on. "Since I kissed you. And then since you kissed me?" A smirk lifts his mouth. He raises an eyebrow, expectant, as though he honestly believes I'll answer him.

If truth be told—which it won't be—I've lost count of the number of times I've thought about him since Friday night. I also thought about him a few times before Friday night, but he doesn't need to know that either.

Instead, I bluff it. I smile, shaking my head at his arrogance, before looking down to play with my cup. I should tell him I don't want him and that I haven't thought about him at all since Friday. I don't though. What I do is replay the kiss in his office, and then in the hallway, over and over in my head.

"That many, huh?" he says, sounding pleased. When I look back up at him, he's grinning at me. It's that small half-smile that gives him a mixture of arrogance and boyish charm.

Damn him.

"It's okay, Doctor. I've thought about you a lot too. About how good your tongue felt in my mouth and how hard you made me."

I gasp out loud, and his eyes blaze, unashamed.

When I'm certain my voice won't betray me, I fix him with a pointed stare. "What is it you want from me, Jake?" I whisper in exasperation. "What is it you think white roses will achieve, exactly? Do you think that's all it takes? That a bouquet of flowers is all it takes for me to spread my legs for you? I'm sorry, but I'm not that girl."

Did I just say that out loud, in the deli I frequent twice a week? I look around to check no one heard me. It's fairly noisy though, and thankfully, the clattering of crockery and the noise of the milk steamer seems to have muffled my crudeness.

His expression changes. Playful to serious. He lifts his coffee cup to take a sip, and unlike mine, his hands are steady. They're also extremely sexy like I remember them being.

"What do I want from you . . .?" he repeats with a sigh. He looks thoughtful as he sits back in his chair again. "I want everything from you, Alex. I want to spend the rest of my life with you. I want to make you fall so fucking in love with me that you forget your own name. Can you let me do that, yeah?" His face is serious. Totally and utterly serious.

My breathing stutters to a complete stop. I can't feel my legs or my face, white-hot heat burning me up from the inside. He stares at me with that serious face for one, two, three beats and then chuckles and runs his hand through his hair.

"Kidding. Too much too soon?" He quirks a brow.

How long passes before I can speak I don't know, but finally, I find my tongue. "Um, actually, no. It wasn't too much at all. In fact, I think I might be in love with you already. Let's get married and have four children? Two boys and two girls?" I sit back in my chair and try to keep my face serious too, like he did a moment ago.

I manage it for about four seconds before a small laugh escapes my mouth. Jake grins a grin that practically sets my womb on fire. He really is gorgeous. Ridiculously so. I feel stupid from it.

"Married? Sure." He nods. "Kids? Absolutely. But how about you let me take you to dinner first, yeah? You might hate the noises I make when I eat or something." He leans toward me again, biting his lip adorably.

From this new closer distance, the clean, masculine scent of him floats toward me and up my nose, both citrusy and woodsy. He reaches his hand out to mine, and I think he might take it, but he doesn't; instead, he draws a shape on the table between our hands. It seems like an eternity since we kissed against the wall in that cold hallway, and I crave contact with him again.

How different things seemed in that hallway two nights ago. Not only another me, but another Jake too. A Jake who sends me roses and asks me out for dinner. A manageable Jake.

As I fiddle with my pearl pendant, I try to remember all the sensible good-girl reasons to stay away from him. But they're ... gone. I can't remember why I was against this at all. I'm so attracted to him even though he's not my type, and he sent me flowers and sought me out twice because he wants me. Shallow and short-sighted reasons to do this with likely the biggest player I've ever met, but I can deal with the consequences later. I'm a big girl.

"Okay," I hear myself say, "I'll have dinner with you." When I look up from our hands, mine pale and small next to his large, tanned one, his eyes flash wide.

In a second, though, he's serious again, nodding as he stands up from the table. "Okay. Saturday. Eight o'clock. I'll pick you up. I'll be on my best behavior, I promise. Don't want to shock you *too* much on our first date." He smirks.

Our first date.

He leans in to bring his mouth to my cheek, his lips hovering there a moment. When he kisses me, it's soft and chaste, but it still sets my blood on fire, my pulse throbbing so hard beneath my skin I'm sure he must be able to see it. When he stands up straight, he smiles that smile again. The one that makes me want to point at every other woman in the place and go, "See? Do you see what I'm up against? I don't stand a bloody chance!"

"I'll see you Saturday then, Doctor," he says, the side of his mouth turned up in a smirk. Then he turns on his heel and strides out of the deli without looking back.

It takes me five whole minutes, after my breathing returns to normal and my brain begins to function again, to realize I've agreed to go out with him at the same time I'll be on a date with Sam.

Oh, crap.

SEVEN

DEBATE MY CONUNDRUM FOR THE NEXT TWO DAYS. AND BY "DEBATE," I mean, "magnify the situation to be much more than a diary complication about which date I should move," in true Alex fashion. I extrapolate it, magnify it to the maximum zoom available, and turn it into a major life crossroads. Perhaps it's a sign to cancel this whole thing with Jake entirely. Or maybe this is my way of being a coward and doing the sensible, expected thing.

Who do I want to be from now on?

On Thursday night, I realize it will have to be Jake I cancel on. Sam has been casting furtive glances in my direction all week, and canceling now would bring awkward repercussions at work, which I always want to avoid. Part of me thinks if the date goes badly, it will be bad at work too. To get over this, I reason if it does go badly, all I need to do is think of it as not being a date at all; it's a few drinks at the pub with someone from work. I've done that with Sam before.

I pour myself a glass of chardonnay and flop down on the couch to compose and recompose my text cancelation to Jake. Then I worry he might call me, so I decide to be an even bigger coward and wait until the morning. That way, if he rings me, I can't answer because I'll be at work.

Alex: So sorry to do this at such short notice, but I've double-booked myself on Saturday and can't make it. Can we do dinner another time? A x

I send it, turn off my mobile, and try to forget about it for the rest of the day. And I almost manage it too. Though, when I leave the surgery that night, I'm certain I'll see him standing outside. I don't. And when I turn my phone on as I get into the car, there's no angry text waiting for me either.

There is complete radio silence. It does nothing to settle the ball of anxiety brewing in my stomach.

"So, what did you go for outfit-wise?" Robyn asks, having called for my pre-date pep talk. I can hear her munching on what I assume is a carrot stick down the other end of the line. She's on her wedding diet, and they're her replacement for crisps.

"My black skinny Calvin Kleins, black-and-white-striped silk top, and flat red ballet pumps. I'm going for French casual." I nibble at my nail.

"Sounds perfect. How are you feeling about it now?"

I feel sick, actually. I haven't heard from Jake, so I have no clue how annoyed he is, whether he'll ever ask me out again, or whether he's still even chasing me. Frankly, Sam is the last thing on my mind.

"Fine, I suppose," I lie. "Sam's nice. It'll be nice."

"Wow, calm down, babe!" she says sardonically. "Listen, Al, he *is* a lovely guy, and cute too. In that geeky, clean way you like them. He's perfect Alex material."

Perfect Alex material. If only she knew "perfect Alex material" was now tattooed, nightclub-owning knife wound victims. We finish up, and I promise to call her tomorrow to fill her in.

Sam, of course, arrives on time. In fact, he's early, ringing the doorbell slightly before 7:00 p.m. and carrying a lovely hand-tied bouquet of sunflowers. Not white roses.

"Oh, Sam, you didn't have to," I say as he hands me them.

He shrugs. "Oh, I know. You like them though, and they were just asking to be picked from your neighbor's garden," he jokes. "Though, you probably have them all over the house, don't you?" He looks around in curiosity.

"Actually, I don't." I shake my head. "They're really lovely, thank you. Go through to the living room while I put these in water." I gesture toward the front room and go to the kitchen to get a vase.

They *are* lovely. I'm not surprised he remembered sunflowers are my favorite. I normally have them in my office at the surgery, and Dad sends me them every year. Sam is the sort of person who remembers those kinds of things. He's nice like that.

I fetch a vase from under the sink and fill it halfway before settling the flowers into it. Sam is browsing the contents of my bookshelf when I come back and set the flowers down on the side table that holds the phone.

He turns to face me and gives me a warm look. "You look really pretty, Alex," he says shyly.

"Thank you. You scrub up okay yourself." I smile.

He's wearing light-colored brown cords with a dark blue denim shirt and smart trainers. His face is clean-shaven, and though he isn't wearing the black-rimmed glasses he wears for work, he looks good without them too. His hair is a dark chestnut brown, longer than Jake's, and he wears it in a trendy unkempt style. It occurs to me then that he looks like a student despite being my age. Christ, I hope he has ID on him.

"Yeah, it's good to get the civvies on." He smiles. "You have a really lovely house, by the way. No Fred?" He looks disappointed. Of course he also remembered my cat's name.

"Oh, no, he's out on the tiles. Every night from six until nine is party time for Fred. He won't be home until he's scented every square inch of the village. Then once more for good measure," I tell him, and he laughs softly.

"Well, that's a shame. Wanted to introduce myself to the man of the house."

"You'll meet him later," I say, and Sam's eyes widen a fraction. Then I realize why: because I've intimated I'll invite him back here after. Ignoring the hopeful look on his face, I lift my bag from the couch and nod. "Ready?" I ask.

In the hall by the door, I grab my blazer and lift my phone, checking one last time to see there's still no response from Jake. Perhaps he's already moved on, seducing some other girl with an elaborate ruse as we speak, fucking his barmaids on the sofa in his office. I ignore the slight burn of anger that idea creates.

Outside, Sam's BMW is parked behind my Mini on the driveway, and he unlocks it as we start down the path.

"Sam, we can walk there. It's only five minutes down the road," I suggest.

"Oh, right, yeah, of course, great." He nods and locks his car again, and we head off down my street.

The Pig and Hen sits at the entrance to the village, opposite an ancient wishing well that now functions as a roundabout. I give him a mini tour of Shere as we go, pointing out Ken's bakery where I get my Saturday croissants. I tell him they also do the best éclairs I've ever tasted outside of Paris, and he makes me promise to bring some to work next week to prove it.

It's a nice warm summer night, and it shows the village off at its best, and likewise, Sam is bright and easy to be around. It pushes all thoughts of a certain mercurial male to the back of my mind.

The pub is busy as always, but we find a small table next to the large open fireplace, which is thankfully unlit tonight. As we enter, Stuart, the owner behind the bar, gives me a wave, his gaze moving curiously to Sam. Since I'm normally with my dad or Nick when I'm here, I'm hoping the fact I'm on a date will mean people will stop trying to set me up with every single male relative they have.

"So, what are you having?" Sam asks once we're seated and I've hooked my jacket over the back of my chair.

"A half of the cloudy draft cider, please."

"Oh, you said it's good."

"It is, but it's super strong, so if you're driving, you may want to have a taste of mine and get something else." I give him an apologetic smile.

Sam is funny and sharp in a witty, dry way—a side I've only really glimpsed at work where he's almost always professional and reserved, which isn't him at all. I'm not sure how long Sam has liked me, but I definitely felt a shift in his behavior toward me after Ben and I broke up. Then, a month later, at his thirtieth birthday—which I dragged Rob along to—he suggested we "go for a drink sometime." It only took him another six months to follow up on it. I suppose this could mean he doesn't like me much at all, or he's as indecisive about things as I am.

Sam was also engaged, and though he never talks about it, I'm pretty sure he had his heart broken too. It's why the girls at the surgery fuss around him in a way I'm not entirely sure he appreciates. So perhaps that's why it took him so long to ask me out. Heartbreak tends to kill your confidence with the opposite sex even if you convince yourself you're absolutely fine.

We somehow get onto the London club scene, which is apparently his idea of hell. He asks about my night with the girls last week at the opening, which of course causes unbidden thoughts of Jake to fill my mind, supercharging it. I say "unbidden," but really, they don't need much bidding. He's been hovering on the periphery of my thoughts all night.

We chat about movies and music, and I find out he plays piano too—something else we have in common. It's starting to feel a bit eerie. I started playing at six, he at seven, though unlike me, he says he stopped when he left high school. I never stopped but have barely played a note since Ben moved out. Most of the tunes I know best are emotional and mournful pieces that make me teary, and I don't want to cry over him. He doesn't deserve that.

Honestly, I think I forgot how much I enjoy dates. The buildup, the getting to know one another, the deciding whether you even like each other. Of course, there's always the chance the date will be truly awful, a prolonged stumble through awkward conversation and even more awkward silences until it's over, but tonight isn't like that at all. Sam and I have so much in common, and I thoroughly enjoy his company. It's easy and relaxed, and it's why we get on so well at work. Is there a sexual attraction there? Before last Saturday night, I'd have said yes, sure. Now? Now, I don't even know how to measure sexual attraction unless I compare it with how I felt pressed up against Jake Lawrence on Saturday night.

Could I ever be this comfortable with Jake?

The answer is immediate: Christ, no. He makes me far too edgy and hot for comfort and chat. And what would we even talk about anyway? Jake would just stare that stare at me, turquoise eyes glittering, the occasional lip bite thrown in. Then he'd do that sexy smirking thing for good measure.

I realize I've missed an entire three minutes of Sam describing a documentary he watched last night about the sinking of a passenger ferry while I've been sitting here imagining what a date with Jake would be like. Sam, thankfully, doesn't seem to notice. I tell him to give me the name of the documentary and store it dutifully in my phone.

I have a couple more half-pints of cider, and Sam has a small taster of a weak-strength craft beer, and then, almost too soon, it's 11:30 p.m. and Stuart is calling time.

"Night, Alex. Night, Sam. Was nice to meet you," he says as he holds open the door for us and we head out into the night air.

"Thanks, Stuart. See you soon," I say, noticing my voice is slightly too high.

As soon as the fresh air hits me, I feel the intoxication level increase. Then, rather embarrassingly, as we turn the corner onto my road, I stagger slightly, and Sam has to move closer to take my arm to steady me. I could honestly hug him for it, because falling over pissed in the middle of the street would certainly ruin the sensible image of Dr. Alex Marlowe I've been cultivating around here for the past three years.

"Oops, thank you for that," I laugh as he releases his arm from my shoulders. "God, that cider is quite strong. I think three is the limit," I say in my ridiculously high voice. *Please don't hiccup. Please don't hiccup.*

"You had four, Alex." Sam chuckles.

"Christ, did I? Okay, then four is the limit!" I nod, and he laughs harder.

"Wow, nice car," he remarks. "Expensive postcode you live in, Alex. Douglas paying you more than me?"

Through my drunken haze, I glance at the car parked across from my driveway at number 15. The Taylors have another of their flashy friends over. I'm still certain they're swingers. The car itself is flashy and sleek with tinted windows, but apart from that, it looks like any other flashy car. It's what Rob would call "a drug dealer's car."

"Eh, wait a minute—don't you live in Teddington?" I exclaim, turning to Sam. "In a five-bed detached?"

"Yeah, but I inherited that, remember? I'm still a socialist at heart." He puts a fist in the air playfully.

I frown at the inheritance thing, but then I remember: he told me earlier about a rich, childless uncle who left him everything when he died. "Hmm, still . . . glass houses, Dr. Wardley." As we walk up my driveway, I feel Sam close to me, his touch light on the small of my back as he guides me over the rougher gravel as if he's scared I'll trip and fall.

"Oh, it wasn't a slight in any way. And in fact, your postcode means your life expectancy is a lot higher than the average cider-drinking female, so that's good." He tries to stay serious, but I slap him lightly on the chest, and he breaks into a laugh and throws his hands up, saying it's factually true.

At the door, I'm tempted to ask him in, mainly because it's been a good night and I've really enjoyed his company—far more than I thought I would. But then I've also had four pints of strong cider, and my judgment is more than a bit impaired.

"I had a really nice night, Sam. Thank you. I'm glad we did this." I lean back against my front door and look up at him. He's about as tall as Jake, I think, but not as muscular and so doesn't feel as intimidating. Or as dominating. Or as warm.

"You sound surprised," he jokes, sliding his hands into his pockets.

I try to decide if I want him to kiss me. How different from Jake's kiss would it be? I doubt he will kiss me though, since it took him eight months to ask me ou—

Then he's kissing me.

I stand there momentarily stunned, my hands at my sides before I bring them up to rest them on his arms. His own hands stay in his pockets, head tilted to the side, his mouth soft and careful as he kisses me on my door-step like a teenager. His kiss is warm but cautious, and there's no urgency to it, no possessive taking or claiming. He smells of clean linen and tastes of orange, and it's . . . a nice kiss. I'm sure if I wasn't bulldozed by a different kind of kiss from a different kind of man a few days ago, it would have far more of an impact.

Then he isn't kissing me anymore.

He takes a small step back and looks at me warily, checking to see if he's overstepped a line. "Sorry," he says. "I thought I'd do that before I over-thought it too much."

"No, I get it. It was fine," I tell him. "I'm the queen of overthinking, trust me."

He pouts his lips slightly. *"Fine?* Oh, well, I was hoping for mind-blow-ing, but I guess fine will do for now . . ."

I laugh. "Sorry, that's not what I meant. It was . . . nice."

"Nice is better, I guess." He nods, mouth soft.

Suddenly, I get the strangest feeling we're being watched, and I turn to look away from him down the driveway shiftily. Small village con: nosy neighbors. Sam takes this as his cue.

"I guess I'll head off now then. I had a great time, Alex." His voice is sin-cere and hopeful, and not for the first time tonight, I feel as though maybe this *could* go somewhere.

"Me too, Sam. We should do it again sometime." The words are out be-fore I can stop them, but I don't care, and I don't think it was drunk talk. I like him, he's nice, and we have far too much in common to cast it aside, surely?

Sam's face lights up. "I'd really like that. Okay, so, see you Monday," he says, backing away from me toward his car.

"Night."

I stand there for a moment and watch him reverse out, waving a small goodbye before reaching into my bag to get my keys out. Once inside, I lock the door behind me and retrieve my phone from my bag to check for a text I know isn't going to be there. It's off, having died during the evening. The battery really must be going on it. I need to admit defeat and upgrade the bloody thing. I take it through to the kitchen and plug it in to charge.

I put some dinner out for Fred and fill the kettle for some tea. As soon as I flick the switch on the kettle, the doorbell goes. Sam must have forgotten something. Though, I can't imagine what since he was only in here five minutes. Maybe he got the sudden urge to sweep me upstairs to bed and make crazy, passionate love to me. The idea makes me giggle for some reason. Sam is definitely not the type.

I walk through the hall and quickly unlock the door, expecting to see an apologetic Sam. For the second time that week, I feel the breath leave my body, my legs threatening to give out.

Jake is standing at my front door looking completely, mind-bendingly gorgeous . . . and completely furious.

EIGHT

H E'S GLARING AT ME, NOSTRILS SLIGHTLY FLARED, MOUTH IN A hard, angry line, and his body practically trembling with rage.

I can't move. I'm frozen to the spot, open-mouthed. In my shock, I still register he looks completely edible in jeans and a casual red-and-white-checked shirt. The skin of his throat is stubbled and slightly golden, and it makes my mouth water. His hair is mussed as though he's been dragging his hand through it.

As we stand looking at each other, I decide anger looks extremely sexy on him. Okay, even in my head I know how wrong that sounds, but there's something about his body tensed and on edge that makes him look even more delicious than normal. It was the same at the club when he was facing off with Matt. His ferocity has a sensuality to it. God, what the hell is wrong with me? Ferociously sensual? Sexy anger? Also, his anger is directed at me. I caused it.

"So, he's what came up, is he?" he hisses, finally cutting through the charged silence.

I blink, opening my mouth to tell him something, anything, to explain it wasn't really like that, but I don't get the chance.

"Are you fucking him?"

I flinch, stunned. "Excuse me?"

"Are you fucking him?" he repeats. Okay, so, apparently, my ears heard him perfectly fine the first time.

I frown, cheeks hot. "Is that any of your business?"

"Since you agreed to go out with me, yeah, it is."

I'm not entirely sure I agree with that. Having dinner with someone doesn't give them the right to know who you're sleeping with. *Does it?* I haven't done the whole dating thing for a while, but I'm certain it hasn't changed that much.

Because he's close and rather intimidating, I take a small step back, into the hallway. Jake reads it as an invitation though and follows, stepping inside the door and into the vestibule. Okay, maybe now I should be afraid. He's in my house. Jake Lawrence is in my house. It's not frightening though; it's only surreal. Again.

"Well, are you?"

What possesses me to answer him I don't know. "No. I'm not fucking him," I reply quietly. The word sounds vulgar and ill-fitting in my mouth. Unlike how it sounded from his: raw and coarse and entirely natural.

He says nothing at the admission, registers no emotion at all. He just continues to stare at me hard. It occurs to me he might be trying to decide whether I'm telling the truth.

Uncomfortable, I turn on my heel and head toward the living room.

"Don't walk away from me, Alex," he says quietly this time. It's the kind of tone you use on a misbehaving child. I feel him following me, his presence like a force field near my own.

Pacing over to the window, I turn to face him, folding my arms across my chest. I almost gasp at the sight of him there by the fireplace in the room where I read, where I stroke Fred, where my Mum and Dad drink tea when they come over. "Surreal" doesn't seem to do it justice suddenly.

"Why are you here, Jake? Don't you think it's a bit late to be turning up at people's houses?" I glance at my watch—it's midnight—and then back up to his eyes.

"I was in the neighborhood," he says, gaze dark and challenging.

I narrow my eyes, trying hard to ignore the dull throb thrumming between my legs at the sight of him here, looking like that, when I feel like this. Christ, I need him to go. I really don't trust myself around him.

"Well, you should go," I state. It sounds half-hearted though, and he must think so too, because he smirks.

Even though I have no intention of following through with it, I go toward the phone on the table next to where Sam's sunflowers are. He's closer to it though, and quicker than me all around. He reaches down to lift it from its cradle before I'm anywhere close.

Maybe I'm being utterly naïve in not being afraid of him. I think about all I know of the man in front of me—which, granted, isn't much. But from what I know and what I've seen of him, do I think he would hurt me? He certainly has a temper, and his threatening behavior toward Matt last week wasn't for effect, which makes him potentially violent. But he could have hurt me the night at the surgery and he didn't, and he's known where I live for weeks now and hasn't been near me.

The thought is clear and sharp in my head: He isn't going to hurt me. Not physically anyway.

I still startle like a cat when he moves. He doesn't go toward the door to leave. Instead, he moves toward my floral armchair and sits down, keeping his eyes firmly on me as he does. His eyes are softer now. Not as dark, nor as angry. Okay, perhaps still a little angry and a little dark, but they're not seething with rage like they were when I first opened the door to him.

The sight of him there in my armchair is so incongruous I almost want to laugh. His muscular, ferocious form sitting in my Laura Ashley armchair isn't an image I ever thought I'd see. I don't laugh though. I don't think he'd appreciate the joke.

I feel utterly sober, as though the four pints of strong cider with Sam never happened. Except they did. And that's the problem here.

When I take a few steps toward the sofa, that strange current that sparks between us seems to intensify, the heat and crackle more obvious the closer I get to him. I wonder if he feels it. He settles forward, elbows on his thighs, and puts the telephone on the floor between his feet. When he runs a hand over his mouth and squeezes the bridge of his nose between his eyes hard, I wonder if he has a headache. He also looks tired, and that makes me wonder if he's sleeping all right and whether he snores.

"I knew what would go through your head," he starts. "Knew you were going to spend all week regretting saying yes and looking for a way out of it. I expected your text sooner though . . ." He gives me a look, and I feel a burn of embarrassment flush over me. "Surprising you seemed to work well the other day, so I thought I'd give it another go, figured you'd either let me in or would be busy, so I had nothing to lose." He shrugs and looks up at me, eyes startlingly soft. "And I wanted to see you."

He wanted to see me, and I canceled on him for someone else. No— not canceled on him. Stood him up.

"I saw your car and the BMW, but all the lights were out, and I got . . . I don't know . . . worried. I tried calling you, but your phone was off. So, I waited." His eyes darken again.

Then he saw me giggling arm in arm with Sam, looking like a couple enjoying each other. I feel guilty and embarrassed again, so I look down at my hands, away from his eyes.

"So, you're not fucking him, but you and him are—what? Together? You're with him?"

I shake my head. "No, I'm not with him. He's a colleague. We work together."

"So, you kiss all the guys you work with, or just him?" he asks, a sarcastic edge to his tone. "Work's night out, was it? Spend the night talking about stitches and urine samples over dinner then?"

It was in fact stool samples, but I doubt it would be helpful to correct him right now. I decide to be sarcastic instead.

"Oh, and how about you? Slept with any of your barmaids recently? Or are they just overtly possessive of their boss?" I snipe. God, I sound jealous. He notices too, sitting up straighter and fixing me with a stare.

"Is there something you wanna ask me, Alex?" he asks quietly.

My breath catches in my throat at the intensity in his eyes. The unabashed directness. I swallow. *Have you slept with your barmaid since the night in your office? Have you slept with anyone since the night in your office? Do you still think I'm amazingly beautiful and out of your league?* There's a long, heavy silence until finally, Jake shakes his head, letting out a loud sigh.

"So, you canceled on me for him. Seriously?" He sounds incredulous, like he can't understand how that could ever possibly be the case.

"It wasn't like that . . ." I shake my head. "You blindsided me the other day. You appeared out of nowhere, and I momentarily forgot I had plans tonight." Surely, he's noticed how my being around him makes my brain turn to jelly. How I forget things such as breathing and sense. I certainly can't diary manage effectively in his presence.

"But that's not the total story, is it?" he asks, searching my face the way he often does. "You were gonna cancel on me anyway, weren't you?"

Was I? If I didn't have plans with Sam, would I have reached the same conclusion: that Jake Lawrence is not the sort of guy I should be messing around with?

I look down at my hands again. "I don't know," I tell him, because I honestly don't. When I look back up, he's worrying the inside of his cheek with his teeth, still watching me closely.

He gives a small nod.

"But I should have let you know earlier in the week either way. I'm sorry for the short notice. It was rude of me." *It's just, it took me longer than I thought to decide what kind of person I want to be for the rest of my life.*

He frowns. "The short notice wasn't the problem, Alex," he says. "I'd still have been pissed off. I still am."

"Oh, you're pissed off? I never noticed."

His mouth twitches with the hint of a smirk.

A long moment passes between us, lighter than before, but heavier with something new. I let it gain a bit more mass before I have the overwhelming need to fill it.

"You're scary when you're angry, you know?" *Scary and sexy.*

"I know," he replies.

"You could do some damage with a temper like that."

He looks very serious then. "I'd never hurt you, Alex. Ever." His voice is quiet but strong with sincerity.

"Okay." I nod.

He mirrors it.

We sit in silence for a little while longer before I catch sight of something in the corner of my eye. I turn to see Fred saunter into the living room with his tail in the air in greeting. He doesn't hesitate before walking straight over to Jake, stopping with his paws turned out to stare up at him. Jake smiles softly and reaches down to scratch Fred behind his ear and then smooths his hand over his back, soliciting an almost immediate chorus of purrs from my normally moody tortoiseshell. Fred is indifferent to nearly everyone and regards everyone else with a quiet disdain, so his reaction to Jake makes my mouth part in shock.

"He's Fred," I tell him with a shake of my head. "He isn't usually so friendly."

Jake looks up at me briefly before returning his attention to Fred. He knows how to stroke a cat, which surprises me because few people do. Does that also mean he likes cats? In my head, I tick off another box on the pro list.

"I like how cats give nothing away," he muses, still stroking Fred. "How you never know what they're thinking. Well, normally . . ."

As I look from Jake to Fred and back, I marvel at how far we seem to have come in ten minutes. A thought enters my head then—something I wanted to ask him if I ever saw him again. Something that completely slipped out of my head at the deli when he blindsided me.

"Why did you call your club Surgery?" I ask quietly.

"You know why," he says.

A rush of warmth floods my cheeks. I can't breathe.

"Do I?" I ask, my voice thin and barely-there.

He lifts his head and offers me a small half-smile. "Okay. I liked the name. It felt . . . right," he says, watching me intently.

I still can't breathe properly. It is a good name, I have to admit. That's why it felt right. Because it's a good name.

"What is it you want from me, Jake?" I ask.

He stops stroking Fred, and his stare intensifies. It's that hungry stare of his—the one that strips me away to nothing. I feel raw and naked and wide-open, stripped bare of everything.

"You know the answer to that too, Alex."

I laugh nervously. "Oh, yes, that's right. You want to make me fall ridiculously in love with you so we can live happily ever after with our reams of children."

He straightens up, eyes darkening again. "Is this all a fucking game to you, Alex? 'Cause I don't react well to people playing fucking games with me."

I harden my stare on him. "Jake, the game was your idea. You wanted to chase me, remember?" I can see his mind ticking over as he bites the inside of his cheek furiously.

"Chasing you wasn't a fucking game, Alex. It was a means to an end."

I've noticed that when he wants to make a point, he says my name at the end. Like a punctuation mark.

"What end?" I ask.

"Catching you. Having you. Being with you." The shrug almost makes it look nonchalant, but the look in his eye is anything but.

I can't breathe again. He's watching me closely—too closely—and I wonder what my face is saying. It feels bright hot.

"Those good-girl reasons catch up with you then?" he asks with a note of playfulness. "Why else would you have canceled on me and not him?"

I can't take my eyes off him as I consider what to say to make myself sound less pathetic than I am. "It seemed sensible," I say finally.

"Standing me up? Messing me about? That seemed sensible?" His voice is laced with something dark.

I swallow and shake my head again. "No, of course not. Messing you around wasn't my intention, Jake. I promise you that. I'm not like that. I mean, canceling you and not him. God, I don't know. This . . ." I motion between us. "It's not something. It doesn't . . ." I flounder. I don't have the words to describe what this is. It's a lot of things: nonsensical, terrifying, intense, exciting. I don't want him to think I'm insane though, so I don't say any of these things. But he's waiting for something, I think.

"Sam is . . . a nice guy," I offer.

"And I'm not," he says. A statement, not a question.

"That's not what I meant."

"You don't want him, Alex." It's another statement.

"What? What are you even talking about? How wou—?"

"When he kissed you, I saw it," he cuts me off. "You don't want him. That much was fucking obvious from a distance. It's one of the only things that kept me in that car and stopped me from kicking his fucking head in. Seeing that you didn't want him."

Wait—is he saying that if he'd seen any sign I wanted Sam, he'd have hurt him? Why can't I decide how I feel about that? I know it should disgust me. Horrify me.

Christ, I can't think straight with him this close to me. I need him to leave. It's much safer fantasizing about him alone.

I stand up from the sofa and grab a hold of the pearl at my neck again, for strength this time. "Well, your eyesight must be spectacular."

He nods, looking up at me as I stand. "Yeah, it is. It's genetic. I've really good genes," he scoffs as though laughing at a private joke.

"I think you should go now, Jake." I run a hand through my hair as I sigh. "It's getting late, and I'd like to go to bed." *And fantasize about you there.*

"I could come with you. I'm a pretty good cuddler." He smirks.

I feel the goose bumps spread and ripple across my body in anticipation. Oh, I imagine that's true. He's so warm and muscular and smells divine. Yes, he'd be a great cuddler all right.

"I enjoy sleeping on my own, but thanks for the offer."

"That's not a no," he points out, smirking deeper.

So, I still can't say no to him, and he knows it. God, if he asks me to take my clothes off and let him have me here on the floor, I'm in serious bloody trouble. He bites his lip, and I decide the next time he kisses me, I'm going to do that. Bite his lip. I want to bite down on it hard enough that he cries out. I lick my lips absently.

He stands from the chair, closing the distance between us. "Okay, Alex, answer me one question, and then I'll go."

The closer he is, the less I can breathe, I've noticed. "Fine."

"He a better kisser than me?"

There's a smirk playing across his perfectly kissable mouth. He looks smug. Because he knows the answer.

I do a half-shrug thing. "I don't remember, to be honest." All lies. I remember perfectly well. I'm not likely to forget either.

He takes a quick step toward me, and my instinct is to step back—and I do, until I feel the living room wall at my back and he's crowding me again. Our default position, it seems.

"You're a terrible fucking liar, baby," he breathes. Is he angry again, or turned on? Strangely, I can't tell the difference.

Without my heels on, I'm a lot smaller than him, my entire body fully eclipsed inside his. He brings his arm up to brace it against the wall above my head and leans in so his face is only inches from mine. It hits me then. His scent. I almost close my eyes from the sheer pleasure of it. That woodsy, citrusy mixture that somehow smells completely natural. Unartificial. It's the clean, intoxicating aroma of spice and lemon and something sweet. It makes my mouth water again.

At this distance and under this light, I notice his stubble growing in across his jaw, and it matches his hair exactly. A rich, sandy brown. God, he's beautiful up close. His nose the perfect length, those eyes somewhere between deep green and deeper blue, completely dazzling, his lips full and wet against his slightly tanned, smooth skin. That's when I realize he isn't even touching me. He's not touching a single place on my body, yet I feel as though I'm on fire. Burning up from the inside out. Just as I'm wondering why he isn't touching me, he brings his hand up and draws his thumb over my lower lip.

"Yeah, you remember all right." His voice is a hoarse whisper as he stares longingly at my mouth before gently forcing my lips apart with his thumb and pushing it inside.

I taste salt and heat and spice as his thumb grazes the inside of my lip and the tip of my tongue. I about manage to resist the urge to bite or suck on it. It's such a simple thing, him putting his thumb in my mouth. It's barely anything at all, yet it feels powerful, erotic. I feel it all over my body—my throat, my chest, my nipples, my legs. I feel it most in the dull, throbbing ache between my legs.

Oh my god.

An instant later, his mouth is on mine, and I can't think anymore. His taste explodes on my tongue as a dam bursts in my belly. Our mouths mold together in a rush of wet heat and hot breath, and I hear him moan. I do what I thought about doing earlier and bite down hard on his bottom lip, sucking it into my mouth. He doesn't cry out; he just groans deliciously low in the back of his throat. It makes my legs tremble. I bring my hands up and place them flat on his chest as if I'm going to push him away, but of course, I don't. In fact, I pull him closer with a need so desperate it scares me.

Then he pulls away, leaving my mouth wanting. He's not angry anymore. Now, I have no doubt he's turned on. Because *I* turn him on. Oh, what a heady feeling that is.

"That's how you kiss someone you want, Alex. *Me*. You want," he states confidently, arrogantly.

I should be angry and embarrassed by his assertion, but I'm not. I'm annoyed at him pulling away.

"You're quite possibly the most arrogant man I've ever met."

He smirks sexily. "Then tell me you don't want me. Tell me you don't want me to fuck you. Tell me you only fuck nice guys. Nice guys you don't want."

I'm damn well tempted to, if only to see the cocky look drop from his face. Instead, I smile back.

"So, of all the things I could tell you, that's what you want to hear? That I don't want you. Really? You're a strange man, Jake Lawrence . . ." The cider has made me brave, or perhaps I left my brain at The Pig & Hen.

Something dark flickers across his eyes, and he steps forward, pressing himself into my body. He narrows his eyes, angry again. "Are you trying to drive me mental?" He scrubs his hand over his mouth, looking tense, and then pinches the bridge of his nose and squeezes his eyes shut.

Okay, I need to check these headaches with him. Do they come with dizzy spells? What if it's something serious?

"Fucking hell, I need to know where your head is, Alex. I need to know what the fuck is going on here." He sounds utterly confused now as he fixes me with that intense stare again. "You know, normally, when I want a girl, I get her, simple as that. This shit doesn't fucking happen. *Ever*. It's a done deal."

Is he actually serious? Oh, god, he is.

I press my hand to my heart and sigh dreamily. "You know, I think that might be the most romantic thing I've ever heard," I drawl sarcastically.

He narrows his eyes again as his jaw tenses, his brain ticking loudly. Oh, yes, he's definitely not used to this. Women *definitely* spread their legs at the bloody sight of him. It makes me stiffen, and I fix him with a withering look.

"You must be used to guys falling over their feet trying to impress you, huh? Expensive jewelry, expensive restaurants—the lot. Were there love letters, Alex? Yeah, I fucking bet there were." He chuckles, and it sounds mean. "Tell me this though: How many times did you wish that instead of a love letter or a five-course at the Dorchester, they'd take you home and fuck you raw and hard? Your Oxbridge-educated twats don't have it in them though, do they?" He gives me a look that borders on pity.

I'm not breathing now. At least, I don't think I am. *Raw and hard?* I'm not breathing again. I'm so bloody turned on. All I can think about now is him fucking me raw and hard, which, of course, is exactly what he wants me to do. Which is exactly why he said it. Which is exactly why he's looking at me the way he is now. Sexually arrogant.

From nowhere, the image of him pushing me against my living room wall, yanking down my jeans, and thrusting himself into me, hard, explodes in my mind. My toes curl into the carpet as my fingers clench with want.

Christ, I need to get away from him. Now.

As I go to move, he shifts his foot, wedging his thigh between mine to stop me. I can feel the heat of his thigh, thick and muscular, against the inside of my own. I swallow.

"Oh, we aren't done here yet, Alex," he informs me.

I blink. Rear my head back to glare at him. Okay, now, who on earth does he think he is? This is my bloody living room, in my bloody house.

Seething, I narrow my eyes on him. "Oh, we aren't in some back hallway of your bloody club this time, Jake. This is my house, and I'm in charge here, not you. I say when we're done." To me, my voice still sounds too girly and breathy, so I weigh it down when I speak again. "We are done. Move."

But he doesn't move. He doesn't give an inch.

"You get more fucking beautiful every time I see you, do you know that?" he whispers, licking his lips with his tongue slowly, deliberately.

My heart feels as if it's going to beat its way out of my chest. Then I feel something on my hip, near the hem of my top. Scorching heat. He's touching me.

"So fucking beautiful," he breathes, cocking his head to the side as he stares at my lips. He skims his hand across the waistband of my jeans, tugging on the button gently. If he unbuttons my trousers, I will be gone. No turning back. I won't stop him. "Are you turned on, baby?" he asks me.

God, I love the feel of his hands on my skin—my low skin. My body keels ever so slightly toward him, and the need to move against the heat of his thigh almost overwhelms me. The ache between my legs is near painful. I close my eyes as he brings his mouth to my neck, close to my ear.

"I'm turned on too, Alex. I'm so fucking hard for you. Fuck, I'm always *so* hard for you," he groans obscenely.

The knot tightens. I feel his fingers then, looping around mine to guide them to the front of his jeans. I try not to gasp as I feel the truth of it. He's extremely hard and very large, and I have to resist the urge to look down and see my hand on it. Touching him there. I want him to undress and let me see it. I want to touch it, skin-to-skin. I want him to push me to my knees and make me take it in my mouth.

I swallow, dry-mouthed, painfully turned on, hating how easy I've made all this for him.

"Are you imagining how good it will feel inside you? When I make you come with it?"

Oh, good god. Did I just orgasm? From only those words? I honestly can't be sure. My eyes flicker open to find him gazing down at where my hand rests over his jean-clad cock. He groans quietly, rocking our foreheads together.

"Tell me you want it, Alex. Say it," he says.

I won't say that. Ever. Could never. As though I've been burned, I draw my hand off him and give him an indignant stare.

"Don't you have a business to run or something?" I try to sound bored again, but I don't. I sound breathless and turned on, and I have the most vivid sense of déjà vu. Here I am again, wedged between the wall and his bloody hard place. The same as last Saturday night.

"I have good staff," he says, and I almost want to ask if he means good staff like Gemma. "You know what I think, Doctor?" He sighs, leaning back, away from me.

Great, we're back to "Doctor" again.

"What do you think, Jake?" I sigh. "Please, enlighten me."

"I think you're a cocktease."

My mouth drops open, and I blink up at him as the word settles in. "A cocktease?" I flare. How dare he! When did I tease any cocks? Okay, maybe teasing Jake's a moment ago was intentional, but he put my hand on it, didn't he? *He* started it. I look at him aghast. He looks pleased with himself again. "I have never . . . Ugh, get the hell away from me." I push at him, and this time, he steps back.

As I march away from him, Fred, who's languishing on Jake's floral chair, gets up suddenly and scuttles out of sight. He knows to run from my wrath when he sees it.

"So, let me get this straight," I say, whipping around to face him. "You, a man I've met twice, turn up at my bloody house in the middle of the night—uninvited, I should add—barge your way in, and then, because I don't allow you to fuck me hard and raw against my living room wall, I'm a cocktease? Is that it? That's actually what you're saying?"

He's leaning against the wall as if he's waiting on a bus, an out-of-place look of nonchalance on his face. Suddenly, he pushes up and walks toward me. I narrow my eyes at him, giving him the look I only reserve for figures of hate in my life. Of which, to date, there has been only one other. Another tall, arrogant male.

"Four times," he says.

"What?" I snap, irritated.

"We've met four times. The first time when you fixed me. The club, the café, and then tonight. I'm a man you've met four times." He dares to sound reasonable.

"I don't care." I shake my head. "It's not the bloody point. How dare you say something like that to me in my own house? I am not one of your barmaids. Now, we're done, and this little game of yours is finished. I want you to leave right now. I want you out of my house." I point at the door in case he's forgotten where it is.

"Okay, I was wrong. I fucked up. I'm sorry." He gives me a wide-eyed look, genuine, innocent. "I was wrong about what I said."

I narrow my eyes, setting my mouth in a straight, angry line. Oh, this had better be good. Really good. He had better grovel, preferably on his knees. Okay, maybe I like the idea of Jake on his knees a bit too much . . . I'll give him a bloody cocktease. And that doesn't sound right even inside my head. I fold my arms, waiting.

"I was wrong," he says again. "When I said before that you get more beautiful every time I see you, I was wrong. You get ridiculously fucking sexy. I mean, you're beautiful too, but right now, utterly pissed off." He whistles. "Fucking hell, you're killing me here, Alex."

I can only stare at him, wide-mouthed and speechless. *Did he just...? What on earth...?* The small, boyish smile tugs at the sides of his mouth, and it almost works. Almost.

No, I can't listen to him. He's womanizing me. That's what he does. Of course it's what he does.

"I am not a cocktease," I hiss.

The smile widens over his pretty mouth as he adjusts the front of his trousers. "Oh, I beg to differ, baby."

I make a frustrated sound and turn away, but he reaches out to grab a hold of me, turning me to face him.

"What are you doing, Jake? Let go," I say weakly. His heat and smell are far too close, and they're overpowering. I'll succumb if he pulls me any closer to his body. I know it.

I'm weak. He makes me weak.

"Alex, please stop . . . Please calm down, yeah? Let's talk about this. It needs sorting, baby." His voice is soft and soothing like a concerned lover now.

Oh, I really do like it when he calls me baby. I never thought I'd like being called that.

Womanizer. Be stronger, Alex.

As I make a last attempt at freeing my arm from his grasp, he lets go. I'm not expecting it though, and the release causes my arm to snap backward, my hand connecting forcefully with something fleshy and hard. As I look around at him in shock, I see the blood running down his face from his nose.

Oh, bloody hell.

NINE

COVER MY MOUTH INSTANTLY. "OH MY GOD, JAKE, THAT WAS A complete accident. I didn't mean to hit you. Let me see," I say, moving toward him.

He touches his hand to the blood and inspects it. Then he gives me a look that might be shock or awe and tilts his head back.

"No—forward, here, like this," I instruct, and he puts his hands out to stop the blood from dripping on my white rug.

As I reach up, I see the chunky antique turquoise ring that is now officially a weapon. I yank it off and throw it onto the chair as though the ring is the villain of this piece, not me.

"Here, sit down. I'll get some ice . . ." I lead him to the sofa and leave him there to go through to the kitchen, shaking my head as I do.

What on earth was that? I don't act like that. I wonder vaguely when my period's due. He has such a flammable effect on me, as though around him, every single nerve in my body is a live wire, and one tiny spark from him will set it off.

I burst his bloody nose. Oh, dear god.

When I get back to the living room, I find him sitting back on the sofa, holding his nose with his head tilted back even though I told him not to. Though, since I burst *his* nose, I don't feel like scolding him for it. As I come to kneel beside him on the couch, he glances at me sideways and flinches.

"You didn't come back with a baseball bat, did you?" he jokes.

My cheeks flame as I shake my head and kneel up to gently wipe away the blood around his mouth and nose. "I'm so sorry." I grimace. Oh, his perfect, innocent nose. Bloodied and sore because of me.

He shrugs. "I probably deserved it, to be honest."

I shake my head firmly. "No, you didn't. No one deserves to be smacked across the face. It was a complete accident. I don't know what came over me . . ."

"Well, unfortunately, not me," he says, staring at me.

I look back at him confused, and he's smirking playfully now. Oh . . . I get it now. I blush slightly and bite back a smile. Well, at least he still has a sense of humor.

"I really am sorry," I say guiltily.

"I'm sorry too. I was wrong to say that to you." He looks guilty as well. "I did it for a reaction, I suppose. Got one."

I look at him for a long moment. He wanted a reaction from me? That's hilarious. So, my attempt at mounting him against my living room wall wasn't reaction enough?

"You got one all right," I whisper.

He looks at me seriously now. His voice when he speaks is low and soft. "You know, if you hadn't canceled on me, this wouldn't have happened."

"Oh, is that right?" I say, raising an eyebrow. "How do you know?"

He smiles adorably, and I go back to wiping and dabbing. Erasing the evidence.

"You're making this fucking difficult for me, you know?"

"I know . . ."

He sighs, the weight of his stare heavy on my face. "I meant the part about you being fucking gorgeous when you're angry, by the way. Pissing you off has its upsides."

I should look away from his eyes, where it's safer. I finish wet-wiping around his face and mouth, and then I bring the freezer bag with ice to his nose, settling it gently on his cheek. He winces as it touches his skin, and I wonder how long the ice will take to melt since his body is so hot. Then I laugh inwardly at my double meaning.

"So . . . do you need to monitor me through the night?" he asks.

"We'll keep it here until you can't feel your face anymore, or until it melts. Whichever's first," I say, and he nods, turning his face forward.

I take a long look at his profile as he shifts to get comfortable, spreading his legs and slouching down lower so his head is resting on the back of the couch. My eyes take this as an invitation to glance down at his body, my heart speeding at the faint outline of the bump in his trousers. The image of him relaxing in my house makes me feel strangely content. Seeing him sitting comfortably on my sofa, seeing him stroke my cat. Bizarrely, I also enjoy tending to his burst nose.

I glance away from his crotch and back up to his face, where it's safer.

Though, as soon as my eyes land on that perfect face, I remember there are no safe places to look at.

"You said another time, maybe. Did you mean that?" he asks, deep voice breaking the heavy silence. "I mean, were you ever actually gonna have dinner with me? The truth, Alex. No more games." He doesn't look around at me, just stares upward, head resting on the back of the sofa.

I resent him calling it a game again. It wasn't a game because I wasn't playing. Or if I was, I had no idea what the rules were.

"Yes," I whisper. Though I'm not certain my brain wouldn't have talked me out of it, I know I wanted to see him again. More than I've ever wanted anything. It's only that I *was* certain it wasn't a good idea.

"Because you wanted to, or because I blindsided you?" he asks, turning his head to look at me.

"Because after you blindsided me, I wanted to." I smile.

He returns it before an instant later it melts away, his eyes darkening as if a shadow's passed overhead. "So, how long have you been seeing him for?"

I shake my head. "I'm not seeing him. I wouldn't have agreed to have dinner with you if I were. Tonight was the first time we've gone out. As I said, we work together." I look down and brush a piece of imaginary fluff off my jeans.

"You planning on seeing him again?"

"Oh, you mean even though I don't want him?"

"Even though you want me," he says. Sexual arrogance.

I fix him with a narrow gaze and shake my head again. God, his eyes are a remarkable color, the irises moving like green liquid fire under certain light. Under this light.

Beneath my cool fingers, the ice pack melts slowly, which I'm glad about. I'm not ready for him to leave yet.

"He's a nice guy, Jake," I say, clearing my throat.

"Yeah, you said that before, Alex." His voice is quiet. "Is that the kinda guy you want then? *Nice.*"

"As opposed to what?" I ask.

He holds my stare for a long stretch, and I manage not to look away this time. Then he sighs again. "You know, I never normally have to work this fucking hard with a girl. Never."

"Yes, and you said *that* before. Any girl you want, you get her. It's a done deal. I remember." An image of womanizing Jake flits through my mind, and

I see him fucking nameless, faceless women raw and hard over his desk, on the sofa, against the window. The heat curling in my belly shifts, transforming into something else—something with a sting to it.

When I look back at him, he's biting the inside of his bottom lip in the way he does. His eyes are still intense and dark.

"But you're not any girl, are you, Doctor Alex Marlowe? I knew that from the start. I knew you were . . ." He stops himself from saying any more.

I can't breathe again. "You knew I was what?"

He examines me as if he's trying to decide something, then he blinks and shakes his head. "Never mind," he says, tilting his head back away from me again.

I feel as if I've missed an opportunity to get inside his head. As though the bravado and sexual arrogance cracked just a smidge to reveal a glimmer of something else beneath.

"I mean, I have no fucking clue what's going on here, Alex. You say you'll go out with me, but then you stand me up for some guy in a pair of cords who you aren't into? Help me out, will you?"

I sigh, irritated. I don't want to talk about Sam anymore. "Jake, we're going around in circles here. I explained why I did that . . ." I meet his eye. "You told me yourself the reasons I had for staying away from you are entirely valid, so how can you be angry at me for doing so? You're being unreasonable . . ."

"Yeah, well, I'm an unreasonable sort of person, Alex." His voice is heavy, his eyes too.

To lighten the mood, I raise an eyebrow. "Well, that's good to know."

His face is serious, but then the corner of it tugs into a smile. I feel mine do the same, and before I know it, I'm smiling back at him.

"I mean, you smacked me in the face for calling you gorgeous, so it looks like we can both be a bit unreasonable sometimes . . ."

I frown. "That's not why I smacked you in the face. I mean, that was an accident. A complete accident."

He's grinning now. An adorable grin that makes his eyes sparkle and his nose scrunch slightly. He has an incredible duality to him, I realize. One moment he can look adorable, almost sweet, and then the next, he looks as if he's thinking the most obscene thoughts.

"Okay, well, I promise never to smack you in the face again. Contrary to what you might think, I don't condone violence."

"Dunno . . . it has its uses." He shrugs. "You went from wanting to kill me to being my primary carer in about ten seconds. That was useful."

I roll my eyes. "I didn't want to kill you. I was annoyed with you." *And embarrassed you might have had a point.* "But please don't make light of it— it isn't funny. I feel terrible about it." I glance at his nose again. God, I hope we've caught it in time and it doesn't swell tomorrow. Or worse, he has a black eye.

"No, it wasn't funny. It was pretty fucking painful. Not a bad back-hander." He grins.

I think he's going to add "for a girl," but he doesn't. With a shake of my head, I shift the ice pack lower. Then I lean up, pulling his collar down at one side to inspect the wound I all but forgot about. He takes a sharp inhale of breath before turning his head to give me better access. My mouth waters at the sight of the skin on his throat—smooth and tanned with a thick cord of muscle running from his jaw to his collarbone. I suddenly have the over-whelming urge to run my tongue up it, to feel and taste his warm vital skin as the scent of him invades my nose. Then I want to kiss around his jaw un-til I reach his mouth, and suck and bite on that full bottom lip.

"How has this been healing?" I ask in a strange, faraway voice. I keep my gaze fixed on his neck, afraid he'll see my desire written plainly across my face with his amazing hereditary eyesight.

Carefully, I peel back the small white square padding on the crook of his neck to peek underneath. The sutures look good, though I'm certain he'll be left with a scar across the top of his shoulder. A flurry of anger toward the person who did this flares up inside me.

"Yeah, it's been fine. I don't mind it," he says, and I frown. He doesn't mind it? He doesn't mind the fact someone tried to kill him with a kitchen knife?

Fixing the padding back in place, I take a deep breath. "Can I ask you something?"

He turns his head back to me, eyes wary under his long, dark lashes. He nods once.

"Why didn't you want to go to the police about this? I mean, some-one hurt you badly. They could have killed you. Why would you let them get away with it?" He could have died. He could have been paralyzed. The notion makes my gut tighten with unease.

"What makes you think I let them get away with it?" he asks, quiet.

Something prickles over my skin at the depth in his eyes. So, he paid them back. There can be no other inference from that.

His eyes continue to stare at me, their deep turquoise blue standing out brightly against the healthy, tanned skin of his face. He really is stunning up close like this. Beautiful, really. Yes, he's also dangerous and intense and mercurial, the kind of man my good-girl reasons should be screaming at me to stay away from, but they've gone quiet now. I want him. I'm not even going to bother denying it anymore. It takes far too much effort.

As I see it, I have two options: I move across the sofa and kiss him, which will lead to my sleeping with him, because that's what I want—more than anything, it's what I want; or I move across the sofa, remove the ice pack from his face, and politely wish him good night. I'm sure he can tell what I'm thinking. I'm sure he can tell I'm weighing up all the ways this night could end and being completely and ridiculously unable to act upon any of them.

When I shift forward, our bodies are so close I can smell his spicy, masculine scent that makes me dizzy. His mouth opens, and I think he might lean up to kiss me, and I hope he does because it means I won't have to decide. He licks his lips ever so slightly, but he doesn't move any farther, doesn't reach his mouth up to mine. My breathing feels light but labored, his low and hot, as we both stare at one another.

Then I reach up and remove the ice pack from his face. "I think that should do it," I say breathlessly before standing up.

I leave him sitting there as I walk through to the kitchen to empty the contents of the bag into the sink. With my hands on the sink, my head bowed, I watch as the remnants of melted ice run slowly down the plughole.

Why am I like this? Why can't I ever take what I want? I want him. Why does it *need* to be anything more than tonight? Why do I need it to be? I'm sure as anything he doesn't.

But then it wasn't so long ago I had my heart broken. I can't go back there so soon. Not with a guy like him. A guy who fucks women raw and hard and doesn't have to try this much to do it.

With a deep breath, I turn around, getting a shock when I see him standing in the doorway of my kitchen watching me. How long has he been there?

"Do you want me to leave you alone now, Alex?" he asks quietly, eyes unreadable.

I look down at my watch and see it's slightly after 1:00 a.m. He's only been here for about an hour? It feels like days since I opened my front door to see him standing there.

It's been a long day, and I should be exhausted, but I'm not. I'm on edge, frustrated, excited, magnetized. Too many adjectives again. I can't help it. He's so close and so attainable. The fantasy of him in the flesh no longer seems that dangerous.

"It is late, and I'm tired," I lie.

He moves into the kitchen. "That's not what I meant."

I frown at him, confused.

"I meant, do you want me to stop chasing you and leave you alone now?"

My stomach bottoms out as though I've hit turbulence, and my fingers dig into the worktop to hold myself upright. Oh. That kind of alone. His eyes burn through me as he waits for my answer. Waits for me to say he can have me, or he should leave me alone.

I'm convinced now that this kind of attraction is something you only read about. It doesn't happen to actual people in real life. Or if it does, they don't overthink it to the point of insanity as I've been doing. They grab it with both hands, no matter how unlikely it may seem, no matter the consequences. But then, that's not real life either, is it? To say to hell with the consequences. It isn't mine at least.

"I never asked you to chase me, Jake," I whisper, stalling for time.

He lets out a breath and stalks across the kitchen toward me. My heartbeat speeds up the closer he gets, and when he stops in front of me I think I stop breathing completely. He reaches his fingers up under my chin and tilts my head to meet his eyes, his eyes roaming mine, looking for something. I want him to find it. I try to imagine what he's seeing, hoping for once how much I want him *is* written plainly across my face, because then I won't have to say it out loud.

"No, you didn't ask me to chase you." He shakes his head, his voice sad, almost. "And if you asked me to stop now, I would. I can take a hint. But I know you want me, Alex, and it's confusing the fucking life out of me. So, I need you to say it. I need you to tell me."

This is a turning point. He will leave me alone now if I ask him to. He'll walk away, and I don't know how to feel about that. What I do know is if I tell him to leave me alone, anytime I walk down a London street—or likely any street—I'll search every nameless face, hoping one of them will be his.

Hoping one day, when I least expect it, I'll bump into him, like what happens in movies. In my fantasy, he'll have been hoping to bump into me too. We'll have an awkward, "Hi, how are you?" before the next scene of us kissing and making love desperately. Ridding ourselves of the memory of the night I stood him up and smacked him in the face.

That's the fantasy. Though, in reality, if I bumped into him in the future, he'd be married to a glamour model, and I'd be single, alone, and bitter because he still looks as good as he does now.

"Is that what you want, Alex? You want me to leave you alone?" His voice snaps me out of my thoughts.

Okay, real life now. Not chick flick-inspired fantasyland. I need to rationalize this. I'm good at rational.

Is that what I want? To move on and continue with my life as it was before him? To never set eyes on him again? A weird sense of panic skitters down my spine at the thought of that—of never setting eyes on him again.

His thumb is at my mouth now, and as he strokes it softly over my lip, my body sizzles. Yes, actually sizzles. I'm sizzling from a man's touch, and I'm contemplating not seeing him again. Am I bloody mad? Have I lost my mind?

No, not seeing him again is not an option.

No.

Jake smiles. It's small and starts in the corner of his mouth before spreading across it slowly. I wonder why he's looking at me like that, and then I realize: I spoke aloud. I didn't think the word "no"—I said it aloud.

"I didn't think so," he breathes. He runs his hand slowly down the side of my cheek and brushes my hair behind my shoulder, exposing my neck to him, then he skims his fingers down, his touch leaving scorch marks as they go. When he leans down and kisses open-mouthed across the path his fingers just took, it occurs to me how gentle all his touches have been. They're not at all what I expected. Not when I first saw him, and not in my fantasies where he's always commanding and rough.

I hear him inhale and moan softly.

"Fucking hell, you drive me crazy, Alex . . ." he moans against my throat, dizzying me.

I'm stunned by him. Stunned in the real meaning of the word—as in, he constantly shocks me into a semi-conscious state. When he reaches my ear, he nuzzles below it and then softly begins to suck on my earlobe, biting down on it gently. *Oh . . . my . . . god . . .* A small, loose moan escapes my mouth.

When he twists his head to kiss me on the mouth, it's sudden and shocking, and I have to dig my feet into the ground to stop my legs from buckling. My arms slide up and around his neck to pull him into me, deepening the kiss. He's greedy with it, sucking and biting and licking at my mouth, my lips, my tongue. When he pushes his hips into me, I feel the hot hardness of his arousal against my jeans. Without warning, he moves his hand to the waistband and pulls open the top button quickly.

Breaking away from his mouth, I shake my head at him.

He gives me a look, apologetic and uncertain, before I slip out from between him and the counter and away, turning back to him when I reach the kitchen door.

"Well? Aren't you coming?" I ask, breathless. "I assume you haven't changed your mind about wanting to come to bed with me. I've high hopes for your cuddling ability."

He blinks in shock before a look flashes across his face that practically sets my womb on fire. It's similar to the look he gave me in the deli when I agreed to go out with him, only magnified by a thousand. How does any woman have a chance against him when he looks at them like that?

They don't. *I* don't.

My entire body trembles as he walks toward me, his movements slow and measured, before wrapping an arm around my waist and pulling me into him. His free hand, he slips around my neck, possessive. When he speaks, his voice is low and serious.

"Doctor, I've wanted to go to bed with you since the moment I laid eyes on you." His thumb strokes the skin of my cheek, soft. "Doctor" doesn't sound so impersonal this time. It sounds erotic. Carnal. "You think there's any fucking chance I'm letting you go now?"

TEN

Before I have time to respond, he wraps his hands around my butt and hoists me up, spreading my legs so I'm wrapped around his waist. A small, surprised gasp escapes my mouth, and Jake smiles.

"Come on, Alex. Don't tell me that's the first time you've ever been swept off your feet."

I giggle. And so, like I never thought he'd be gentle, I also never thought he'd be cute or sweet. Then his mouth is on mine again, and I can't do any more thinking about what I thought he'd be. Jake carries me out of the kitchen and up the stairs as though I weigh less than nothing while I mumble against his mouth that he should watch his head because the ceilings are low.

When we get to the top, he halts but doesn't put me down, his breathing only slightly labored. I pull back from his mouth to find him looking at me expectantly.

"Gonna need some directions here, baby," he says, amused.

Oh, right—to my bedroom, because he's never been in there before.

I give him a shocked face. "A man asking for directions? How novel."

"So, you're hot, smart, and funny? Fucking hell, a triple threat."

I grin. "Feeling inadequate, are you?"

"Always with you, Alex. Always," he says before giving me an impatient look.

I can only stare at him a moment, distracted, before nodding toward my bedroom. He nudges open the door with his foot and carries me inside, his mouth finding mine again until we reach the bed, where he sets me back down on my feet.

He takes in my bedroom with a strange look on his face. The English country cottage style probably isn't to his taste. He probably prefers dark and sexy over cozy and calm. Except, with Jake in it, in all his forbidden sexual glory, it doesn't feel cozy or calm.

"So, this is where you dream about me then?" he says, a smirk playing over his mouth.

I bite back a smile, heat rising to my cheeks. "So bloody sure of yourself, aren't you, Jake Lawrence?"

"Yeah, almost always," he mumbles, his eyes intense as he stares at me.

I realize then that in a few seconds, he's going to be naked. The thought sends a blast of something hot through me, and the tops of my thighs tighten again, my tummy swirling with need and anticipation. I do not know when I became so shallow, or when lusting over a man became normal behavior for me, but I'm almost certain this is strictly a side effect of Jake. He makes me do strange, out-of-character things.

My eyes dip down his body to see the lusting is most definitely reciprocated, the unmistakable sign of arousal visible through his jeans. Involuntarily, I lick my tongue across my lips.

He moves quickly then, stepping forward so he's on me again, kissing me hard. The right amount of tongue coupled with the right amount of sucking and enough bite to drive me insane. It's addictive. Hypnotizing. When his hands go to the front of my jeans again, I let him unzip them all the way before he slips a hand inside to clasp between my legs, over my underwear.

I hear his sharp intake of breath.

"Fuck, baby, look how wet you are," he whispers against my mouth. "That all for me?"

My cheeks feel so hot, partly from embarrassment, but mainly from the lust sparking through my body. As he strokes me in tender circular motions, I drop backward and onto the bed, moving immediately to push my jeans down over my hips. He slips his hand out and helps me, sliding them down the rest of the way while I pull my top over my head. When I'm laid out on the bed in nothing but my underwear, he pauses, taking a moment to drink me in.

Internally, I congratulate my foresight in choosing one of my most expensive lace underwear sets. Jake, a hand over his mouth, looks hungry. When he moves toward me, I bring my foot up, pressing it gently against the hard front area of his jeans to keep him at bay. He glances down at my foot then up to my eyes with a bewildered expression.

"Your turn," I say with a small smirk of my own. My transformation to wanton, shallow nympho is complete. "I'm almost naked, and you're not." It's embarrassing, the way I pout.

But then his mouth curls up into that sexually arrogant smile, and I think I might orgasm on the spot. "You want me naked, Alex? That what you're saying?"

I nod, and Jake licks his lips, not moving a muscle for what seems like hours. Finally, his hands come up to the button of his shirt, and he unbuttons it before moving straight on to the next one.

"Mmm, slower, please," I tell him, and he huffs out a quiet laugh.

"Your house. You're in charge," he says with a serious look. It makes me wonder exactly what it would entail if we were in his house, where he would be in charge. The idea sends jolts of pure pleasure up my thighs and into the place where they meet.

Slower, Jake continues to strip out of his shirt, his hands steady and controlled, whereas mine are having trouble holding me up. Only one thought comes to mind as his shirt hits the floor, and it's not complex. It's three simple words:

Oh my god.

I didn't think men had bodies like his in real life. Not really. His is the kind of body you see on billboards or in men's health magazines. I was sure he looked after himself, worked out, and ate well, because I saw and felt the hard lines of his body over his clothes, but he is . . . something. All ridged muscles and hard lines. His tattoos are stunning to look at too. They cover every corner of his perfect body and arms, black, swirling shapes and words, which are all intricately and skillfully done.

I've never been into tattoos, never really understood why people want to mark their skin permanently with designs that will lose their allure and importance over time. I'm not thinking that now though, nor that this permanence of ink spoils his perfect body. I'm thinking the opposite: the result is breathtaking. As I bring my eyes back to his, I find again that he's watching me intently, looking pleased by whatever he sees on my face.

He moves his hands to his belt and unbuckles it slowly. Why on earth did I tell him to go slowly? What was I thinking? He unbuttons the top button of his jeans and then stops, leaving them hanging there, open, so I can see the dark hair leading down into tight white boxers.

Christ, I honestly think I might orgasm just by thinking about what's in there. He's sex personified, his body practically made for it, and the look on his face promises it.

"Why did you stop?" I ask.

He bites his lip sexily. "Because I like seeing that look on your face."

"What look?"

"How much you want me."

Every hair on my body stands on end, my spine buzzing with need, my cheeks hot. He moves toward me again, taking something out of his pocket and placing it on the nightstand. He uses his knee to nudge open my legs and reaches out to tilt my head up to him.

"How much do you want me, Alex?" he asks quietly.

As I stare up at him, my chin level with the opening of his jeans, I realize I can't think straight, let alone speak. I look away shyly, my eyes flitting to the nightstand to see what he took out of his pocket. The lamp illuminates the foil packet. Surely, he didn't think . . .?

I turn my head back to him, frowning slightly. "Did you come here expecting this?"

I stood him up. He was livid. And yet somehow, he still expected I'd fall into bed with him. That's sexual arrogance to the nth degree.

He looks at the condom packet. "No, of course not. I'm just . . . prepared." He shrugs.

I honestly don't know what to think of that. So, women throw themselves at him with that much frequency—and he complies with that much frequency—he carries condoms around with him. Perhaps the medical practitioner in me should be glad he's safe and sensible with his sex life.

Oh, what does it matter either way? It's too late for second thoughts. There is absolutely no way I'm not having him. Not now.

"Well, aren't you a good little boy scout?" I say with a hint of sarcasm. He notices because his eyes darken.

"There's not a lot that's good about me, Alex. You should know that right now. I'm not one of your *nice guys."* His voice is serious, and the sliver of doubt I had a moment ago magnifies.

But then he leans down and kisses me hard, his tongue slipping into my mouth to drown away all the doubts.

He pulls back and licks his lips. "So, I really fucking want you to take my trousers off now. But since this is your house and you're the boss here, it's totally up to you."

I glance at the hardness straining his trousers. God, I want to see him— all of him. I want to touch him, taste him. Moving forward so I'm perched on the edge of the bed, I reach up to unzip his jeans, my eyes locked on his as I do. Then I put my hands on his hips and pull his boxers and jeans down together, a small gasp escaping as I'm faced with the full, glorious, naked sight of him. He's almost fully erect, the end moist, and like the rest of him, he looks utterly edible. It dawns on me almost immediately that he's rather large. Of course he is. His sexual arrogance makes total sense all of a sudden.

He steps out of his jeans and boxers and kicks them away. "Lie down, Alex," he commands as I'm still dazed at the sight of him.

So, Jake gives orders in bed too? As I move to obey, I decide I don't dislike it. From this angle, lying back on the bed, he looks even bigger. I'm not entirely sure he'll fit inside me.

He seems to catch onto my thought direction, because he looks down at himself and then back up at me. "Pretty impressive, huh?" he says with a low chuckle.

Hilarious. He's making a joke of his enormous cock.

"You could have someone's eye out with that." My tone is nervous as I smile back at him.

"Don't worry, I promise to be gentle with you," he says, playful, and then his hands are on my knickers. He has them down and off in one quick movement before he picks up my foot to kiss the inside in soft, sensual kisses with his open mouth. Then, without taking his eyes off mine, he drops to his knees, pushes open my legs, and lowers his head between my thighs. The feel of his mouth there is sudden, shocking, and wanton.

"Oh my god, Jake," I moan, fisting the sheets as he licks at me hungrily, his lips and nose pressed flush against me. As he pushes his tongue inside and fucks me with it, I let out a loud gasp. He moans too—a raw, animalistic sound that vibrates where his mouth is.

Jake's mouth is masterly as always as he withdraws his tongue and instead begins to suck and nibble, flicking his tongue expertly over the throbbing, magnetized spot. When I open my eyes and look down, he's watching with a rapt expression, eyes darkened with lust.

He lifts his mouth away, and I whine from the loss of it.

"Fuck, I've thought a lot about how your cunt would taste in my mouth, Alex," he hisses, and then his mouth is back on me. *Good god.* He thought about how my *what* would taste? Did he actually say that word? I swallow, gasping for air as his mouth finds a perfect pace.

"Jake, please don't stop . . . I'm . . . god . . ."

"Are you going to come for me, baby?" he asks, muffled against me.

I nod, reaching down to grip at his hair, pulling his head closer into me as I move against his mouth.

"That's it. Come, Alex. Come for me. In my mouth, that's it . . . yes, baby . . ." He groans low in his throat, and it's enough. Jake pulls me through the orgasm, milking me with his mouth as rolls of exquisite, bone-softening pleasure course through me.

When it's over, my legs trembling around his wide shoulders, I lean my head to look down at him. He's sucking softly and loudly at the inside of my thigh, eyes heavy and hungry with desire. He places a kiss against my buzzing clitoris before moving up my body, his erection pressed hotly against my thigh.

I feel my wetness on his mouth as he kisses me lazily, masterful tongue stroking against my own. He circles my nipple with his thumb and finger until it's hard and tender before pulling the fabric down and around it to expose it to the air. The cold air stings only for a moment before he moves his head lower and covers it with his mouth. Teeth scrape gently, tongue flicking softly, until it feels almost painful before he moves to repeat the process on the other.

"Mmm, I could get used to making you come," he whispers against my breast, the feel of his light stubble on the sensitive skin making it tingle and throb.

I smile down at him, my fingers tracing back and forth across the dark shapes of the tattoos on his shoulders. "I could too," I whisper.

He grins and kisses a trail across my breasts and down to my belly, where he makes gorgeous little groaning noises.

"Let me see you again," he says.

For a moment, I wonder what he means, but then he kisses the top of my left thigh and I understand. I open my legs for him. Have I ever been this brazen in my life?

He doesn't touch me; he just looks at the most intimate part of me with his mouth slightly open. "I like that my mouth has been here now, and that I made you come with it," he says, leaning forward to kiss me where I came.

The desire to have him inside me is torture. Why is he torturing me? He's being too gentle, like a feather, when I need a riding crop.

"Did you think about it?" he asks, glancing up. "About me inside you?" His voice is low and sexy.

Biting my lip, I nod, and he smiles from the corner of his mouth. It's so bloody sexy. Everything he says and does is so bloody sexy. When he dips his finger inside me, I gasp quietly, and he makes a soft growling noise, watching my face intently.

"Tell me you want me to fuck you."

"I want you," is what I say—all I *can* say—breath turning shallow as he adds another finger and moves them deliciously. "Please, Jake." With a look, I show him where I need him, and a wicked smile spreads across his face.

"I need you ready for me," he whispers, leaning down to lick at my clitoris ever so softly. My back arches up off the bed into his mouth.

Ready for him? Is he blind? Deaf?

When he slides another finger inside me, I almost break apart. It's not nearly enough, but it's better than two, and it fulfills some of the need throbbing between my legs. Not enough. But it's something at least. When I spread my legs open for him to move his hand easier, I hear him murmur in appreciation. He moves up my body again, finding my mouth, while his fingers move in me, and he dips his tongue between my lips in the same rhythm.

"Fuck, baby, I want to be in every part of you," he says against my lips as his fingers spread me wider while he fucks me with them. It's good. *So* good.

Suddenly, I realize how selfish I've been. I've barely touched him. Which is bizarre, because all I've wanted to do since I set eyes on him is touch and kiss and taste him. I move to put my hand between his legs, wrapping my grip around his velvety-smooth hardness.

"Alex, don't," he groans, jerking away from my touch.

He doesn't want me to touch him?

"I can't touch you?" I frown up at him.

"Yes. Fuck. Of course you can. It's just . . . I'm struggling a bit here. If you touch my cock right now . . ." He shakes his head. "No fucking chance." He leans down to kiss me again, fiercer this time, teeth scraping my lip.

"Jake, I'm going to . . ." I moan as I move against his fingers, urging them on.

He breaks away from my mouth to look at me, his face a picture of gorgeous enthrallment. "Look at me when you come, baby, yeah? Look at me when I make you come."

He seems to sense my climax a moment later and separates our mouths to lift his head and watch as the heat crashes up and outward. I dig my fingers into his back as wave after wave of hot, numbing pleasure washes over me. Our eyes stay locked until my body slows and the white heat of my climax ebbs away.

I feel soft and warm and totally spent—and he hasn't even made love to me yet.

As I lie there with my eyes closed, enjoying the soft buzz that's settled on the surface of my body, I feel him looking at me. I can feel the heat of his eyes on me. Normally, I'd feel self-conscious in this kind of situation with a new lover. Not that I've had many new lovers, but lying here scattered, pleasured, and spread open would normally make me vulnerable. Nothing is normal with him though. Nothing about being with him feels even remotely normal.

It all feels extraordinary. If I'd known for a second it would feel like this, I would never have fought it. Never. Every woman deserves to feel like I feel in this moment: totally desired, completely satisfied, and alight with the anticipation of what's still to come.

His weight shifts, and he presses a gentle kiss to my lips before leaving my body space. When I open my eyes and see him move to the nightstand, I have the overwhelming desire to touch him somewhere, and so I reach up to scratch my nails gently down his back, which glistens with a light sweat. He turns around and gives me a look filled with so much want my body feels needy again.

Have I ever come twice and been ready so quickly for a third? No, but then I've never been looked at like *that* by him before.

"Hmm," he says, quirking an eyebrow at me. "Why are you still not naked? You have me at a disadvantage here." He smirks. I hear the foil rip and see his hands move between his legs.

"I'm almost naked."

"Almost isn't enough."

"I was distracted."

"What were you distracted by?" he asks.

I put my finger to my mouth and look upward as if I have no clue.

"Well, I like that I distract you."

Sitting up, I reach behind and unclasp my bra, trying my best to make it look smooth and seductive, though I'm not sure taking off a bra can be done anything but awkwardly. Unless you're a stripper.

When he turns back around to face me, his eyes blaze, causing that warm spreading sensation in my stomach to start again. He moves over me, settling himself between my thighs, his slightly intimidating hardness lying thick and hot against my hypersensitive skin. While he holds himself up with a strong-muscled arm, he continues to stare down at me. The atmosphere seems to shift from erotic to something else—something more intimate and intense.

"So beautiful . . ." he says, fingers skimming the shape of my lips. "You're so fucking beautiful, do you know that?" He leans in to kiss me, chaste and soft. "I've been thinking about this since I saw you." He sounds almost shy. It's not how I thought he'd talk in bed. "Fuck, I haven't stopped thinking about being inside you, Alex."

And there it is. How I thought his pillow talk would sound.

"Look at me," he says, shifting his body over mine.

My eyes flutter open to stare at him. God, he looks serious. And strong. Dangerously strong. The corded muscle of his neck and shoulder pulls tight as he holds himself up. Yes, he's a man made for having sex, for making women come. I should count myself lucky to have at least one night of pure, unadulterated lust with this man.

He nudges his cock closer to the space between my legs, teasingly, temptingly. "Do you want me inside you now? Is that what you want?"

Cheeks flushing hot again, I nod.

Leaning down, he licks his tongue into my mouth as he moves the tip of his cock to press against my opening, resting it there.

"I want you to look at me when I put my cock inside you," he says. "If you close your eyes, I'll stop, okay?"

I'm not thinking straight enough to analyze the point of this, but I'm pretty sure I'd agree to anything at this moment, so I nod.

He pushes in, and the scorching heat of him is immediate, the feel of him making me gasp aloud before he begins to push himself into me. It's so painfully slow my entire body thrums and trembles under the building pressure. His face is a picture of focus as he alternates between looking at where he's entering me and back up at my eyes.

It's without a doubt the most intense sexual experience of my life.

When I feel him fill me all the way up, the sensation becomes too much, and my eyes close on a soft, desperate whine.

Quick as a flash, I feel him pull out, so I'm left with only the feeling of emptiness and confusion. My eyes fly open to glare at him.

"What did I say?" he asks, looking slightly amused, I think.

My head isn't functioning properly, so, for a moment, I don't know what he's talking about. Then I remember.

"Sorry. I was trying . . ." I say meekly.

"Mmm, then try harder," he says, voice low as he starts to push himself in again.

This time, I make sure my eyes are open and looking up into his as he does. The feeling is more intense the second time, and more like rapture. He's a tight fit, but I feel my body grab onto him from the inside, greedy and possessive. I dig my hands into the soft skin of his muscular back to pull him closer and balance out the sensation.

"Fucking hell, Alex . . ." he moans as his eyes close over. Perhaps the eye contact part is over now because he's all the way in. He is all the way in, isn't he? He has to be—there can't be any more of him.

He brings his head down and kisses me, holding onto my bottom lip gently with his teeth. To ease the torturous pressure of him throbbing but not moving inside me, I undulate under him, tilting my hips up. He lets out a delicious moan I'm certain I'll fantasize about for the rest of my life.

"Do you want me to fuck you hard or slow, baby?" he asks, a small smirk settling on his face now.

Oh, so he's a sadist.

"I don't know, Jake. Please . . . just, please . . ." I pant pathetically, desperately, as I hold his gaze.

"Always so fucking polite, aren't you?" he says. "One day, I'll get you to beg me to fuck you hard, Alex. I promise you that."

"Okay . . . whatever you want, only, can you . . .? I need you," I manage.

At my words, a strange look passes over his face that I don't entirely understand, but it feels intense. I think I've done something wrong again because slowly, he pulls out of me. Oh, god, no. Please, no. His face is a mask of concentration as he withdraws, but then his eyes flash wide and he thrusts into me fully. Deliciously. Finally.

The noise that comes from my throat is unlike any noise I've ever made. His groan is rough and scratched, and I love it. He shifts, leaning up to watch himself moving in and out, and the sight of him doing it is so completely erotic I find I can't look away.

"Fuck, Alex . . ." he moans as he thrusts, alternating between hard and gentle and deep and circular in a perfect harmony of movement. He kisses and licks at my mouth as his hands roam my body: my hip, the flat of my tummy, my nipple, my throat. And then his fingers are in my mouth, and I'm sucking on them as he watches me.

As I feel myself get close again, I pull his mouth to mine and kiss him hard, biting down on his lip, which only makes him fuck me harder. My hands try to pull him deeper into me, clutching at his hair and scratching at his back to do all I can think of to feel him closer.

"I want you to come around my cock, Alex," he growls close to my ear. "I want to feel you come while I'm inside you."

Holy Christ.

He speeds up his thrusts as he brings his fingers between my legs to find the nub of pleasure between our bodies. Then he circles it magnificently. With his mouth at my neck, biting and nibbling, he orders me to come for him—which, a second later, I do.

"That's it, baby." He kisses my neck and throat and fucks me as the climax courses through me. "That's it."

Jake's movement changes, and he sits up, pulling my legs around his waist. With his hands finding my hips, he pulls me onto his cock, rough and sharp. He's close. I can see it on his face, feel it in his movements—careless and hurried now. Sliding one hand up to my throat, I think he's going to do something I'm not quite ready to deny him, but he doesn't. He just rests it there, the other hand gripping my hip, as his orgasm shudders through him. He tilts his head back and curses before cowering over my body to kiss me, holding onto my mouth and sucking my tongue as the curses turn to long moans. His moans are low and raw and primal, and they touch something deep inside.

I can't think. Or breathe. He feels so good, and I'm so hot. I feel boneless and weightless, my body soft with pleasure.

"Fucking hell . . ." he breathes raggedly against my neck. He slows to a stop and kisses down my mouth to my chin, where he bites me softly, growling playfully as he does. It's an adorable little sound that reminds me of a puppy.

He stays inside me for some time after he comes, kissing my throat, neck, forehead, and nose before finally touching his lips to mine. He's a ton of muscle on top of me, but he's not suffocating. Not at all. He's a comforting, necessary weight, like a paperweight in a windy room.

Then—because I thought that, of course—he shifts and pulls out, coming to lie on his back next to me. His skin is sticky and sucks against my own as we both lie there and wait for our breathing to return to normal. When I glance around to look at him, I'm certain he looks sated and satisfied. I really hope he is. I hope it was as good for him as it was for me.

The next thought that hits me is how incredible he looks postcoital. His face is flushed, his hair mussed, and his lips wet and kissed raw. Pride and something else shoots through me. *I did that. Me.* When he turns his head to look at me, lust roars again at the sight of that sharp canine smile as his mouth pulls up at one side. Christ, he's incredible. A sexy, gorgeous, deadly incredible that makes me feel way out of my depth.

"Well, I knew it would feel like that with you," he says, still breathing hard.

My breath falters. *"Like what?"*

He shrugs and closes his eyes, letting out a sigh. "You know. Like that."

Do I know? I know it felt amazing and intense and mind-blowing. Is that what he means? Is this always how sex is for him? I'm not always that good. It's never been that good for me.

"It was definitely . . . something."

He opens his eyes, and a worried look crosses his face. "I didn't hurt you, did I?"

"What? No. You didn't hurt me."

He relaxes and nods, smiling again. "Well, Doctor, I wish I could say the same about you. I think you ripped the skin off my back, and my lip might still be bleeding." He pouts his lip out. "You always so violent? What the fuck happened to your bedside manner?"

A wave of embarrassment washes over me. Christ, I scratched and bit him. I lean over to inspect his lip. It looks a little swollen and a lot kissable.

"Hmm . . . I think you'll live."

"Well, that's good." He leans up and kisses me. "Because I wouldn't mind doing that again. *A lot.*" His voice is low, and I feel him still semi-hard against my leg. It's a good thing I'm lying down because I may have just swooned.

He wants to do it a lot. I can almost hear the hallelujah music in my head. Then it's muffled by the sudden need to pee.

"I'll be right back," I say, springing up from the bed.

As I walk around the bed, I glance at him, and I swear the image of him lying naked and semi-hard on my bed incurs a double take. He looks like something from a fantasy, all hard muscles framed by tattoos and the lustful, wicked grin. Definitely one for the memory bank. When I'm old and gray, at least I can say, "Jake Lawrence—what a fine specimen of a man he was."

I laugh to myself as I walk to the en suite, picking up my bathrobe from the chair and wrapping it around my cooling body. He watches me the entire way, and I revel in it.

"That won't be on for long, Alex . . . trust me," he says sleepily.

I shake my head at him as I close the en suite door. In the bathroom, after washing my hands and brushing my teeth, I stand in front of the mirror to look at myself. Then I smile like a fool at my reflection.

I look well and truly seen to.

I had intense, mind-blowing sex with Jake Lawrence, and not just in my head. It happened.

I try to arrange my hair into something acceptable, but my mind wanders, and then I'm running my fingers over my mouth and closing my eyes as I remember the feel of his lips on mine. I shake myself out of it, because why on earth am I standing in the bathroom fantasizing about him when I have the real thing naked in my bed?

His arm's flung over his eyes as I near the bed, and it doesn't move as I climb into it next to him. His body is still and his breathing even, and soon, I realize why. He's sound asleep. Gloriously naked and sound asleep in my bed. He's on top of the quilt, and so I pull the throw from the foot of the bed over him and watch him for a moment, marveling at his beauty.

It'll be strange, having someone sleeping next to me after all this time. I decided pretty quickly after Ben left that I enjoyed having my king-size bed to myself. But as I look down at one gorgeously asleep Jake Lawrence, I'm more than happy to make an exception.

I wonder vaguely if he dreams, and if so, what about, before reaching over his body to switch off the lamp. As soon as my head hits the pillow, my eyes close, and I drift off to sleep feeling satisfied, comfortable, and warm next to him.

I also feel a weird sense of pride that I managed to tire him out.

ELEVEN

WHEN I OPEN MY EYES, MY BODY IS TURNED TOWARD HIM, HIS arm weighty and possessive across my body as he sleeps. I like how it feels there. I also like that he doesn't appear to be a snorer. His breaths are deep and calm and even. I can live with someone in my bed who isn't a snorer.

I shift slightly so I'm flat on my back, but he doesn't flinch, out cold and dead to the world. Well, I suppose that's what giving someone three orgasms in quick succession will do to you. Not "someone" though. Me. I was the one he wore himself out pleasuring. I sigh girlishly and take the opportunity to just watch him sleep. Is that creepy? Maybe, but since I don't know if I'll get the chance to do it again, I'm not going to beat myself up about it.

He has long, thick lashes, I notice. Unfairly feminine, and they rest across the smooth, tanned skin of his cheeks. There's no swelling around his nose at all, thank god. My eyes drop to the plump lips that did exactly what they promised last night and more.

The covers are below his waist, giving me a full view of his magnificent inked body, and as my eyes move down to the dark sprinkling of hairs that disappear below the sheets, my mouth actually waters. The wicked thought that crosses my mind causes me to glance back up at his face, fearful the volume of my dirty mind has somehow woken him up.

Christ, he's ridiculously good-looking, really.

My next thought is that I really hope this morning isn't awkward. Last night, I was tipsy on cider and overcome with lust, and everything always looks a lot more fragile and a lot less pretty in the harsh light of day.

Well, everything except him.

He looks the same. Probably better, actually, with the sunlight hitting the hard lines of his body and his gorgeous sleeping face. A disarming thought enters my head: I want to keep him for a while. I want more than one night or a couple of nights with him. I want to call him when I've had a bad day, have him sit next to me at an event that calls for a couple.

Oh my god, I'm in trouble. I let my gaze drift down his body to linger on the ink across his abdomen. It reads "C W," followed by an artistic, abstract heart and a date marked in roman numerals. Somehow, my foggy morning brain manages to work it out: November 4, 2016. A date four years ago that means something to him. A woman from his past who means something to him. I imagine Claire or Catherine or Carla or some other name of a girl I obviously now loathe.

Okay, I seriously need to get a grip. I also need to pee again and drink some water because I have morning cider mouth.

I slide out from under his arm and shimmy gently over to the edge of the bed. It's then I notice Fred sleeping soundly at the foot of the bed between Jake's legs. I nod at him. Can't really blame him for that.

I scrub my teeth while I pee, splashing some water on my face to put some life into it. When I come out of the bathroom, I see he's awake, though still lying where I left him.

He turns his head to smile at me. A small, lazy thing. "Morning."

"Morning." I can't help but smile too, something like embarrassment rushing to my cheeks.

"What's the chance of some breakfast then?" He yawns, but the heat stays in his eyes. It makes my legs weak. "I'm fucking starving."

Something clenches tightly below, and I feel my face flush. It's an innuendo. I'd have to be blind and dumb not to get it.

"I'm not sure what I have in," I say apologetically. "I can make you some toast?"

"I'll take whatever you're offering, Alex," he says, the intonation loaded.

I brush a hand through my hair and look away from him briefly. I hear a rustle of bedcovers and the sound of him stretching. He rolls his shoulders and twists his neck to one side, then the other. There's a clear crack. The movement disturbs Fred, who stands up and yawns, stretching too, before jumping off the bed and out of the room.

"Ah, I fell asleep on you last night. I'm sorry." He looks unapologetic, his mouth playful.

"Technically not on me. Beside me," I joke.

He grins, scrubbing a hand through his bed hair. "Well, I'm sorry anyway."

"You were tired. I covered you." I shrug. Seriously? I may as well have told him I'm carrying a watermelon.

"All that pent-up frustration, I guess . . ." he says with a small smirk.

I swallow, mouth flooding with want all over again. Neither of us speak for a few heavy seconds, until I clear my throat.

"So, I'll get you coffee then. And some toast." I nod and move toward the door. I hear him sigh quietly.

"Okay if I use your shower?" he asks.

Jake in my shower, naked and wet.

"Of course. There's one in there, and towels in the cabinet next to the sink." I indicate my en suite. "I'll leave you to it then."

Fifteen minutes later, I'm in the kitchen blowing over my scalding coffee when I hear him coming down the stairs. I'm not fully prepared for the weird flip my tummy does when he strides into the kitchen looking fresh, clean, and his hair still damp from the shower. He looks better every time I see him, I think. It's unnerving.

He stares at me as he rubs his wet hair with my fluffy cream towel.

"It might be a little cold now, sorry." I indicate the plate of buttered toast. "I can stick some more on if you want."

He picks up a slice and takes a large bite, chewing happily. "It's perfect, thanks."

"Coffee's in the pot. Milk and sugar are there."

I watch as he pours himself a cup and immediately lifts it to his mouth. No milk or sugar. I wonder then if maybe he's a soya or almond milk person, which, given his physique, would make sense. He sips quietly as he takes another bite of his toast, eyes flicking between his cup and me, then around my kitchen.

Weirdly, the silence doesn't feel uncomfortable. Hot, definitely. Heavy too, the tension between us still there, still loud. It feels different though. Less dangerous, but more intense somehow, memories of last night so vivid as I stand looking at him.

"You have a gorgeous place, by the way," he says, taking me completely by surprise. He turns his head out through the French doors to my garden.

"What—? Oh, thank you." The garden does look gorgeous right now. It's rosebushes and wildflowers bathed in buttery orange sunlight.

"I kinda imagined you living somewhere like this. Somewhere nice, you know? Quiet." He looks back at me.

"Isn't 'quiet' just a polite way of saying 'boring'?"

He raises an eyebrow. "You think I'm *polite?*"

I laugh into my cup, cooler now as I lift it to my mouth.

"You happy here?" he asks, making me blink.

"Um, yes, I am."

His eyes flicker with some unnamed emotion before he nods once. "I'd really love to get out of London," he sighs. "Gets you down sometimes, you know? So big yet so fucking small at the same time." He sounds tired. Though, Jake strikes me as a true London boy. I couldn't imagine him anywhere else.

"I do know. I lived there for a bit. I mean, it's a great city. So much happening all the time. It can sometimes feel like the center of the universe. But I guess I fancied a bit of peace and quiet." I shrug my shoulders.

"When did you live in London?" His eyes are wide with interest.

"During my residency at Tower Hamlets—so, like, four years ago."

He nods. "Whereabouts?"

"Islington."

Jake nods again, gaze piercing. "Fuck, the peaceful life. Sounds fucking perfect, to be honest," he muses, taking another sip of coffee, staring hard at me over the rim.

This time, the silence does feel uncomfortable. Darker.

"Jake, I feel the need to clear something up."

His gaze narrows, focused.

"Last night. What happened . . . I don't normally . . . do that. One-night stands, I mean. They're not my thing. I don't do them. Normally." Christ, why do I sound like an idiot who hasn't quite grasped the English language yet?

He chews his lip from the inside as he ponders my statement. Then he takes another sip of his coffee. "So . . . then I guess that makes me special?" he asks, the corners of his mouth turning up.

I feel a stupid grin threatening to break out. "You know what I mean."

"Yeah, I know what you mean, Alex."

Then, because the atmosphere feels kind of playful, I fix him with a look. "And I'm also not a cocktease."

He frowns, confused. "A what?"

"A *cocktease.*"

"I still didn't catch that." He puts his hand to his ear.

"Seriously?"

"Nah, I did. Just really like hearing the word 'cock' coming out of your mouth."

I roll my eyes. "You're unbelievable."

"Unbelievably special, I know," he says, and I can't help but giggle.

We drink the rest of our coffee in a charged silence, Jake munching on another piece of toast, his hair slowly drying in the hot air of the kitchen. So, it looks as though last night did nothing to abate my attraction to him. Now I know how he can make me feel I want him more, not less. The whole "sleep with him once and move on" plan is starting to look like a complete and utter failure.

Abruptly, he puts his cup down on the worktop and walks toward me. "Could you do something for me?" He stops in front of me, leaning in close as if he might kiss me.

I can smell him—that distinctly *Jake* smell that turns my head soft and my legs weak. How can he still smell like that when he's just used my pomegranate bodywash?

"Have a look at my back, will you? I had a look at it in your mirror upstairs, and I don't know what I've done to it."

I frown, confused, as he begins to unbutton his shirt. He holds my eye as he does, turning around and shrugging the shirt off his body. I feel my mouth drop open, unimaginable heat flooding my face. Oh my god. Scraped down his back is a group of red scratches where I've clawed at him like a bitch in heat.

"I'm pretty sure I didn't have these yesterday . . ." he says quietly.

I can't find any words to say. Not one. I'm mortified.

He glances over his shoulder. "I'm starting to think you like hurting me."

"I'm a doctor. It's my job to fix you, not hurt you," I tell him a little breathlessly as I stare transfixed at the angry red welts. They aren't serious. I've not broken the skin at least. They're . . . strangely hot.

"Yeah? I think I'd like to be fixed by you, Alex." There's a heaviness in his words that's not sexual this time.

I swallow. "Well, good news is, I didn't break the skin, so no need for a tetanus." I feel him laugh softly. "I'm sorry though . . ."

With no warning, he turns around and kisses me hard, stealing the breath right out of my lungs as he presses me back against the worktop. His hands slide around me before dipping lower, caressing the backs of my thighs beneath my robe.

"Don't apologize," he murmurs against my lips. "I like having your sex scars on me." When he slides his tongue into my mouth again, I moan, my hands smoothing up over the hard lines of his arms to his shoulders, then around his neck. When he moves to untie my robe, I don't stop him. I don't want to. "Do you have any idea how fucking crazy you make me?" he growls quietly.

I can only make a small sound at this. The feel of his hands slipping under my butt to pull me into him, his hips moving deliciously against me. Wanting. God, I love how he feels when he's this close to me. His experienced mouth and tongue, and his body warm and comforting, pressed hard against my own.

He stops kissing my mouth and pulls back to look down at me. There's a wicked glint in his eye now. "Don't move," he says before lowering himself so he's kneeling in front of me.

My breathing starts to spiral out of control as I realize what he's going to do, here in my kitchen. He delicately peels open my robe, leaning in to place soft, gentle kisses across my stomach, beneath my belly button, across to my hip bone. Lifting up my leg, he drapes it over his shoulder. I have to lean back on the worktop to steady myself as he presses his mouth to the inside of my thigh, licking the flat of his tongue up the inside of it. He looks up to meet my eye before moving his mouth inward, mixing gentle bites with soft licks until his breath is ghosting over my opening.

"Do you want me to make you come with my mouth again?" he asks as he presses his lips to the highest point on my thigh.

I can only moan softly as he rests his cheek against me and inhales deep.

When he turns his head up to me, I see the expectant look on his face, and I know he actually wants me to answer that.

"Please," I manage meekly.

He doesn't hesitate, groaning filthily as he licks his tongue the entire length of me before his mouth latches onto where I need it most.

My god . . . The heat of him is searing, a jolt of pleasure shooting through my whole body as he finds the bundle of nerves and fixes upon it. When I feel his hand slide between my legs, his fingers meeting his mouth so he's stroking and sucking at the same time, my legs almost give out.

Then he pushes his tongue inside.

"Jake . . ." I gasp. *Christ.* He's really going to make me come right here in my kitchen.

It grows rougher, the sounds from his mouth low and dirty as he fucks me with his fingers and his tongue with an expertise that takes my breath away. My orgasm comes fast, without any warning, rushing at me violent and loud.

"Oh my god, Jake, please don't stop!" I scream as the pressure snaps, flooding over me in hot waves.

I hear and feel him moan, sensitive against my climax, as he continues to lick and suck the pleasure from me. He makes a sucking noise and licks his tongue into me one last time before settling my leg back on the floor and standing up.

I blink up at his flushed face, dazed and trembling, as he fastens my robe. Then, as though he's enjoyed an extremely messy meal, he wipes the back of his hand across his mouth and licks his lips. It's probably one of the most erotic things I've ever bloody seen.

He leans in and kisses me lazily on the lips, licking his tongue against mine. "As good as your toast was, that was a lot fucking tastier," he says. "Now, I have to shoot off, but you owe me a date, Doctor, and I always collect on what people owe me." He bites back a smirk before bringing his hand up to stroke his thumb softly over my lip. "I'll call you to arrange, yeah? And this time, you won't stand me up." His eyes are deadly serious. Expectant too.

"Okay," I manage.

He nods, satisfied, then leans in to press his mouth to mine. "See you soon," he whispers against my mouth before he backs away from me and out of the kitchen.

When I hear the door close behind him, I burst out laughing—a stupid, girlish giggle fueled by light-headedness from one of the best orgasms I've ever had.

TWELVE

THE REST OF THE DAY I SPEND IN A RECURRING DAYDREAM ABOUT firm muscles and tattoos, multiple orgasms, and words of a sexual nature. I go for a run in the afternoon to try to expel some of the sexual tension that started building in my body when he left. I run until I'm sore, but when I get home—red as a beetroot, breathing fast, and dripping with sweat—I'm still groaning aloud thinking about his body and how he felt inside me. Sexual tension most certainly not expelled.

By early evening, I'm convinced I'm obsessed with him. I can't seem to stop thinking about how he sounded and felt, and neither can I stop my eyes from closing over and the small moan that comes from my throat whenever I do. *After a single night with someone? Seriously?* Also, his smell seems to have imprinted itself on my brain, because even though I showered for a lengthy period after my run, I can still smell him on me.

I manage to exist in a Jake-filled reverie for most of the day until 8:00 p.m., when Robyn calls me for details on my date with Sam.

Sam, who has almost disappeared from existence.

"Hey, babe. Sorry I never called earlier—spent the entire day at Dan's mum's talking about the wedding. I swear she drains any and every scrap of excitement from it. I feel like buggering off and doing it in secret after today. Vegas, baby. Fancy it?"

"You'd regret it forever, Rob," I tell her. "You'd cringe every time you looked at the photos of your Elvis impersonator reverend, but sure, I'll come. I've always wanted to see Vegas."

"Ugh, you're right. I want my bloody castle! Damn that woman!" she says lightly.

Rob doesn't always see eye to eye with Dan's mother, but it's mainly because they have such similar personalities rather than any real enmity for each other. They both love Dan fiercely, and it's become competitive now. Since

Rob and Dan got engaged, I've listened to her complain about his mother pushing her way into the wedding arrangements a little more every day.

"You know, she's probably making such a big deal of this because of Mark's divorce," I suggest, hopefully sounding diplomatic.

"I know, I know. I just wish she would extract herself a bit. Today, it was the font on the name cards and whether Dan's Aunt Flora is close enough to the toilet because of her arthritis. We must have spent four hours rearranging everyone, only to go back to my original layout. It was pointless. Anyway . . ."—she takes a deep breath—"back to you. How was your appointment with the doctor?"

For a single moment, I flirt with the idea of telling her about my appointment with Jake instead. It would certainly help to take her mind off Dan's mother. I'm sure my sleeping with the sexy nightclub owner is a pretty big deal. But I'm also sure she'll think it's a terrible and ill-advised big deal and likely talk me out of ever doing it again, and I don't want the judgment right now. I'm enjoying basking in the sexual afterglow too much to swap it for anything else.

"It was fine. Sam is really sweet, you know, but I don't think it's going to go anywhere. I don't think it can." *Mainly because I'm sleeping with someone else.*

Robyn makes a disappointed noise, and I decide to go on.

"And there's still the complications at work, Rob. I honestly don't think Douglas would approve of two of the potential partners sleeping together. It's kind of unprofessional," I say, hoping my tone gives nothing else away.

Vaguely, I wonder if sexual subterfuge is even a thing, and if so, what tone of voice it has.

"Hmm, yeah, I guess," she says, but she still sounds disappointed. "Maybe it's not the ideal time to start something with him when one of you is going to be taking over the partnership spot. Well, at least you put yourself out there. Maybe you can come back to it later."

"Maybe. We get on really well as friends. I think it's best to keep things platonic when the spark isn't setting you on fire, you know?"

"Yeah, you're right. But I want you to get back out there, Al, meet someone new. Someone who deserves you. Someone passionate and special and right for you." She sounds almost sad.

I ignore the image of Jake projected on the inside of my

mind—passionate and special and right for me. Two out of three isn't bad, I suppose.

"Rob, I'm really, honestly fine being single. Try not to worry about me so much, will you?"

"I know, I know you are. Oh, but on that note, Mark asked about you today. He was there at Julia's too and casually dropped your name into conversation. *THEN* he asked if you were seeing anyone yet!" Her voice is lighter, tinged with excitement, I think.

I've always found Mark, Dan's older brother, handsome in a stand-offish, arrogant kind of way. In a Ben-type way. He makes me nervous for some reason. Though, I've always thought that was because of his job. Police officers have always made me a little nervous, honestly.

"The divorced brother of your fiancé? Yeah, babe, because that's far less complicated than the colleague/rival I went out with last night."

"Oh, but imagine if it worked out with you two. We'd be sisters!" she squeals.

"You're already like a sister. I don't need to marry Sherlock to solidify it."

Robyn makes an exaggerated noise of disappointment.

"So, when is the dress reveal then?" I ask, desperate to change the subject. Rob bought her dress in New York, and it's being shipped over to a boutique in London in the next week or so.

"It arrives next Friday! So, we'll go on Saturday. You're still free, right? 11:00 a.m.?"

"Of course! I wouldn't miss it."

"Oh, Al, what if I don't like it when I see it again? What if I made a hasty decision?"

"Then Dan will buy you a new one." We both laugh because it's true. Dan adores her and would buy her ten dresses if it meant getting her up the aisle to become his wife. "It will be gorgeous though, sweetie. The pictures looked divine." I absently twirl my hair, inspecting the ends. I really need a trim. Then I wonder if I'll ever go wedding dress shopping.

"I wish you'd been there. You're my style guru. I'm scared it's out of style now—you know, dated?"

She's worried about this for nothing. It will be stunning. I know the shop in Manhattan where she bought it, and it's couture. Plus, Robyn would look stunning in a potato sack.

"Rob, it will be gorgeous. I can't wait to see you in it."

We finish up with me saying I'll call through the week to confirm. I'll have the situation with Jake sorted out much clearer in my head by then too and will be in a much better position to discuss it with her. At least, that's what I'm hoping.

Later that night, I'm wondering why he hasn't called to arrange our date yet when I realize only a crazy, desperate person would wonder that. He's been out of my house precisely eight hours, and I'm wondering why he hasn't called yet. Seriously?

Then I realize I'm counting the hours since he left my house. I *am* a crazy, desperate person.

When I get back to the office at 3:30 p.m. after my Monday house calls, he still hasn't called. That's when I begin to think maybe I'm not going to hear from him at all. Maybe the "see you soon" comment was just his way of being polite. The date thing too. Maybe that's what one-night standees say to each other as they leave you post-orgasm in the kitchen. Sort of like when you say, "Let's keep in touch," to an old school friend you have no intention of keeping in touch with.

But then I remember the look in his eye when he said this wasn't a one-night stand. He meant it. So, what the hell is he playing at? Typical bloody male, staying away and playing mind games, making me doubt, question, and overanalyze everything. Except I do that anyway.

Christ, I really hate this. I forgot how much I hate this. Being single looking for love is not the barrel of laughs romantic comedies would have you believe.

As I pass reception, Anna gives me a knowing look, which I can only assume is to do with Sam and our date. He must have told her. He and Anna are friendly, but I didn't think to the point of swapping date gossip.

Great. This is exactly what I wanted to avoid: knowing looks and tilted heads and the "aw, poor Sam" comments between the girls on the desk when it doesn't work out. Sam inspires a certain kind of protective-ness in other females, I've noticed. I'll be the scarlet woman come Friday, I'm sure.

I smile back awkwardly and head for the shelter of my office, closing the door tightly behind. I almost gasp at the sight waiting for me on my desk. An enormous bouquet of red roses sits proudly in a vase.

Oh, god, please don't let them be from Sam. Please don't let them be from Sam . . .

My heart beats wildly as I walk over and open the sealed card clipped into the middle of the bouquet. Handwritten again.

How many other colors do these come in . . .? P.S. Thanks for breakfast yesterday—so tasty . . . See you soon. J

Heat breaks out across my whole body, rippling and warming my insides. He sent me flowers and an innuendo. He wants to see me soon. It wasn't a polite brush-off.

I tell myself I never really had any doubt about it, but I feel as if I could jump up and down on the spot with relief like an overexcited toddler. I fish my phone out of my bag and deliberate far too long over the words and the tone and whether I should end it with a kiss. I mean, he made me orgasm four times. He gave me oral sex in my kitchen. A kiss at the end of a text is hardly an overstatement.

Me: They're beautiful, thank you. Breakfast was . . . my pleasure . . . A x

Okay, I need to be (partially) sensible here. Think about this sensibly. About what this is. Are we seeing each other now? And is that sensible? I weigh up the pros and cons in my head.

Cons: I need to know I'll most likely get hurt by him. He certainly doesn't seem like someone who does relationships. He could break my heart. Except, isn't that always the case when deciding to get involved with someone? Heartbreak is a serious possibility regardless of who the person is. It isn't a reason to forgo it entirely, otherwise we'd all be alone with pets.

The potential for heartbreak is a surmountable possibility I will have to deal with when it happens. I have experience in that department. I'll get over it. Over him.

Pros: He's gorgeous, charismatic, passionate, and amazing in bed.

Okay, of course, I know none of that is enough to sustain a relationship long-term, but this isn't a relationship. This is a—

A sharp knock on my office door pulls me from my thoughts.

"Yes, come in."

Sam pokes his head around the door, his shy smile all but disappearing when he sees the bouquet on my desk. Okay, how to explain this one?

Thankfully, he doesn't ask or make any reference to the roses before he opens his mouth to speak. "So, I had a nice time on Saturday," he says, a note of nervousness in the way he fidgets ever so slightly with his hands before sliding them into the pockets of his cords.

Oh, so I have to do this now then. Time to be a grown-up, I suppose.

I take a deep breath. "I did too, Sam. But I . . . Well, I spent the weekend thinking about how . . ."—*I don't want to be touched by anyone except Jake Lawrence right now, or for the foreseeable*—"you and I work so well together here. And get on so well—which I think is *why* Saturday was so nice. But I don't think it would be good for work, or the partnership, for us to get involved, you know? Like that. I hope that makes sense." I hope the look on my face is kind and genuine and not patronizing.

I meant everything I said. I did. It's just there is also the Jake-shaped side issue on top of it. As I watch him, I try to gauge Sam's thoughts. His face, normally composed, has a look of slight disappointment, I think. But not animosity.

Sam nods slowly before he speaks. "I totally understand, Alex. It's fine," he says with a small nod. "And I had a really nice time on Saturday too."

I nod, smiling. "And I hope things don't change—between us, I mean. I don't want things to be strange between us."

"Nah, and they won't be. I promise. A bit of bad timing, I guess." He shrugs. "No one to blame for that but myself."

After he leaves, I think about it some more. Though a bit of guilt lingers, I decide not to give it too much space in my head, because even if Jake didn't come crashing into my house on Saturday night, Sam was never going to be the guy I end up with.

My phone goes off with the text message alert.

Jake: No, baby, it was my pleasure—trust me. So I was going to take you out on Saturday, but I can't wait that long to see you. I'll pick you up at 7. J x

I blink. He wants to take me out tonight? Christ, it's 4:00 p.m. already. Way to catch me off-guard, Lawrence. I have two more appointments this afternoon and my meeting with Douglas and the other GPs at 5:00 p.m.

No, a 7:00 p.m. pick up is far too much of a tight squeeze. By the time I finish up here, get home, and debate an outfit, I won't have any time to groom myself.

I text back I'll be ready by 8:00 p.m. To which I receive the response:

Jake: No changing, no moving, no canceling. See you at 7. J x

I should be indignant at his demanding, unreasonable tone, but I'm not. I can't wait to see him. I have butterflies already. Butterflies a grown woman should be embarrassed about.

I finally get out of Douglas's office before 6:00 p.m., always somehow being the last to leave as he insists on chatting to me about Dad. They're old friends and play golf once a month together. The journey home takes me forty minutes because of a contraflow on the A3. While I sit in the jam, I'm tempted to text and try to push him to 8:00 p.m. again, but I decide against it. I will just have to be quick—really quick—and if I'm not ready, he'll have to wait until I am.

I rush into the house to feed, kiss, and cuddle Fred before dashing upstairs to shower and change. I have twenty bloody minutes. Twenty minutes to scrub and preen and pick something to wear.

I let the shower run while I throw some potential outfits on my bed. Where is he likely to take me? Dinner, he said. Well, that narrows it down . . .

I hate not knowing where I'm going. I could end up totally underdressed, or worse: completely overdressed. Clothes are normally my thing. I always know what to wear; I'm *good* at clothes. Summer dress for a picnic, fitted work dress and blazer for a conference, LBD for a dinner party.

Simply the thought of seeing him makes me buzz with the sort of nervous excitement that makes my head loud and scattered. I was nervous before my first date with Ben who, at the time, was a charming older consultant at the hospital, but at least I knew where he was taking me. Kyoko Japanese & Teriyaki Restaurant. Damask shift dress and wedge heels. I inwardly cringe at the thought of a damask shift dress, but then it was 2009 and things were different.

I'll have my shower first and then decide what to wear. I can't stand here debating at the cost of cleansing.

As my post-shower body butter absorbs, I decide on a cream, sleeveless Ralph Lauren dress with a brown leather belt and bag. It's a warm night, so I'll wear tan sandals and keep my legs bare. That should work in a restaurant or bar. It won't work in a kebab shop in Hackney though, should he decide to take me there.

I decide on a nude lace underwear set, which I also got from my favorite boutique in Paris. As I put it on, a shiver runs through me at the thought of him taking it off later. Can I even sleep with him on our first date? I mean, surely since I already have, it doesn't count in the same way. I keep my makeup neutral with a peach eye shadow and pale lip gloss and finish by drying my too-long hair straight and boring. I leave it down about my shoulders and surprise myself by being ready for 7:10 p.m.

Then I wonder where the hell he is, because he's late.

I check my phone as I go downstairs, but there's nothing. He wouldn't call or text if he was driving, so I assume he's on his way. Then I remember the contraflow before the cutoff, and I relax.

Ten minutes later, as I finish the glass of Riesling I poured to try and calm my nerves, he still hasn't arrived. 7:25 p.m. I lift the copy of *Vogue* from the basket under the coffee table and flick through the pages as my head swirls with the possibility I'm being stood up. Perhaps as payback for Saturday night. Would he do that? God, surely not.

I certainly won't lower myself to standing at the window watching for him, so I go into the kitchen and pour myself another glass of wine, smaller this time. I take a few huge gulps and feel the effects straight away as it begins to soften the muscles at the back of my neck and lift the weight of irritation. However, then a wave of light-headedness washes over me, and I feel tipsy. Though, this is probably because I haven't eaten since 12:30 p.m. and my dinner date is late.

I wonder if I should be worried about him. What if something's happened to him? I'm being paranoid, of course, but what if he's been in an accident and I'm standing here assuming he's stood me up?

Before another panicked thought can move through my brain, the doorbell goes. I let out a sigh of relief and glance up at the clock, trying to decide if thirty minutes is ridiculously late or just slightly rude.

I take my time ambling to the front door, stopping by the mirror in the hall to check for obvious signs of a worried-I-was-being-stood-up face. My cheeks are slightly flushed, but that's surely the anticipation and the wine, and it gives me a healthy, bright appearance. With a deep breath, I reach for the handle, deciding at the last moment to go for playfully annoyed. I can't have him believe I've just been sitting here thinking he wasn't coming. Of course he was coming. Why wouldn't he be coming?

When I open the door, his head is down as he stands back, hands in his pockets. When he lifts his head, my heart falters at the sight—at the apologetic and slightly uncertain look in his eye. Of course, he looks ridiculously gorgeous from top to bottom. As his eyes meet mine, the apology vanishes, replaced with something else. Something I've seen before. Desire. Lust. I flush warmly from head to toe.

He lets out a breath as he looks me over. Then he whispers hotly, "Fuck."

THIRTEEN

JAKE'S DATE OUTFIT MAKES HIM LOOK AS IF HE'S JUST COME FROM a *GQ* photo shoot. He's wearing a charcoal-gray wool jacket with the collar turned up slightly, and a lighter-colored gray V-neck T-shirt underneath. Dark jeans and brown suede boots. The white of a small bandage peeks out from the right-hand side of this throat. The overall look is effortlessly stylish yet casual.

So, apparently, clothes are his thing too. As are no clothes.

My inner anger fades instantly and completely as every nerve in my body stands to attention. It looks as though he's had his hair trimmed too, which is bloody adorable. I stop the simper that threatens just in time because I still need to look annoyed.

"Okay, so you turn up"—I glance at my watch—"almost half an hour late and then swear at me? Interesting dating etiquette." I nod. I wonder whether to fold my arms for additional effect, but I decide against it.

He grins sexily, and it makes my legs feel weak. "You look . . . fucking amazing," he says, running his hand over his mouth.

I shiver at the compliment but sigh for effect. "Flattery will only get you so far, Lawrence," I say evenly. "It's rude to keep your date waiting about. You know that, right?" When I smile, he nods and lets out a small groan before stepping up onto my doorstep.

"I do know that. And I'm so fucking sorry." His face is inches from mine, and his smell invades my personal space. Though, it doesn't so much "invade" as it's welcomed with open arms as I breathe him in. "I'm a fucking idiot," he says in a low, warm tone before pressing his mouth to mine.

I moan softly at the welcome hot feel of his mouth as he licks into my own. The kiss feels hungry and desperate, and when he pulls me into his body and lets out a deep noise I almost want to drag him inside and tell him to forget all about dinner.

He pulls back first. "Okay, so, as much as I'd love to stay here and do that all fucking night, I want to take you out. Like, on a proper date." He takes both my hands in his and kisses me again, a peck this time. "You ready? You look ready."

I catch a breath from somewhere and nod. "I'm ready. Just let me grab my bag. One second."

He waits at the door for me, and I follow him down the driveway to his car. It's not the car that was parked outside my house on Saturday night, so it must be new. Or maybe he has two. It's an Audi this time and still flashy, but not as flashy as the other one. He opens the door for me, and I get in. Inside, it's dark leather and smells new. He presses a button on the dash to turn the engine on and causes a burst of loud rock music to explode into the car. He moves to turn it down then off, throwing an apologetic look at me.

"You drive with it at that level?" I ask, incredulous. His poor ears.

"It blocks out everything else," he says with a small shrug.

As we drive through the village, we pass a few of my neighbors, and I'm glad the windows are tinted. Sam at the pub on Saturday and then another man tonight would be tantamount to brazen hussy behavior around here. Small village cons: Lots of old people with conservative views about dating.

"So, where are you taking me?" I ask, turning to look at him. His profile is gorgeous, of course—full lips, a straight nose, and a youthful, healthy complexion. His eyes are focused firmly on the road ahead, but he turns to glance at me, playful.

"Not The Dorchester anyway."

I laugh a little. "You know, I've never actually been to The Dorchester. Well, not for dinner at least."

His mouth twitches with a smirk. "Well, this is a place I like. Nothing fancy, and I know the owner, and the food's amazing."

It could be my imagination, but he seems nervous. Edgy even. He licks his lips again, which he does a lot. I'm not sure if it's a nervous thing, but it gives his lips a constant kissable look. I want to kiss him. My eyes drift down to his hand resting on the gear stick as he puts the car into a higher gear. His hands are as sexy as I remember them. Long, shapely fingers. Smooth, tanned skin. Is there any part of him I don't find attractive?

"There's a contraflow just past junction five. Oh—is that why you were late?"

He looks away, into the side mirror. "Ah, no, I just got caught up with something at the club. The contraflow wasn't there when I came down."

I'm about to ask him what happened, but something about his manner and the way he bites the inside of his cheek stops me. It's none of my business anyway. Instead, I nod at his profile. Though, he senses I'm looking at him and flicks his eyes to me, tense, before looking back at the road.

Okay, I need to try harder at not staring at him.

"So, it's in the city, the place you're taking me?" I ask to make conversation. This silence between us is mildly uncomfortable, but I'm also hoping it'll help me think of something other than deep, sexual growls and wet, warm tongues.

"Yeah. Is that okay? It's where I know." He sounds apologetic.

"Of course. That's fine." I nod eagerly before turning my head back to look out the window.

The car journey continues in a strange yet heated staggered silence. It feels as though we're both thinking things that would make our parents blush. He asks me about my day at work and whether I had any lives to save. When he asks if I have any plans for the weekend, I think it's because he's going to ask me out again, but he doesn't.

Perhaps he's waiting to see how tonight goes first.

Some twenty minutes later, we pull up to a quaint restaurant at St Katharine Docks, and Jake reverses—with some skill—into a tight parking space. Outside, I smooth down my dress and hook my bag over my body as he gestures toward the restaurant. It's a two-story building with a pretty wraparound terrace. It looks busy, but not overly so.

When he slips his hand into mine as we walk toward the door, my stomach flutters, which is ridiculous because what age am I? Thirteen? Also, it seems chaste for him. Who knew Jake was a hand-holder? I like the feel of his firm hand in mine.

As we get closer, I see it's an Italian, and as soon as the door opens, the familiar scent of pasta, garlic, and bread fills my nose, making my stomach growl. Immediately, a man in his late fifties perhaps comes toward us, beaming, with his hand out. Jake shakes his hand and turns to me.

"Leo, this is Alex," he says softly.

"Ahh, Alex, it's a pleasure to meet you, *cara* . . ." He leans in to kiss me on both cheeks. "I'm Leo. Welcome, welcome." Leo smiles in a fatherly way while Jake scans the restaurant with keen eyes, as though he's carrying out a risk assessment.

"You've got my table, yeah?" Jake asks him, and Leo nods before leading us to the back of the restaurant where a cozy, secluded booth with green leather seats, a dark wood table, and those candles made of wine bottles awaits.

Leo offers to take my jacket, and Jake shrugs out of his too. Though, as he does, an image of him stripping for me in my bedroom blasts loud and hot into my mind, and my mouth waters. Swallowing, I slide into the booth trying to appear nonchalant and not as though I'm having mind-sex with Jake.

"Some wine for you both?" Leo offers.

I nod, and someone hands him a bottle of red. It's barbera and has an expensive label, and I watch as Leo pours a small taster into a glass and slides it to Jake. He shakes his head and gestures toward me. With a nod, Leo offers me the glass instead.

I lift it to my nose to have a sniff before taking a small sip. It's good. Not French, but still rich and full-bodied and perfect for Italian food.

"It's lovely. I'll have a small glass please," I tell Leo with a polite smile, and he pours us two large glasses of what I'm sure must be his best wine.

Jake presses the top button on his phone and turns it facedown on the table then looks up at me again. Yes, he definitely looks nervous or on edge. His normally cool demeanor is unusually ruffled. It makes me smile.

"Anything else for you at the moment?" Leo asks my date before looking at me.

Jake doesn't look at him, just shakes his head and keeps his eyes on me.

"Um, some water, maybe?" I say to Leo, who nods politely and departs. "So . . ." I begin.

"So."

The way he looks at me, the way my mind can't stop flitting back to the other night, means I have to break his gaze before a server appears with some bread, olives, and dipping oil. A jug of water and two glasses are placed down too.

I'm utterly starving, and so I lift an olive immediately and pop it into my mouth, almost groaning aloud from the pleasure. Then I take a long, welcome sip of the wine before turning back to the menu. I don't see Jake even give it a cursory glance. I'm so hungry I want to order one of everything, but I know it's because my stomach feels unloved and wants to be showered with gifts.

After a few seconds, I glance back up and see his head tilted as he watches me. He still hasn't looked at the menu.

"Are you not eating?" I ask.

"I know what I'm having," he says, eyes glittering. Eyes that look darker than I've ever seen them under this candlelight.

"Really? So, what do you recommend?" I take another slow sip of my red wine. "Mmm, this is lovely," I say as I swallow.

Jake follows my lead and takes a small sip from his glass. His face screws up at the taste, but god, does he try to hide it. I stifle a giggle.

"Yeah . . . It's strong." He swallows slowly, with difficulty.

"You don't like red wine, do you?"

His shoulders sag slightly. He looks disappointed in himself. "No, not really. I don't really like wine at all. Except champagne. I'm usually a beer or Jack man, though I don't go in much for spirits these days." He pushes the wineglass away as though it's insulted him.

"So, why did you order it?"

"'Cause it's expensive and I thought you'd like it, so I was prepared to give it a shot," he tells me, gesturing to a server over my shoulder. Jake orders a half-pint of Peroni and hands his glass off to the waiter, saying it's fine but just not to his taste.

He was prepared to give it a shot for me. It makes me feel fluttery and warm.

"So, you were going to recommend something?" I ask, dropping my focus back to the menu.

"I don't normally have a starter here—the mains are huge even for me, and I will always pick dessert over a starter—but the chicken ravioli is amazing, as is the spaghetti meatballs."

"Chicken ravioli sounds delicious. I'll go with that then."

I close my menu maybe thirty seconds before Leo appears to take our order. Jake orders "the usual," and I go for the chicken ravioli. When Leo leaves us, Jake takes a long sip of his beer and smiles at me. It's that small, knowing smile that makes me think he's thinking X-rated thoughts.

"It's a nice place . . ." I say, breaking the silence.

"'S'not The Dorchester." He shrugs. "But I like it."

"I've heard The Dorchester is wildly overpriced anyway."

Jake licks his tongue over his bottom lip again. "So, tell me about yourself, Dr. Marlowe."

I have to stifle another laugh because this is a man who has seen me naked and given me multiple orgasms, one of which was in my kitchen. "You already know way too much about me, Mr. Lawrence. How about you tell me something about you? I know nothing about you."

He sits back in his chair as he considers this, his leg grazing against mine as he does. The heat of him blooms warm through his jeans against my bare skin.

"You know *nothing?* Well, that's not true now, is it? You know lots about me." He smirks.

I think about this. "Okay, I know your name, phone number, where you work, and that you like Italian food but not red wine. That's not lots, Jake. It's barely anything." I take another sip of the wine, which tastes better on every swallow.

Jake leans forward on the table then, closer, resting his hands under his chin. "Come on, baby. You know way more than that." His voice is a low, sexy whisper that seems to dance over my skin. "You know I get hard just from looking at you, can make you come standing up with just my mouth, and you know I could have someone's eye out with my cock." He finishes with a gentle bite of his lip.

Holy Christ. I can't breathe.

The look on his face demands a reaction of some sort, and he gets it. A chemical one. Heat floods my cheeks, and my tummy clenches tight, the tops of my thighs vibrating desperately. *Breathe, Alex. You're in a public place. Just breathe.*

I swallow. "Don't think I don't know what you're doing . . ." My voice sounds weightless.

He grins. "What am I doing?"

"Changing the subject."

"Hmm, maybe. But talking about how hard you make me is the only subject I'm interested in. Oh, and making you come with my mouth. I'm pretty interested in that too." He laughs. It's a quiet little sexy laugh that almost makes me orgasm in a crowded restaurant.

"You really can't help yourself, can you?" I look at him over my glass, giving him a small shake of my head, cheeks hot. "That mouth of yours . . . Completely . . . filthy."

"Maybe I really like the way you pretend you don't like it, me talking to you like that." His voice is low and hot, his words hanging in the air for a moment. Finally, he breaks his stare to lift his beer, taking a thirsty gulp of it. I try not to watch the way his throat bobs deliciously as he does. "Tell me though, do you prefer when I'm talking about what I want to do to you, or when I'm doing it?"

At that moment, Leo and a waitress arrive with our food. Leo places the steaming-hot plate delicately in front of me, and I watch the pretty waitress place Jake's spaghetti and meatballs in front of him. Though she steals more than a few glances in his direction, he ignores her completely, still looking at me with that sexy smirk of his, wondering which I prefer. Him talking about it or doing it.

Leo comes back with the black pepper and parmesan, but I wait until he's gone and out of earshot before I lower my voice to launch a little conversation stopper of my own. I choose my professional tone—the one I use with my patients. Hopefully, it will have more effect that way.

"Well, granted, Jake, when you're fucking me with your mouth or your cock, your filthy mouth has a distinctly erotic effect, so I'd say they both have their place. However, I'd much prefer it if you didn't espouse your learned and graphic sexual vocabulary over dinner. Later though, when we aren't eating, please tell me just how delightful my cunt tasted." I keep my eyes on him as I carefully stab a forkful of ravioli before sucking it off the fork into my mouth.

He was right—the chicken ravioli is amazing.

I manage to swallow and take a sip of my wine while he remains speechless, staring at me in shock or awe, I'm not sure. It sends a thrill straight through me all the way to my toes to know I can have that effect on him.

I bite back a smile and swallow another mouthful of the delicious ravioli.

FOURTEEN

I T TAKES ABOUT TWO WHOLE MINUTES BEFORE HE SEEMS ABLE TO SPEAK again. When he does, his voice is low and serious.

"Okay. You win, Alex. The dinner table isn't the place for that kind of language. Mainly 'cause it makes me want to drag you out of here and—" He stops himself.

Oh, he's trying. How sweet. Except now I'm burning to know exactly what it makes him want to do.

Since I don't want to be a hypocrite, I bite my tongue and say nothing.

He spoons a large, twisted forkful of meatball into his mouth, and we chew in silence for a couple of minutes, with him shaking his head as if he can't believe what I just said. Though, to be honest, I can't believe what I just said either.

"So, where are you from?" he asks, casual, the sexual tug-of-war fading away slowly.

"Um, I grew up in Camberley. You?"

"Bromley. Brothers or sisters?" he redirects immediately, sliding another mouthful between his lips. He's a really polished eater, I notice. Elegant with his fork, chewing each bite economically, not getting anything anywhere except in his mouth. Admirable given he's eating spaghetti. Maybe I shouldn't be surprised since everything he's done so far with that mouth has been some kind of human art form.

"Both," I say. "An older brother, Nick, and Natasha—she's older too. What about you?"

A dark cloud rolls over his eyes, and he visibly tenses. "Um, a brother. We don't talk."

I only nod at this. Something about his expression tells me he doesn't want to discuss it. I file it away though for the future.

"What about your parents?"

"What about them?"

"Are you close to them? What do they do?"

"We're close. And they're both retired now. My mother was a university lecturer, languages, and my dad was a doctor. I suppose technically still is." I take another bite as he nods.

He looks thoughtful and a touch distant as he stares at me, then he goes back to his food, then he stares at me again. I don't know what to make of the long looks, the slight narrowing of his eyes, or the thoughtful bite of his lip. It's as if he's processing every single piece of information I give him and digesting it along with his spaghetti and meatballs.

"Is that why you became a doctor? 'Cause of your dad?" he asks.

"Partly. I mean, my dad's amazing, the best man I know, and there was never any pressure or anything like that. But I look up to him. I suppose I wanted to make him proud." I get a flush of embarrassment at how saccharine that came out.

Thankfully, Jake doesn't look as if he's about to throw up. No, his eyes are just intense and warm. I like the way he looks at me. It makes me feel aware of every nerve ending in my body.

"I'm sure you do," he says, and it's so genuine it makes my tummy flip.

I smile and take another bite of my ravioli. He starts eating again, but then he stops and reaches over to refill my wineglass.

"Not too much," I say. "School night and all."

He fills my glass up, stopping below halfway. I like that he didn't just go ahead and fill it up anyway despite what I said. Most people would have. *Ben* would have.

"What about your parents—are you close?"

He tenses, his gaze darkening before he reaches to take a long gulp of his beer. "No."

Again, the look on his face tells me not to push it. So, I don't. No relationship with his parents or his brother. It should maybe send an alarm bell of some kind ringing through me, but it doesn't. Some people don't have great relationships with their families.

"Well, my sister lives in California now with her husband, so I don't see her as often as I'd like, which is sad, but we Skype every week. When she's not out living her best life running along the beach with her dogs and doing Pilates with Malibu housewives." I give a grunt of disgust, and Jake smiles, the tension easing off his shoulders visibly.

"But your brother is here?"

I nod. "He lives in London, and we see each other a lot. Too much, prob-ably." I widen my eyes playfully. "But we do a family vacation every year to France. My parents have a house there."

"That mean you speak French?" He raises an eyebrow.

"I get by," I say shyly. I speak French well. Some Russian too. But he never asked that, so I don't mention it.

"Would you say something in French if I asked you to?"

"I'm not a performing monkey, so no."

He laughs softly, and it's the most gorgeous thing. His eyes crinkle gen-tly at the corners, and his entire face seems to transform. Beautiful and light. Jesus, he really is a stunning man. Unfairly so.

"So, what does your brother do?"

I give him a frown. "Come on, we've spoken enough about me. I want to know something about you. *Besides* what I already know, that is."

He shifts in his chair and puts down his fork, wiping his mouth with his napkin. His plate is completely cleared. Every morsel is gone.

"I'm not that interesting, baby." He shrugs.

"So modest." I sigh. "Anyway, surely it's up to me to decide whether I'm interested. And since I'm here on a school night, against my better judgment, that means I am. Interested." I lean forward.

He watches me for a long moment before leaning forward too. Our faces are close enough now that I can see the white of the small scar across his eye-brow. His scent overcomes me in waves, and I'm helpless not to inhale deep.

"I'm flattered you're interested, Alex. That you're here with me on a school night, against your better judgment. But there's nothing worth know-ing that you don't already know." I catch the side of his mouth pull down slightly as he says this.

I frown. "Christ, you don't enjoy talking about yourself at all, do you? I never imagined when I first met you, you'd be a guy who wouldn't like talking about himself." I say it in a way I hope sounds playful, not insulting. He doesn't look insulted. "Only, how do we get to know each other in that case?" I lift my glass and take a sip of my wine.

His eyes soften, and he smiles a suggestive smile. "See, this is where I'd say we already know each other pretty fucking well . . ." I feel his leg rub against mine under the table. He's trying to distract me again.

"That's not an answer either though, is it?"

A twist of irritation—I think—flares in his eyes, and he sits back. Sighs. "Let's say I'm not a big sharer or talker, yeah?"

I think this is almost funny because when he's in bed, he is the most sharing, talkative person I know.

"But I'm a good listener, so it all balances out in the end, I guess."

I ponder this for a moment. Being a good listener certainly isn't a terrible quality in a partner. I mean, *potential* partner. An idea pops into my head.

"Let's . . . Why don't we try something?"

He looks at me warily, and I sit back too, resting more comfortably against the leather booth. Oh, this might work. Might even be fun.

"Okay, and I promise I'm not trying to interrogate you or anything, but how about tonight, as it's our first date, you give me three questions? I'm allowed to ask you about yourself. You can't refuse to answer any of them, but it's completely up to you how much you want to tell me." I turn my head slightly as if to say, "Are you game?"

His eyes narrow, and he runs his forefinger lightly across his bottom lip as he mulls it over, staring at me in that piercing way he does, as if he's performing the act of visual dissection. Finally, he sighs.

"Deal," he says, though he certainly looks tense at the notion.

Just then, Leo appears from my right to clear away the plates, asking us confidently how our food was. I tell him it was wonderful while Jake looks at him with a nod. He returns his eyes to me immediately when we're alone again.

As I debate with myself over my three questions, I try to think about what I need to know versus what I want to know. Because they're different. I begin to understand what Aladdin felt like trying to work out the most clever use of his three wishes.

"Okay," I begin. "Why aren't you a big sharer? Is it really because you think you're uninteresting, or is it a trust thing?" And there goes my wasted question. He'll never answer that—not properly anyway.

Jake smirks then affects a playful frown. "That sounded like three or four separate questions rolled into one. Trying to outsmart me, Doctor?"

Yes, so I like the way he says "doctor." I like the way it rolls off his tongue almost sensually. I don't know how he can make such an ordinary word sound like that, but then "toilet paper" would probably sound hot coming from his mouth. From *that* mouth.

"You could say it was one question with a multiple-choice answer section." I give him a sweet smile.

He takes a moment to consider his answer. "Well, if I told you neither of the above, you'd think I was cheating you out of a question, so let's say it's more of the second and less of the first. Mainly, it's because I hate sharing my shit. I share when I have to or when I trust someone." He shrugs. "Think of me like Fred. Wary until I know I'm in safe hands."

I want to tell him *I am* safe hands. I'm a bloody doctor, for Christ's sake—how much safer does it get? But on the other hand, I think what he's saying is extremely sensible. Prudent. It still doesn't tell me anything about him though.

"I also don't date, so this getting-to-know-you stuff is a bit weird for me, I guess," he adds, running a hand over the back of his neck.

"Why don't you date?" I say, too eager.

He grins. "That your next question then?"

Damn him. I let out a breath and narrow my eyes as I take another sip of my dwindling wine. I feel as though I'm playing chess with him, which would be terrible because I'm terrible at chess.

So, he doesn't date. I suppose I'm not surprised at that, because he doesn't exactly come across as a dinner-and-flowers kind of guy—even though here we are, at dinner, and he's sent me flowers . . . twice. A quiet, warm glow hums through me with that knowledge. I mean, yes, it could be a total lie, but something about the way he's looking at me tells me it isn't.

Do I want to ask him why he doesn't date? It surely has to be commitment phobia or he's newly single. In the end, I decide to shelve the question entirely. It's something we can talk about another time. I'm more interested in Jake the man. What drives him, what his ambitions are, what he wants out of his life.

"No, it isn't," I confirm. "Tell what made you want to open a nightclub. Was it something you always wanted to do?"

He seems to think about this one harder than the last, which is strange. Surely, questions about your personality and trust issues are more difficult?

"No. What I always wanted to do was be a fireman," he says before shaking his head as though it's a ridiculous idea. Did he just give me an additional piece of information for free? "The club was an opportunity I couldn't pass up. I'd been thinking about it for a few years, putting the money away for something, then this popped up. I kinda hoped it'd be the start of something. Not having to work for someone else anymore. A fresh start, you know? What a fucking fantasy that turned out to be." He laughs again, but it's bitter. He looks annoyed. He really can switch emotions so quickly. It's faintly unsettling.

"Why was it a fantasy?"

When he lifts his head, his eyes are on fire. His face looks colder, meaner, as though he's trying to keep a lid on whatever's making him angry. Maybe my questions are.

"Last question, I take it?" He raises his eyebrow at me.

I want to know why it's a fantasy. And why he's angry about it. But I also want to know about his family, where he grew up, and what he does when he's not naked in my bed. But I can't have them all. Not tonight anyway.

Not until he knows I'm a safe pair of hands.

"No. Tell me something about your childhood," I say finally. That's not a proper question, and I know it. It's more of a general topic, designed to start a discussion about why he doesn't speak with his parents or his brother. I think I see him wince, but it could be my imagination.

"Come on, Alex. That's a bit vague. My childhood?" His tone is mocking and cold, and I know my little gambit here has failed.

"Oh, come on, Jake. Seriously? This is bloody ridiculous—can't you see that? How on earth can I get involved with someone who has so much difficulty having a two-way conversation? I mean, why am I here? Why were you so keen to do this if you don't want me to know anything about you?" I ask, hating the way my voice sounds high-pitched.

He stares at me, biting the inside of his mouth that way he does when he's thinking about something especially hard.

"It's impossible. This will never work." I let the statement hang in the air for a few seconds to see if he'll counter it, but he doesn't. With a sad sigh, I slide along the booth and get up from the table.

"Sit down, Alex," he says in a low, firm tone.

When I look back at him, his eyes are hooded and dark, commanding me to do what I'm told. He nods back to the place I was sitting.

"Please," he says, softer.

I know if I leave now, it'll be the equivalent of a child stomping off because they didn't get their way. I'd also be cutting my nose off to spite my face, because I still want him despite the mystery he's so artfully trying to weave around himself. If he has trust issues, surely all I need to do is be patient. Wait until he sees me as a pair of safe hands.

I slide back into the booth and sit down across from him. Immediately, his gaze softens, though I still wonder if he's regretting asking me out.

"Well, this is going great, isn't it?" His tone is softer now too.

"It was. Now it isn't," I say, shaking my head.

He nods and purses his lips.

"Look, I'm not trying to pry into your life, Jake. I'm just not used to being on dates like this."

"No, I'll bet you're not," he scoffs, running a hand over his mouth. Then his face turns serious again, and he leans back in his chair and lets out a loud sigh. "Okay, Alex. You want to know about my childhood . . ." He shifts in his chair a few times, clearly struggling to find a comfortable position—or getting ready to exit the booth entirely, perhaps. That's how uncomfortable he looks.

Suddenly, I hate myself for forcing him into this, but I've come this far and can't exactly back out now.

"I grew up in Bromley—or was dragged up until I was eleven and they took me and my brother into care. My mother had issues deciding whether to feed us or buy two bottles of vodka and get her mates around every other night. We never won often." He looks away for a moment, and I continue to hold my breath, my face impassive. He brings his eyes back to me. "I bounced around for a few years, mainly in north London, but Jon was a few years older, so as soon as he hit seventeen he joined the army. But as I moved about a bit, we lost touch pretty quick." Another rub of his mouth with his hand, and he drops his head. "When I was sixteen, I met a guy who felt sorry for me and gave me a job, and that was that. Three weeks ago, you met the finished product, I guess." He shrugs, nonchalant.

The casual look on his face is almost convincing. He's trying to persuade me nothing about his story affects him in the slightest—not the fact his mother chose alcohol over him or that he has no idea where his brother is now. But I'm *not* convinced. Somewhere in there is someone who cares.

I realize I'm still holding in a breath, and so I let it out quietly. "Jake, I'm sorry . . ." I begin.

"I don't want your pity, Alex," he cuts me off. "Fuck, that's not why I shared. It's exactly why I didn't want to. I don't want you looking at me with pity. Never like that." His eyes flare hotly.

"That's not why I was apologizing," I tell him. "I was apologizing for forcing you to talk about something you didn't want to talk about . . . But thank you. For sharing."

His mouth softens. "Well, if I could have thought of another way of stopping you from leaving, I'd have done that instead. Trust me."

Okay, so he has no idea I would have only got as far as the door before turning back.

I'm not quite sure how to lighten the heavy, sad tone that's settled on both of us, so I decide to use flattery. Mum always said men like being flattered as much as women do.

"Well, I wouldn't have left. I like the finished product far too much." I smile.

He cocks an eyebrow. "So, you played me?"

I shake my head and take my last sip of wine. "Not intentionally. I was annoyed at the silly game. I know I started it, but I suppose I was hoping you would come after me."

His mouth curls up into a wicked grin. "Oh, I'll always come after you, baby. Promise." He winks. Actually winks, and I can't help but burst into a stupid giggle.

When my laughter clears, I lean forward over the table toward him. "See? That wasn't so bad. Sharing."

He leans forward too so our faces are only centimeters apart. "It was fucking awful." He shudders. He takes my left hand in his, holding our fingers together, palms touching, and traces his fingers softly over mine. It's soft and lulling. He lingers on the one next to my pinkie, running his fingers up its length, and then he moves along to my forefinger where I wear my Tiffany Elsa Peretti ring, a graduation gift from my parents. An emerald set in platinum with "Dr. A Marlowe" engraved on the inside.

I look up from our hands to find him staring at me. His face is serious but his eyes soft as he leans in and touches his nose to mine, rubbing them softly together. It's utterly adorable.

"So, you like the finished product, do you?" he says, sounding cocky.

My breathing quickens, and I need for him to kiss me, so much so my mouth tingles and aches from the want. The warmth of his breath tickles my lips as his fingers continue to caress my own, and I feel a *lot* like someone falling for someone. Someone I'm not supposed to.

A million bloody pieces, Alex.

"I do." I nod. "I mean I don't know anyone as successful, as well-dressed, or as hot who was 'dragged up in Bromley.'"

He chuckles. "Yeah, well, I'm gonna bet you don't know anyone from Bromley, baby."

"Well, I know one." I giggle.

He leans in then and flicks his tongue over my lips before kissing me. His kiss is soft at first, teasing, his tongue licking into my mouth for a moment before he tilts his head to deepen it. More intense. The knot of pressure in my stomach that's always there when I'm around him expands.

God, I want him. I want to kiss every inch of his body until my mouth is raw and sore.

"So, you think I'm completely hot?" he says against my mouth.

"Completely," I whisper as he pulls back.

"Well, the feeling is completely mutual, Doctor. You drive me fucking crazy." He shakes his head and looks down at our entwined hands once more.

I drive *him* crazy? I feel completely self-certifiable around him. As if I have a whole other personality I didn't know about. It's dangerous when you can't think straight.

So, being with him is dangerous then. Which I suppose I always knew. No earth-shattering revelation there. It's just that it's also exciting and intense and, for now, completely necessary, and these things are far stronger. Far louder.

Jake pays for dinner, and we walk together out of the restaurant, his arm wrapped somewhat possessively around my waist. Again, I like how it feels there, like when I awoke with it over me. My head is light and fuzzy from the wine, but there's no point in kidding myself—it's also light and fuzzy from him.

When we get to his car, he stops and turns me around to face him, nuzzling me back against the passenger-side door. He presses his warm body into me and reaches up to brush my hair back behind my shoulder as he looks deep into my eyes. His face is so open to me now, blinds up, curtains pulled wide, and all that shines back is desire and lust.

"Thanks for dinner," I whisper, overwhelmed.

He nods as he brushes his thumb across my jaw and then my lip. "Thanks for having dinner with me. For not standing me up again."

I shake my head, about to apologize, but before I get the chance, he leans forward and captures my lips. I moan as he slides his tongue inside, as he sucks at my mouth and moans low into the kiss. He kisses me like no one has ever kissed me. He tastes like heat and spice, and the sounds he makes as he tastes me are like nothing else. My hands go around his waist and under his jacket to pull him in closer, and we kiss like that, on the street, like teen-agers, for what seems like hours.

Yet when he breaks away, it feels as if it wasn't nearly long enough.

I blink open my eyes, and he makes his little playful growling noise from low in his throat—something that is becoming a familiar Jake trait to me.

"Mmm, yeah, we need to stop before I get carried away," he says.

I want him to get carried away.

He takes some of my hair in his hand and runs the ends through his fingers. "Now, in my fantasy date with Alex, I take you home and fuck you better than you've ever been fucked in your life," he says, and I can't help but laugh. "But I want to show you how much of a gentleman I can be and get you home in one piece. So, help me out here, yeah?" He sighs.

Jake kisses me lightly on the mouth once more, groaning as he pulls back to open the car door. *Fantasy date with Alex.* He has a fantasy of a date with me? Internally, I want to squeal. He gets in, turns on the engine, and stops, sensing me looking at him.

"What?" He's smiling almost shyly.

"Nothing." I look away from him and out the front window.

"What happened to all that sharing stuff? Not nothing." He leans back against the driver's door, eyes wide and expectant. He's right.

Okay, how to word this without sounding like a crazy person . . .

"I suppose . . . well, I was thinking about how you are absolutely nothing like how I imagined you would be when we first met." I give a small half-shrug.

"How you *imagined* me? Wait—what? Does that mean you fantasized about me?" He grins.

I reach across to hit him gently on the thigh, sighing impatiently. When I look back at him, his expression has turned more serious.

"Sorry. What do you mean?"

"I don't know. The night I first met you . . . I guess I had an idea of you in my head about how you might be outside of all . . . *that.*" God, what on earth has happened to my ability to express myself in words? "You're just . . . different."

Jake looks at me for a long time. A really long time, actually. Too long. "No, Alex. I'm pretty sure I'm exactly the person you thought I'd be. I'm dif-ferent with you is all." His voice sounds sad, regretful even. He nods and then turns around, releases the hand brake, and pulls out into the traffic.

FIFTEEN

ROBYN CALLS ME SOMETIME BEFORE LUNCH ON TUESDAY, CATCHING me completely off-guard. She never calls my office line, which should have been the first clue. Though, when I check my phone later, I see a text and two missed calls from the morning.

"So, who's the guy?" she starts, voice accusatory, almost shrill.

"What?"

"Dan saw you last night in town. Said you were snogging the face off some guy. I figured it couldn't have been Sam because you cut that off, and I know it wasn't the prick . . ."

Oh, god. Embarrassment rushes over me. A little panic too, though I'm not sure why.

"Where was this?" I ask tentatively. Of course, I know where it was; I'm trying to buy myself time to formulate an explanation, decide exactly how much I'm going to tell her about this thing with Jake. I need to stop calling it a "thing."

"At the docks. He'd a late client meeting there and saw you outside a restaurant. I told him he should have gone over and said hello, but he said he didn't want to *interrupt.*"

"Interrupt" is said with inflection. As if we were having sex outside the restaurant, not kissing.

"Well . . .?" she presses.

I close my eyes and let out a breath. "Of course it wasn't Ben."

"And it wasn't Sam?"

"No."

There's a pause. *"Righttt, so . . .?"*

As much as I love Rob, as much as she's my best friend and there are no secrets between us, I resent that I don't get to keep Jake to myself a little longer. I ignore the part of me that asks why I want to. Why I'm not bursting to tell her about this new, exciting thing in my life.

There I go again . . .

"Can you come over tonight? I'll tell you all about it."

There are a few seconds of silence on the phone before she speaks. "Yeah, okay, I'll come straight after I finish. About seven?" she says as she hangs up. Okay, so she's definitely put out that Dan found out about this before her. Not that I blame her. I'd be the same if the situation was reversed. I know I would.

Just before lunch, Anna buzzes through to tell me someone is asking to see me. Someone who isn't a patient. By the girly lilt to her voice, I know who it is.

I stand up and get ready to chastise him for coming to my office, but then he walks in, and like always, all rational thought leaves my head. My brain turns to syrup—warm, sticky, and slow-moving. He takes off his sunglasses as he comes in, and before the door has even closed behind him fully, he's pulling me into him, kissing me deep and rough, his tongue sliding easily between my lips. When he pulls back from my mouth, he looks me over from head to toe appreciatively.

"So, I thought since I'm not allowed to send you flowers anymore, I'd send you something else instead." He reaches out to take my hand and places it over the front of his jeans.

A small gasp escapes my mouth at the semi-hardness there.

"Thought you might fancy lunch." His hands slip around my waist before he begins to slide my dress up my thighs.

"Jake, stop. Are you mad?" I peel his hands off me and take a step back, glaring at him.

He pouts sexily. "You sure?" He eyes the high bed against the wall and gives me a wicked look. "I'm fucking starving." Oh, lord, he's serious. "Okay then, fine. Not here. Back at yours? How long do you get for lunch?" He licks his lips, and my stomach flutters with want.

When he kisses me again, it's more chaste, less urgent, his hands staying by his sides this time. Kissing him in my office feels wrong, but I let him do it anyway because I'm weak. Go home and have him for lunch? It feels wild and out of character, and I want it so bloody badly. My desk phone buzzes again, startling me out of my lust-filled trance. Jake makes a small noise of irritation as I pull away from him to answer it.

"Yes?" I say in the most normal voice I can muster.

"Hey, Alex. I'm just checking if that's you out for lunch. Will I hold your calls now?" Anna still has the lilt to her voice. It's knowing too.

I look at Jake whose eyes are on fire and unflinching, already roaming my fully clothed body as though I'm already naked. I'm not seriously considering saying no to him, am I?

No, I'm really not.

"Yes, please, Anna. When's my next appointment?"

I hear tapping on the keyboard. "Mrs. Kavanagh at 2:00 p.m.," she says.

"Okay, thanks, Anna." I hang up. I'm really doing this.

I walk back to him, shaking my head in disbelief. It feels completely wild. *I* feel completely wild.

"Okay, meet me at my house? I keep a key under the white plant pot by the door," I tell him. He frowns at that. "I'll leave in ten minutes. I don't want it to look too obvious."

He leans in to kiss me again, soft and slow, licking at my mouth in that way that's become familiar. "Leave in five minutes. It already looks obvious." He gestures down to his crotch again, and my cheeks flame. "See you soon, Doctor," he says with a lick of his lips before exiting.

Oh, god. Anna and Katie are going to know. They'll see him and then me, and then they'll know. They probably already know. I'm really glad Sam is on calls today.

I pace the office for seven minutes wondering what the hell has become of me. Leaving work in the afternoon for sex with a man I've known for a fortnight . . . Just as I begin to have a modicum of self-doubt, I recall the sight of his naked, muscular, tattooed body, how he felt moving inside me, and the sounds he made when he—

I moan aloud before grabbing my bag and rushing out of the office. I try not to run past the reception desk, but I'm certain I notice a flicker of a smile from Anna as I pass.

As I drive to my house, I continue to rationalize my behavior. Or, to be more precise, overanalyze it. I certainly don't recognize myself these past few weeks, but I'm also not about to deny myself this *because* it feels out of character. I'm sure bungee jumping and skydiving feel completely out of character too, but people still do it. These are the kinds of experiences that warm you on a deathbed or chill you in their absence. Regret over something not done is the worst thing imaginable. I don't want Jake to be a regret chilling me on my deathbed; I want memories of him to warm me later on.

I glance at the clock on the dash as I pull up to my house. 12:23 p.m. The sight of his car parked in my driveway sends a small thrill through me, joining all the other thrilling feelings inside me right now. I like knowing that he's in my house, that he's there waiting for me. Glancing into the living room first to check he's not sitting watching TV or something, I tiptoe tentatively upstairs. An image of him naked on my bed, dealing with his erection while he waits for me, floods into my mind, overwhelming me. I swallow.

The bedroom door is ajar, no sound at all coming from inside as I push it open gently. My heart feels as if it's about to beat through my chest, and so I take a few deep breaths to try and slow it. I feel ridiculously turned on already.

The room is warm, the soft yellow sunlight spilling through the sheer curtains giving it a sort of dreamlike quality. Jake's scent is heavy in the air, and it unsettles me how recognizable it is to me now. I'm only a few steps into the room when I feel him behind me, hands skimming up the bare skin of my arms, heat pressed against my back.

"What took you so fucking long?" he breathes against my ear.

I turn to face him, but he stops me, holding me in place facing away from him as his mouth ghosts over my neck.

"Don't move," he whispers before reaching up to unclip my hair so it tumbles down. His fingers sift softly through the lengths for a moment before I feel him press his mouth against it and inhale.

I close my eyes in bliss, dropping my head back onto his shoulder as he moves his mouth down the column of my neck. Through my dress, I feel the outline of his erection, and it only turns me on more. Knowing I've done this to him. Knowing he wants me this much. It's heady. Powerful.

"We don't have a lot of time, Jake. I need to get back to work soon," I whisper as he continues to kiss, nip, and lick my throat. I think he could make me climax from this alone. As I reach behind me, my hands connect with bare flesh, and I know then that he's completely naked. He's naked, and I'm fully clothed, and the idea of it is almost too much.

"Shh," he says, voice low and hoarse. "Let me enjoy this for a bit, yeah?"

When I push my butt back into him, teasing him a little, I feel him groan against my neck. He uses a hand on my hips to do it again, grinding me into him, groaning low on each thrust. The sound causes a tingle to travel along my spine, between my thighs, the need building with every touch. He skims a hand over my butt and slips it through the slit of my dress, between my legs, fingers grazing the outside of my knickers.

"So hot and wet already, baby . . ." he groans.

I inch my legs farther apart, not much, but enough for him to confirm what he already knows. I want to turn around. To see his eyes and kiss his mouth. But now, the feeling of him stroking me gently is too nice for me to interrupt.

"Were you wet in your office thinking about me?" he asks, low.

I feel my fingers curl with need into the taut muscle of his thigh.

"Were you wet in the car?" He moves his other hand up to the zip of my dress, tugging softly. "Were you?"

The heat of the room, of him, and the gauzy, dreamlike sheen over everything makes something bold overcome me. "Yes," I whisper.

He makes a low, desperate sound, which I feel between my legs. "Christ, baby, I can't stop fucking thinking about you." His voice is rough, a touch frustrated perhaps, his accent peppering every syllable. The zip of my dress is open, but he hasn't made a move to take it off me yet, and it drives me insane. "I hated how we left things last night. Dropping you off and driving home alone. I wanted you so fucking much," he says as he places open-mouthed kisses at the top of my spine. "Do you know what I had to do when I got home?"

I sway against him as his fingers dance between my legs and his mouth moves over my neck.

"Do you?"

"What?" I whisper.

"Guess. It involves my hand and an image in my head of you, naked." He groans low in his throat again, and something snaps inside me.

I turn around to face him, kissing him hard. It's quick after that, desperate and rough, as he pulls my dress off my shoulders and down. It gets kicked away when his arms wrap around me, and I move him back to the bed. My hands fist roughly in his hair as the need to consume him overcomes me, fierce and loud. He doesn't seem to mind, making a delicious growling noise and falling back onto the mattress, taking me with him.

"Fuck . . ." he breathes as I begin to kiss down his body, one thing only in my mind now.

I want to taste him.

He looks dazed as I stand, pushing his legs apart to lower myself between them. I run my hands up his thighs, which are thick and hot under my fingers. He sits up on his elbows, making the muscles in his stomach flex. He looks utterly enthralled.

God, something flares in me then. I want this to be the best he's ever had. My overachieving brain kicks into action suddenly.

Holding onto that thought, I shift forward on my knees and bring my mouth to where it needs to be. I lick my tongue gently over the tip first, tasting the salty bitterness that sits there already, circling the head softly, teasingly.

"Fuck, baby . . ." he groans, head falling back to expose his throat.

I run my lips down one side, following it up with my tongue, before closing my mouth over him to take him in deep.

His intake of breath is loud and sharp, the noise he makes deliciously filthy—a deep, low groan that makes me tremble. His fists grip the sheets as I begin to move, sucking harder as I reach the head before sliding my tongue across the slit. His stomach tenses, clenching tight as he arches up off the bed, his thighs opening wider. Oh, I like him like this.

When I slide my mouth off to catch my breath, replacing it with my hand, he lifts his head and gives me a look filled with such desire it takes my breath away. He reaches forward and slides his hand into my hair then smooths a thumb over my lips, tugging me forward again needily. When I close my mouth over him, he falls back onto the bed and begins arching his hips upward into my mouth. It doesn't take long before I feel him curse loudly, his hand tangling in my hair.

"Alex, baby, I'm going to come. You need to stop . . ."

Stop? I ignore that and instead swipe my tongue over the top before drawing him as deep into my throat as I can. He curses again before his whole body stills, a thick, wet warmth flooding into my mouth. When he finally comes to a slow stop, I slide my mouth off gently before planting a small, soft kiss on the end.

He's still breathing fast when I lie next to him on the bed, though he opens his eyes and turns to gaze at me. He looks blissed-out and relaxed, and it makes his eyes shine beautifully. God, he's so bloody gorgeous. Almost ridiculously so.

"Well, that was fucking amazing." He leans over to kiss me, licking his tongue purposefully into my mouth to taste himself.

"An improvement on my previous bedside manner, I hope?" I laugh at the cheesiness of the joke.

He laughs too, but then he goes still, staring at me intently.

"What?" I ask.

He blinks, shaking his head. "Nothing," he says, leaning over to kiss me deeply again. He kisses a path down my jaw to my neck, breathing deeply as he settles his mouth over the crook of my shoulder. "I love how you smell here," he whispers.

"It's Chanel," I whisper.

"It's Alex." He makes a playful little noise and then he's moving his mouth down to stop at the cup of my bra. He tugs it gently with his teeth.

"So, you can't stop thinking about me?" I say, gazing down at him. It's light, but I'm curious. Curious to know what this is, what it could be, where it's going.

He looks up, eyes heated. "You're pretty fucking addictive."

My breath hitches. "Sorry about that."

"Don't be." He places a kiss between my breasts and flicks his eyes up to me. "I like thinking about you."

Inwardly, I swoon. He really does have a way with words. And I hate that I seem to be falling for them. *I never have to try this hard to get girls.* Instead of dwelling on that, I lie back and enjoy the feel of his mouth as it works its way across my bra then back up to my neck.

"You know what I like better than thinking about you?"

"Mmm?" I ask, eyes closed.

"Being with you," he says, and then his mouth is on mine again, deep and hungry. When he pulls away, I feel him shift, holding himself up on his elbows so he's looking down into my eyes. "I never actually thought this would happen, you know? Not really."

"Never thought *what* would happen?"

His eyes are fixed on me, but they're distant too as though he's miles away, holding onto some memory. "Us," he says.

I can't breathe. *Us.* If we're an "us," then we're not a "thing."

"I never thought I stood a fucking chance with you. I mean, what are you fucking thinking, Doctor?" He's half-grinning, half-frowning now.

Just as I'm about to disagree with this, a loud vibrating noise comes from the nightstand. His mobile. He ignores it for a few seconds, seemingly miles away as he gazes down at me. Then he places a very gentle kiss on my mouth and moves off the bed.

"I'll be back in one minute," he says. "I want you naked."

He grabs his phone from the table and goes into the bathroom, closing the door behind him all the way. As I quickly undress, I try my best not to listen. I can't hear any words anyway, but his tone sounds urgent and angry, and it makes it difficult not to focus on it. Then he stops speaking entirely. It's another moment before the bathroom door opens and he comes toward me. As always, this full sight of him stuns me. So powerful and strong. Dangerous.

"Sorry," he says. He has a look of intent on his face now, and I know we won't be doing much more talking. I watch almost open-mouthed at the sight of him putting on the condom, enthralled by the way he grips himself and strokes himself to full hardness again before rolling it over the length. He stares at me as he does it, eyes hot and dark with lust.

"I need to be inside you now, Alex," he says as he climbs up onto the bed, settling himself between my thighs. There's no warning before he shifts down my body and spreads my legs open for his mouth. "Fuck. Still so wet for me, baby . . ." He sighs before teasing along the seam with his tongue. The groan that drips from his throat makes my toes curl, then he starts to work at me, lazy but hungry movements of his lips and tongue, until I'm a gasping, writhing mess. How easily I come apart for him.

"Jake, please, I need you now," I whine.

He obeys instantly, moving up my body with easy grace. He raises one of my legs and hooks it around him before sliding all the way into me. I'm always shocked by the size of him—by the way he makes my body feel so deliciously stretched out.

"I always want to fuck you so hard, but I never want to hurt you," he groans as he begins to move. It's slow but deep. I want it harder.

"You won't hurt me," I whisper, reaching my mouth up to his. "Harder, Jake, please. I need it harder." I dig my nails into the hard-muscled skin of his back and hook my other leg around him as I urge him into me.

Again, he complies immediately, his thrusts turning rougher and sharper until I can't breathe and it borders on painful. I've never been able to come like this, yet I feel it rise quickly inside me. The push of his body into mine, the sound of his groans and breath on each thrust, the pure lust in his eyes whenever he looks into mine.

"This what you needed, baby?" he asks, voice low and rough.

I can only nod, unable to find any words. When he angles his body differently, I almost scream at the jolt through my entire body. I cling to him as my orgasm rushes at me, great waves of white, rolling heat.

"That's it, Alex, that's it." He slides his hand between our bodies, fingering me as he continues circling his hips. It's mind-bending. I never want it to end.

I scream his name as I come around him. A few seconds later, I hear him gasp and curse before his body tenses and he shudders his release inside me. As he comes, he brings his lips to mine, licking into my mouth as he fucks into my body, all the while telling me in hot whispers how good I feel.

"So fucking perfect, Alex . . . so perfect."

After, he moves his body so we're side by side, his head turned into the crook of my neck. His breaths are quick and hot against my cooling skin, and the scent of him drifts up into my nose. I let out a soft laugh and turn to him. Jake's mouth lifts into a lazy smile.

"That was . . ."

"I know. Fuck," he sighs.

We lie like that for a moment before the sound of his mobile going off again cuts through the lazy afternoon air. He doesn't move to get it, just lies there, nose pressed against my neck, until it stops. He reaches up and growls softly as he skims his lips over mine, biting me lightly on the chin. I smile with my eyes closed.

When his phone starts to ring again, he curses, sits up, and grabs the phone off the nightstand. I watch as he storms into the bathroom. He's not all the way in before he answers though.

"What the fuck now?" he growls down the phone.

I almost recoil as he closes the door behind him. Something—and I don't know what—compels me to get out of bed and cross to the bathroom door. As I press my ear against it, I hear his voice low and fierce.

"When?" Jake's voice tenses. "Well, I'm not about, okay? Deal with it, will you? I don't know—tell him you haven't seen me." Silence. "No, because it's got fuck all to do with him, has it?" Longer silence. "Listen, for once, can you do this without making a fucking mess, yeah?" Silence again. I hear him curse once, and then there's only more silence. It makes me take a few steps back from the door.

His eyes are dark and angry as the door's pulled open, and it's frightening how quickly his expression changes. From hard and cold to soft and warm in an instant. He doesn't seem to be trying to figure out what I may have overheard, thank god. He just drags his gaze over my nakedness in definite appreciation.

"Sorry, I was about to knock. I wasn't sure how long you were going to be. I need to shower and get back."

He strides toward me and pulls me into his body, pressing his mouth to the top of my head.

"Everything okay?" I ask tentatively.

He sighs loudly. "Just work stuff. Sorted it."

I feel his heart beating fast through his chest. I wonder then if there will ever be a time where I can ask him what's wrong and he'll tell me.

He lowers his head to burrow his face into my neck. "Mmm, don't shower."

"What?"

"I fucking like the idea of you at work, smelling of me." He pulls back and smiles wickedly. "You're going to be late if you shower." He looks at his watch then holds it out in front for me to see.

Christ, is that the time? I *am* going to be late if I shower.

"You're filthy," I tell him. Despite that, my stomach flips at the idea of being at work, smelling of him.

"Yeah, I know." He nods, unashamed, as he leans in to kiss me. It's slow and sensual, and I feel the heat start to build again.

When people talk about being weak at the knees, it's normally always an exaggeration. This isn't. My legs buckle slightly.

"Just stay here with me instead," he breathes between kisses. "Let's go back in there and fuck again."

I almost groan with want. I want to do that. Mentally, I run through my diary to find the next available day where I can do that. Saturday.

"Another day, maybe . . . I'm already running late, remember?" I say.

He gives me his adorable little boy pout and presses into me once more.

While I brush my teeth, he stands behind me, hugging me close to his chest and watching my every move in the mirror. Every so often, he leans in to kiss the top of my head or the side of my neck. It feels intimate, and a stir of something fond bubbles up in my chest. I like the sight of his strong, tanned, tattooed body close to my smaller, paler one. He makes me feel safe.

That slow-motion fall also feels a little speedier now. I haven't hit the ground yet, but it's coming up to meet me fast. This is going to bloody hurt.

"I'm telling my best friend about you tonight," I say, mouth half-full of toothpaste.

He stands up straighter, his expression changing imperceptibly.

"Her fiancé saw us together last night."

"You haven't told her about me already?" He lowers his head to bite my shoulder softly. "I thought girls told each other everything. So, she's got no idea how big my dick is?" He's grinning now, and I can't help but laugh.

"I suppose I wasn't sure what there was to tell before." I drop my head to spit out the toothpaste as neatly as possible before leaning down to rinse my mouth. As I do this, Jake gathers and holds my hair, making it look like the most natural thing in the world.

Falling.

"And what'll you tell her now?" he asks.

Honestly, I have no idea what to tell Robyn. She can read me like a book. I won't be able to hide anything from her.

"Um, how about that you are a completely hot sexual deviant who could have someone's eye out with his cock?" I burst out laughing, cheeks reddening as I turn to face him. His face is open and warm as he looks at me.

When he leans down to kiss me, I'm certain my brain switches off entirely, so lost in him that we might have been kissing for hours, not seconds.

"Okay, now I'm *really* running late." I slip away from him reluctantly.

In the bedroom, I pull out clean underwear and quickly slide it on before going to shake out my dress and climb back into it. Jake dresses quietly too, watching me as he does, a hot look on his face. He comes up behind me and fastens my zip, kissing me gently on the back of my neck as he buttons the small button. By the time we get to the bottom of the stairs, I'm so bloody late, and the hall clock reads 1:35 p.m.

"When can I see you?" Jake asks as he finishes buckling his belt.

"I'll call you tonight?"

He nods. "Thanks for having lunch with me, Doctor. It was really fucking tasty."

I blush. "It was my pleasure—again." I honestly don't know who I am anymore.

Jake pulls me into him and makes that soft growling noise as he nestles his mouth against my neck. "I'll wait for your call then, Doctor," he says as we exit the house. "Oh, and I don't like this key in the pot thing. It's not safe." He's frowning exactly as he did back in my office.

I roll my eyes. "It's not London, Jake. It's safe here."

He cocks an eyebrow suspiciously.

"Anyway, only you and my neighbor know it's in there, so . . ."

"Yeah, well, I still don't like it, Alex."

I shake my head dismissively at him but still get a thrill at the fact he's being overprotective. "I'll call you later," I say as I get in the car.

He gets into the Audi still shaking his head at my plant pot key. He follows behind me down my street and through the main part of the village before flashing his lights and taking a left.

I sigh girlishly as his car disappears out of sight, then I put my foot down to try and get back to work before 2:00 p.m. If meeting Jake for lunch is going to be a regular occurrence, I seriously need to time it a lot better.

SIXTEEN

MANAGE TO COAST MY WAY THROUGH THE REST OF THE AFTERNOON
in a somewhat professional manner. Even Mrs. Goldman fails to rattle me
when she comes in at 4:45 p.m. Perhaps Jake is good for me. A calming,
relaxing influence I should welcome with open arms. *And open legs.*

Before I head home, I check my phone to see a message from him
from earlier.

Jake: I'm hard again thinking about you covered in me. Call me tonight.

My heart flutters in my chest as I quickly tap out the response because
I don't want him to think I'm being rude.

Me: Smelling of you isn't so bad . . . Thanks again for lunch. I'm starving again . . . A x

I giggle at my saucy wit and shove my phone into my bag. Time to go
home and tell Rob.

I manage a quick dinner of feta and olive salad before the doorbell goes.

"Hey." I smile too wide as I stand back to let her in.

"Hey, babe. You okay?" She pulls me into a fruity one-armed hug and
shrugs out of her jacket, which she hangs up on the hook by the door.

"I'm good. You want tea or coffee?"

"No, I can't stay long. So . . .? What the hell's going on, babe?" she says
as soon as we're in the living room. No messing about from Robyn, ever.
It's one of the things I love about her.

I take a seat on the sofa. "Okay, well, first, I'm sorry you had to find out
from Dan like that. I'd have been confused too, so I'm sorry." I give her my
most sincere look.

She nods, thoughtful. "Are you pissed off at me about something?"

"What? No, of course not. Why would you think that?" I shake my head, puzzled.

"I don't know . . . I feel like we've barely spoken this week, and now this. It's like I don't know what's going on with you."

I almost want to laugh at that because I don't know what's going on with me either. Jake is a bull in my china-shop life. I look away from her guiltily. Guilty I've hidden Jake from her. Guilty I've kept this new, exciting, terrifying thing from her when we always tell each other everything. I mean, she told me about how my brother went down on her in our parents' conservatory once. She was the first person I told about Ben's affair. The first person I call or text when something remotely funny or exciting happens. Nothing is hidden between us. Nothing until now, that is.

"I'm sorry. I did keep this from you, but it wasn't because of anything you've done." I shake my head. "It was just . . . I don't know."

"So, who is he? Why all the secrecy? Is he married or something?"

I look at her in horror. "What? No. God, no. He's not married. He's . . . no."

"Then what's the big deal? Who is he?" She gets up from Jake's armchair and comes to sit beside me on the sofa, eyes wide with expectation.

I feel the stupid grin spread over my mouth though I try to stop it.

Finally, she loses patience and gives my knee a shake. "What? Bloody tell me!"

"Jake. He's Jake." I laugh nervously. Saying his name aloud immediately makes me feel as if the albatross around my neck has just broken free, flapped its wings, and flown away. The name means nothing to Rob, of course, so she stares at me blankly.

"Jake. Okay, I'm gonna need a bit more than that, babe."

"I met him at the club a few weeks ago—the opening." It's not a lie.

Robyn's eyebrows move together while she digests this. "The nightclub? You never mentioned you met anyone." She shakes her head. "Oh, wait—the guy you were dancing with? The tall one who disappeared?"

Who? Who is she talking about? Then I remember: Matt.

"No, not him. It was after that."

"After that, you went home with a headache . . ."

"Before the headache. After the dancing guy. When I went to the toilet and got lost." My face begins to feel warm as though I'm digging myself back into a hole. "I was tipsy, and we got talking, and, well . . . I gave him my number."

Robyn chews the information over in her head. "That's great, but why all the secrecy about it?" She looks genuinely confused.

I shrug again. "I honestly don't know." Again, not a lie. "I suppose at first, I never thought anything would happen. Then I thought you'd think he was a terrible idea. I mean, he's ridiculously attractive and owns a nightclub. I felt impulsive even going out with a guy like him. I suppose I was waiting to see how it went before telling you."

She nods. Then a small, sly smile grows on her face. "So, he's ridiculously attractive?"

"It's insane, Rob, seriously."

She laughs at this. "So, this is the *real* reason you kicked the eligible Doctor Wardley to the curb then? The nightclub owner." She's grinning now.

I do a half-shrug-nod thing. I didn't exactly kick him to the curb; I was just powerless in the face of the human sex tornado that is Jake Lawrence.

Rob's quiet for a moment before she speaks again. "So, it's obviously progressing well. Dan said you looked close."

"I thought Dan said I was *snogging the face off him."*

"He did say that." She laughs again. "Honestly, at first, I thought it might have been Ben. I was going to disown you."

"Yeah, well, that's not ever going to happen, so don't worry."

She hits me lightly on the knee. "Ugh, I can't believe you kept this from me!"

"I know. I was waiting to see what happened, love. I felt sure you'd talk me out of it, and I didn't . . . want to be talked out of it, I suppose." I was already doing a grand job of that all by myself.

She nods. "So . . . have you slept with him yet?"

I give her a look that tells her everything.

"Oh my god! Dr. Marlowe, you secret nightclub owner-shagging slut!" she squeals before collapsing into a fit of giggles. Then she demands to know every detail of every encounter to date.

I tell her what I can without feeling as if I'm spilling Jake's secrets. Which is mainly that he's completely hot, totally intense, and the sex has been amazing, including this afternoon's lunchtime dalliance.

"Well, I for one want to meet this guy who has turned you into a harlot!"

she says. "Oh, bring him to dinner with us on Friday night?" She's practically jumping off the sofa with excitement.

I forgot about Robyn's dinner party.

"Dan and I were thinking we'd finally get you and Mark together, but now you can bring Jake, and it'll be perfect! Though, probably not for Mark, but he'll get over it." She laughs again.

Invite Jake to Rob's. Is that where we are now? Are we two people who go to dinner parties together? We're having a lot of sex. I flush again. Then I remember I haven't showered yet. I can't imagine Jake would want to come to a dinner party with Rob and Dan and their friends anyway.

"Um, I don't know, Rob. I'm pretty sure he works Friday nights," I say, watching her deflate visibly. "But I'll ask him and see what he says."

I know what he'll say. He'll say he works Friday nights.

It's just before 9:00 p.m. when Robyn leaves. After she does, I go upstairs and run myself a steaming bubble bath, relaxing into it as I dial his number. Pathetically, I'm excited to hear the sound of his voice on the phone.

It rings twice before he picks up.

"Well, you took your time," he says softly, no greeting. His voice is deeper and very masculine.

"Sorry. Rob just left, and I thought I'd run a bath before calling you." I stretch out my legs, running my toes across the taps. The bubbles pop and crackle around me.

He groans softly. "Wait—you're in the bath right now? Naked and wet?"

"Baths normally involve both of those things, yes." I smile.

"You are fucking killing me here, baby. I'm not gonna be able to sleep tonight thinking about you naked and wet. Wait—I'm always thinking about that." He huffs out a low, sexy laugh.

"Deviant," I say. "So, what are you doing? No club tonight?"

"Nah, we're closed Monday and Tuesdays. I'm watching the football. West Ham game from earlier, so don't tell me the score, yeah?" I hear the smile in his voice.

"Oh, I'll try not to let it slip," I say. "So, a West Ham fan then? Must bank that little nodule of information away somewhere. Extremely sharey of you."

He chuckles. "Told you I wasn't that interesting, didn't I? So, are there bubbles?"

"Always. Lots of bubbles. It's also very, very hot." I sigh. Jake curses on the other end.

"I could come over there, you know. Could be there in, say . . . twenty minutes? Water would still be warm. Your bath is big enough for two, if I remember right."

He sounds utterly serious. I'm utterly tempted. I close my eyes at the thought of him climbing naked into the bath with me, his body slippery and wet, and me wedged between his thighs. I almost groan out loud from want.

No. I can't have him thinking I need to see him every minute of every day, even if it is probably the truth. That would be giving him far too much power. He has too much power over me already. A few nights apart will do us good.

"You'd be breaking the law if you got here in twenty minutes, and that wouldn't be good. Anyway, I'm exhausted. It's been a long and eventful day . . ." I say pointedly.

"You saying no to me again?" His voice is low but playful.

"No," I say, and he huffs out a deep laugh. I really, really wish he were here.

"Good. Because I don't take rejection well."

"Oh, really?"

"Wait—I don't know how I take rejection 'cause it's never happened before. It nearly happened with this gorgeous doctor I was mental about, but she came around in the end."

I'm smiling like a fool now. "Well, she sounds like a pushover." I slip down lower into the water.

"Nah. She just doesn't know what's bad for her," he says.

My heart stumbles slightly at the warning. Which is what I assume it is. Another one.

"Well, I'm not rejecting you. I'm . . . delaying you."

He groans again. "Fine. So, how'd it go with your friend? Tell her about your sexual deviant, did you?"

"I did. She, um . . ." *Here goes.* I take a deep breath. "She invited you to dinner at her place."

"When?"

"Friday night. She's having a few friends around. I told her you work Friday nights and it probably wouldn't suit."

"I'll come," he says. A strange, warm ripple courses over my body.

"Oh. Okay."

"Unless you don't want me to."

"No, no—I do. I thought, well, you don't know any of them, so you'll be kind of on your own." Why am I trying to talk him out of this? Why am I so terrified suddenly?

"I assume you're going."

"Of course I am."

"Then I'm not gonna be on my own, am I?"

"No, I guess not."

He sighs. "Alex, do you want me to come or not? Tell me what you want me to do, and I'll do it." There's a sliver of impatience in his voice.

What am I doing? I care about him. I *might* be falling for him. I want him to meet my friends. I should be happy *he* wants to meet them.

"I want you to come," I tell him. And at that moment, I realize just how much.

"Okay. Then I'll come."

"Okay," I whisper.

"Okay," he echoes.

"She'll be delighted. She can't wait to meet you."

"I want to see you tomorrow," he says, ignoring the statement. "Can you have me for lunch again, or dinner? I'm not really fussy."

I giggle as a ripple of goose bumps break out over me. "Um, actually, I can't. I have a seminar in the afternoon, so I'm out of the office from lunchtime. I won't be home until god knows when. Anyway, I don't think I can make a habit of meeting you at lunchtime for sexual deviance." Oh, who am I kidding? I could absolutely make a habit of it.

"Why not?" he asks, sounding serious. "C'MON!" he shouts then, and I almost jump out of my skin. "Sorry, Sakho just scored a class goal from a corner," he tells me. "So, where's your work thing at? In town?"

"Yes. The Lancaster. Two until five." I could do without wasting half a day listening to sales pitches, but Douglas wants a report on what this newest patient management system is all about and whether we need to buy it, and since Sam went to the last one, and Helen before that, it's my turn.

"So, meet me after. You could stay the night," he says.

"Stay the night? What—you mean, at your place?"

"Yes, at my place. Where else?" He laughs. "I'll make you dinner."

"You cook?" The idea is amusing to me for some reason. I can't imagine him pottering around his house doing menial things such as cooking. I imagined he sustained himself on sex and the swooning of desperate women. Desperate women like me.

"I cook a bit."

Stay at his place. It's a chance to find out more about him—what kind of place he lives in, what kind of things he surrounds himself with. I could knock on Ed and Betty's in the morning and ask them to mind Fred.

"Okay then. That would be nice. I'll come to yours and stay the night. Text me your address so I can figure out the tube?"

"Nah, I'll pick you up. About five? Which Lancaster is it? There's two."

"The one at Hyde Park. Are you sure? The tube will be easier at that time."

"I don't mind. More time I get to spend with you, isn't it?"

Beneath the cooling water, my toes curl, cheeks flushing from a different kind of heat. "Okay, well, I'll see you at five tomorrow then. I'll let you get back to your game. I've some cleansing to do anyway, and the water's starting to get cold."

"So, you're washing me away, are you?" He makes a "tsk" sound. "Ah, well, I'll have to cover you in me again tomorrow."

"You are a deviant." I smile. In my head, I imagine his hands and his body and his smell on me. Robyn's right: he has turned me into a harlot.

"You don't even know the half of it," he growls quietly. "See you tomorrow. I'm off to have a cold shower. Night, Alex," he says before hanging up.

Before I get into bed, I pack my small overnight case so I don't have to do it in the morning. I can still smell him on the pillows and the sheets from this afternoon when I climb under the covers, meaning I'll have to change them. But not tonight. Tonight, I'm happy to go to sleep with the scent of him in my nose and the promise of him in my head. I take a deep breath in, and I'm asleep in seconds.

SEVENTEEN

MAKE IT TO THE LANCASTER AT 1:45 P.M. AND SIGN IN AT THE ARRIVAL desk. The badge reads "Dr. Marlow," and so I write the "e" on with my black pen before making my way to the toilets to fix my hair. It's flat, and my updo needs a brush through and redo. It's also a good way of avoiding having to network in the lobby.

I'm a terrible networker. Always have been. Probably because I'm also a terrible small talker. I'm always one step away from oversharing or offending someone, so I tend to try and avoid it altogether.

As I'm coming back out of the ladies, because I'm not looking where I'm going, I run smack into a body coming from the opposite direction. I lift my head to apologize and stop dead.

Oh, god. Please. No.

Ben. Or "Mr. Ben Cooke," as the badge reads. Spelled correctly, of course. No rubbish handwritten letter "e" for him. He forces his eyes wide before he smiles.

"Hey, you," he says warmly. Completely at odds with my insides-full-of-eels sensation at staring my cheating ex-fiancé in the face after almost six months. He's still handsome. In an older, snobbish, arrogant way, which, for some bizarre reason, I used to be attracted to.

"Ben. Hi. Um, how are you?" I ask tightly, glancing over his shoulder for some means of escape. Then I look down, smoothing my skirt as I inwardly curse myself for asking how he is. I couldn't care less about how he is. I hate my inbred politeness and good manners sometimes.

"I'm good, Lex. You?" He nods.

I tense at the sound of the nickname. I hate that he still thinks he can shorten my name.

"Really good, actually." I nod, and I mean it. *I've been having the best sex of my life with a man younger and hotter than you, you arrogant, cheating prick.* I don't say any of this though—but, bloody hell, I want to.

Ben nods. "How's Fred? Does he ask about me?" He smiles at his own joke.

"Actually, no. He's good too though. Still bringing in the decapitated heads of small, winged creatures, but it's what he enjoys, so . . ." I shrug, and Ben chuckles lightly.

"Well, you will not believe this, but we are at the same table," he tells me. "I had a quick look at the seating plan, as I always do, and Dr. Marlowe without an 'e' is at table four with me." He smiles again.

Good god, seriously? Twice in one week, the laws of probability have entirely screwed me over. Yes, I should definitely put the lottery on.

"Um, great . . ." I mutter as I walk away from him toward the conference room with about as much enthusiasm as someone going to their execution. I think about asking someone to switch tables with me. I also think about turning around and leaving this thing altogether, but of course, that would be immature. It's three hours of my life. I can get through it like an adult.

As I walk into the room, I check the seating plan on the off chance he was mistaken. Unfortunately, he wasn't. Ben and I *are* at table four, which I see is near the center of the room. Without glancing back once, I weave through the other tables to get to my seat.

I sit, and Ben takes the seat directly to my left, as I knew he would, before introducing himself to everyone. He starts with the woman on his left and then stands to shake hands with the others at the table. He gives each of them a flash of his perfect (cheating prick) smile before sitting back down, his leg grazing mine under the table as he does. I look longingly at the spare seat across the table, but I think having to look at him all afternoon would be marginally worse than having to sit next to him.

After introducing myself to an older lady to my right, I get my phone out to send Rob a message telling her of my current predicament and asking her to pray for me. Then I message Jake to ask what he's making for dinner, adding I wish this thing was over already.

My phone buzzes with his response almost instantly.

Jake: I wish it was over already too, 'cause then you'd be here. J x

Then:

Jake: I haven't decided yet. Any preferences? Anything you don't eat?

I ponder the question for a moment before responding:

Me: Not really. And I'm not allergic to anything except bad cooking! No pressure. A x

Jake: Oh, I'm not worried. Prepare to fall even more in love with me after you taste my cooking . . .

He sends a winking emoji, and I'm powerless to stop the grin spreading over my face. From the corner of my eye, I sense Ben looking at me, and so I slide my phone into my bag and focus on the stage.

Throughout the first two speakers, Ben grazes my elbow and leg constantly—on purpose, I'm sure—until I physically have to move my chair a few inches away from him. At one point, he leans over and refills my water without being asked, and the lady's next to me. His face is all butter wouldn't melt, and the woman practically swoons. I feel like telling her butter would most definitely melt and that he's a lying, cheating prick in fact, but that would be an overshare. So, she continues looking at him the way older women tend to look at Ben.

Today, he looks every inch the surgeon, clean-shaven and dressed impeccably in a dark pinstripe suit, white shirt, and patterned yellow tie. I can't help but compare his profile with Jake's. It strikes me how utterly different they are in almost every conceivable way.

I thought Ben was everything I wanted once. I looked up to him, respected him. I was the naïve medical student to his older, handsome consultant. I suppose it laid the foundation of how I would always feel with him. Young and naïve. I was certainly naïve. Completely oblivious to his sneaking around behind my back for months with some medical sales executive. Though I wonder if it was less about my naïvety and more about my lack of attention. Perhaps if I were paying attention, I'd have noticed something wasn't right. And perhaps if I were paying attention, he wouldn't have felt the need to fuck his sales exec.

I wonder if I could ever stop paying attention to Jake.

Ben catches me looking at him and smiles. I look away and concentrate on the speaker instead. I certainly don't need him to think I'm thinking about him like *that*.

The speaker talks about why patient management systems need to change as the patient becomes more demanding, and "rightly so." We don't just provide a necessary service; we provide a competitive service, blah . . . blah . . . blah. Personally, I think all patients want is a good service, but that isn't a moneymaker.

It carries on like this for another hour as I struggle to take down the necessary points of note, my mind mainly filled with images of what Jake's place will be like and how badly I want to see him. As soon as they finish the second presentation, they announce the coffee break, and though some delegates at our table don't move, I practically spring up and race for the door. They probably want to spend the coffee break networking, which I can't be a part of. I make my way to the coffee station and pour myself a weak one with a splash of cream.

"I saw your mum and dad the other night," I hear from behind me.

I roll my eyes before turning around to face him. He's a networker—why isn't he sitting at the table networking? So, he saw my parents. Unfortunately for me, Mum and Dad are still good friends with his parents, Harrie and George, and their paths cross often.

"Really? Was Laura there too?" I smile as I lift my cup to my mouth. I hate myself for even mentioning her name. He'll think I care. Which I don't. I sip my coffee and look away from him.

"Um, no." He shakes his head. A few beats of silence ensue before he speaks again. "Alex, I thought your mum might have said something . . ." He studies me. I say nothing. He clears his throat. "Laura and I aren't together anymore. I ended it. About a month ago . . ." He's watching intently for my reaction.

I nod but say nothing as I continue to sip my coffee. I knew Mum was bursting to tell me something when I spoke to her on the phone last night, but she knows better than to instigate Ben conversations with me these days so must've opted not to mention it.

"Oh, right." I press my mouth into a flat line to stop myself from saying something like, "I'm sorry to hear that."

He shrugs and smiles softly at me. "Have you done something to your hair?" He casts a look over it.

I almost gag on my coffee. Is he flirting with me? He has got to be joking. For an instant, I think he's about to reach out and touch it, but he doesn't. Thank god.

"No, absolutely nothing," I say, planting my coffee cup down. I need to get away from him—from this. I turn back toward the conference room, though I only get a few steps away before I feel his hand on my arm.

"Alex, wait a second, will you?"

Only because I don't want to cause a scene in the crowded lobby, I stop walking. When I turn around, he has his serious face on. His earnest, humble face. His butter wouldn't melt face.

"What is it, Ben?" I sigh.

"I thought we could go for a drink after. Have a chat." Then, I imagine because my face demands an elaboration, he adds, "About us."

I blink in surprise. Does he seriously think a drink and a chat is all it would take for us to become us again? Oh, Christ, he does.

"Ben, there's nothing to talk about."

His jaw clenches ever so slightly. He never did like being disagreed with. "Lex, there's plenty to talk about," he chides.

"No. There *really* isn't."

He looks as though he's about to say something else, but since I don't want to hear what it is, I turn and walk away from him, back to my seat. I don't look to see if he's following.

The second half of the seminar begins, but Ben doesn't return to the table. Only because it makes me on edge not knowing when he might appear, I glance back toward the door a few times, but he doesn't show. It relaxes me to know he's likely not going to return now, and so I settle in for the last portion of the seminar.

The final speaker is by far the most interesting. He's the software developer and speaks passionately and enthusiastically, so most of the room is completely convinced by the end. The question-and-answer session starts immediately after, but since it's 4:45 p.m. and I want to freshen up before Jake arrives, I decide to give it a miss.

As I leave the ladies' room and head toward the front door to wait for him, I pull out my phone. There's a message from him at 4:20 p.m. saying he was leaving his place and will be here before 5:00 p.m. I get to the front of the hotel and have a quick look outside but don't see him. He's probably caught in peak commuter traffic.

I turn to head back across the foyer to the waiting area and freeze. Ben is watching me intently, a sad, lost look on his face. He looks me over from head to toe and begins to walk toward me. I sigh, my entire body tensing up. I really don't want to deal with this now, here, ever. Why is he even still around?

"I thought you'd left," I say.

"You mean, you hoped I had?" He raises his eyebrows.

I shake my head and look down. Of course I hoped he'd gone, and we both know it.

"You missed the best speaker," I say, desperate to steer the subject away from any kind of "us" chat. Desperate to keep things neutral. "He convinced me anyway," I add.

He smiles. "Really? How did he manage that? I could do with some pointers . . ."

"Ben, don't . . ." I start.

"Alex, you were right," he cuts in with a nod of his head.

I'm startled and momentarily speechless. I was right? With Ben, I was never right. Few people ever were.

"I didn't take care of you properly for a long time. I took you for granted. I knew you were drifting away from me, but I didn't know how to pull you back . . . Then Laura came along. She wanted me. There was a spark there again, for the first time in a long time, and it was easy to forget what I was doing was wrong. It was selfish, and I'm sorry. For hurting you and lying to you."

I'm in shock, I think. Because he never said sorry. Not once. He never once admitted any fault during the entirety of our breakup. He always maintained *I* pushed him away; *I* didn't love him anymore.

Now, he's apologizing to me. Christ, maybe he has changed.

I wonder then what might have happened if he'd said sorry sooner. Would I have taken him back? If Jake came crashing into my life like he did and I was still with Ben, what then? The thought makes me feel uneasy, so I dismiss it.

"I appreciate that, Ben, but it doesn't matter now. It's over," I say.

Ben moves a step closer, into my body space. He's taller than Jake by a few inches, and I have to crane my neck to look up at him. He's too tall now.

"Alex, please, can you let me—?" he starts, but his eyes catch onto something over my shoulder. Something that makes his expression change entirely.

When I turn around, I see Jake standing inside the revolving door, his gaze confused and dark. Immediately, I step away from Ben and his unwelcome proximity to my body. I think about how to explain this to Jake. I can't tell him it isn't what it looks like because that's utterly cliché, and somehow, it's almost *always* what it looks like.

Despite the glint in his eye, he still looks completely divine. He's wearing a light blue T-shirt and blue jeans that hang slightly loose on his hips. His hair is mussed and wet as though he's not long showered, and his cheeks are pink and glowing, which all adds to the almost youthful look he has on today.

"Alex?" Ben says. The way he says my name makes me think it isn't the first time he's said it in the past few seconds. "Alex, do you know him?"

I nod, feeling dazed. Then I turn back to Ben and take hold of my case.

"I have to go. It was nice catching up," I lie. There I go again. It wasn't nice catching up. *Stop saying things you don't mean, Alexandra.* "Tell your parents I was asking for them," I throw over my shoulder as I walk toward Jake.

It wasn't what it looked like. It wasn't anything.

"You were late again," I say with a small pout as I stop in front of him.

He's still glaring over my shoulder, so I lean forward and slip my hand around his waist before pressing my mouth to his. As his eyes close, I hope maybe the kiss will make him forget about the thing that wasn't what it looked like.

Of course, I know Ben is watching, and I also know kissing Jake like this in front of him isn't the nicest thing I've ever done, but Ben's feelings are really low on my list of priorities right now.

When I open my eyes and pull away from his mouth, Jake is staring at me, his expression unreadable. "Looks like you had someone to keep you company," he hisses.

I take his hand and pull him with me toward the exit. "An old friend. He's just gone through a breakup."

"An old friend who's clearly into you," Jake says, linking his fingers through mine.

"Well, that's unfortunate for him then, because I am into someone else." I smile.

My words cause his expression to lighten somewhat before he looks back at Ben in what I can only describe as an extreme warning. "Does he know that? Or do I need to go over and have a word with him? Make it clear you're fucking taken."

Somewhere inside, a part of me practically purrs at the thought of being taken by Jake. The other part of me would love to hear how the conversation in which Jake tells Ben I'm taken would play out.

"Um, I think he got the message."

When he turns back to me, he only smiles, tension dissolving from his body before my eyes.

"Come on then—let's see if these domestic skills of yours are as good as you think. I'm starving. It's been a loooooong day."

"Starving? Pretty sure I can sort that out." He winks.

I at least have the manners to blush slightly as he leans down and opens the passenger door for me. I climb into the seat as graciously as possible in my dress before he closes the door and puts my case in the boot. Once in the driving seat, Jake leans over to kiss me, running his hand up my bare thigh and slipping it under the hem of my dress. My whole body reacts, a bright, sharp shiver coursing over me as I return the kiss, heating under the sound of him moaning low against my mouth.

"You look completely fucking hot, by the way, Doctor," he murmurs into my mouth, his fingers curling into the skin of my thigh, needy but tender too. "Been thinking about you all fucking day," he says, nuzzling against my neck.

I keep my eyes closed and smile. "It's nice to see you too."

He brings his mouth back up to mine and licks at my lips before pulling away to start the engine. Then he turns to look at me expectantly.

"Seat belt," he orders after a moment.

When I reach behind me to pull it on, I see Ben getting into a black cab, talking animatedly on his phone. Since he's looking in my direction, I assume he knows I'm inside, though, thankfully, the tinted windows mean he can't see me looking back.

As soon as my seat belt clicks into place, Jake pulls out into the traffic, and we head east along Hyde Park.

"So, long day?" he asks, glancing at me briefly before turning back to the road.

"Long and boring. These things normally are. Not as exciting as the nightclub business, I'm sure."

He nods. "Yeah, you have no idea the lives I'm saving daily in that place. It's fucking exhausting," he sighs, and I giggle.

As I slide back in the chair, I feel something ridged dig into my back. I reach behind me to grab it, pulling out a small plastic fire engine toy. I give it a confused look as I hold it up.

"Aw, yeah, Paul said his kid lost that somewhere," Jake says absently, looking back to the road. "He borrowed the car the other day while his was getting serviced. Toss it in the back."

I reach behind me and place the toy on the back seat. "So, what did you get up to today?" I ask, turning to look at him. "I hope you didn't spend all of it in the kitchen. That would be way too 1950s housewife."

"Not quite." He smiles, not expanding further. Something tells me not to press it either. No matter—I'm going to see where he lives. Where he spends his time when he's not with me. I'm inordinately excited. It's ridiculous, really, considering all that's happened between us so far. But I feel as if this is my first *real* chance to get to know a side of him I haven't seen yet. One he hasn't let me see yet. You can't hide things in the place where you live and feel utterly relaxed. My house reflects me and my personality—trinkets I've collected from places I've been, books I've read, photos of me and my family and friends in every room. Jake's home will open him up to me finally, I'm sure of it.

Yes, after tonight, I'll know a lot more about the self-confirmed mystery that is Jake Lawrence.

EIGHTEEN

ABOUT TWENTY MINUTES LATER, WE ARRIVE AT THE ENTRANCE TO an underground garage at a converted warehouse on St Katharine Docks, not too far from where he took me for dinner. Jake presses a button on his dashboard, and the large roller door opens. Inside, he parks smoothly into a space marked 10/1. Unbuckling my seat belt, I take a deep breath to steady the butterflies that have started fluttering in my stomach.

I'm going to see where he lives.

This is a seminal moment, surely. Bringing me one step closer to being "safe hands," as he called it.

Jake gets my case from the boot and walks around to meet me as I'm closing the passenger door. He slips his hand into mine and gives me a cute smile then pulls me toward the entrance to the stairwell. A bank of elevators sits on one side, and he lets go of the case to press the button to call one. While we wait, he circles his thumb softly over the skin of my hand, glancing at me with that same sweet smile: relaxed, but with definite promise behind it. I want to kiss him again.

I lean forward, closing the distance between our mouths, but as I'm about to touch my lips to his, the doorway to the garage swings open, making me pull back. Through it struts a tall, tanned girl dressed in a tight white crop top and high-waisted jeans, her heels adding at least six inches to her height. As she comes to stand next to us, I get a waft of strong, thick perfume that, mixed with the butterflies, makes my stomach churn with something oily. She looks around at Jake and smiles brightly.

"Hey, Jay. How are you?"

Jay? She calls him Jay? Oh, I don't like that.

"Yeah, good, Dawn. You?" He flashes her a small, tight smile and nods before turning to watch the counter crawl down to garage level. He gives my hand a gentle squeeze.

172 | SCARLETT DRAKE

"Great, thanks, yeah," she says, swinging the set of keys at her hip. "How's the club doing?"

"Really good, yeah." Jake doesn't give her more than a glance this time before the lift springs open and he stands back to let me in. He gets in behind me, and Dawn gets in last, and we travel up in a strange silence until she exits at level 5. As she does, she glances back at Jake with a look so subtle she may as well have given him a lap dance.

I look sideways to see his reaction, which, from here, appears to be one of mild awkwardness. It's all the confirmation I need.

Jake steps forward to press level 10, and the doors close.

"I guess you never called," I mumble.

He looks at me, frowning slightly. "What?"

"Dawn." I incline my head. "Afterward. You never called her, did you?"

He thinks about it for a moment, and I'm sure he's going to deny it, but then he shakes his head. Gives a half-shrug.

"Nah, I didn't call." He's watching me carefully. I nod, and he takes a step toward me. "It was months ago. It only happened once. Never shit on your own doorstep, they say."

"Well, Miss Nuts Magazine there is still into you."

Another shrug. "Yeah, well . . ."

"So that's your usual type then?" I ask, then I immediately curse myself. Why do I need to know that? The question came from nowhere of substance; it popped into my head and then out of my mouth.

He closes the distance between us and lowers his lips almost to mine. "Baby, I've never had a type until you," he says quietly.

My cheeks feel warm, and I can't help but let out a soft laugh. "Is that so?"

"Yeah, it is."

He leans in to kiss me then. Deep and warm and slow. The kind of kiss that feels like foreplay. When the door opens on a ding, he recovers far faster than I do, and he has to pull me out behind him because I'm still dazed.

He leads me down a long brick hallway with a polished wood floor and a floor to ceiling window at the far end, through which I see Tower Bridge. We come to a stop at a shiny copper door with the number 10/1 etched into it, and he unlocks it and leads me inside.

"Go through," he says, gesturing for me to go ahead. Behind me, I hear him lock the front door.

My first thought is that his place is like something out of a stylish living magazine. Large and open, the ceiling lower in the kitchen before the lounge and dining area open up into a double-height mezzanine level behind me. A black wrought iron spiral staircase is visible past the kitchen. Straight ahead is a large corner window, floor to ceiling, with an impressive view of the docks and bridge. The kitchen to my left is all white gloss and stainless steel, completely modern and utterly spotless. The living area looks comfortable and stylish too, with a large dark brown leather corner sofa and a huge flat-screen TV on the exposed brick wall. In the far corner, I see an acoustic guitar and amplifier.

I turn back to him, eyes wide. "You play the guitar?"

"Fuck, I wish," he says with a shake of his head. "I'm teaching myself. I'm terrible at it."

I wonder if he's being humble again. Like when he said he's not interesting. I turn back around to look at where the staircase goes and can only assume it's to his bedroom.

God, this place must be worth a fortune. The London club scene definitely pays. When I turn back to look at him, he's leaning against the wall by the kitchen watching me, a strange, almost distant look on his face.

"I'm impressed." I smile. "You have a really beautiful place."

He pushes up off the wall and comes toward me. "Yeah, well, it never normally looks this good."

I flush and shake my head as he pulls me into him, dipping his head and kissing me slowly, deeply. I loop my arms up over his shoulders to stroke the back of his short, cropped hair as his mouth moves over mine, tasting, teasing. God, will I ever tire of kissing him? Not likely.

"I'm glad you're here," he says, pulling back and licking his lips.

"I'm glad I'm here too. Thanks for inviting me."

He presses his mouth to mine again. "Lemme give you the tour," he says, moving behind me. He rests his chin on my shoulder and wraps his arms around my body, raising a hand to point as he turns me. "Kitchen, living room, and spare room. Door down there on the right is the bathroom."

"This place is worryingly tidy, Jake," I remark with some awe. "Please tell me you didn't spend all day cleaning . . ." I can't believe how immaculate it is. So neat and spotless. I'm not sure what I was expecting, but I don't think it was this. He's surprised me again.

"Nah, I have someone who helps."

I spin around to face him. "Oh my god, you have a cleaner?"

He nods, apparently confused. "She comes in twice a week. She was here this morning. I'll tell her you like her work."

"So here was me thinking you were just an exceptionally tidy man, and instead, it was some poor woman who made it look like this." I laugh.

"Oh, don't feel sorry for her. I pay her fucking well." He's grinning as he reaches out to take my hand and pull me toward the stairs.

Smiling, I follow him up the curved staircase to his bedroom, which is as impressive as the lower level. The double-height windows mean he has an unobstructed view of the London skyline from his bed. Along one wall is a row of mirrored and walnut wardrobes, a matching walnut tallboy against the wall, and a low wood bed, thick curtains along the mezzanine to allow him to close out the light. The bedroom is colored in muted white and gray with thick gray carpet.

"Are you going to tell me this is where the magic happens?" I ask playfully as I turn to him. The words make me wonder exactly *how many* women he's brought up here. He's a man who looks like him with a bachelor pad most guys can only dream about. Dawn from the elevator has certainly been here. Gemma from the club too. Countless others, surely.

Christ, I hate my brain.

"Hmm. Well, I could tell you that," he says, pressing his mouth to mine, "or I could show you . . ." He turns me so my back is to him again, and then his mouth is on my neck, sucking gently, biting softly, nudging the space below my ear with his nose. He inhales deep, and a ripple of goose bumps break out across the skin of my arms, the back of my neck. I close my eyes on a soft moan. "You smell incredible, baby . . ."

I do? I wonder if he knows his smell drives me insane. He dips his mouth lower, and I tilt my head to the side to give him more space to cover. His mouth is warm and wet, and the sound of his mouth as it moves is delicious. My hands skim over the muscle of his thighs needily as he slides my dress up from behind.

"Alex, I kinda need to fuck you now," he says, low.

The words light a fire inside. Yes, I need him to do that now too. My hand slips behind me, between our bodies, to graze the front of his jeans, and I feel immediately how aroused he is. It's thrilling knowing how much he wants me. Knowing I make him like this. That I can do that to a man like him. It's an odd, heady kind of power.

Turning around, I move to brazenly unbuckle his belt while he grabs the hem of his T-shirt and pulls it up and off. His hands come around my shoulders seeking the zip of my dress, which he tugs down. Loose, it falls from my body, allowing me to step out of it.

As soon as I do, our mouths meet in a rush, and he pulls me back toward the bed. I grip onto him to steady myself as he finishes removing his jeans, pushing them roughly down his thighs and kicking them off. He sits down and pulls me onto his lap so I'm straddling him, knees pressed into the bed on either side. His hands roam over my body and around to my back where he deftly unclasps my bra. As the straps slip down, his mouth leaves mine, and he lifts his head to stare down at them.

"I fucking love these, you know . . .?" he whispers as he lowers his head to take one nipple into his mouth. He moans a raw, masculine sound as he suckles it and flicks it with his tongue, his long stubble tickling the sensitive skin around it.

I hold his head and run my fingers through his soft hair, pulling on it as he sucks more. When his fingers move between my legs, he lets go of my nipple and groans, lifting his head to look up at me.

"Fuck, baby . . . Look at how wet you are already . . . Is this for me?" His voice is low and filthy, and it only tightens the knot of heat between my legs. There's no embarrassment, only desire, his words having the same effect on me as they always do. Loosening. Emboldening. He doesn't seriously want me to answer that, does he?

He's still looking up at me as his fingers dance close to where I need him. Soft pushes of the pads of his fingers against my underwear. God, he does.

"You know it is . . ."

He smirks and reaches up to kiss me, licking into my mouth. "Tell me what you want, Alex . . ." He slips his fingers inside my knickers and strokes one up the entire length of me, causing me to arch against him. My face feels so deliciously hot, my body on fire.

"Jake . . . please . . ." I pant against his mouth.

"Tell me what you want, baby," he says again.

"You. I just . . . I want you."

He smiles at this. A small, soft thing, which is at odds with his words and fingers. Securing a hand around my waist, he moves suddenly, flipping me onto my back on the bed. He repositions his body over mine, fingers trailing over my shoulders, collarbone, and neck as he stares down at me. Closing my eyes, I enjoy the soft dance of his fingers across my skin.

"I fantasized about this, you know?" I hear him say.

I open my eyes to look at him. "You did?"

He nods, eyes drifting away from my face to my lips, and then to my neck, where his fingers glide over the skin. "The first time I saw you, I fantasized about this." His tone is soft. "Imagined fucking you here on my bed. I wanted you in my bed."

I feel a deep clenching in my belly in response. "You imagined all of this while I was stitching together a potentially life-threatening knife wound? How . . . kinky."

He grins a little. "Bet you get that a lot, huh? Patients fantasizing about you."

I laugh. "I don't think so, no . . . I think it's just you."

"Bullshit. Look at you." He gestures. "If you were my doctor, I'd be fucking sick all the time."

I giggle at that, giving him a soft shake of my head. "Your lines are something else, you know that?"

He frowns, leaning up. "Why do you always think I'm giving you a line?"

"It was a joke. Sorry."

"It wasn't though, was it? You always say shit like that whenever I tell you how I feel." He sounds angry as he sits up fully. "You always think I'm bullshitting you. Why?"

Do I? I guess I do, and clearly, it's something he doesn't like. Except all I can think about is the fact I'm naked and splayed out before him, and suddenly, I feel very exposed. I shuffle up the bed and lean back against the headboard, pulling a pillow over myself. I stare at him. He's still waiting for an answer.

"I guess I'm a little cynical that way," I start, shrugging slightly. "Guys like you . . . well, you have a way with words, and . . . I don't know." God, this is a terrible attempt at an explanation.

"Guys like me?" he says quietly, eyes narrowing.

Is that what I said? Christ. I grimace slightly. "I meant *guys*. Generally. I mean, you practice this stuff, saying things girls want to hear. I didn't mean it as an insult, Jake. It's more of a compliment when you think about it. Because you're good at it . . . *really* good."

He's frowning, hard. I see the cogs ticking over in his mind for a few dreadful seconds before he shakes his head.

"You honestly think I say shit like this to women?" He laughs, the sound thin and cold. "Fucking hell, Alex, I don't bring women back here. Ever. And I don't fantasize about doing it either."

Now, it's my turn to laugh. "Oh, really? You've seriously never brought a woman back here?"

"No," he confirms.

"Oh, really? Not even Dawn from the elevator? What, are you going to tell me you were a virgin before we slept together?" My voice is ridiculously high.

He stares at me for a moment longer and then sits up and steps off the bed entirely. I watch as he walks over to the glass barrier at the edge of the mezzanine and looks out at the view, shoulders hunched as he runs a hand over his face.

"You want to know how many women I've been with, Alex? That it?" He turns, and he looks so staggeringly gorgeous topless and angry that I forget for a moment we're in the middle of an argument. "Would that help? If you knew how many women I'd fucked but never called after?"

I feel a horrible twist in my tummy. Why on earth would I want to know what number I am to him?

"No, of course not." I shake my head.

Jake looks away from me and stares at a point on the floor while he works at the inside of his lip with his teeth. He looks sad, I think. Regretful. It makes me feel guilty. From day one, I assumed him to be a player; a man who fucked women, didn't do relationships, and who'd break my heart when he moved briskly on to the next one. I guess I figured he'd be okay with that assumption. I never expected it to hurt or insult him.

"Don't you think this is funny?" he says.

"What is?" I frown. I'm pretty sure nothing about this is funny.

"That I'm the one on trial here, but since I met you, I've had to stand watching you with three different guys."

I feel as if he's slapped me across the face. Oh, god, that's unfair. He's right, but Christ, it doesn't make it any easier to hear. The fact I'm sitting on Jake's bed naked only adds to it.

Well, this evening certainly isn't turning out how I wanted it to. I want to go home. I feel cheap and sad, and I want to go home right now.

With a nod, I slide across the bed slowly, bending down as gracefully as possible to retrieve my underwear from the floor. He watches me as I pull on my knickers then lift my bra.

"You're leaving?" he asks.

To this, I just give him a look, stepping into my dress to pull it up my body.

"Please don't," he says, moving toward me.

I pause to look at him, and he sighs, taking a step closer.

"I shouldn't have said that. It was a fucking dick move. *I'm* a dick. I'm sorry." His eyes are wide-open and sincere. "Stay."

I don't want to leave. I want to stay. More than that, I want to rewind ten minutes and take back the stupid comment about him being the biggest man-whore in London. I want to go back to the way he looked at me when I first walked into his apartment. Anyway, he can't be the biggest man-whore in London because I'm pretty sure my brother is.

His hand comes up to cup my face, and he strokes my cheek softly as he nibbles on the inside of his bottom lip, waiting. "Please stay."

I feel myself soften, the horrible chill of the argument melting away. "I shouldn't have said what I did either," I admit. "I'm sorry too."

He debates his next words for a moment before wetting his lips with his tongue. "Look, Alex, you're not a million miles off . . . I may not have brought women back here or wowed them with my *lines*, but I've never treated them right either." He sighs loudly. "I've been a cunt to a *lot* of women. But I can't do anything about it now. I just need you to know it has nothing to do with us or you. We all have nasty shit we'd rather not think about or talk about or share with someone we're trying to impress." His mouth tugs up into a small smile.

I raise an eyebrow. "You're trying to impress me?"

"Always. And always fucking failing at it."

I lean up on my tiptoes to kiss him. "You're doing fine," I whisper.

His smile grows against my mouth as our lips meet, my tongue teasing his gently. With an arm around my waist, he pulls me into him, and I hear him moan. God, I love when he makes that sound. When I pull back, his eyes are heavy-lidded.

"Actually, I'd like to redact that. You've failed at impressing me with your cooking. I'm about to pass out from starvation."

He grins before leaning forward to stroke his nose softly against mine.

It's that same sweet gesture he did in the restaurant that night, and I find I still love it. It's soft and intimate and totally unexpected.

"Well, I can fix that," he says as he pulls back. He looks almost excited. "Prepare to be fucking impressed." He moves away from me and steps into his jeans, buttoning them quickly before lifting his T-shirt. I watch his lean, muscular, tattooed body flex with the movement as he does. I'm bloody starving.

He seems pleased by my appraisal, that sexually arrogant look on his face again as he rights his T-shirt and drags a hand through his hair.

"Will you tell me about your tattoos one day?" I ask as I walk toward him, turning so he can zip up my dress from behind.

"What do you want to know?"

I shrug. "What they mean, which one came first, if you're getting more."

He makes a soft noise as he finishes zipping the dress. I turn to face him. His eyes are intense again. Dark with want.

"They remind me of where I've been, what I've done, where I'm going. The angel on my right bicep was first, and yes . . ."—he steps forward into my body again, pressing himself against me—"I plan on getting a few more."

I wasn't expecting a detailed explanation, and so I don't have a follow-up question ready, but I like that he answered. So now I ask questions, and he answers them. It's progress.

"Would you cook for me naked if I asked you to?" I say.

He pulls back and fixes me with one of those heavy, sexy stares. "Course I would. Would you be naked too? You know, so I'm not at a disadvantage."

I bite back a smile, giving him a confused look instead. "I don't see how you being naked is disadvantageous for anyone."

"Okay, maybe not for you, but it might be for the guy handling hot food." He points at himself. "So how about you get naked for me while I cook, and I'll get naked for you after?"

"I've just got dressed." I tut.

He makes a small disappointed noise and smiles, nodding. "Okay, let's both wait until we've eaten then, yeah?" He brings a hand up to my chin and pinches it tenderly between his thumb and forefinger. Another cute gesture that only makes me fall a little more. Leaning in, he pecks me on the lips, then he takes my hand and leads me downstairs. "Come on, Doctor. Time to be impressed."

NINETEEN

"WINE?" HE ASKS OVER HIS SHOULDER AS I TAKE A SEAT ON one of the barstools.

"Mmm, yes, please." I nod.

I could check my emails while he cooks, I suppose. Being out of the surgery all afternoon always makes me anxious about what I might walk into in the morning. I slip back off the stool to go get my laptop from my work bag and take out my MacBook. He sets a large glass of red down in front of me as I sit back down.

"Thank you." I take a long, welcome sip. It's good. Rich and dark and maybe even French. He must have gone to some effort to pick it for me since he doesn't drink wine. An image of him asking the woman in Waitrose which wine he should get for me is adorable.

He lifts a remote and presses a button before something folksy floats through the sound system into the kitchen. It's a far cry from the angry rock playing in his car the night of our date.

"You have work to do?" he asks, nodding toward the computer.

I shake my head. "Not really. I just need to check my emails quickly."

"Well, this won't take too long. About forty minutes, maybe. Did most of the prep earlier," he tells me.

I relax on the stool and watch as he goes about the kitchen removing things from various places: green vegetables and an oven dish from the fridge, a large silver pot from a cupboard beneath the sink, utensils from their hanging places above the cooker. I've opened my laptop and switched it on, but I haven't even looked at the screen, too absorbed in watching him being domesticated. It's curious. Again, unexpected. He has a gracefulness of movement I've never noticed before. His body is strong and powerful, but it's never clumsy or heavy-handed. Everything he does, he does with assuredness and confidence—even rinsing potatoes and chopping asparagus.

I sigh girlishly and log into my personal email first. There's one from

Tash that I open immediately. My sister, house hunting again in Malibu. Apparently, Brad got the big promotion at work they were hoping for. She wants to Skype on Sunday night for a catch-up. I type out a quick reply congratulating Brad and arranging a time for Sunday.

Now Rob knows, and we're an "us," and I'm spending the night at his flat, I think it's time to mention Jake to Tash. I'll tell her, and she'll squeal and want to know everything, of course. She won't say anything to Mum or Dad if I ask her not to—which I will. They're a step too far for right now. Mum will want to grill him over roast lamb and potatoes and find out through a variety of far too personal questions whether he's good enough for me.

Suddenly, I remember about Robyn's dinner party on Friday, and a small, nervous ball forms in my tummy. As I look up, I see him put a pot steamer on the hob. As though he senses my stare, he looks up too and smiles a boyish smile at me, making my insides stir.

"You're so fucking impressed right now, aren't you?" he says.

I nod, sipping my wine. "Mmm, I've never wanted you more. You slaving over a hot stove for me—definitely one of my fantasies."

"One of?" His smile turns heated. "So then, later, I'll get you to tell me the rest, and I'll see what I can do about them." He holds my stare for a moment before moving to pour water into a pot from the boiled kettle. As he does, I wonder how that conversation would go. *You against that window in your office. You in an upstairs room of a party while everyone else is downstairs. You in a slightly public place. You on my Steinway . . .*

I feel my cheeks flush and look away from him, back down at my emails.

There doesn't seem to be anything urgent in either my personal or work emails, and so I close the laptop and take another sip of my wine, resting my head on my hand to watch him work. He really is ridiculously gorgeous. A fierce, dangerous kind of gorgeous that's always excited me. Even here, cooking me dinner, he has that same edge, and it gives me a heady feeling to see him like this. I somehow manage to stop myself from doing another pathetic dreamy sigh before sitting up.

"So, you never said what you got up to today. Apart from watching your well-paid cleaner earn her wages."

He chuckles. "I went to the gym for a few hours, prepped the dinner, popped into the club for a bit."

A few hours in the gym? Well, that explains a lot. I wonder how many days a week he spends a "few hours" in the gym. It's impossible to stop the image that floats through my mind then. Of him working out, dripping with sweat, groaning with exertion. I lift my wineglass and take a deep, thirsty gulp. He notices my glass is almost empty and reaches out to take it, moving to refill it without a word. When he returns, he bends down to kiss me, deep and sensual. He licks his lips as he pulls back.

"Wine tastes better from your mouth," he says, eyes fiery.

I smile, cheeks warm. "They do say you develop a taste for it over time."

"Oh, I've got a taste for it all right . . ." It's said low and filthy and with so much innuendo I can't help but laugh. Jake smiles back.

The sound of a pot boiling over grabs his attention, and he goes toward it.

"You're distracting me even with your fucking clothes on, Alex."

"Well, I want your best culinary effort, Lawrence, so perhaps I'll sit in here, shall I?" I throw a glance back at him over my shoulder as I move into the living room.

"Yeah, probably a good idea."

I pick my handbag up on the way past and fish out my phone as I flop down on his large corner sofa. There are missed calls from Mum and Nick and a text from Robyn asking if Jake can make dinner on Friday so she knows how many places to set. I decide to ignore Mum for tonight. She'll only want to know where I am, and I don't like lying to her, so I hit the button to return Nick's call.

"Hey, sis, how's it going?" He sounds chirpy.

"Great, you? You called. Everything okay?"

"Yeah, everything's fine this end. You spoke to Mum tonight yet?"

"She called, but I missed it. Why?" I ask ominously.

"Where are you?"

I look over at Jake, who's busy setting the cutlery on the large wooden dining table by the window. "At a friend's, in town."

"A guy friend?"

I sigh. "Maybe."

He makes a whistling noise. "So, you saw Ben today, huh?"

"At a conference I was at, yes. Why? What's going on?"

Nick makes a weird groaning noise as if he'd rather not be discussing this. "So, apparently, Harrie rang Mum tonight. Ben told her he saw you with some guy today. Christ, I sound like some gossiping old lady. And he told her he *didn't like the look of the guy* or something, so Harrie told Mum that, and, well, you know what Mum's like. Then she worried when she couldn't get hold of you and so called me. But you're fine. Which I told her you would be."

I feel my entire body clench and my teeth grit. Bloody Ben. So now I'll have to have a discussion about Jake with my parents whether I want to or not. Jake, who he has already planted a bad seed about in their minds. Bloody wanker.

"He's unbelievable," I say through gritted teeth, shaking my head.

"Yep. Still a total prick then?"

"Some things in life are constant," I mutter.

"So, who's the guy? Someone new?" Nick asks, curious. "Got Ben's knickers in a twist seeing you with him, looks like." He sounds pleased by this.

When I turn to look over at Jake again, he's bent over, staring through the glass door of the oven.

"New, yes. I'll tell you when I see you next," I promise. "Listen, can you do me a favor though? Call Mum back and tell her I'm fine. I can't go into this with her right now. It'll end up about Ben, and I don't want to go there. Not tonight."

"Sure, I'll call her back," he says. "Oh, before I forget, are you free Saturday? To come through? There's someone I want you to meet." His tone is almost shy, and it shifts my attention immediately from Ben to Nick.

"Oh my god, you've not met someone," I gasp.

He makes that same groaning noise again. "Are you busy or not?" I practically feel him squirm down the phone.

"Tell me."

"Oh, for Christ's sake, Al. You sound like Mum, you know?" he groans impatiently.

Sensitive. It's not normally a tone I hear from him about his love life. Yes, this is serious all right.

"Yes, I'm free. What time?"

"Come over about 4:00 p.m.? I'll book a table somewhere for the three of us. We can meet up with Seb later. Cleo and Tom, who you've met before, are up from Brighton."

"At least tell me his name, Nicholas." I'm grinning like an idiot.

"Jin," he sighs, but his voice is warm when he says the name.

"Jin . . .?" I giggle childishly. "Like the drink?"

"No, Jin, like the hot piece of ass you'll be meeting on Saturday."

I burst out laughing. I really shouldn't take anything away from the significance of this though; my man-whore brother finally mentioning someone of importance to me is huge. It isn't a part of his life he flaunts loudly. Not because he's ashamed, but because Mum and Dad still didn't know he prefers men to women. Mainly because Tash and I have been quietly holding onto this massive truth for him for the past ten years since a tearful, nervous coming-out on his twenty-first.

"Okay, I'm going now, Alex," Nick groans. "See you Saturday."

"Can't wait to meet him."

"Goodbye . . ." he mutters.

"Bye, and Nick, remember to call Mum for me!" I squeeze in before he hangs up. I turn around to find Jake staring at me from a few feet away.

"Nick. Your brother?" he asks, looking as though he hopes he didn't misremember.

I nod. "Yes. He's met someone. This is big. I'm meeting them on Saturday." It's automatic, the use of the gender-neutral pronoun. Years of practice so as not to inadvertently spill his secret to anyone. I don't particularly want to keep it from Jake though, and I suppose I'm also curious to know whether there's any prejudice there. So, I add, "Meeting *him*, I mean. His boyfriend." It sounds strange coming from my mouth. Nick has a boyfriend. I almost want to squeal with excitement at what this might mean.

Jake's eyes widen a fraction, but he smiles warmly, nodding. Something eases inside me.

"This is almost done, if you wanna sit down."

"Oh, I want to sit down. I'm utterly famished." I pick up my wineglass and go to take a seat at the dining table, which he's set with black fabric place mats, water, and contemporary cutlery.

Jake brings the wine over and tops my glass up again before setting the bottle in the center.

"Have I mentioned I'm so impressed?" I say, looking up at him.

"Let's wait until you've tasted it, yeah?" He smiles.

I watch as he takes an oven dish from the oven and plates it up. I'm utterly in awe of how relaxed and not at all stressed he looks. If I were cooking for him at home, I'd be sweating and panicked and worried about poisoning him. But I'm not the greatest cook.

Suddenly, I don't care about any of that though. Suddenly, I want to slave over a hot stove for him. Suddenly, I want to be some 1950s housewife who does his washing and has his dinner ready and waiting for him when he comes home.

Jesus Christ, what is wrong with me? As he puts the plate down in front of me, my stomach growls at the sight of his creation.

"It's Parmesan and red pesto chicken with steamed potatoes and asparagus," he announces unceremoniously. "Hope you like it."

It looks and smells divine, and I pick up my knife and fork, cutting into it immediately. On the first mouthful, I know he can cook. It's heavenly—succulent, juicy, and cooked to perfection. I give him a wide-eyed stare.

"Jake, this is amazing," I say with my mouth half-full.

He smiles and nods, looking pleased, before picking up his cutlery to tuck into his own. "They serve it at Leo's place. He gave me the recipe."

We eat in comfortable silence, mainly because I'm starving and want to eat this delicious plate of food rather than talk. I can tell he's watching me though, and as I look up I momentarily worry I look more like a caveman. Frankly, I'm too hungry to care.

"So, are you still okay for Robyn's dinner on Friday? I'm not promising the food will be as good as this, but she normally does something edible."

He nods, chews his food, then swallows. "If you still want me to come, I'll come."

"I do. I want you to come. I'd like you to meet her."

He nods again. "So, Robyn was with you at the club that night?" he asks before putting another forkful in his mouth.

"Yes. She was the tall, gorgeous blonde."

Jake shrugs before his eyes turn heated. "I don't remember. Was sort of focused on someone else that night."

My mind drifts back to that night in his office when I laid eyes on him for the second time. How completely certain I was that I'd never see him again, and how completely relieved I am to be wrong.

I stretch my feet out under the table, grazing my bare feet against his slightly. As I look back down at my plate, I see I'm only a few more mouthfuls away from finishing the entire thing. It was delicious.

"Well, that was incredible," I tell him as I set down my knife and fork atop the plate. "You'll have to make it again for me sometime." I wash down my last mouthful with the rich wine, and it's only then I glance at the bottle. It's Bordeaux.

So, he bought me French wine.

"I definitely will." He nods, still chewing.

I can't believe I finished my entire plate before he did. I push the plate away and sit back in my chair to observe him. Then I remember watching someone eat isn't polite, so I look around his stunning apartment and try to imagine him living here. Doing normal day-to-day activities such as lounging on the sofa, watching TV, and eating cereal. Not cleaning though, because he has a cleaner for that.

Ben once mentioned getting a cleaner, citing we were both too busy for housework. What I think he was saying was that he wasn't happy with my domestic skills and I needed help.

"I'm glad you stayed," Jake says, nudging into my thoughts. He's finished eating and so sets down his cutlery and picks up his bottle of beer.

"Me too. I like it here."

"So, you're impressed then?" He gestures toward my empty plate.

"So impressed. Who knew you could cook? Or that you had a cleaner?"

"I did."

I laugh and feel him reach out with his feet to touch mine, gentle, soft. "Yes, well, it's not as if you're forthcoming with this kind of stuff now, are you?" I keep my tone light.

"If you'd asked me whether I could cook or if I had a cleaner, I'd have told you."

"Does that mean I can ask you something about yourself right now?" I sit back in my chair and bring my glass to my lips, gazing at him over the rim.

He doesn't shift in that uncomfortable way he did at dinner as though he wanted to bolt. "Only if I get to ask you something too."

"I've got nothing to hide."

He raises an eyebrow. There's something mischievous in his eye. "That a yes then?"

"Yes. Go on. Ask me whatever you want."

He pretends to think about it, because I'm sure as soon as the idea came into his head, he knew what he wanted to ask me. "Did you think about me after we first met? After that night. After you fixed me."

My breath catches at the intensity in his eyes. At the raw openness in them. I wonder how disappointed he might look if I say no. I swallow thickly, too hot all of a sudden.

"Yes."

He likes this. The side of his mouth lifts into a satisfied smirk. "What did you think about?"

"Does that mean I get two questions too?" I sip my wine, my eyes locked on his.

"Okay, baby, deal."

A brief flutter of triumph moves through me. I'm not planning to ask him anything serious—no way do I want to return to the heavy atmosphere that reared its head at dinner the other night—but he doesn't know that.

"I thought about how I might like to see you again." I give him a small smile and take another sip of my wine.

"That all?"

I thought about you turning up at the surgery and fucking me silly in the back of your car. "Mm-hmm. That's all."

He chuckles. "Well, if it makes you feel better, I thought about you a lot too. I'm happy to go into a bit more detail, but I'm pretty sure we banned that sort of talk from the dinner table." He smiles sexily at me, just for a change.

"We did," I say, but it's too breathy. Too needy.

We stare at each other like that for a few heavy seconds before he shakes his head as though to clear it and moves to stand up. When he reaches over for my plate, my brain finally kicks back to life, and I stand too, lifting my plate as well so we both have a handle on it.

"Let me clear them. You cooked," I offer.

He shakes his head and nods toward the sofa. "Nah, loading the dishwasher is another of my skills," he says. I'm about to insist, but his eyes go serious. "Go. You're distracting me again." He gestures toward the sofa and pulls the plate out of my hold.

I sigh dreamily and refill my wineglass before padding across to the sofa.

After flopping down, I pick up my phone to text Rob and tell her Jake will be there on Friday. There's a text. From Ben. My light, happy, relaxed mood disappears in an instant.

Ben: We need to talk, Alex. Call me please. Love Ben x

The "Love Ben x" makes my blood boil. I swipe angrily out of his message and tap out the text to Rob before throwing my phone back in my bag, fuming.

A moment later, Jake strolls into the lounge, fresh beer in hand and

T-shirt faintly damp at the front from the sink. He sits down next to me and moves to lift the remote, flicking the TV on. He spreads his arm along the back of the sofa and gives me a look of invitation, so I slide across and into his body, tucking my legs up and under myself. It feels warm and comforting, and the smell of him as I lean my head on his chest is intense. I feel him place a kiss on the top of my head, inhaling deeply.

"There's probably nothing on," he says as he flicks through the channels. He lingers briefly on a football match and then mutters an apology and turns it over.

"It's fine—watch it if you like. I'm enjoying lying here," I tell him. I feel warm and full. It's partially from the wine and great food, but mainly, it's from his arms. I also like the idea of being curled up next to him watching TV.

"Do you like football?" he asks lightly.

"Not particularly." I smile with my eyes closed. It's one of the few things I hate. My underhanded, manipulative ex being another. "But I'm happy if you're happy," I add.

He leans down to plant a kiss on the top of my head again, his free hand stroking gently over my arm—soft, light touches that tickle and tease at the same time.

"I'm happy," he says and promptly turns the TV off. "So, tell me about your sister in America. Natasha, is it? You must miss her," he asks, hand moving up and into my hair.

My eyes close over. Having my hair played with is one of the things I love most in the world, and having him do it only makes it better.

"Mmm, I do. She's so happy there though, so I don't think she'll ever come back. Which I don't blame her for at all—I'd go in a heartbeat. My parents would be devastated though. And I'd never want to leave Nick."

"You'd leave the UK? Move there?"

I sigh longingly. "California is another world. The weather, the lifestyle. It makes everything here seem tiny and boxed in. Wet too." I laugh. "I think about the life my children would have over there, and I'd really want *that* for them, you know?"

"So, you want children then?" he asks.

My eyes fly open. God. Did I seriously mention having children on a second date? Panic peels over me. I try to keep my voice distinctly non-nutcase-like as I answer.

"I meant more generally. That if I do, when I do, the idea of raising children somewhere like California really appeals to me." I shrug, hoping it comes off as nonchalant.

"Does your sister have kids?"

I shake my head and sit up so I can see him. Tash and Brad have been trying for a while now, and though I know she isn't too fussed about when it happens, I know he's definitely more impatient about it all. "Not yet. I'm hoping for a niece or nephew soon though." It makes me giddy thinking about it.

He's looking at me now, eyes narrowed in study.

"What?"

"I guess I'm surprised at *you* wanting a different life from the one you have now," he says, sounding genuinely bemused. "Your life here seems pretty fucking good to me. Respectable job, nice house, a family who love you."

Something like guilt stings me. Considering his shitty start, I've had a perfect life here, and in loads of aspects, I do. Of course, to him, it makes no sense to move it thousands of miles away.

"I do have a good life. I'm really lucky, I know that. But I feel like . . . I don't know . . . as though something's missing in it, you know? I've always felt as if I should be living a different life somewhere else. As if I'm missing out on something." I look away from him as I say this because I sound spoiled and ungrateful, and I'm failing to properly explain what I mean.

Though his gaze is heavy, pulling my eyes back to his, his expression is soft. "I know exactly what you mean," he says, nibbling on the inside of his cheek. "I've always felt a bit like that myself, as if I'm living someone else's life or something. Guess I'm surprised at you feeling that way too."

I frown. "Why?"

He thinks about this. Shrugs. "I don't know . . . I guess because you're sorta perfect." His mouth is soft with the hint of a smile. I wait for him to laugh at his own line, but he doesn't.

I can only frown harder. "I'm not perfect, Jake."

"Yeah, well, to me you are," he says almost dismissively before leaning over to kiss my open mouth. The kiss is chaste but deep at the same time, a steady build that turns my insides molten and soft. He finishes by sucking gently on my bottom lip then pressing his lips to the tip of my nose.

As he pulls back from me and I drink in the sight, his kissed red lips and green, sparkling eyes, a weird, nihilistic thought enters my brain. If this doesn't work out between us, how on earth do I ever get over him? How do I forget these quiet moments in which he makes me feel so utterly and completely alive? It's a ridiculous thought. Negative and silly, and I feel a little ashamed by it. But it doesn't change the fact it's true.

After, Jake moves our bodies so I'm lying with my head on his chest as we look out on the London skyline. He strokes his hand lazily up and down my spine. The night is clear and dark, and the reflection of the stars and the city lights across the water is picturesque, almost romantic. It's as amazing as I thought it'd be.

The feel of his steady, vital heartbeat through his chest is loud against my ear, but it's so reassuring, so strong. I feel that same nihilistic thought I felt on the couch: I'll never get over him. It's made all the more ridiculous by the fact I barely know him. But do you need to know every single part of a person for them to have such a huge and lasting impact on your life? I've never believed it.

I remember a man I met in the Louvre once. I went alone one day while Rob lay nursing her hangover in the hotel. I met him in the Denon Wing beside a painting of Napoleon where he told me how he was a descendant of Napoleon through his sister. We only spent about twenty minutes in each other's company, but I think about him now and then whenever I see an elderly man at the deli, or whenever an elderly male patient comes in to see me.

In any case, I don't need to know everything about Jake to feel what I feel for him. It doesn't mean I don't want to though.

"What are you like when you're not with me?" I ask, my voice sleepy. His stroking across my spine doesn't waver or stop.

"Hmm?" He also sounds sleepy.

"You said before that you're different when you're with me. I keep wondering what you meant by that."

I feel his body tense slightly. "Did you come to any conclusions?"

"Not really. I have one context for you, and it involves you being naked." I laugh.

He's covered with his light gray sheet, but I see the faint outline of his growing erection. My mouth waters slightly.

"Well, that's me at my best, baby. What other context do you need?"

I smile and run my hand over his ridged stomach, across the lettering that makes me want to eradicate all his exes from his memory. No—not all of them. The one he cared about enough to etch permanently into his skin. I itch to ask him about it. About her. I turn my head to stare up at him, and my stomach somersaults. He looks breathtaking in this light. Just fucked. His mouth tilts into a lazy half-smile.

"Seriously though, what did you mean by it?" I ask.

Something flits over his eyes, and I think he's not going to answer. Make some excuse up about him not being interesting or that he was joking. But then he takes a long, deep breath and speaks.

"I guess I'm saying that . . . well, I'm not good enough for you—I'm aware of that." He says it with the same sincere tone he used to tell me I was perfect. I move to sit up, to disagree, to tell him not to be ridiculous, but he stills me with his eyes. "So, when I'm with you, I try to be better, I guess. That's all I meant."

It's a beautiful sentiment, I suppose, but it still makes me frown. "What makes you think you're not good enough for me?" I try not to let my voice do that high, accusatory thing it does sometimes.

He cups my cheek. "I don't think it; I know it. You deserve better."

I sit up taller then. "Jake, stop saying that. I—"

"I'm not the person you think I am, okay?" he says, cutting me off. He seems to think better of his tone and reaches out to take my hand, pulling me closer.

I frown, confused. "What does that even mean? Who is it I think you are? Is this you now? Here?"

He nods. "Yeah, fuck, when I'm with you, this is who I want to be. But I'm still not a nice guy, Alex. I meant that when I said it."

There's something like a warning in his eyes. Not warning me away from the subject, but away from him. I consider this for a moment then lean in to press my mouth to his. His lips are wet and soft, and the kiss turns heavy far quicker than I expect.

"I thought we already established I don't want a nice guy," I whisper against his mouth.

He lets out a small, needy groan. "That's because you don't know what's good for you." His voice is low, licked with need.

Something unfurls inside me, and I hook my leg over his thighs and sit up so I'm straddling him. His head falls back against the headboard to look up at me, arousal clear in his eyes.

"*You're* good for me, Jake," I say, my eyes fixed on his. When I grind my hips into him, he lets out a delicious groan. So, I do it again. "You're so good for me."

"Fuck, baby . . ." His hands slide around my hips, holding me in place as he rocks upward, his cock thickening against my thigh. He drops his mouth to my nipple and sucks one into his mouth as I continue to move on top of him.

I think I could come from this—from the feel of muscle between my legs and the wet heat of his mouth sucking at my skin.

One day, I'll know all of Jake's secrets. Every last one of them. But it won't change how good *this* is; how good *he* is for me. It can't. It's not possible. I won't let it.

TWENTY

I AWAKE TO THE SMELL OF TOAST AND FRESH COFFEE AND THE distinctly chilly absence of him. Jake's digital clock by the bed tells me it's 6:20 a.m. I should move, but it feels beyond me. I'm comfortable and warm, and the sheets around me smell like him. When I stretch my body out to shake off the sleep, I'm sore. A delicious, Jake-inflicted sore I can more than live with. With a soft groan, I slide over and out of the bed.

It takes me a moment to figure out how to turn his modern shower on, but once I do, I step under the spray with a sigh, closing my eyes in bliss under its power. When I open them to retrieve some bodywash, Jake is standing in the doorframe, watching me with a riveted expression on his face. My instinct is to cover myself, but I resist, letting his gaze travel over my body as I lather the bodywash into my skin.

"Need any help in there?" he asks, the corner of his mouth twitching.

I smile. "I've done this before. I think I can manage."

He nods and proceeds to watch me. He's wearing dark gray boxers, and the sight of his bare chest and thick thighs is distracting. As I glance down his body, I see the unmistakable sign of interest between his legs.

"Ask me to come in there with you," he says, low.

My voice is shaky as my breathing starts to spiral. "Come in here with me."

His smile is slow and sexy as he slides his boxers down his legs and steps gracefully into the stall. He moves closer, tipping his head under the water, then closes the distance between us so I'm pressed between him and the cool marble.

"Fuck, I like you wet," he says, bringing his mouth to the side of my neck as I slide my hands around his body to his perfect behind.

"I like you wet too," I whisper, and he pulls back to smile. Then he kisses me slow and messy, the water running between our mouths and bodies noisily.

"You know, normally, when I'm in here, I'm imagining this is happening. Now, it is."

He's thought about this? About me in here with him? The idea makes me ridiculously hot, ridiculously turned on. He presses his lips to mine again, sucking the water from my mouth.

"Do you imagine that a lot?" I ask as he begins to mouth at the side of my neck, my collarbone, my shoulder. His erection presses thick and urgent against my tummy now.

He chuckles. "Every day since I first saw you," he says. "Sometimes twice a day."

We met almost four weeks ago.

His hands are tender and slow as they sweep across my body, cleaning, caressing. He kisses me again, long and slow, while his hands massage the soap into my skin. When his hands move between my thighs, I automatically part them a little, moaning as he massages the ache he left there.

Ben and I never showered together, not in eight years. We shared a few baths in that time, but showering with him never appealed to me. I always imagined it would be an awkward, mangled experience with lots of cold patches. Perhaps it's all down to Jake, but it's not awkward or mangled at all.

"Put your hands above your head for me," he says softly. When I do, he smooths his hands down over my sides, my hips. "I like you like this too." He bends his head to flick his tongue across my nipple, tauntingly gentle. It makes my fingers curl with need. My arms are starting to weigh a ton though, so I rest them on the strong, wet expanse of his back.

"Now, turn around," he says, standing up again.

I smile at him. "You're very thorough."

"Told you I wasn't anti-bathing." He smirks. "Now, turn around."

When I'm facing the marble, I place my palms flat on the shower wall. He slides a hand down my back and over my butt before leaving my body completely. I hear the sound of squirting and more lathering, and then they're on me again, starting at my shoulders. It's hypnotizing and relaxing but arousing too, and I close my eyes to heighten the pleasure of it.

When he reaches my butt, he massages each cheek gently, hands squeezing and releasing several times. Next, he slides his hand between my legs, grazing the ache that's been building there softly—too softly. I gasp. Then I feel him, the length of him, sliding between my cheeks, hard and wet.

He groans as his mouth latches onto my shoulder and tilts his hips into me. "Open your legs for me, Alex," he says in a rough voice. I do it immediately, and then his fingers are teasing me open before a finger slips inside.

Pressing my forehead to the cool stone, I bite down on my lip as his finger moves against me. As I focus on it, I realize there's something vaguely clinical about it. It's as though he isn't trying to pleasure me; he's simply cleaning me. The heat continues to build though, the knot inside me coiling as I try to stay still and open for him while the inside of my body tightens with desire.

Suddenly, he grabs my hip with one hand and spins me around so my back is pressed against the wall. Then he drops to his knees and lifts my leg to hook it over his shoulder. The look in his eye as he stares up at me is filthy, hungry, and filled with intent. He dips his head and drags his tongue the entire length of me, sliding and sucking along every part. When I look down at him, the sight of his wet, gorgeous body almost makes me orgasm instantly.

I feel his hand join his mouth, and he teases me open more to angle me deeper into his mouth. It's perfect, every nerve focused on that point—the point where his fingers and tongue meet. My legs wobble, and I have to clutch onto him to steady myself.

"Jake . . . god . . ."

"Does it feel good when I fuck you like this, baby?" he asks, replacing his tongue with another finger. He crooks them just right inside me, and I gasp loudly.

His cheek is resting against my thigh as he stares up at me, the water resting neatly on his eyelashes. Instead of responding, I make a small, frantic noise I hope answers his question.

"Does it?" His voice is firmer this time.

"Yes . . . god, yes," I manage, grinding against him, greedy for my climax. I fist my hands in his hair and fix him with a desperate stare. "Please."

He presses his lips to my thigh, sucking loudly. I squeeze my eyes closed tight. Was that his tongue again? It doesn't take too long once his mouth is back on me, so intense is the feeling, so expertly has he built it. My orgasm is an endless wave, pulsing white-hot through my whole body. I'm panting as he raises himself to stand, kissing his way up my body as he does. His fingers continue to move against me—softer now, careful.

I let out a stupid laugh as I open my eyes. "I think I'll be thinking about that in the shower from now on too . . ."

His cheeks are flushed, his eyes a bright, glittering blue-green, and his smile smug. He leans forward and presses me against the wall with his body to kiss me slow and deep again. He's painfully hard against me, and when I look down at him I see he's red and flushed too. I reach out to wrap my hand around him, delighting in the deep groan that falls from his lips.

"Okay. Your turn . . ." I smile.

We pull up to the surgery just before 8:30 a.m., Jake managing to somehow make light work of the heavy rush-hour traffic from Central London out. He leaves the engine idling and turns in his seat to face me. He's wearing sunglasses, so I can't see his eyes, but he's smiling.

"Well, thanks for letting me stay over. And for dinner last night. And breakfast this morning." He made me buttery toast and jam and a coffee from his fancy machine. Meanwhile, he tucked into an egg-white omelet and some grapefruit juice. I enjoyed having breakfast with him.

"My pleasure," he says. "Thanks for the shower." He takes off his shades, and his smile turns to a smirk.

"Hope it lived up to the fantasy." I smile, staring at his mouth. "I'd hate to disappoint."

"Yeah, that's never gonna happen, so I wouldn't worry."

I feel the blush hit my cheeks then my ears. "So, I'll see you tomorrow? For Dinner?"

Jake nods and reaches across the space, casually brushing my hair back away from my face. "Yeah. Tomorrow. Robyn's. The tall, gorgeous blonde." His eyes are playful. "Call me later, and we can sort it out, yeah?"

"I will." I nod.

He leans forward first, placing an almost chaste kiss on the side of my mouth before it deepens to something heavier, hotter. When he pulls back, I'm breathless, and the taste of his tongue swims over my own.

"So . . . we'll talk later," I say.

"Yeah . . . later."

I open the passenger door and climb out, smoothing down my dress and hair as I walk around the front of the car toward the pavement. I hear the window going down, and so I turn back.

"How corny is it if I say I miss you already?"

I smile like a twelve-year-old girl. "Maybe the corniest."

"Okay, then I liked waking up with you."

It's embarrassing how weak my legs go as I bite back a grin. "Me too. It's a pity your bed isn't as comfortable as mine," I sigh.

He puts on a hurt face, but there's a smile hidden there. "Your bed was pretty comfy. I have to agree."

"Well, tomorrow, if you're a good boy and you behave, I'll let you have a sleepover at mine."

Jake grins, and it's adorable, and I feel myself fall a little further. "A good boy, huh? First time for everything, I suppose."

I roll my eyes, but it's playful. "Speak to you later, Jake." I wave over my shoulder as I climb the steps of the converted townhouse.

He waits until I'm in the front door before pulling away, the sound of his car roaring off down the street as I walk into reception.

When I get home from work later, Fred is most definitely grumpy with me. I know because when I open the front door, he's sitting on the bottom step of the stairs staring at me accusingly. He gives me a withering look before sauntering off into the kitchen. No coming to lie at my feet for belly strokes, and no bumping his head against my legs.

On the fridge is a note from Ed saying Fred has been fed and my keys are back in the flower pot. I make a mental note to take over a bottle of wine as a thank-you later in the week. I honestly have the best neighbors a single woman with a cat could ask for.

Though maybe, technically, I'm not single anymore.

I put some food out for Fred and then go to the fridge to see if I have anything for myself to eat, eventually closing it on a bored sigh. I need to do some shopping this week. Mentally, I pencil in a trip to Waitrose for Sunday afternoon before my Skype with Tash—presuming I'm not too hungover after catching up with Nick and his new man.

I can't believe my brother has met someone. Nick's dating someone seriously, and I'm sleeping with a tattooed, self-proclaimed bad-boy night-club owner. Looks as though the Marlowe kids have certainly come of age.

I somehow manage to forage a dinner of roasted veg and couscous from what I have in the pantry and get down to doing some work. I have a paper to examine for the peer review board that I sit on once a quarter, and I haven't even looked at it yet.

It's not long though before I'm no longer thinking about the benefits of a bottom-up merger of GP and pharmacy service provision and thinking instead about how I might be falling for someone I barely know. I think back to our chat last night about how he's "not the person I think he is." What does that even mean? Who *do* I think he is? Do I have a clue? Given how we met, I know our lives are drastically different. Of course I do. But apart from what he shared at dinner about his horrible childhood, how much do I actually know? Is the fact he's largely a mystery part of the attraction for me? Is that something he's doing on purpose, to keep me interested and make me want to know more? I've certainly never met a man like him before.

Once again, that familiar pull urges me toward him. I grab my phone to check for any sign of life. There are no new messages from him, but then I did say I would call. I wonder if he's at the club and try not to think about ruses, seduction, and pretty barmaids. Wherever he is, at least I know he's not stupid enough to be wondering how the hell he's managed to fall halfway in love with someone he barely knows.

I try to get back into my paper, but my heart isn't in it. Instead, I lean over and stroke Fred who's curled up in a ball on the pillow beside me. At some point between the tin of tuna and the quarter pack of catnip-infused treats, he decided to forgive me.

With a sigh, I switch the computer off and resort to running myself a bath. A nice, luxurious soak in the tub is exactly what I need. That will give me the perfect opportunity to overthink me and Jake. I pour lavish amounts of bubble bath into my roll top, light a few scented candles about the bathroom, and put on my favorite modern classical album. As I slide into the bubbles, I reach for my phone again.

Me: About to get into the bath and thought of you. We should find out if it's big enough for two soon :) Are you working right now? A x

I smile, wondering whether if I asked him to come over right now, he would. I put the phone down and slip into the bath slowly, oohing and aahing at the temperature as it stings the tops of my toes and still achy parts. While I wait for him to respond, I enjoy the sound of the soft pop of bubbles around me.

So, I'm falling for him. I can manage it. It's quick, yes, and totally un-expected, but it's likely fueled by lust. Everything's sharp and more intense in these early days. I can almost remember what it felt like with Ben. This feels different, louder, but that's because I'm in it, surely?

Out of the corner of my eye, I see Fred walk into the bathroom, and I turn my head. My mind takes a second to process what it's seeing before I let out a small scream of shock.

Not Fred. Ben.

TWENTY-ONE

"**W**HAT THE BLOODY HELL ARE YOU DOING?" I SNAP, TRYING to lower myself into the water.

"You never called," he says. As if it answers my question at all. "You still keep a key in the plant pot."

I should have listened to Jake. Of course Ben is the other person who knows I do that.

"That doesn't mean you take it out and use it!"

He gives me an odd expression for a moment and then casts a look around the bathroom. "This used to be our house, Alex. We bought it together, remember?"

I can only blink in disbelief. "Used to be. You don't live here anymore, Ben. I want you to leave. Now." My voice is low and firm.

He sighs. It sounds almost sad. "Not until we talk. We need to sit down and have a proper conversation about this. Surely I deserve that much at least?" He must see the look in my eye because he rearranges his face into something softer and adds, "I mean, surely *we* deserve that much at least?"

Oh, his apologetic demeanor yesterday must have killed him. This is the Ben I know.

"I told you yesterday, there's nothing to talk about." It comes out gritted and sharp.

The side of his mouth twitches before he sighs. "I'll wait downstairs, Lex," he says and exits the bathroom.

I sit in the cooling water utterly defiant. I glance at my phone sitting on the ledge and contemplate calling Jake. But what good would that do? I'd have to explain the guy he saw me with yesterday wasn't an old friend, but my ex. I'd have to explain I lied to him. Why on earth did I lie?

Furious with Ben and annoyed at myself, I climb out of the bath and dry myself with hasty rubs of the towel over my body. Then, still half-damp, I wrap my bathrobe around myself and stomp downstairs.

He's sitting on the floral chair, his long—too long—legs crossed casually, finger scraping across his mouth as though deep in thought. The sight of him there looking like he used to look there leaves me cold. I wonder vaguely what he thinks of the color of the living room, which I painted the second weekend after he moved out. A deep green where his canary yellow used to be. Fred sits on the window ledge staring at him suspiciously.

"You have no right to be here. I don't want you here," I tell him, folding my arms as I come into the room.

He turns to look at me.

"Letting yourself in. How dare you?"

"I rang the doorbell, but you never heard it, so I checked the pot. You know it's not safe for you to do that now. Not when you live alone." He has the nerve to sound concerned.

I narrow my eyes. "Did it occur to you that I might not have been alone?"

His lip curls slightly for a second then relaxes again. "Oh, yes, your new boyfriend." He nods. "Is he here? Wouldn't mind introducing myself."

"You should be glad he isn't."

He only stares. "Sounds like you've not told your parents about him yet. Why's that then, Lex? He some kind of dirty little secret?"

"Fuck you," I retort.

His eyes flare angrily. "Don't talk like a common tart, Alex. It doesn't suit you. Unless, wait—is that his type?"

I want to scream some profanity or punch him, but I'm pretty sure those would also make him deem me a "common tart." I need to calm my breathing down, stop my hands from shaking.

"So, *this* is the conversation you wanted to have. No, thank you. I want you to leave."

His expression changes instantly. Becomes softer, apologetic. "No, it's not." He shakes his head. "It's not the conversation I wanted to have. I wanted to talk about us."

"And I told you yesterday, there *is* no us."

He sits forward in the chair, turning his body fully toward me. "I don't see how that can be true though, sweetheart. How can everything we had be gone?" His voice is gentle, and he shakes his head as though he's truly struggling to comprehend it.

I almost laugh. "You can't be serious."

His face is a picture of seriousness.

I take a few steps into the room. "Hmm, okay, how about when you were sleeping with your sales executive four nights a week for months before coming home to me? How about when you moved in with her the day after you left me?"

"The day after you kicked me out, Alex," he corrects.

I ignore that. "How about when you *proposed* to her after three months of living with her?"

"That was a rash mistake . . ."

"But fucking her wasn't? God, you are deluded if you think there is any way of us being together again. I mean, you are." I fold my arms again and straighten my spine, but I feel more tired than angry. Ben's betrayal still hurts on a basic level. Finding out someone you trusted lied to your face over and over again for a long time is hurtful on a basic level. But I don't care anymore because I don't love him anymore. I don't want to look at him anymore.

He's silent for a long time, eyes lowered to the floor as he considers what to say next. He lifts his head and fixes me with a soft, sincere look.

"I regret every day what I did, how I hurt you. We had everything . . ." He shakes his head and drops his eyes again. "I mean, we weren't perfect, and no, you never did what I did, but there were days when it was like . . . Christ, you barely looked at me. Barely noticed when I was in a room. It was as if you were waiting for something else . . . *Someone* else." He sounds desperately sad now, and I know there's truth in what he's saying. It makes a tiny sliver of guilt settle over me.

"And yet you were the one who slept with someone else, not me," I say, my voice sad now too.

It's a long time before he speaks again. "I miss us."

It's not the kindest or the most polite thing I've ever said, but this isn't a time for either of those. "I don't."

He blinks—shocked, I think. It's some time before he reacts at all. He nods once and stands up from the chair, coming toward me. He's taller than Jake, and his height and my lack of shoes mean he towers almost a foot above me. His height used to make me feel safe. It doesn't do that now. It makes me feel small. My state of undress only adds to the discomfort. My hands instinctively go to pull my robe tighter around me.

"Maybe you've forgotten what it felt like," he says quietly, eyes dropping to my mouth.

I've no time to think or respond before his mouth is on mine and he's pushing his tongue inside. I'm too stunned to react right away, until my brain ignites, and I push at his chest. His arms are strong though, and they're around me and pulling me in closer until I'm pressed against him.

"You still love me, Lex, I know you do," he mumbles as I twist my head away from his mouth. I feel his hand slip under my robe, and cold panic spreads over me. It's the only thing I can think of to do, so I bring my hand up and hit him. A slap, full force, on the side of his face. My palm stings from the impact. It does the job though, because he steps back immediately, looking shocked as he brings his hand to his cheek.

"What the hell was that?" I hiss at him.

"I thought if I kissed you, it would remind you." He sounds dazed.

"Remind me of what, exactly?"

"Of us. Of what we felt like."

"God, you really are delusional."

His face turns cold again, a small smile playing at the corners of his mouth. "Or maybe it's that you only go for thug cock now." He puts his hands up.

I flinch as though he's slapped me, my ears and cheeks burning from rage. The insult sounds so disgusting from his mouth it turns my stomach. I think about slapping him again. He's an even bigger prick than I remember.

I try to keep my voice calm as I speak my next words. "So, because you can't keep a woman anymore, you force yourself on them?" I nod, pulling my robe tighter around my body as the smug look evaporates from his face. "Your mother would be so proud of you right now, don't you think?"

It has the effect I want, the embarrassment clear on his face. He's speechless for a moment before he nods, the cool smile settling back over his mouth.

"Oh, you always were a prude, Lex." He sighs as he runs his hand through his hair. He looks smug, and I wonder how smug he'd look with Jake's fist across his face. A sadistic, unfamiliar part of me wants to find

out. "Could have been pretty good farewell sex if you'd let yourself go a little once in a while, bloody hell."

I grit my teeth. "The sex was never 'pretty good' to begin with, so
why on earth would it be any different now?" I ask.

He narrows his eyes again, clearly getting ready to hurl another insult, but he just lets out a small, empty laugh and turns to leave.

"Key," I hiss, holding out my hand.

He stops, turns, and smiles before reaching into his front trouser
pocket to pull out my spare keys with the cat key ring on them. I snatch
them from him.

"When you tire of your bit of rough—or rather, when he tires
of *you*—call me. I'm sure it won't be too long." Then, with one last smug
look, he turns and strides out of the room.

"Don't hold your bloody breath!" I shout after him pointlessly.

I wait until I hear the door close and the engine start up before I go
and lock the front door behind him, my hands still shaking with the remnants of rage and shock. I also lock the back door—something I rarely
ever do—before switching off all the lights downstairs. Fred whines as I
pick him up to carry him upstairs.

Out of everything he said tonight, Ben's words about Jake tiring of
me are the ones that play the loudest in my mind. Am I the kind of girl
men tire of? Did Ben tire of me? He said I stopped paying attention to
him, but maybe that's not really what happened.

I flop Fred down in the bed and go to retrieve my phone from the
floor by the bath. I need to hear his voice, chase away the doubts swirling
loud in my brain.

There's a message from him from almost an hour ago.

Jake: How the fuck am I supposed to concentrate on anything when
you're talking about being naked and wet? This place pretty much runs itself anyway. Say the words and I'm there, baby

God, I want him here now. Strong arms around me, warm body
pressed against me.

I feel like crying. A cold emptiness grows larger and larger inside
me. I thought I was done crying over Ben. Crying over how he makes me
feel. I hate that he still has this kind of power. Am I weak? Is this what

weak women do? Cry and worry over the words of men. Fall for others they barely know. Everything about what Ben said tonight was calculated. Because he knows me. He knows exactly what to say to hurt me. But he knows nothing about Jake, or about what we have, or about whether he will tire of me.

And you do? Is the dissenting reply that comes from somewhere in my head. Then I am crying. Stupid, unwanted tears that would please Ben immensely. Prick. I'm scrubbing at them angrily as I hear the doorbell go, causing me to practically jump out of my skin. He seriously dared to come back here?

As I contemplate what to do, my phone starts to ring in my hand. It's Jake. My chest eases immediately. I wait for a moment to see if Ben will ring the doorbell again before hitting the button to answer.

"Hi," I say. My voice sounds a little breathless from the crying, but I'm hoping he doesn't notice.

"Looks like you listened to me—your key isn't in the plant pot anymore."

I stand up from the bed. "You're here." It's more like a gasp of relief than a question.

"Outside. I wasn't gonna use it without asking, don't worry, but it's fucking cold out here . . ." He makes a "brrr" sound.

Relief washes over me, comforting like warm milk. I rush downstairs immediately and unlock the door.

"Hi."

His eyes roam over my entire body, lingering for a long time on my face. He frowns.

"Hey. You okay?"

I nod, feeling emotional again. He's here. When I needed him, without even knowing I did, he's here.

"I'm fine, just surprised to see you. Happy, but surprised."

He's frowning down at me now. "You been crying?"

He looks incredible as usual. He's wearing a fitted gray shirt open at the neck, tailored black trousers, and he has his suit jacket draped over his arm. His sandy brown hair is mussed as though he's been running his hands through it. I swallow and swipe a hand absently over my cheek, standing back to let him.

"Um . . . no, not really."

He frowns at this, reaching out to brush his thumb across my cheek. "What's going on, baby?"

Truth time, Alex. Get on it. I take a deep breath. "My ex. He was just here."

Some cloud of darkness settles over his eyes, his entire body stiffening. "Your ex was here?"

I nod, biting my lip hard as I meet his eye. "The guy from the hotel yesterday. The one you saw me with."

His eyes flicker again, nostrils flaring. "That guy was your ex?" I can't tell how angry he is because his voice is so low. He's silent for a long time.

I nod.

"Why'd you lie to me about it?"

I close my eyes as I shake my head. "I don't know. I shouldn't have. It just came out, and I didn't want you to think anything was going on, and—"

"He was just fucking here. What do you want me to think now?"

"Nothing! I never invited him here. But he came, and he wanted to talk."

"He wanted to talk." His voice is laced with doubt as his eyes skim over my state of relative undress.

"*Yes.* Talk."

He laughs at this, but it's cold. "All those old feelings come rushing back when you saw him yesterday, baby?"

My eyes go wide. "What? No, of course not. He wanted to talk yesterday, and I told him no. So, he turned up here."

"I guess that's why you looked so fucking close. Makes sense now." It's as if he hasn't even heard me. "Not a guy who's into you, a guy who used to fuck you. A guy you used to be in love with." He runs his hand over his mouth as he shakes his head. I notice his knuckles are red, but it barely registers. I'm too focused on the way he's looking at me and the tone of his voice. From so soft and warm to this. I want to cry again. "Thinking about him all night, weren't you, baby? What about when I was fucking you? Were you wishing it was him?" He isn't shouting anymore, but his voice is low and cold, which is worse. Far worse. I feel sick. How can he think that? Or say that?

It hits me then. This is the other side of him. This is who he is when he's not with me. This is a glimpse of the man people want to cut open with kitchen knives.

I feel the tears burning at the backs of my eyes.

"You think *that* little of me?" My voice sounds far too fragile. I hate it. He at least has the decency to look somewhat ashamed. "You know what, Jake? I've had enough of men making assumptions about me for one night. Think whatever you want. I'm going to bed." I turn from him and storm upstairs without looking back.

In the bedroom, I close the curtains and turn on the bedside lamps. When I turn around, he's at the door looking at me, his face a tense mix of emotions. Unlike Ben's gaze, which chilled me, Jake's makes my body heat rapidly. It always has.

"We weren't done, Alex," he says, his voice softer than it was.

"Weren't we?"

He sighs loudly and walks into the bedroom. "How the fuck can you blame me for being pissed off? You lied to me about who he was, then I turn up tonight and he's just fucking been here?"

I fold my arms and stare him down. "I'm not blaming you for being pissed off, Jake. I'm blaming you for accusing me of something that isn't true. For not letting me explain . . ."

"So why the fuck was he here?"

"I told you. He turned up here. *Uninvited.* To talk."

He looks down my body again, at the bathrobe again. "Right."

I pretend he hasn't spoken. "He let himself in though I told him yesterday it was over. There was nothing to talk about."

"He still has a key to your fucking house?" he cuts in.

"No. He knows about the key in the plant pot because it's something we did when we lived together."

Jake's mouth turns up at one side, almost a snarl.

"He let himself in. I was in the bath."

His face is dark with rage now. "He walked in on you? In the bath?"

I shift uncomfortably on my feet and swallow. I know how this is going to go, but I won't lie to him again. Not on Ben's account.

"He said he rang the doorbell for a while. I had music on, so . . ."

"He fucking watched you? In the bath?" It's not that he wants me to confirm it; it's as though he's trying to comprehend it or decide what to do about it. "You do realize if I ever see this cunt again, I'll kill him, don't you? I will fucking end him," he says. He sounds completely and utterly serious. It's almost frightening. I decide not to tell him about how he kissed me.

"I don't think he'll do it again . . ."

Jake makes a low noise. "Oh, he *definitely* fucking won't. Trust me."

"Jake, I don't want to talk about him anymore." My voice is soft and pleading. "He knows it's over now. That I'm with you now. Now, I need you to believe that."

Jake stares at me for the longest time, seeming to analyze every inch of my face before repeating the process over again. Anger has no negative effect on him in any way—he still looks as heartbreakingly gorgeous as he always does. I'll never tire of looking at him. Will he tire of me though, as Ben said?

Finally, he speaks. "You're *with* me?" His voice is quiet and faintly dubious.

I frown. "Of course I'm with you. Isn't that what this is?"

He lets out a breath. "Alex, I've honestly no fucking clue what this is."

The words scare me, panic flooding me. He doesn't know what this is? He sees something in my face and comes toward me, sliding a hand around my waist to pull me close. His other hand comes up to stroke the side of my face as he stares deep into my eyes.

"But if you tell me that it's you and me . . ." He trails off. "Then it's you and me, yeah? This kind of thing, being with someone . . . it's rare for me. Really fucking rare. Being with you is . . ." He shakes his head again, lost for words.

"Then there can't be an endless supply of secrets between us, Jake. Yes, I lied about Ben, but I've always been open with you. About who I am . . . about what I want and don't want. Can you say the same? When am I a safe pair of hands to you?"

I feel his grip on me tighten, and thoughts toss and swirl behind his eyes. I can see them. Can *almost* hear them.

"Alex, there's so much I want to tell you. So much you should know about me." He stares at where his fingers trace over my mouth.

"About why you're no good for me?"

He nods, chewing the inside of his cheek in that way he does.

I sigh. "But one day, you will? One day, you'll tell me everything?"

He gives me a long look and lowers his mouth to mine. I moan and press myself into him, sliding my arms up and around his neck as he deepens the kiss, his tongue roaming my mouth hungrily.

"Yeah," he breathes. "As soon as I know you won't leave me when I do, I'll tell you everything."

When his hand slides between my legs, I gasp loudly, latching onto his forearms to hold myself up. As he pushes me back onto the bed and begins to untie my robe, I let his mouth kiss away the last of my doubts. Right now, I need to feel his heat and his body and his mouth on me. Right now, I need to feel as though when I finally and completely fall, he'll be right there to catch me.

Jake sleeping is quite a sight if I'm honest. Full mouth slightly pouting, thick, dark eyelashes resting against his faintly tanned cheeks, inked chest bare and muscular. I could quite easily lie here and watch him until the sun comes up. It might be possible since my head is packed full of thoughts and sleep is nowhere to be found. The longer I lie here, the more jumbled and loud I know they'll become. My phone tells me it's almost 5:00 a.m.

Getting out of bed as quietly as I can, I grab my robe from the floor and slip into the hall, pulling the bedroom door closed behind me. The staircase leading up to the attic room is squeaky, but not loud enough to wake him, I don't think.

Upstairs is mainly dark, but the moonlight from the skylight shines down across my beloved Steinway. I try to remember the last time I was up here, and I can't.

Sliding onto the stool, I press my bare foot against the pedal, wincing slightly at the cold. It's a balmy night though, and my body still feels the aftereffects of Jake's anger over Ben. He took me apart with his mouth first, worshiping my body to a delicious orgasm, until I felt weak and pliant. It was rough and commanding after that—hard from behind, fingers twisted in my hair as he whispered low words against my ear. It was possessive, and I only felt myself falling quicker. Despite his words before. Despite knowing he has secrets. Despite all of it.

"Moonlight Sonata" is the first piece I ever truly mastered. I say "mastered," but I still sound amateurish to my own ears even after twenty years of practice. I keep my fingers light on the keys, not wanting to wake him, and after a while, I'm lost in the familiar, melancholic sound. One I always found sad. One that doesn't quite fit my mood right now.

I'm not sad—not at all. Scared, yes. Scared about how completely he's nestled beneath my skin, and by how quickly he's done it. But I'm not sad. Any lingering hurt from Ben's visit was gone soon after Jake took me to bed.

As my thoughts drift and meander, so does the piece, and I skip over some sections and repeat others. Mainly, it flows in an almost hypnotic continuum, and soon, my mind quiets and settles—although he never leaves it entirely. What secrets could undo what I feel for him? It frightens me to think of them, and so I don't. I focus on the music instead. I remember what he did to my body instead. The sounds of his pleasure as he fucked me into the bed. A small, desperate moan escapes my lips.

Finally, my fingers slow to a natural stop.

When I sense movement behind me, I whip around to see he's standing at the top of the stairs. He's pulled his boxers on, but they're tight and do nothing to quell the rush of lust that hits me at the sight of him there.

"Sorry. I didn't mean to wake you up."

"How come I had no fucking idea you could do that?"

"It's never come up." I shrug slightly, smiling. "How long have you been standing there?"

"Long enough to know you have very talented hands. But I suppose I knew that already." He comes toward me. The moonlight illuminates him a little more as he moves across the attic room, and I almost gasp out loud at how gorgeous he looks. Sleepy and more than a little aroused. He's breathtaking, but there's a danger to his beauty, I've always thought. It heightens it, turns it into something else—something darker and more intoxicating.

When he stops behind me, I lean back against him with a sigh. A second later, I feel his mouth at my neck.

"What was that?" he asks. "Sounded familiar."

"Mmm, Beethoven," I murmur as he continues to kiss me, tongue and lips ghosting below my ear.

"So, when you can't sleep, you play Beethoven on your piano, half-naked. You fucking kidding me?" He lets out a small laugh.

I turn and give him a serious face. "I never joke about Beethoven.

Although, there was this one joke I heard once that made me laugh . . ." The words dry up on my tongue as he leans down and presses his mouth to mine, kissing me deep and a little rough. When he pulls back, his eyes are glittering, awe-filled.

"You're fucking incredible, you know that?" His voice is so completely sincere I twist myself around on the stool fully to look up at him, my gaze drifting down to where his erection stands a little more pronounced now. When I glance back up at his face, I lick my tongue across my lips, hoping he gets the intent. In case he doesn't, I reach out and grip him over his boxers, drawing my thumb gently over the tip. It's already a little damp.

"Fuck, Alex . . ." He sucks in a gasp.

I shift forward on my stool and tug his boxers until they fall down his thighs. His cock is flushed pink and very hard, and the tip glistens temptingly, my mouth watering instantly. I grip the base as I lean forward to flick my tongue tentatively over the head, loving the way he groans at the briefest of touches. When I tilt my head to lick his length, the sound he makes is almost feral, hands sliding into my hair. I look up at him. His head is dropped back to expose his throat, shoulders tensing with every movement of my tongue. It sends a jolt of heat between my legs. I love seeing the effect I have on him like this. Seeing him lose control like this.

"Can I fuck your mouth, baby?" he groans, his voice scratched and a little raw.

I give him a half-nod, and he spreads his legs a little, settling his hands on either side of my head. He starts slow, sliding against my tongue in a steady grind before his hips begin to speed up. I close my eyes so I can focus, but a moment later, I feel his thumb move to my cheek, below my eye. He strokes the skin there tenderly.

"Look at me," he says. When I do, he gives me a lazy smile, hips still moving steadily into me. "I want to see your eyes when you suck my cock . . . that's it."

As I feel him hit the back of my throat, I try to relax it. Try to stop the reflex. When I swallow, he makes a desperately dirty noise and curses loudly.

"Fucking hell, Alex . . . that's it. I love seeing my cock in your mouth." He pulls out, letting me breathe and rest for a moment before he slides back in.

This time, he's faster, more impatient, greedier. He's close. The muscles of his stomach tighten, his thighs too, as he fucks my mouth gracelessly.

"Please don't stop . . ."

I pull him deeper into my mouth, as far back as I can again, reaching up to cup between his legs and massage gently. A few seconds later, and he's done, coming warm and thick down my throat.

When his body calms, he slides out of my mouth, loosening his grip on my head. He's heavy-lidded and looks slighty dazed, and it makes my chest ache. Keeping my eyes on him, I lean forward and place a soft kiss on his stomach, below his belly button. Then I sit up and lick him from my lips.

I just gave Jake oral sex at my Steinway. How's that for "prude"? *Fuck you, Ben.*

"Fuck!" he exclaims, smiling sexily. "You do that just as well as you play Beethoven."

I giggle. Then, with a look I hope is seductive, I say, "You should hear me play Bach."

He chuckles, pulling me up off the stool and into his body. Jake skims his thumb over my lip before leaning in to kiss me softly, licking his tongue into my mouth as though deliberately trying to taste himself. Deviant.

"What the fuck did I do to deserve this with you?" he asks after he pulls back. I try to think of a lighthearted response, but before I get a chance to speak, he kisses me again. "Now, come on. We should be asleep. Tomorrow's a big day for you." He takes my hand and pulls me toward the stairs.

"Is it?" I trail after him, puzzled.

"Yeah. You're introducing your hot sexual deviant to all your friends, remember? It's fucking massive. Nervous? Scared they'll hate me?" He looks back and grins, eyes over-wide.

Oh. I forgot about that. Am I nervous? Totally. Scared? Absolutely bloody terrified.

TWENTY-TWO

FRIDAY AT WORK IS HECTIC. I MANAGE TO COMPLETELY MISS LUNCH because I have to arrange an emergency admission for Mr. Caithness who arrives for his 11:30 a.m. appointment complaining of bad indigestion that turns out to be myocardial infarction.

The frenzied day I've had does have an upside though: I've had no time to overthink and worry about dinner. Rob is the only one who matters, and if she doesn't like Jake, it will crush me. Though, in all honesty, it won't make a difference to how I feel about him. Now I'm falling, I can't un-fall.

Rob's always had strong opinions about things, and that extends to my life—whether it's Ben, Nick, or what I'm wearing. If she doesn't like him, it won't matter, but it will burst a hole right through my sexual adventure bubble. Tonight, Jake and I become a real thing. An "us" outside of my bed or his shower or my attic room.

It's almost 6:30 p.m. by the time I'm home, so I text Rob to tell her I'm running a bit late, but not too much. She deplores latecomers to her dinner parties, so I always get there early. I'm hoping she'll be too distracted by Jake to mind much about it.

I'm in and out of the shower in five minutes and decide to keep my hair up to save time. I finish my little black dress off with a dramatic eye and a bold red lip, and I'm done. On my way out of the bedroom, I squirt some perfume and grab my black heels from the shoe cupboard by the stairs. I've not done badly timewise, and so while I wait for Jake to arrive, I grab a bottle of red from the rack and nip across to Ed and Betty's.

Ed appears a few seconds after I ring the bell, smiling in that soft way he has that reminds me of my dad. "Alex, hello. Don't you look nice?"

"Thanks, Ed. Dinner at a friend's tonight. I just wanted to say thanks to you and Betty for the other day, feeding Fred. It was a great help." I hand him the wine, which he takes with a "tsk."

"Oh, no need, Alex. You know we're always available. No problem at all. And he's mainly well-behaved." He smiles.

"Oh, I know you don't mind, but I don't know what I would have done otherwise. I really appreciate it." I know what I *wouldn't* have done, and that's have amazing sex with Jake for a start. For that, I should probably have brought them two bottles.

Ed nods and glances down at the bottle.

"Oh, and I've moved the key from the plant pot, so if you guys wouldn't mind holding onto the spare for me . . . I'm definitely getting a little more paranoid in my old age." Paranoid about arrogant ex-fiancés, mainly.

"Oh, sure, of course, no problem." Ed takes the key from me and opens his mouth to speak but then closes it immediately before offering me an awkward smile. "You know, I thought I saw Ben coming out the other night. Are you two patching things up then?"

Ed isn't nosy or a gossip—I think he just cares. As far as I know, most people around here liked Ben, and as far as I also know, they have no idea he was a lying, cheating prick. Which is why they still offer me a sad smile when they mention him.

As I'm about to explain, I hear a car turn up the road and then stop to turn into my drive. Over the hedge, I see Jake's Audi moving carefully up the gravel. I glance at my watch and smile. He's early.

"No, we're not. He forgot a few things, so he came to pick them up," I say.

Ed nods a little sadly and then glances over the hedge.

"*And* that's my date. I have to go."

"Oh, I see," he says, sounding interested, craning his neck across the hedge to try and get a better look.

Okay, maybe Ed is a *little* nosy.

"Thanks again, Ed. Thank Bets for me too."

"Not a problem, Alex. Anytime. We're happy to do it. Thanks for the wine." He holds up the bottle.

Jake isn't waiting at the door when I get there, and I like that. I like that he feels he can come inside. I laugh inwardly at the innuendo. As I'm taking off my slippers by the door, I hear him coming down the stairs, and I turn to look up.

My mouth all but drops open at the sight of him, my stomach swooping giddily.

Oh my god.

He's wearing a perfectly tailored dark blue three-piece suit with a white shirt and black tie. The tie is tied but loosened, and the top button of his shirt is undone to show me a lick of tanned throat. He's shaved, but there's still a faint trace of stubble across his jaw, and his hair is slicked back elegantly. It's a look I've never seen on him before, and Christ, he suits it. He still has that touch of edginess about him, but it's polished now.

Jake always knows exactly what to wear that will show his body off at its best. Though, I don't even know if he's style-conscious at all. Maybe he simply throws things on and they just *happen* to look this good on him.

As he catches my eye on the descent, I see his slightly panicked expression evaporate, replaced by a slow smile brimming with desire. "There you are," he says, running his eyes over me appreciatively. He rubs a hand over his mouth. "Fuck, you look beautiful." He steps into me, lowering his mouth to mine.

I fold myself into his arms in a soft moan, welcoming the taste of him into my mouth. He tastes like masculinity, warmth, and danger. I'll likely never forget it for as long as I live. When I pull back slowly, I feel dazed.

"And you look so bloody handsome," I whisper, smoothing a hand over his lapel. "Handsome" doesn't quite cut it though. He looks bone-meltingly gorgeous.

He smiles at the compliment, but it's a little brazen, as though he knows full well how good he looks. "Wasn't sure what to wear," he says, looking down at himself. "Never been to a dinner party at my girlfriend's friend's place before. Figured you can't go far wrong in a suit." He shrugs.

"*You* can't go far wrong in anything," I tell him, and he only grins. I stand up on my tiptoes to kiss him again, a light peck this time. "I just need to grab my bag and put on my shoes. Give me a sec." I squeeze his arm and go to the kitchen to get my heels.

"Where were you?" he asks, following behind me.

After I slip into my black heels, I turn to face him. "Next door, thanking my neighbors for cat-sitting the other day." *While you shower-fucked me and made me fall for you.* This, I don't say.

"Right." He nods.

I grab my bag and decide to forgo my jacket. It's a warm night, and we're going from the car to Robyn's and then the car home. There's no need for one.

"Okay, ready?" I say with a smile I hope doesn't look nervy.

As we drive, I try to concentrate on anything but the rumbling thunder in my stomach. It's partly hunger, partly nerves. The music is far mellower than last time, which relaxes me slightly. Jake reaches over to cover my hand with his, letting go only to change the gears up or down before returning it to mine again.

"How was your day?" I ask.

His jaw clenches instantly before releasing. "Fine," he says, tone clipped.

"Okay." I shift around in my seat and stare straight ahead. The matter's closed. Of course it is. From the corner of my eye, I see him turn his head to look at me.

"Sorry. Just work stuff." His tone is softer now. "Things got a bit heated with . . . one of our suppliers. Sorted it though." He smiles, but it doesn't reach his eyes. He reaches over to take my hand in his again. "Everything's good, baby, honestly."

"Okay." I nod, squeezing his hand in mine. "Well, I had a patient have a heart attack in my office today," I say.

"Shit, really? Did you have to give CPR?" he asks, sounding fascinated. It makes me want to tell him I had to perform open-heart surgery on the floor.

"No. It didn't get that far. Ambulance got there before that. It's frightening though because he thought it was nothing. If he hadn't happened to be in my office, he could have died."

"So, you saved his life." He honestly sounds no less impressed by the fact I picked up a phone and didn't have to massage a man's heart back to life. It makes my cheeks warm.

"You'll stay with me tonight?" I ask him.

"That a question or a demand?"

"Mmm, well, I'd like to think I don't need to demand."

"Well, maybe I like it when you're in control."

I laugh at this. "And when am I ever in control with you?" He gives orders, and people follow them, including me.

He sighs softly. "You're always in control, Alex."

"Well then, I guess that means you'll be staying the night with me."

"Yes, Doctor, I will most definitely stay the night with you." He shifts slightly in the driver's seat as he changes gear, spreading his thighs open a little wider. As he does, some sex demon takes a hold of me, and I lean over to place my hand on the muscular thigh. It flexes under my fingers, warm and strong. When I slide my hand higher, grazing it over the front of the rich fabric of his trousers, he groans quietly, the length growing harder instantly.

Heat blooms across my entire body.

He flashes me a look of warning. "Thought you were worried about being late."

"I am."

"So then, you don't want me to find somewhere we can park up . . . ?"

My thighs clench tightly, need curling deep in my stomach. The thought of it.

"We're already really late," I murmur, biting hard on my lip. My ears feel too warm.

He spreads his thighs a little wider still, encouraging me. "True. We'd have to be really fucking quick. I mean, I'm pretty sure I could make you come for me pretty fast . . ."

"Jake," I whisper, my cheeks burning now too. I think about it though. Fast and hard and rough in the back of his car. It was a Jake fantasy once.

We're only about five minutes from Rob's, but we're already half an hour late. Plus, where on earth would we do that around here? It's leafy suburban Epsom. Reluctantly, I draw my hand away from his thigh and place it back in my lap.

"Let's wait," I say.

He makes a disappointed noise. "Your call . . . Gonna be thinking about fucking you in the car on the way home all night now though."

I cover my face with my hand and laugh, but I know I'll be thinking about it too.

There are already a few cars outside Rob's, which tells me we're most definitely the last to arrive. Jake pulls in and parks behind Rob's Range Rover, saying he'll come out and move it if they need him to.

"Guess I'd better do something about this then," he says, glancing down between his thighs. He fumbles with the bulge straining the front of his trousers and gives me an accusatory look.

The heat in my tummy fights against the nerves still lingering there. With a deep breath, I pop open the passenger door and step out into the slightly cooler evening air. I meet him around the front of the car and slip my hand into his. He looks down at them.

"You going to hold my hand the whole night?" he asks, amused.

"Yes. Is that a problem?"

"Might be if I have to use a fork." He grins.

TWENTY-THREE

"**F**INALLY! THE GUESTS OF BLOOMING HONOR ARRIVE!" ROB shouts from the back of the house as I close the front door. She comes out of the dining room, beaming, dressed in a gorgeous white cocktail dress and holding a margarita. Rob is the only woman I know who'd risk wearing a white dress while cooking a four-course meal.

I watch her reaction carefully as she looks at Jake. First, her eyes and mouth go a little wide, and then she glances at me, a question in her eyes almost, then back at him. She blinks dramatically. Beside me, I feel Jake stand up a little straighter before moving and stretching out his hand. He keeps a hold of mine with the other.

"You must be Robyn," he says. "Great to meet you. Thanks for the invite. Nice place." He casts his eye around briefly before looking back at her with a smile.

Rob preens. "Aw, thanks, Jake. It's so good to finally meet you!" As she moves in to give him a peck on the cheek, she gives me a look and mouths what I think is the word "wow" silently. "Well, I don't remember seeing you at the club that night. I'd definitely have remembered." She laughs shamelessly before taking his arm to lead him through to the dining room.

I slip my hand out of his at this point, and he gives me an apologetic look.

"Well, everyone else is here. Dan will get you both some drinks while I introduce you to everyone, Jake."

I'm all but forgotten. I don't take it personally; Rob in hostess mode is different from Rob in friend mode.

As Rob steers Jake away, I make my way to Dan, who smiles brightly at me by the breakfast bar. Dan's *extremely* good-looking in an obvious pro footballer-type way. Except he's not a pro footballer—he's an ex-pro footballer who broke his leg in four places and is now an agent for pro footballers. He's still athletic though, and an immaculate dresser.

Dan holds out a pre-poured cocktail to me as I come over. I hug and kiss him on the cheek before pulling back to give him a look.

"This is all your fault, you realize?" I gesture toward Jake and Rob.

He grimaces and holds his hands up. "Yep. Totally. Pretty big news though. Can you blame me?" He waggles his eyebrows. He means me snogging the face off some guy in the street is pretty big news. Which, given how completely and utterly single I was up until Jake walked into my life, is sort of understandable.

Standing next to Dan is his brother, Mark. Or "Sherlock," as Rob and I call him. Mark hates the nickname, but it's never made much difference to me or Rob—we still call him it.

"Mark, how are you?" I ask.

"Good, Alex, yeah. You?" He sips his red wine as he looks me over.

"Great, yes, all good. I'm starving." I nod as I take a deep gulp of my wine.

"What's . . . Jake, is it, having?" Dan asks.

"He's driving, so a soft drink is fine, thanks, Dan."

As Dan pours a can of Coke into a glass, I glance at Sherlock. He's staring out into the conservatory where Rob still has her arm around Jake.

"Everyone," Robyn says loudly, cutting through the chatter, "this is Alex's Jake."

Jake glances over his shoulder at me and raises an eyebrow. I shake my head and mouth, "Sorry," at him. When he confirms to the room that Alex's Jake is his full name, there's a bubble of easy laughter before Rob rushes through everyone's names and how she knows them. Soon, he's striding back toward me.

"Alex said you're on the soft drinks, mate," Dan says, handing him the Coke. I remember then about the time Matt called him "mate" and how he reacted. I hold my breath.

"Yeah, that's great, thanks." Jake takes the glass with a nod.

"Jake, this is Dan—Rob's Dan," I say with a smile. "And Mark is Dan's brother."

Jake moves his glass to his other hand and reaches out to Dan first, then Mark. Mark smiles, but it doesn't reach his eyes, and I wonder if this is what Rob meant about how my bringing Jake tonight might not be perfect as far as Mark is concerned. I've sensed flirtations from Sherlock in the past, sure—most recently at Dan's birthday a few months back—but I've never taken it too seriously.

"Alex's Jake, huh?" he says, sliding an arm around me. His breath is warm against my neck.

I turn my head to face him. "Yes, and don't you forget it."

"So fucking possessive." He rolls his eyes playfully before nuzzling my neck again. The act isn't missed by Rob, who's coming toward us again.

"Hope everyone's hungry," she says, reaching around Dan to grab her cocktail.

"Bloody starving." I nod. The others agree, and Robyn looks pleased as she gulps her margarita.

"Mmm, so, we should all sort a night at Surgery again—what do you say, Al? Jake? We'll let the guys come this time. Dan, I told you how much you'd love it."

Dan nods, turning to Jake, eyes alight with interest. "Yeah, I'm up for it. Rob said the place was something else."

Jake nods, sipping his drink. "Yeah, course. Anytime you fancy another night there, just let me know. Alex's table is there whenever she wants it."

"I didn't know I had a *table*."

"Put your name on it and everything," he says.

I can't tell whether he's joking, until a moment later, he laughs. I hit him softly on the arm.

"So, tell us about the name then?" Robyn asks. My heart falters a little as I look at her, butterflies rising in my tummy. She's got a mischievous look in her eye. "I mean, you meet Alex, a doctor, the night of your opening and then call your club Surgery. Sounds like a *bizarre* coincidence if you ask me."

"More like fate," Jake says after a few seconds. I feel Rob, Dan, and Mark's eyes on us, but I barely even notice. Jake is all I'm aware of. The corner of his mouth lifts.

"Yeah, okay, you two are adorable. We get it," Rob proclaims before sashaying past me toward the kitchen, pulling Dan with her.

The dining table is a work of art as usual. Elegant candlesticks, stylish cutlery and glasses, and a gorgeous contemporary centerpiece. Rob's skill with interior design is quite something. She runs an interiors Instagram account with a quarter of a million followers, and it's not even her day job.

As Jake and I sit to the left of Robyn, Mark sits directly opposite. It's maybe a bit strange given Dan will be at the other end of the table. As Mark gets up to fill his wine from the bottle on the table, I notice him steal another look at Jake. When he catches me staring at him, his expression lifts immediately, and he smiles warmly. I glance to my right to see Jake in conversation with Dan's friend Damien who is on his left, and so he hasn't caught any of it.

A few minutes later, Rob's signature goats' cheese and roasted vegetable tart is placed in front of me, smelling so good my mouth waters. As I reach over to help myself to some more wine, Jake turns to say something to Damien again that makes them both chuckle. It dissolves the last of the unease inside me, and just like that, I can't remember why I was so nervous about this. It's fine. Rob seems smitten with him, and he's been nothing but charming since we came through the door.

"I haven't seen you since Dan's birthday, Alex," Mark says. "You're looking great."

I notice Jake's head turn at the comment as I lift my glass. "Yeah, that was such a fun night." A moment later, I feel Jake's hand slide onto my thigh, squeezing gently. I twist my head and smile at him and then pick up my cutlery and slice into Robyn's tart.

"Rob, this is amazing as usual. I think you're getting better at it," I say.

She swallows her mouthful. "Aw, you think? Guess we can thank Jane for it," she says grudgingly.

Rob's parents divorced twenty years ago, after her mother fell in love with a guy ten years younger. Rob couldn't forgive her, and it effectively ruined their relationship.

Most of the chat through dinner is about the wedding, which everyone agrees has totally crept up on them, and Robyn all but glows in the chair from excitement while she talks. Dan rolls his eyes in between looking lovingly at Rob. I've no clue why, but for some reason, my mind drifts to Ben and where we might be now had I not found out about his affair. Would I have gone through with it because it would have been expected of me? Because it would have been the *polite* thing to do? I practically shudder at the thought.

Taking a deep sip of my wine, I turn to look instead at the man sitting beside me. He senses me looking at him and lifts his head from his tart to widen his eyes playfully. Something warm and content blooms in my chest.

Despite his joke outside about my holding his hand all night, he barely lets go of mine throughout the whole of dinner. Soft strokes of my fingers and small, private smiles that only draw me in further and make the warmth in my chest burn hotter. Seeing him in this context, outside of just us, naked, is revealing, actually. He's chatty and funny and knows a lot about football—which, since the dinner table is filled with two agents and two footballers, is perfect. He's also charming and funny and great at telling stories in a way that makes people want to listen. I find out during the monkfish main that he was scouted for Fulham Boys Club in school but "lost concentration and ruined it." There's something about how he says this though that makes me think that's not entirely what happened. It makes me think maybe it was more to do with his being taken into care.

There are a few moments of panic when the chat turns to conservative politics. I hear the words "benefit scroungers" from Simon, one of Dan's agent friends, but Jake takes that moment to turn his attention fully back to me, distancing himself completely from the topic. After Rob takes away the empty dessert plates, which she refuses to let me help with, and while everyone else chats loudly under the obvious effects of alcohol, Jake leans in to kiss me.

"You have no idea how much I want to fuck you right now," he whispers.

My stomach swoops deliciously, thighs clenching with want. I feel my face go a deep, sexual red. I look at him aghast while he smiles that slow, sexy smile of his.

"I thought we banned that kind of talk from the dinner table," I whisper back, my eyes dropping to his mouth. It looks luscious and wet, and I think about how it must taste like the dark chocolate and strawberries from Rob's dessert.

"I decided to lift the ban." He shrugs.

"Oh, you decided, did you?" I try to sound annoyed. Which I'm not.

"Yeah, I did."

"Well, as nice as your proposition sounds, we can't leave right now, because that would be bad dinner party etiquette. We've just finished eating." I smile.

The low light of Rob's conservatory makes his eyes look incredibly green as they glitter at me deviously. When he gives me a little pout, I almost orgasm at the table. Something that would also be bad dinner party etiquette.

"Who said anything about leaving?" He begins to stroke the inside of my wrist with delicate, soft strokes of his fingers. "I'm sure Rob and Dan have a room upstairs we could use."

My stomach does another tight, warm clench at the thought. Then I wonder why on earth we'd bother climbing a flight of stairs when I'd let him take me right here. Under the table, I place my hand on his thigh and slide it upward until I meet something semi-hard. His eyes close over a soft groan as he licks his lips. I want to lick his lips. I also want to unzip his trousers and make him come with my hand, but that is *most definitely* bad dinner party etiquette.

What I do is skim my hand gently over his erection before curling my fingers around it teasingly. I see his jaw clench as he bites back the groan. He almost sounds as if he's in pain. When I drop my hand away, he shoots me a glare.

I give him my most innocent smile. "What's wrong, darling? Aren't you having fun?"

He reaches out to skim his hand over the back of my neck, fingers dancing light over the nape. "Mmm, I'm having a little fun, darling," he breathes. I love how strained and low his voice sounds. "But I can think of a few other things I'd rather be doing . . . Starting with—"

"So, Jake, you own a club in the city, that right?" Mark's authoritative voice comes slicing through the carnal haze that's settled in front of my eyes.

Jake blinks a few times, looking mildly irritated at being interrupted, before slowly turning his head to look at Mark. I sit up as he settles his arm along the back of my chair, hand draping casually over my shoulder.

"Yeah, that's right." Jake nods.

Mark lifts his glass, his eyes fixed hard on Jake. It's the same look he's had all night whenever he's looked in Jake's direction: wariness bordering on animosity. I vaguely wonder if it's an alpha male thing. They both have that sort of vibe.

"Whereabouts?"

"Brick Lane."

Mark nods as he turns his glass on the table. "It new, or have you taken it over?"

Jake begins to shift in his chair. I glance at him. His face is impassive. I suppose he doesn't want to answer any of these questions, but he's doing it because he's a guest here, and it would be impolite to tell Mark to mind his own business.

"New," Jake answers. "Building was an old metalworks before."

Jake *sounds* relaxed, but I feel his body tense beside me. He isn't. Mark nods again slowly, and I begin to feel uncomfortable.

"So, what'd you do before that? Before you got into the London club scene?"

I'm about to step in when, to my shock, Jake answers this too.

"This and that," he says. "Working for other people, mainly. Helping manage a few places. Did a bit of personal training for a few years before that."

"You encountered any issues?" Mark asks.

Jake frowns.

"With the club, I mean."

"Issues?"

Mark shrugs. "I mean, the London club scene can be pretty hazardous. Financially, physically . . ." He makes a weird whistling noise. "Seems to me only a certain kind of person would take on that kind of venture *in that part of London* in this kind of climate." There's something hidden in Mark's tone that I can't put my finger on.

Jake nods, holding Mark's gaze directly. "Oh, yeah? And what kind of person is that?"

"Someone brave, connected, or fucking stupid." Mark smiles, but it's that same cold smile I saw earlier. His delivery also causes the whole table to stop talking and turn their attention to either Mark or Jake. They were only half-listening before, but now, with everyone's attention on them, the whole atmosphere intensifies.

I feel rage simmer up inside me, bright and fiery. How dare he say that to Jake here? Here, where Jake's on unfamiliar territory, and Mark isn't. Here, where Jake knows nobody but me. I'm about to speak again when I hear Jake laugh beside me. A small, cold thing.

"Yeah, you're right there, mate. You're fucking right there."

"So, which are you then?" Something like irritation flashes over Mark's face.

With a sigh, Jake stands, pushes his chair back, and smooths the front of his suit down. "I'll let you decide on that, yeah?" He looks down at me. "Where's the bathroom, baby?"

I stand, ready to walk him there, but he stops me. "On this floor?"

"Yes, as you come in the front door, on your left."

He nods, leaning in to kiss me hard on the lips.

"God, could you two get a room?" Rob says from behind us as she comes back into the conservatory with Dan. Dan's carrying a tray of cocktails, which he immediately starts to hand out.

As soon as Jake's out of the room, I round on Mark. "What the hell was that?"

He has the nerve to look confused. "Pardon?"

"You're kidding, right?"

"What happened?" Rob asks, sitting down, head moving between us. "That was rude."

He gives me a wan smile. "Oh, it wasn't intended to be. I was only trying to get to know him. He's a stranger." He shrugs.

"It was more like a bloody interrogation."

"Can someone tell me what happened?"

I give Mark a sharp look. "Mark decided Jake needed some heavy questioning."

"Listen, we don't know anything about this guy, do we? I was just trying to suss him out, that's all." Mark sighs as though this is all some huge overreaction on my part.

Robyn throws Mark a look then. "If you want to suss Alex's dates out, Sherlock, then do it on your own time, not at my dinner parties. We're not in some mirrored room at your cop shop now."

This is enough to shut Mark up. It normally is. He stands and follows Dan outside where a couple of the others are smoking and drinking their cocktails. The conservatory doors are open, letting in a nice cool breeze, soft twinkling lights casting a warm glow over the large decking area. Low chatter fills the air, and I wonder if they're gossiping about whether Jake is well connected, brave, or fucking stupid.

"You're not going to go now, are you?" Rob asks. "Did he piss Jake off?"

"No, I think he's okay. It was . . . weird."

"Guess he's jealous you brought the hot nightclub owner to dinner," she says, throwing daggers at Mark's back.

I glance behind me to see Jake is on his phone in the hall now. He doesn't look angry or annoyed, and when he lifts his head, he gives me an easy smile.

"Soooo, he's one hundred percent not what I imagined at all," Rob says. When I look back at her, she's also looking at Jake as she sips from her glass. "I mean, when I asked Dan what he looked like, all I got was, *'Ummmm, I dunno, ummmm, fit-looking, ummmm, kinda tall.'* Well, he got fit-looking right. He's certainly fucking fit. But he's not . . . I don't know . . . the kind of guy you ever go for."

"I haven't gone for a guy in eight years, Rob. Maybe my type has changed. Maybe the polar opposite of Ben is a good thing."

"Yeah, he's definitely that," she laughs.

"Oh, he came over last night. Ben." I take a drink and wait for her reaction.

Her mouth falls open. "Whaaaaaat?" Her eyes are wide.

"I met him at a seminar on Wednesday. He wanted us to go for a drink and *talk*."

Rob rolls her eyes.

"I said no, obviously, but then he turned up at the house last night, used the spare key to let himself in. He tried it on."

Robyn's mouth goes even wider before her eyes narrow to slits. "That is fucking out of order."

"Shh—Jake doesn't know about that part. I think he'd kill him . . ." I glance behind me again. I can't see Jake now, and I have a moment's panic that he's left.

"I'll kill him too. What a fucking wanker," she hisses quietly.

I nod, lifting my margarita to sip at it. It tastes a little bitter against the previous glass of red wine.

"Ugh, well, you don't even need to think about him anymore. Fuck that cheating prick." She sounds riled up and still looks angry, but an instant later, her face transforms into a wide smile.

"Soooo, Jake, did Al tell you she's playing piano for us at our wedding?" Rob announces from nowhere as Jake slides back into the chair beside me. "I'll bet you didn't know she was a pianist."

I almost groan out loud. Nerves and dread flicker in my tummy every time I think about the wedding. I made a promise to her when I was fourteen that she's holding me to and which I resent her for immensely now.

Jake turns to me, eyes and voice soft. "Yeah. I heard her play last night for the first time. She was mind-blowing . . ." A look crosses over his face then, heated and soft.

My cheeks heat at the memory of how gorgeous he looked as he came in my mouth.

"Ooh, you did? Lucky you—she never plays for anyone!" Rob exclaims. "She must really like you."

I turn my head to her, and she winks playfully.

"Did she tell you about the time we went out for Dan's birthday to some cocktail bar in Soho and forced her to play some Coldplay song? The whole bar was singing along. Afterward, the bar gave us a bottle of champagne and offered her a Saturday gig. Oh my god, it was brilliant." Rob collapses into a fit of laughter, and I can't help but laugh too.

"Hijacking the piano in a cocktail bar half-cooked on champagne is slightly different to playing sober at the wedding of your best friend. I'm going to mess it up, I bloody know it."

"We'll get you half-cooked on champagne again, don't worry, babe," she says, still giggling.

With a sigh, I slide closer to Jake, resting my head on his shoulder. I feel his mouth kiss the top of my head gently. He doesn't appear to be tense or angry about Mark's questioning, and whatever phone call he took in the hall isn't lingering either. I feel my whole body relax into him, well-fed, light from the wine and cocktails, and content in his arms. It feels nice.

"You're going to be fucking amazing, baby," he whispers.

I turn my head to look at him, my breath catching slightly at the utter belief in his eyes. I realize then that I want him there with me when I have to stand up in front of two hundred people and play. I *need* him there looking at me the way he did last night. I've always felt like a different person with him—one who takes risks and leaves her comfort zone. He makes me feel as if I can do anything.

Some of the others start to float back inside to their seats, but Mark thankfully stays on the patio, seemingly in deep conversation with one of Dan's friends. Around us, the table chatters easily under the influence of wine, cocktails, and good food, but I'm too relaxed to join in.

Jake and Dan return to their earlier chat about football and some signing at Chelsea they both agree is a huge waste of money. While he chats, I enjoy the heat of his body and the soft feel of his hand as it rubs across my bare shoulder. When I feel my eyes begin to close over, I know it's time to go home. I glance at Rob, now sitting contentedly on Dan's knee, and she smiles, giving me a small nod.

"I think I'd like you to take me home now," I tell him softly.

"You sure?"

I nod sleepily.

"Okay then." He smiles, pressing his lips to my forehead.

"Okay, guys, I'm sorry to be a party pooper, but I'm knackered. Long, long day. We're going to call it a night," I say to the table as I stand.

Robyn and Dan walk us out, Dan and Jake slightly ahead, joking about something together.

"I hope you aren't *too* knackered, babe. I think he has other plans for you," she whispers as she pulls me into her.

When we reach the front door, Jake and Dan shake hands, and Robyn leans in to hug him, reiterating how nice it was to *finally* meet him. Then she turns to squeeze me tight.

"Have fun," she whispers in my ear.

"We always do," I whisper back, and she giggles dirtily.

From inside the car, I wave back at Dan and Rob who are cradled against each other at the front door. I want that, I think then. With Jake. I want to host dinner parties with him and wave our friends goodbye from the door with him. He gets in and starts the engine, but as usual, he waits for me to fasten my seat belt before lifting the handbrake and reversing out of the driveway.

I feel content and relieved and happy. He met my best friend, and it was fine. Aside from Mark, whose opinion doesn't matter in the slightest, there was nothing to worry about. So, I wonder why I have a little knot of something in the pit of my stomach, or higher up in my chest.

Except I know why. I know what the knot is. What it represents. Why it's a knot in my chest but something lighter and more fragile in my stomach. I just can't let my brain know about it yet. Because it's far too soon. Or maybe it's far too late.

Jake flicks a switch on the steering wheel, and the radio comes on, playing some heavy house music like the sort they play at his club. He leaves it on but turns it down low. Because I feel sleepy and not in the mood for talking, I turn my head to stare out the passenger window, letting my eyes close over with the slow, smooth movement of Jake's car. I always get sleepy in the passenger seat of a car, the slow rocking lulling me into relaxation.

It's like this for a good ten minutes until Jake breaks the balmy silence.

"So, did I pass?" he asks quietly.

I roll my head to the other side to look at him, taking in his profile as though committing it to memory for the final time. The shape of his perfect mouth, his long, straight nose, the lightly tanned, smooth skin of his face, glittering green eyes framed by thick, dark lashes. He's so bloody beautiful.

Then I know it *is* too late. The thought I've been trying to hide from my consciousness pops into my head. It's not a soft landing.

I'm no longer falling; I've fallen.

I'm in love with him.

TWENTY-FOUR

FEEL EVERYTHING ALL AT ONCE. I'M A MYRIAD OF EMOTIONS LIKE MY mother.

I mean, I have no clue where his head is right now, and I'm in love with him. Well, okay, I never know where his head is, but I *know* he's not bloody in love with me. He's not an idiot.

"Well? Did I?" he presses gently.

I swallow before answering him and hope to god my voice won't betray me. "Mmm, flying colors springs to mind. You can be really charming when you want to be—has anyone ever told you that?" I ask quietly. If my voice is quiet, then there will be less emotion in it. Less "I'm in love with you" in it.

He grins. "It's not the first thing people say about me, no . . ."

"Did you have fun?

He thinks about it for a ridiculously long time. "It was a great tart."

I smile at him for a moment before turning straight ahead to focus on the road. What the hell am I going to do? I'm such a bloody idiot. Head over heels for a man I've known for less than a month. God, this probably happens to him all the time, women falling in love with him at the drop of a hat. I'm just another one. Another idiot.

"What are you thinking about?" he asks.

"Oh, nothing. Just tonight. I'm really glad you came." I reach across to take his hand, squeezing softly. "I'm sorry about Mark. He can be a little overbearing at times. It's automatic, I think. Because of his job."

Jake frowns slightly. "His job?"

"Yeah, he's a detective sergeant now, I think. With the Met. He's never normally quite as bad as that," I explain.

An odd look passes over Jake's face, but only for a moment. Then it's gone. "He's a copper?" There's an edge to his tone that I don't understand.

Then it hits me. I sit fully around in my chair to face him.

"Jake, I never told him about what happened that night. About how we met, about what happened to you. I never told anyone. Even Rob thinks we met at the club opening."

He glances around at me, eyes narrowed. It looks as if he's trying to figure out whether I'm lying or not, which hurts me. It hurts me he doesn't seem to believe me. He turns back to focus on the road, saying nothing.

"Jake, I could lose my job if anyone found out I did that—treated a stabbing without recording it." I'm sure if Douglas ever found out, he'd go easy on me, especially if I put it down to inexperience or an oversight. Or that it happened during a drop-in where the rules are slightly different.

"So, why didn't you?" Jake asks. He keeps his eyes on the road, biting the inside of his cheek the way he does when he's tense.

"What?"

"Why didn't you report it? I mean, if you could have lost your job. You're a good girl, Alex. Why *wouldn't* you report it?' His tone is sharp. "To your detective friend, maybe? One phone call. Easily done."

I don't honestly even know how to answer that question. Why didn't I report it? Suddenly, loudly, frighteningly, the magnitude of what I did hits me. What the hell *was* I thinking? Would I have kept my mouth shut if it were anyone but this man sitting in front of me? Was I unconsciously trying to protect him because, deep down, I wanted him? Hindsight doesn't offer me any clues on it. But at no point after it happened or since has it even occurred to me to report it.

When exactly did I become the girl most likely to ruin her career for a beautiful face and a bit of sexual chemistry? Oh, wait—I do know the answer to this: five and a half weeks ago.

"You know why," is what I say. It's the same answer he gave me the first night we were together. When I asked him why he named his club after the place we met.

He offers me a strange, sad look and turns his eyes back to the road. We drive the rest of the way home in silence. I'm fully awake now, the soft hum of contentment gone. My stomach churns loudly with fear and love and confusion, and every time I chance a look at him, he looks equally anxious. His hands grip the steering wheel hard while he nibbles away at the inside of his lip.

By the time we pull into my driveway, the tension has built to an almost oppressive level. The car is stuffy with it, and I can't breathe properly.

As soon as he turns the engine off, I get out of the car immediately, desperate for some air. I'm almost at the front door when I realize he isn't following me. I turn around to see him standing by the driver's side with his hands deep in his pockets, staring at me. My heart constricts at the sight of him there, so faraway.

"Aren't you coming in?" I ask. I think maybe I sound desperate, and I hate that I do. But then I think maybe I am desperate.

He says nothing for a moment, and I think he's about to refuse. I'm almost certain he's going to get back in the car and leave altogether. But then he walks toward me, steely gaze trained on me. When he's close enough I have to look up to see his face, I find he still looks miles away. His scent floods my nose, but it doesn't do anything except make me feel even more desperate. Mentally, I plead for him to kiss me, to come inside and take me upstairs, to hold me, make love to me. All these things I'm sure will make whatever this is now go away.

"What's wrong?" I ask, my voice horribly fragile. I honestly don't know how we got here or how to get back, and it's terrifying. I don't want to be here—not now. Not now that I'm in love with him.

He sighs. "What the fuck are we doing here, Alex?"

I pull back slightly, frowning at him. "What does that even mean?"

"It means, fuck . . ." He looks exasperated as he drags his hand through his hair. "You and me—what even is this?"

Something horrible crawls along my spine, and I feel my stomach bottom out a little. "What are you talking about?"

"Come on, Alex. You know what I'm talking about." He laughs, but it's small and cold.

Do I? I'm certain I don't. Not at all. All I know is that tonight, when I realize I'm in love with him, he feels like this. All I know is that I feel sick.

"You seriously think I fit in there tonight? With your mates?" he adds.

"You're not even making any sense. Everyone loved you tonight." *Like I love you.*

His head snaps up, a sharp look in his eye suddenly. "Yeah, well, that's not true now, is it, babe?" His tone is one he's never used with me before. I don't like it. "Your detective friend spotted that a mile off, didn't he?"

That's the second time he's called Mark "my detective friend." I don't like that either.

"He's not my detective friend, Jake. And I told you, he does that with every—"

"Everyone new, yeah, you did tell me that. He's looking out for his mates, yeah, I get it. He also wants to fuck you though. Or maybe he already has." He cocks his head, something nasty in his eyes.

"He hasn't," I say.

He holds my gaze for a long moment, trying to decide whether to believe me, probably, before he turns away. Panic grabs at me, and I feel utterly helpless then. I've no idea what's caused this. If I caused it. How to fix it.

When he looks at me a second later, I wish he didn't. The look in his eyes is so unbearably cold. So distant. I straighten my spine and take a deep breath.

"I'm not having this kind of conversation with you in my driveway, Jake," I tell him in a firm voice. "If you want to have a deep and meaningful—which would be a first—then you can come inside and do it." I unlock the door and push it open, leaving it wide for him to follow. Though there's every chance he won't. There's every chance he's going to walk back to his car, get in, and leave.

As I dump my bag and jacket by the stairs, I glance back. He looks undecided, but when our eyes meet, something happens, and he moves, stepping inside before closing the door behind him. Relief floods through me as I slip off my shoes and head straight to the kitchen.

I'm filling the kettle when he appears at the door, watching me wordlessly, the thick, heavy tension from the car moving into the room now. A moment later, Fred appears, and I watch as Jake bends down to stroke him. I recall then what he said the first night he came to my house, about how he likes cats because they never give anything away. Was that another warning he gave me? How on earth can I be in love with him when he's kept himself a virtual stranger?

Who I am when I'm with you, that's who I want to be.

Maybe I'm not in love with him. Maybe I'm in love with the idea of him. Of the mystery and excitement he brings to my life. It's cliché, but at least it makes sense. Maybe I want him because he's everything I'm not. Everything *my life* isn't.

While the kettle boils, I lean back against the worktop and watch him. Fred's flat on his back now and purring loudly as Jake scratches at his belly.

"Tell me what's going on, Jake." My voice sounds sharp in the quiet.

He stops and stands up, lifting his head slowly to look at me. My chest aches. He still looks unbearably gorgeous, his beautiful mouth set in a firm line and eyes glittering with something that frightens me. He doesn't speak.

"Is this about Mark? Or my friends? Or is it about me?"

He sighs softly. "It's always about you, Alex." For the first time in what feels like hours, his eyes flicker with something warm.

"Can you stop being cryptic, just once, and talk to me?"

"I am talking to you." Some lazy smile plays over his mouth, and my temper rises further.

"Seriously? This is funny to you? Tell me what the fuck is going on, Jake, or I swear to god . . ."

He hesitates for a moment before moving toward me, strides long and determined as he crosses the kitchen. An instant later, he's pressing me against the counter with the front of his body, and I practically vibrate from his closeness. There's a definite hardness at his crotch, and he pushes it into the front of my body. He still wants me physically anyway. There's comfort in that, I find.

"Not a lot of people dare talk to me like that, baby," he says in a low tone. He doesn't sound angry, just a little dazed. Aroused too. He leans in, eyes closed as he touches his forehead to mine. He pushes his hips into me and groans softly.

On my tiptoes, I reach up to bring our lips close, but I don't kiss them. I want him to be the one to kiss me. No—I *need* him to be the one to kiss me.

Suddenly, he grabs my chin and tilts my head back away from him to stare down into my eyes. He looks turned on now, and I feel my entire body weaken with need, my legs quivering as they try to hold me up. The fact I want him with this kind of ferocity scares me half to death. I doubt I will ever feel like it for anything ever again. What has he done to me?

With his eyes open, he leans down to kiss me. Except he doesn't kiss me; he just licks hotly into my mouth, his tongue sliding over my lips and then inside. When he finally closes his mouth over mine, I moan softly against him. He does the same.

I marvel again at how perfect our mouths feel together—the delicious slide of our tongues, the quickening pace of our breaths. It's terrifying to me that he could ever think he doesn't fit with me. Needy, my hands travel up his body around his neck, tangling in his hair. Using his knee to nudge open my legs, he lifts me up to settle me on the counter and stands between my spread thighs, crotch pressing into the needy space.

His moans turn deeper, dirtier, more desperate as he pushes his tongue farther into my mouth, tasting every part of it. I reach between us to grip hold of the hardness between his legs, stroking him through the soft fabric of his trousers. He bites down on my lip and grips my face tighter, a tremble moving through him. For a while, I lose myself in the feel of him, in the noises that escape from him, at the need radiating from him, until suddenly, his mouth is gone.

He lifts his head up but doesn't move away, meaning I can still stroke my hand along his thick length where I sit. So, I do. When he talks, his voice is a tight whisper.

"You should do yourself a favor, baby, and tell me to leave right now."

"No," I reply as I stare up into his eyes. As I thumb over the tip, the head. I ignore the tortured look in his eye and reach my mouth up to his again, capturing his bottom lip softly between my teeth before kissing him almost desperately.

"I'm serious, Alex," he says against my mouth. Yet he doesn't pull away even an inch.

I move to kiss the corner of his mouth, soft licks of my tongue across the seam as I stroke my hand over his length. He's painfully hard now. Hot and thick and leaking slightly between my fingers. There's a physical ache inside me from how much I want him to make love to me.

"Alex, you need to stop . . . fuck . . ." he protests. But again, he doesn't move away, and so I don't stop. He groans louder, steps in closer, and wraps his arms around me to pull me into the heat of his body. "You have to be the one, baby." He almost sounds in pain now. I'm so bloody confused. "You need to finish this. Tell me it's over."

I drop my hand and lean back to look at him, cold, sobering confusion settling over me. "Why would I do that?" I ask. It's a genuine question. What would ever make me tell him that? "I'm never going to do that, Jake. Ever."

I love you.

He gives me a lost look and steps back, out of my touch. Then he turns his back to me and pinches the bridge of his nose, his shoulders high and tense. When he spins to face me, his gaze is dark again. Dangerous almost. I'm not afraid though. I've never been afraid of him. Being without him is the only thing that scares me now.

"You seriously don't have any fucking clue what you're doing, do you?" He shakes his head. "You never have . . ."

I match the ferocity of his gaze with my own. "I'm not a bloody child, Jake. Of course I know what I'm doing."

"No, Alex, you don't. This . . ."—he motions between us—"this is a fucking terrible idea, and you need to end it right fucking now, before—" He cuts himself off.

I can only stare at him dumbly as the words sink in. As my mind catches up. As it processes what I'm certain he's saying. I feel sick. But more than that, I feel stupid. And angry.

"You pursued *me*, Jake, remember?" I say, anger flaring again. "I tried to stay away from you, tried to listen to all those good-girl reasons that told me this would happen eventually, but, Christ, you wouldn't bloody let me, would you?"

He looks guilty now, and I'm glad of it. I slide down and fix my dress, run a hand through my hair.

"You could have said no, you know?"

"What?"

"To dinner. Tonight. If that's what this is about. If this was all getting a bit too serious for you, why say yes? I gave you an out, didn't I? I didn't force you to come. If you wanted this to be something else, something that was just about sex, you should have said no." *You should have told me that's what "us" meant. I could have prepared.*

When I finally look back at him, he has a sort of bewildered expression on his face as if I've spoken in Russian. Soon, the bewilderment turns to a scowl.

"Are you fucking serious?" he asks. I hold his eye until his scowl gets too difficult to hold onto and I have to look away. "Look at me, Alex," he says, and then suddenly, he's close again. "I said, look at me." He takes hold of my chin and forces my head up. "You know it's more than sex. You know that. You fucking *know* that, Alex."

I stare into his eyes. He looks so genuine. So confusingly genuine.

"I thought I did. But I'm so confused right now, Jake, that I'm beginning to think I never knew anything. Not really." I shake my head out of his grip because it only adds to my feeling of powerlessness. It's impossible to think straight this close to him.

I go to push past him, but he stops me, trapping me against the worktop between his arms. As he stares deep into my eyes, I feel as if he's trying to tell me something. He looks hurt and sad and a little lost, and I feel guilty about it. Then I feel angry about it because I don't know what he has to feel hurt about. Five minutes ago, he told me to stay away from him and to end it, and now he looks heartbroken I'd suggest this was all just a bit of fun for him.

Is this what he does to women—plays mind games with them?

"Alex, I don't ever want you to think that. You're more than that to me. You've always been more . . ." He trails off, leaving the sentence hanging in the air between us.

"Then why have you kept me at a distance this whole time? Isn't it because I was only temporary? I mean, why let her in at all when she's not going to be about for long? Isn't that what it's been all along?" I stick my chin up, eyes hard.

His nostrils flare angrily, and he shakes his head. "No. That's not it. Fuck, you deserve to know who I am. You deserve to know everything about me so you can decide. But I'm a coward. And I don't want to lose you or hurt you. I never wanted that . . ." He stops and runs another hand over his mouth before squeezing his eyes shut.

"You told me five minutes ago to end it, but now you're saying you don't want to lose me? That doesn't make any bloody sense, Jake, and you know it . . ."

I can practically hear the cogs in his mind churning as he squeezes his eyes closed with his fingers again. Suddenly, his shoulders drop, and when he opens his eyes again, he looks calmer, dark clouds in his eyes chased away.

"You're right." He nods. "Fuck it, ask me. Anything you want to know, and I'll answer you. Tonight, I'll answer any fucking question you want." His voice cracks slightly as he licks his lips.

An odd wave of panic washes over me then. Inexplicable panic at the idea of him telling me things he was unwilling to tell me before. Tonight, when he wants me to end things. *When I'm sure you won't leave me when I do.*

I shake my head. "No. I'm not playing twenty questions with you again, Jake. It wasn't much fun for either of us last time, as I recall."

As a show of determination, he pushes himself into me again, and again, I feel his hardness, obvious and urgent, pressing against my thigh. I stifle a moan. He could be inside me so easily. My dress has risen high up on my thighs, so he need only unzip his trousers, pull down his underwear, and he could be inside me. I moisten a little as his fingers dig into the upper skin of my bare thighs. God, I still want him. Despite everything, I want him more than I've ever wanted anything. No matter what is happening in my mind or outside of our bodies, my need for him is a constant, unstoppable, living thing. My fingers itch to unbuckle his belt and pull him into the space be-tween my legs.

"You say you don't know me, and you're right," he says. "You need to know me. *Really* know me. You need to know who I am when I'm not with you. So do it now. Right now. Ask me."

I swallow the lump in my throat. So, he's prepared to tell me every-thing. Anything I want to know. After all his evasions and subterfuge, he's prepared to finally open himself up. But not because I'm safe hands or be-cause he trusts me. Because he thinks it'll make me run. Maybe he thinks it will make me hate him. This man in front of me, who I'm in love with, wants to break my heart.

Vaguely, I wonder what I would ask him. What on earth could he tell me that would change my feelings for him? A wife, maybe? A family? Yes, that would do it. I'd still be in love with him, but there would be no work-ing through that.

Suddenly, I don't want to know anything. Suddenly, I want him to keep his secrets. Every single one. Why do I need to know what he's like when he's not with me anyway? What a stupid, pointless, needless thing to want to know.

I'm about to tell him something of that sort or ask him to forget the whole thing and fuck me instead when I feel a vibrating sensation against my inner thigh. His phone. He stares at me expectantly while the insistent vibration continues. It looks as if maybe he hasn't even noticed it, but then he lets out a breath, reaches into his pocket, and pulls the phone out. He visibly recoils from whoever it is, then he swears quietly under his breath.

"I need to get this," he says.

Of course he does. He always needs to get it. He turns his back on me and moves away, out into the hallway.

"You'd better have a good fucking reason for this," he growls. As a good reason—I presume—is explained to him, he closes his eyes and pinches the bridge of his nose yet again. "What the fuck are you on about? And how many times have I told you never to fucking go there?" Silence. "Yeah, well, that's never gonna happen, is it? Where is he?" Silence. "About forty-five minutes. None of your fucking business." A sigh. "Just wait fucking there. I'll be there shortly."

He's leaving. My heart drops as he comes back into the kitchen looking tired and angry. I know some of that is my fault, but I also blame some of it on the person on the phone.

"You're leaving," I say. It's not a question.

He nods. "I'm sorry. I have to." He looks as if he wants to say something more, but of course, he doesn't. I suppose my window of opportunity to ask him anything is closed. I chance it anyway.

"Any chance you'll tell me why?"

He lets out another deep breath. He looks so lost, so conflicted, as if he has so much going on in his head that I couldn't possibly begin to understand it at all. Who knows—maybe I wouldn't. Which means I can't help him. Which means I'm useless to him.

"Not right now, but I will," he says, his voice soft. "I'll try and come back tonight, otherwise I'll see you tomorrow. We can talk then. Properly." He nods decisively.

"I have plans tomorrow."

He looks angry again. "With who?"

I contemplate being secretive in order to give him a taste of his own medicine. But what's the point in widening our current schism any further?

"I'm seeing my brother," I tell him.

He nods, chewing his lip. "But he lives in town?" I nod. "So, I'll see you later on then, after. Call me, and I'll come pick you up," he says as if that's it settled.

"So, you aren't coming back tonight then?" I try not to sound as if I'm pleading.

"I don't know." He looks at his watch and drags a hand across his neck. For some reason, I feel guilty for making more demands on him and being useless.

I take a few steps toward him, desperate to try and comfort him even though I'm not sure if comfort is what he needs. I just want to do something that makes me useful to him. He looks down at me and opens his mouth to speak, then he closes it again and pulls me into his arms. It feels nice. I close my eyes and take a deep breath of his scent. I feel starved of it.

"Is everything okay?" I whisper against his chest. I'm not even sure what I mean. *Are we okay? Are you okay? Will we be okay?*

"Don't worry. I need to go," he says and places a gentle kiss on the top of my head, his heart beating hard against his chest. The sound of it only adds to my sense of fear and anxiety. "I'm sorry," he says, and it's as if he's apologizing for a whole host of things and not only having to leave me now. "I'll call you later, yeah?" As he steps out of my body and turns to walk out of the kitchen, every step he takes serves only to magnify my anxiety. The front door closes without a word, and I hear the sound of his car crunching down the driveway, and then he's gone.

Upstairs, after I've taken off my makeup and changed into my pajamas, I place my tea and mobile on the nightstand, turning the volume up and the vibration on so there's no chance of missing him if he calls. The knot in my stomach that appeared when we got into the car at Robyn's has transformed so it now feels like a living, breathing thing, rotting and keening and afraid in the pit of my belly. I still feel sick. And terrified.

I'm in love with him. I have to be. It wouldn't feel like this otherwise.

As I'm brushing my teeth, I wonder whether to call him. No. I doubt it would help anything. Whatever he left to do sounded important and critical, and I doubt a call from a useless, emotional female who knows nothing about what's going on will help his situation. Plus, he said he would call me.

I have the worst sleep I've had in a long time, waking every hour wondering why he hasn't called, texted, or come back yet and if his drive home has convinced him we're done.

TWENTY-FIVE

NICK CALLS ME BEFORE NOON TO CHECK I'M STILL COMING OVER to meet Jin. He sounds excited and nervous. I try hard to get caught up in my brother's budding romance, hoping it will take my mind off Jake, who still hasn't called.

"I can come and get you if you want? I know you hate driving in town," Nick offers.

"No, it's fine, I'll drive. There's something I need to do first." My voice is distant.

I'm going to go see him. I decided that when I woke up this morning and felt better immediately. Less useless anyway. If it's over, then I want him to say it to my face. I also need to know he's alive. Someone tried to kill him a few weeks ago, so how do I know it's not serious?

"You okay?" Nick asks.

"Hmm? Yeah, fine, just tired." I scrub at my eyes. "I never slept great, that's all. I'm really looking forward to meeting him." I lift my voice to try to sound chirpier.

"Cool. Well, I've booked a table at Ècole at 7:00 p.m.—you know, the French place we went to for Mum and Dad's anniversary. It was nice there. I liked it anyway. And then we can go meet the rest of the guys after. If you're up for it, that is. Seb's dying to see you. But no pressure." He takes a deep breath after speaking, and I laugh a little.

"What's funny?"

"Nothing. You're babbling. It's sweet." I smile. He makes a tutting noise, and I smile harder.

"Yeah, and so what about you and the new guy? Mum mentioned it last night—can't believe you told her. It's serious then?" Nick asks.

I literally have no idea how to answer that. It's really serious right now. I have no idea where he is, why he hasn't called, or whether he's ended things. Whether *I* should.

But I'm in love with him. I feel sick again.

"Maybe, yes. We can talk about it later."

"Deal. Okay, I'll see you later then," he says brightly.

After I hang up on Nick, I check to see if Jake tried to contact me, but there's still nothing.

The light of day offers me no further clues. Last night, I was certain it was because he sensed my feelings and wanted to run from them. This morning, I'm not sure. Something happened after dinner, and I need to find out what it was. Something so bad he wanted me to end it. Something that convinced him we aren't meant to be together.

I feel sick again.

I arrive at his building at St Katharine Docks about forty minutes later but spend another fifteen driving around to locate a parking space. After I park up and get to the front of his building, I'm confronted by the confusing high-tech intercom. I know his apartment number and that it's on the tenth floor, but the intercom on the front door doesn't appear to correlate to that, and there are no names to help either. While I'm deciding which random button to press, a guy leaves, smiling politely as he holds the door open for me.

In the elevator, the knot in my stomach starts to vibrate again, gaining mass. I can't decide if I'm more annoyed or scared. What if something happened to him? What if whoever hurt him the night I stitched him tried again? Another wave of nausea washes over me.

What makes you think I let them get away with it?

No. Jake can look after himself in that way, I'm certain. But if he's safe, why not call? Surely, he knows I'd be worried about him. What could have been so urgent it's prevented him from contacting me? Unless, of course, he didn't *want* to talk to me.

In front of his door, I take a deep breath and press the doorbell. It's ridiculous, but I feel as if my whole life is about to be determined by whatever happens when the door opens. By whatever it is he has to tell me.

We'll talk tomorrow. Properly.

There's no answer, and so I wait for a moment before pressing it again. It didn't occur to me he might not be home. As I pull my phone out to call him, I hear movement behind the door before it's clumsily unlocked and opened.

I'm not sure what happens first—either my stomach bottoms out or my breath catches in my throat. But I can't breathe. Not fully anyway.

Her hair is blonde with purposely accentuated dark roots, and it's mussed in the sort of way that advertises the fact I've dragged her from sleep. She's dressed in a bathrobe—one that looks too big for her. She's roughly about my age, I think, maybe a little younger, and pretty in a hard-faced kind of way. She's clearly fallen asleep in a full face of makeup, because her mascara is smudged under her eyes, and her lashes—which, from here, look false—are clumped together above her dark brown eyes. I must be at the wrong door.

Good lord, please let me be at the wrong door.

"Erm . . . I was . . . looking for Jake." I glance behind her at the number etched into the door. It's his door.

Her eyes narrow suspiciously before a small smile moves across her face. "He's . . . um . . . indisposed right now." She glances behind her as she pulls the door closed. "Can I pass a message on for you?"

As my mind scrambles, she yawns, running a hand through her hair.

A thought pops into my head then—a random, pointless thought. He wasn't lying when he said he doesn't have a type. We couldn't be any more different. She's petite, tanned, and blonde. And I'm none of those things. I wonder if it would be worse if Gemma from his club had opened the door, or Dawn from the elevator. I decide that no, it wouldn't be worse. It would be equally as bad.

I swallow and shake my head. "No. No message," I say. Something about the look in her eye tells me it wouldn't reach him anyway. I smile some ridiculously polite smile at her before turning on my heel and starting down the hallway, my legs slightly unsteady beneath me.

The familiar burn of mortification and humiliation settles over me like a hot fog. Like how I felt when I pressed play on the answer message from The Hilton Covent Garden when they called to say Ben had left his BlackBerry in his room after he checked out early that morning. They had thoughtfully called "home" to let him know, adding quietly at the last minute that his "wife" had also left some underwear. Somehow though, this feels worse. Probably because I should have known better. Probably because I *did* know better but decided to fall in love with him anyway.

I glance back once to see her watching me from the doorway with that same small, smug smile on her face. It's larger now.

An image of Jake lying naked on his back waiting for her to return to bed blasts into my mind, and I feel my fists curl. Then I imagine his body being touched and kissed by her, his perfect mouth moving its way over hers as he pushes himself inside. It causes a blast of white-hot rage to wash over me and stop me dead in my tracks. No. I'm not going to be this person—not again.

Spinning on my heel, I march back to his apartment with a rod of steel in my spine and bang hard on the door. It's opened right away this time, and I smile sweetly at the surprised face of Jake's tart.

"I'd like to speak to him, thanks," I say as I barge past her into his apartment. The TV is on—still on from last night, seemingly, as I register some children's program with dancing teddy bears, but there's no sign of him in the living room or kitchen. He's indisposed in bed then. I whip around to face her, glancing up toward his bedroom.

"He's not up there," she says, coming to stand against the wall by the kitchen. The animosity emanating from her threatens to drown me. She's still smirking, but it occurs to me that maybe she's not smirking at all. Maybe it's that she has a mean set to her face.

"You said he was indisposed." I look up toward the bedroom again. Do I want to go up there? Catch him red-handed? I'm about to call him down when she speaks.

"He's out," she says, folding her arms across her chest as she looks me over from head to toe, unimpressed. Oh, god, I dislike her intensely. She looks cruel and cold, and her pretty face and figure do nothing to dispel that.

I glower at her. "You do know that being indisposed isn't the same as being out, don't you?" I say. My tone is condescending, and to her credit, she notices. She narrows her eyes on me and stands up straighter.

"So, you're his doctor bitch then," she says.

I blink, feeling as if I've been given an electric shock. How the hell does she know about me? Did Jake speak to her about me? I feel sick again.

I stand taller too and narrow my eyes as well. "And you are . . .?" I ask.

"Vicky," she says as though she expects it to mean something. It doesn't.

I shrug. "He's never mentioned you, sorry. But if you could mention to him that the doctor bitch dropped by, that would be great. He'll know who you mean," I say before walking past her to the door.

She says nothing as I pass, only eyes me with disdain. There's a moment where I think she might attack me. I feel it seeping from her, and I brace myself for it. But she doesn't. Only mutters something under her breath I can't hear.

This time, I walk down the hallway without looking back. I feel sad and angry and idiotic all over again.

I drive the half an hour to my brother's feeling like a coiled spring, and when I pull up to his house, I've no memory of getting there at all. It's clever, really. How he did it. How he decided to push me away. This way, he gets to break my heart and still keep all his secrets. Yes, so bloody clever.

God, I am a naïve idiot. I let him play me like a naïve idiot. His lines were just that. Lines. I was right to mistrust them. Except why didn't it stop me from falling for him anyway?

I'd never have considered myself naïve or an idiot, not until two men in relatively quick succession decided I was. There's a part of me that wonders if this is down to the fact Jake and I never had a conversation about exclusivity. I suppose I never thought we had to. Naïve, probably.

Nick opens the door smiling wide. He steps forward and pulls me into a welcoming hug. As he does, the warm, brotherly comfort causes the dam to burst and the tears to flow. Hard and fast, my body heaving with great, pathetic sobs.

I cry hard on Nick's shoulder for almost five solid minutes, during which he leads me into his living room and has me confirm everyone in our family is alive and well. He rubs my back, telling me it's all going to be okay in soothing brotherly tones. I'm grateful for the words of comfort, but he doesn't know it's going to be okay. He doesn't even know why I'm crying.

Nick also has the Marlowe reassurance gene sewn into his DNA.

When I finally stop heaving, he hands me a tissue then gets up and brings me a large glass of cold white wine, which I take and gulp gratefully. He sits next to me on the sofa and gives me a concerned look.

"What the fuck is going on?" he asks. His eyes are filled with concern, and it makes me want to cry again, but I manage not to.

"I'm an idiot," I manage. "I've been such a bloody idiot. *Again*. I mean, when did I become this person, Nick? This person that men treat like this?" Anger sharpens my words.

He sits back and nods in realization. "So, the new guy's a prick too then?" He sighs, looking angry. When I only give him a look, he reaches across and puts his hand on my shoulder, squeezing it in comfort. "You're not that person, Alex. This is their fucking problem, not yours." He sounds a little guilty, I think. When I look up at him, he smiles. "So, you want to tell me what happened? Get a male perspective on it?"

Christ, no. I don't want to talk about any of it. I'm here because Nick wants to introduce me to a guy. For the first time since he realized who he is, he's ready to share that with us. And here I am, crying on his shoulder about how messed up relationships are. It's selfish. I'm selfish. I'm not going to let Jake do this.

"No." I shake my head. "I don't want to talk about it. I'm fine. Just angry and feeling stupid, which you know I hate. Tell me about Jin instead." I smile, wiping my nose with the tissue. "When is he getting here?" I want to know how much time I have to make myself look less unhinged. I don't want to embarrass my brother by looking like some ball of emotional mess on his sofa when I meet him for the first time.

He looks at his watch. "He should be here shortly."

"Okay, so tell me about him. How long have you been seeing him?" I ask, curious.

"A few months. He's a chef, owns a Korean restaurant in Soho." He smiles.

"Seriously?" I widen my eyes, impressed. "Is that where you met?"

He nods. "At Seb's birthday back in March. The meal was insane, so we got him out to thank him, and, well, he was . . ." Pink spreads across his cheeks. "Beautiful. Funny. And he put up with us when we were so fucking pissed. We hit it off."

I've never heard my brother this enamored. This shy. It's lovely. My heart contracts again at the feeling of my loss. My own fault. I shouldn't have been so naïve. I shouldn't have fallen.

"So, it's serious then?" I ask tentatively.

Nick looks at me, a glimmer of uncertainty in his eyes. He rubs his hand over the back of his neck. "Fuck, Al, I think so. He's . . . so smart. And so passionate about everything—food especially. And he's so fucking beautiful . . ." He trails off, looking shy.

I'm smiling too, caught up in his enthusiasm. "Well, he must be pretty special if he's got you nervous and grinning like a teenager."

As he smiles, I stand and tell him I'm going to go tidy my face.

Nick's large bathroom mirror isn't too harsh on me, all things considered. I brush out my hair and touch up my mascara and liner before adding a little blush and highlighter to my cheeks. Lack of sleep is always my worst enemy, not tears or heartbreak. I adjust my floral belted dress and pinch my cheeks then try smiling at myself in the mirror, but it looks and feels forced. I need to try harder. I can't be the harbinger of doom tonight—it means too much to Nick. I'll get through tonight and deal with the Jake aftermath tomorrow.

When I walk back into the living room, Nick is lifting my glass through to the kitchen, presumably to refill it, so I follow him in.

"So, I spoke to Tash today," he says as he hands me my refilled glass. "She thinks she'll be here the second week of August. I told her she can stay here for a few days and then we can all go over together. You wanna take the shuttle again?" He leans back against the counter and sips his wine. I do the same, savoring the taste of the Sancerre, and nod. Fayence sounds so tempting suddenly. The second week of August is only six weeks away though, which means I need to speak to Douglas on Monday so he can arrange the cover.

"You could bring Jin." I smile and widen my eyes at him.

He rolls his eyes and nods. "Yeah, that will go down well. 'Mum, Dad, this is my boyfriend—oh, and we're both gay.'"

I tilt my head at him. "Okay, but you said this is serious. Meaning you're going to have to have them meet him at some point. Meaning you're going to have to *tell* them at some point."

"I said I *thought* it was serious. Let me be sure first, will you?"

It sounds like another excuse. Another delay. But I only smile. This is Nick's decision, and whatever he decides is right is, well, right.

"Of course."

He takes another sip of his wine, and I follow him back into the living room.

The wine is doing its job, the tension starting to lighten in my shoulders and neck and my body relaxing. I find wine has the most calming effect on me. Not the best direction of thought for a GP, most likely, but it doesn't make it any less true. I still have the strange vacuum of loss in my stomach though, the horrible knot of emptiness, but perhaps once I've eaten . . .

Nick chats enthusiastically about a new Netflix show he's obsessed with for a bit before my phone starts to ring loudly from my handbag. I startle, putting my wine down to reach in and get it. If it's him, I'm not answering.

It'll only ruin my mood. Plus, I don't want a shouting match with him in front of my brother.

It's not Jake though—it's a number I don't recognize, so I make a puzzled face and shrug at Nick as I press to answer the call. I've not even managed to get the word "hello" out before he's bellowing down the phone.

"Alex, where the fuck are you?"

As I stand up and walk away from Nick toward the balcony, I wonder briefly where he's calling from to make it an unknown number. Whether it's Vicky's number.

"Oh, so now I'm one of the people you bark at down the phone?" I ask, proud of how calm my voice sounds.

"Alex, tell me where you are right now," he says again, a little calmer, but not much.

"I told you last night, I'm seeing my brother. Now, I'm going. Goodbye, Jake," I say, proud when I manage to maintain the calm despite the whirlwind inside.

"Alex, don't you dare hang up on me!" he shouts. "Look, I need to see you, speak to you. Vic told me you came here. Fuck, baby, why did you have to do that?" His voice sounds a little desperate now, but my mind is stuck on one thing: he called her "Vic." He has a nickname for her. Like people have nicknames for people who mean something to them.

I'm going to throw up. Oh, no wonder she looked so smug. I thought the fact I'd never heard her name before meant she was unimportant, but no, she has a nickname. She's important all right.

"I did *that* because I was worried sick about you. Because you left me like that last night and never called. Though it seems it isn't my place to worry about you, is it?"

"The fuck did she say to you?" he growls.

I want to laugh. He's trying to blame her. First me for going there in the first place, and now her. Unbelievable.

"Who, Vic? Oh, we never got to chat much. After she called me your 'doctor bitch,' the conversation sort of dried up."

I hear him mutter a curse. When I look over at Nick, he looks concerned and a little angry, ready to jump in if need be. I give him the signal that I'm okay.

"Alex, please tell me where you are. I'll come to you. I'll come now."

He's pleading. I don't like how it makes me feel, Jake pleading.

"I need to see you, talk to you. Explain." I wonder if he wants to tell me how her being half-naked in his apartment wasn't what it looked like. "Please, baby."

I straighten my spine at the same moment I hear the doorbell ring. Nick hesitates for a second before going off to answer it. I wait until he's out of the room before speaking.

"Oh, don't you bloody dare. That 'baby' crap is finished," I hiss. "Oh, and explain? *Please.* When have you ever *explained* anything to me? I had to get you to converse with me under duress, for god's sake. Don't let desperation change the habit of a lifetime. Begging doesn't suit you, Jake. I'm going now. This is over." My voice sounds so unbelievably controlled I'm almost proud of myself. If I weren't on the verge of tears again, I might even gloat.

"Alex, I mean it, don't ha—" I hear him shout, but my hand closes over the disconnect button.

As I turn around, Nick enters with a tall, extremely beautiful man by his side. Nick still looks worried, but I fix on my most genuine smile and walk toward them.

TWENTY-SIX

"**Y**OU MUST BE JIN." I smile.

"Babe, this is my little sister, Alexandra, but we call her Alex. Or Al, or Doc," Nick says.

I can only blink at his use of the word "babe" for a moment before bringing my gaze back to the tall, handsome man beaming back at me. I've never imagined what Nick's type might be because I've never seen him with a guy before, and so I had no idea what to expect. Jin is stunning. A little taller than Nick, with the most flawless skin I've ever seen on a man.

"Alex!" he says. "You're exactly like in your pictures—gorgeous." His accent has a strong American inflection, but with a current of Korean woven through it. Large brown eyes and a big smile only enhance his elegant features as he lowers into a small bow before rising to pull me into a gentle hug. "He's been hiding you all for so long I was starting to think he was an orphan. Or an alien. Or something else altogether . . ." He flicks his eyes back to Nick and winks as Nick hits him playfully on the arm.

"Drink?" Nick asks, hand resting on his forearm.

Jin nods and all but pulls me toward the sofa as Nick goes to the kitchen.

When my phone rings a second later, I decline it immediately and turn the thing off.

"So, you're a doctor like his dad?" he asks, eyes wide and gleaming with interest. "And your dad, of course."

I nod at this.

"It's so great. Nick said he'd have loved to have gone into medicine but just wasn't smart enough. He's so proud of you, you know? He talks about you all the time."

I blink in surprise. Did Nick want to go into medicine? How did I not know that?

"Honestly, Nick is one of the smartest guys I know, so that's just him being modest. Which isn't his thing normally—but you'll know that by now." I laugh, and Jin nods in agreement. "So, Nick said you're a chef? That you have your own restaurant?"

"Yes, I do." He nods. "It's fairly small, but I honestly think we have the best Korean food in London."

"Ugh, I love Asian food. I need to come and try it."

"Please do! You're so welcome, Alex."

He's got an infectious, charming way about him—much like Nick does, actually. There's a lot to be said for being attracted to a personality type close to your own, I suppose. Jin's witty and intelligent, and I can see why he caught Nick's attention. Plus, the way he looks at him as he talks and watches when he leaves the room is adorable.

If I hadn't liked him, Nick would have been devastated. Exactly how I would have been if Rob hadn't liked Jake last night. None of which matters now.

Was that really only last night? Christ, what a day.

Dinner at Ècole is comfortable and fun, and I feel less like a gooseberry than I feared. While I drink too much wine, Jin tells us stories about growing up in Busan and why he decided to open a restaurant in London. His family has money, it sounds like, and supported his move to the UK. He studied at Hull, learned English from American TV shows and movies, and now thinks of London as a second home. Nick watches him, completely enraptured, and it makes my heart giddy and warm. It's lovely to watch. And because Jin and Nick are cute and funny, I don't need to think much about what's going on inside my head. I only need to watch, listen, and drink a lot of wine. Too much wine.

After dinner, we take a taxi to Soho to meet some of Nick's friends, including Seb, Nick's oldest friend who practically grew up at our house, and Seb's sister, Rebecca. A few of Jin's friends are there too, and everyone is in high—extremely high—spirits. This is going to be messy. Actually, when we arrive, it already looks pretty messy. Shot glasses clutter the table, buckets holding all colors of wine. I can already feel the hangover settling over me.

To be honest though, messy is probably what I need tonight. Messy should keep my mind off him and his tart.

As we approach the table, I wave at the friends of Nick's I know before Jin introduces me to a female friend as "Nicky's beautiful baby sister." I squeeze into the seat next to Sebastian and lean across to hug him, trying to remember the last time I saw him.

"Alex! How are you doing? What's happening?" he says, squinting at me through his drunken haze. I wonder how many of these empty shot glasses are his.

"I'm bloody great, Sebastian, you?" I lie, looking around the table for some non-carbonated wine to consume. I don't want to start on champagne at this point. Tomorrow will be a washout if I do that, and tomorrow, I have lots of crying and self-pitying to do.

I've no choice in the matter of avoiding champagne though because Seb stands up and pours me a glass. Because I don't see any other wine and the bar is busy, and because I have terrible willpower, I take it from him.

"Thank you," I say as I take a sip. It tastes great, actually. Though I can't think of an occasion where champagne wouldn't taste great. Even now, heart-broken and stupid.

"So, you've met Jin then?" Seb says, smiling. We both cast a glance over at them where they stand, heads close, Nick's arm resting on Jin's lower back.

"I have. He seems perfect."

Seb nods. "Yeah. Fuck, he's almost ridiculously hot, isn't he?" He shakes his head in disbelief then quickly looks back at me. "I mean, for a guy. Which isn't my thing. At all. Anyway, you and Uncle Ben still over?"

I laugh loudly. Partly at his conversational acrobatics, and partly at the nickname, which I forgot about entirely. "We are very much still over, yes."

He grins. "Seeing anyone else yet?" He raises his eyebrows flirtatiously. He doesn't like me like that, and we both know it—it's just how he acts around me and Tash.

"Yes, Sebastian, I am seeing someone. Sorry." I smile back.

He makes an exaggerated noise of disappointment and drops his head back.

"But there's a nice attractive girl over there. Go try your luck with her." I indicate toward a pretty dark-haired girl standing at the bar, looking in the general direction of our table. Not that I can blame her—there are a lot of attractive men sitting here. It's just unfortunate she's not exactly their type. Though, perhaps she's looking at Jin's female friend.

"But you know it's you I want, Doc. You know I've always had a thing for Nicky's sisters. You and Tash are like my dream women. She still married?" he asks, and I laugh again, shaking my head. "Drink?"

I hold up my glass. "I have one."

"Shot?"

"Absolutely not. A glass of water would be great though."

He rolls his eyes and mouths something that looks like, "Boring," before meandering off in the direction of the bar.

It's the sight of Nick and Jin catching up with their friends and looking so much like a new couple that causes the note of loss to sing over me. I'm happy for him—of course I am—but I can't help thinking about what I'm desperately trying not to think about. It pulls at the last of my resolve.

I reach into my bag to take out my phone, switching it back on.

Soon, the notifications begin to flash across the screen. Eight missed calls, two voice mails, and a few texts. Each message is angrier than the last. Except for the most recent one, sent an hour ago, which simply says:

Jake: Alex, please let me explain. It's not what you think it is.

I laugh even as my heart constricts. *It's not what you think it is.* Even so, my fingers itch to dial his number. Not because I want him to explain how it isn't what I think, but because there are things I want and need to say to *him*. Words that will fester and rot if I don't speak them aloud.

As I'm debating whether to ring him, another text comes through. His name flashes up on the screen, the text below it.

Jake: I'm going to your house. I'll wait for you there. We need to talk.

Of course he's going to my bloody house. Because that's what he does. He turns up at my house. I'm tempted to stay at Nick's, but I can't leave Fred all night, and it's too late to ring Ed and Betty.

Christ, I don't want to run the Jake gauntlet in person tonight. Not this inebriated. I don't trust myself around him. It's highly possible if I see him, I'll do something stupid and naïve.

With a sigh, I stand, maneuvering my way out of the row of joined-up tables. Nick catches my eye and comes toward me.

"You're going?" he asks.

"I need to nip out and make a call."

His eyes darken instantly. "Tell me you're not going out there to call him, Al."

"I just have to make one call. Then it's done. Promise." I give him my most reassuring smile. "It's fine. I'm fine, honestly. Go back to Jin."

Nick watches me closely for a minute, checking whether I am indeed fine. He sighs but doesn't look convinced. "Fine, but come over when you're done. Jin's mate Sophia is nice—you'll like her. Plus, he's only going to hit on you all night if you sit there." He casts his eye over my shoulder as Seb collapses into the booth, a tray of shots lined up on it. A glass of ice water too.

"Nickyyyyyy-boyyyy! Shot for you and Jin!" Seb calls out, gesturing him over.

"I'll be back in five." I give him a gentle pat on the arm and squeeze my way outside.

The air is muggy and close, and the street outside is busy with smokers and tables as I dial his number. It barely has a chance to ring before he picks up.

"Where the fuck are you?" he growls. His voice sounds hoarse and scratchy as though he's been using it to shout all night.

"Do you ever answer your phone with the customary hello?" I ask dryly as I move away from the front door to a quieter spot.

"I am not fucking playing here, Alex. I'm in the car on my way to your house, so you will have to fucking speak to me at some point. Just tell me where you are, yeah?"

"Well, since I'm not coming home tonight, I hope your seats recline all the way back."

He sighs, his voice softer when he speaks. "Please, Alex. I'll come to your brother's. Tell me where it is." The softer tone disarms me a little. Cools my rage some. Like it's supposed to. "I need to see you, baby."

"I don't care what you need, Jake. I don't *want* to see you." I'm proud of how calm I sound. This is good. I can do this. "In fact, I never want to see you again," I add.

There's a long silence before he speaks. "I'm not gonna ask you again, Alex. Tell me where the fuck you are."

That does it. I'm gone.

"How bloody dare you!" I snap. My businesslike, detached indifference evaporates, replaced by a drunken woman scorned. "You fucked someone else! You couldn't get away from me fast enough so you could go fuck someone else. Last night, you wanted me to end it, so here I am, ending it. It's over. Whatever this is . . . was . . . is finished now." It surprises me how quickly my rage fades, tears of frustration welling in my eyes instead.

He says nothing. Not a word. No angry demands or apologies. Nothing.

He doesn't deny it or offer an excuse, and I can't help but wonder why. Am I not even worth that to him?

While the sound of his silence stretches endlessly down the phone, I begin to feel self-conscious about who might have heard my outburst. I'm far enough away from the front of the bar that only passersby would have heard, all gone now. The only person close to me is some drunk Scottish guy shouting on his phone. My stomach lurches. He's shouting the name of the pub and the street it's on over and over again for everyone to hear—including Jake.

Oh, dear god.

"I know where you are. I'll be there in ten minutes. *Don't* move," he warns and hangs up.

I need to move. Of course, if I go home, he's going to come there too, but at least we won't be fighting in front of Nick and his boyfriend.

Back inside, I look for Nick or Jin but can't see either of them. When I ask Seb where they've gone, he points through a drunken haze to the dance floor in the lowered area, where my brother and Jin are dancing with a crowd of others. When I tap Nick on the shoulder to tell him I'm leaving, he guides me off the dance floor and back toward our table, leaving Jin with his friends.

"Are you going to see him?" He eyes me suspiciously, an air of disappointment about him.

I shake my head. "No. I'm just tired, and it's too loud, and I can't drink anymore. You know me—a lightweight. Listen, I love Jin. I love *you* with him, and I'm so happy for you. Say goodbye to him for me." I pull him into a hug, feeling emotional all of a sudden in a way that isn't about Jake or his harlot.

When I pull back to look at Nick, he's smiling, face lighter than it was a moment ago.

"Come on—I'll walk you out until you get a taxi." He turns toward the door, tugging me with him.

A shiver of fear runs over me at how badly it will go if Nick sees even a glimpse of Jake's temper. A hand on his shirt, I tug Nick back.

"Nick, it's fine. I'm going to walk up to the end of the road and get water and milk from the shop anyway. I'll get a taxi from up there. Stay."

He looks as though he's about to argue with me.

"You're worried about me getting from here to Tesco on my own? Seriously? I used to live in London, remember?"

Finally, he acquiesces and pulls me into a hug again. "Thanks for tonight," he says, smiling again. "He loved you too."

As I step out of the pub, I feel a little lighter, my joy at Nick's happiness chasing away some of my misery. I head up toward the supermarket, checking my phone as I go, pleased to see no further contact from Jake. Though that's probably because he's driving. I quicken my steps.

I'm scrolling through his other messages when I hear a car engine sound behind me, a door opening and slamming closed. I don't even need to turn around to confirm it. It's him. I can just feel it.

I turn around slowly to find him staring at me. His eyes are blazing, and his mouth is set in a hard, angry line. He's angry, but there's something else on his face too—something like panic, maybe. My stomach does a stupid swoop at the sight of him, and I hate it. I hate the effect he has on me.

He's dressed so simply in jeans and a T-shirt, but as always, they hang so perfectly on his perfect body. It's ridiculous, really. As he takes a step closer, my body prickles with heat, needy. Without much effort, I force my mind back to this afternoon, to Vicky in a bathrobe calling me his "doctor bitch." I go to turn and take a step away from him, but he's too fast, his hand shooting out to pull me back. His touch seems to brand me, scorching my cool skin.

"Let go of me, Jake." I glare up at him in warning.

"Baby, please," he says. I feel the place on my arm where he's holding me get warmer. He steps into my body, and his smell floods into my nose, delicious and clean. Jake. *No . . .* I can just about deal with him touching me, but I can't deal with him this close and his smell.

To steady myself, I close my eyes.

"Get in the car," he says, low.

When I open my eyes to look up at him, his are dark and serious. "I'm not going anywhere with you. Now, let go of me."

His mouth twitches, and he takes a deep breath as though struggling for patience. "I'm not going to ask you again, Alex. Get in the fucking car."

I flinch at his tone before straightening my spine and glowering up at him. "It doesn't sound like you're asking, Jake."

His face softens a little. "Will you please get in the car so we can go somewhere and talk? I need to explain, baby. Please." His tone is so soft and low and lilting it makes me want to move in close and curl myself up in his arms and have him hold me. That's my stupid naïvety again.

I take a step toward him and press myself into his body, edging my face up so our lips are close. My action and whatever he sees on my face makes him loosen his grip on my arm. I see his gaze drop to my mouth, his tongue darting out to lick his bottom lip absently.

"Go fuck yourself," I whisper with venom before pulling my arm out of his hold. As I glare up at him, his eyes narrow, and he smiles. It's slow and devastatingly sexy.

"Do you remember what I said about how you look when you're angry?" he asks quietly. My mouth almost falls open as something warm and traitorous moves through me. "Now, baby, I promise you, if you don't get in that fucking car right now, I'll put you in it." His voice is low and filled with promise. It sounds a lot like it does when he tells me what he wants to do to me in bed. I wonder if he said those same things to Vicky, and my fingers curl into fists.

"You wouldn't dare."

He cocks his head a little, still smiling. "Wanna bet?"

A few people are staring at us now. Maybe because it's Saturday night in the middle of Camden and a couple having a domestic always draws attention.

"You all right there, love?" a male voice says from behind me.

I hold Jake's gaze for a moment before turning around. Two guys look from me to Jake warily. I wonder what they see. They're both young and fit-looking and dressed smart for a night out.

"Do yourself a favor and fuck off, mate, yeah?" Jake says. It comes out as the verbal equivalent of swatting a fly.

An uneasy look crosses both of their faces as they look at me. Jake has a dangerous edge to him generally, but now his dial is cranked up full he looks ferocious. I don't blame them for regretting getting involved.

"I'm fine, thank you." I offer them a half-hearted smile. They look relieved, I think, and then they're backing off, crossing the road to put some distance between us.

I whip my head around to glare at Jake again as he grabs a hold of me. "Stop bloody manhandling me. You're embarrassing me," I hiss.

"Are you going to get in the car?"

"Do I have a choice?" Short of screaming bloody murder in the middle of the street and embarrassing myself further, I don't see what option I have.

He looks at me a little sadly. "Please, baby, for me," he says, and I feel myself soften. I'm such a bloody idiot.

"Fine," I hiss.

When he lets go of my arm, I rub it as though he's hurt me, glaring at him hard as I walk to the passenger side of the car. He doesn't move until I've slammed the door closed. Then he gets in and closes the door, turning to stare at me, the weight of his eyes suffocating. I stare out the passenger window instead.

"Alex, please, look at me," he says.

I close my eyes for a long moment and take a deep breath before turning to face him. His body—which outside was coiled and hard like steel—seems to relax, though his face still looks tormented and anxious. I'm able to look at him for maybe ten seconds before I have to look away again. It hurts too much. Being this close to him tightens my nerves and stretches my willpower. I feel his heat from here, smell his smell too, and I hate myself for still wanting it on me. When, from the corner of my eye, I see his hand move up toward my face, I pull my head back, away from it.

"Don't you dare," I warn.

His hand freezes mid-air before he lowers it slowly and turns around to face the front. Then he sighs deeply and pulls on his seat belt.

"Can you put yours on too, please?" he asks as his clicks into place.

Everything inside me wants to defy him even in this. Huffily, I reach across and pull the strap over my chest to secure it in its socket.

Though my wine haze is fading fast, I still feel slightly disoriented as he starts to drive through the tight, busy streets of Camden. I'm not entirely sure which direction we're going in or where he plans to take me to "talk," but then I see the River Thames ahead. He takes a left turn so the river is on my right and carries on along the riverfront. I know exactly where he's taking me. I feel ill.

"Don't even think about taking me back to your place, Jake," I tell him.

When he doesn't respond, I turn to glare at him. His expression is resolute and determined.

"I need to take you there, Alex," he says eventually. "To explain properly."

"This should be good." I laugh emptily. I'm intrigued though. Except there is no intrigue. Last night, he begged me to end things and then drove away from me to be with her. Nothing intriguing about that.

God, I want to scratch her eyes out and then turn my fury and rage on him. But I also want him to soothe me and kiss me and tell me she meant nothing. Tell me it's only me he wants. I'm pathetic. My mind decides I haven't suffered enough, and so it forces me to imagine him naked and moaning her name as he thrusts into her on the same bed he fucked me on three nights ago.

God, I need some air.

I reach over and hold the button on the door down to lower my window, breathing the cool night air in deep as I try to calm the noise in my head. I glance back at his profile. His face is almost totally in darkness, only the glow of the streetlights to illuminate it. It hits me then—a strange, empty realization, really—that it's him personified, the light teasing me with glimpses of him, only to snatch him away, back into the dark. One moment, I think I can see all of him; then, it's as if he's a complete mystery. But I've never seen him fully, have I? I've only ever seen what he's chosen to show me.

When we pull into his garage a short time later, he switches the engine off, takes a deep breath, and then turns to face me. He looks uncertain and anxious, but there's fear and lust there too, and it's too much for one person to look directly at. So, I look away.

"Alex, I know you fucking hate me right now and hurt, and I don't blame you for it—it's what I deserve. But I need you to know the truth about what you saw today, and if you come upstairs with me, I can show you and explain." His tone is beseeching now.

I blink at that. *Show me?* What the hell can he have to show me?

"Show me what? The scene of the crime? I saw that this afternoon." I fold my arms and turn away from him.

"Please, Alex."

"And if I say no?" I ask.

"Then I'll take you home right now or call you a taxi. Whatever you want."

I whip my head around to face him. "You weren't so reasonable ten minutes ago when you threatened to force me into the car. What's changed?" My voice is so hard and cold I barely recognize it.

"I know." He looks ashamed now, pinching the bridge of his nose. "I'm sorry. Fuck, Alex, I never want to force you to do anything. I never wanted any of this." His voice cracks slightly. He sounds so sincere.

I can't think straight again. He's doing it again.

"Is she still up there?" I ask.

His eyes widen in shock before narrowing with confusion. "No, of course not." He shakes his head.

I close my eyes and take a deep breath. Don't I need to know every-thing? Every truth he keeps promising me. When I unbuckle my seat belt, he does the same, watching me intently as I open the door and step out of his car. I walk ahead of him into the foyer, and once we're in the elevator, I try so hard not to look at him.

I fail.

He's staring at me intensely, eyes filled with concern. It unsettles me that a large portion of my anger is gone. That I feel more tired than any-thing. More resigned.

He gets out first, and I follow him to the door of his apartment, which, bizarrely, isn't locked. He holds open the door, and I walk through to the living room.

Sitting on the sofa is a large man who looks vaguely familiar as he stands. I remember then that he was one of the guys from the club that night. He helped throw Matt out. He looks surprised to see us as he flicks the TV off with the remote and turns to nod at Jake.

"Cheers, Paul," Jake says. "You can head back, mate."

Paul nods. "Guessing we won't be seeing you down there later." He in-clines his head in my direction.

Jake shakes his head then follows Paul to the front door. From my stance in the living room, I watch him show Paul out and lock the door be-fore coming back toward me.

When he's a few feet away, he stops and slides his hands deep into his pockets as he stares at me. I fold my arms again, giving him an expectant look. He takes a deep breath and walks toward me, stopping only when he's close enough that I can smell him, but not so close that I can feel the heat of him.

"Alex, I've kept things from you, I know that. Important things . . ." He hesitates and rubs the back of his neck. "But I need you to know, it wasn't because I wanted to hurt you. Fuck, I never wanted that." He shakes his head. "I wanted to tell you so many times . . ."

"You wanted to tell me what?" My voice sounds so small. So afraid.

He reaches out to touch me, but I withdraw from him again as the fear crawls over me. He looks as if I've injured him by pulling away, but he nods as though he understands.

"I was gonna tell you eventually. I . . . Fuck . . ." His voice is raw and so utterly unlike him. It does nothing to chase away the fear building inside me.

Jake offers me a small, sad smile and then turns toward the room off the living room—the one he called his spare room. He stops when his hand is on the handle and looks back, his eyes beckoning me forward. For a moment, I can only stand there, immobile and utterly confused, until my feet finally begin to move toward him.

He turns the handle gently and pushes open the door. The room is in almost complete darkness, but there's a small blue glow coming from a night-light on a chest of drawers to my right. As my eye moves around the room, I have to stifle the noise threatening to escape my mouth.

There in the corner, in a small white wooden bed, is a little boy, fast asleep. He's about three years old and has Jake's nose and full, plump mouth.

TWENTY-SEVEN

THE RESEMBLANCE IS UNMISTAKABLE. THIS IS JAKE'S CHILD. THE features are almost all Jake's, except in miniature—the full mouth, the long, dark eyelashes, and the long, straight nose. He even has the adorable sleep pout Jake does. I wonder what color his eyes are. His hair is blonde though, lighter than Jake's, but children's hair often darkens as they get older. He's hugging a soft toy lion tightly to his chest as he dreams whatever children dream of.

When I look up at Jake, he isn't looking at his son; he's watching me.

I drop my eyes again to the bed. I don't even know how I feel. It feels as if I've been punched full force in the chest, my heart crushed beneath shattered bones. It feels like a new kind of heartbreak, and I'm not entirely sure why. I stare at the little boy for a few seconds more before walking quietly out of the bedroom and taking a seat on the sofa in the living room.

I don't look up when Jake takes a seat across from me. It would hurt too much.

Neither of us say anything for a long time, the sound of traffic below and his steady breathing all that fills the large space while the silence between us stretches on and on. When I do finally look at him, he's sitting forward on the chair, tense as he nibbles away at the nail on his index finger. He drops it from his mouth immediately and narrows his eyes on me. Not angrily, but as though he's trying to work out whatever the expression on my face is telling him. I'm not even sure what my expression is. Because I don't even know how I feel. Of course I don't. I don't know anything. I never have.

"Why would you keep this from me?" I ask finally. It seems the most obvious place to start.

"I don't know."

"That's a lie," I say, and his head snaps up. "You made a conscious decision over and over to keep it from me. To lie to me. You do know. Why?"

"I've never *lied* to you."

I want to laugh at that. "Okay, Jake, let me rephrase it. Why didn't you tell me the truth about having a son?"

He nods. "I should have told you. I *wanted* to tell you." He sits forward, and the leather chair creaks as he does. "I . . . I'm just not used to talking about him, that's all."

"With women you're sleeping with, you mean?"

"With *anyone*," he clarifies. "Plus, I thought . . ." He shakes his head and runs a hand over his mouth. "Fuck, I dunno. I thought he'd end up being another reason for you not to be with me."

"What are you talking about?" My voice is sharp and hot. I need to try and temper it. Hysterical isn't going to help anything, I know that. I *feel* hysterical though. He has a child, and he never told me.

"You ran from me, Alex, more than once. You didn't want to get involved with me in the first place. If I'd told you about him, do you honestly think it would have convinced you to give this a go?"

I feel my face screw up in an ugly way. "You think you having a child would have made a difference to me?"

"I just meant . . . I dunno, yes, maybe. I thought it would have complicated things further, yeah. And I didn't want to make it harder for you to see me as someone you could be with." He looks down guiltily.

"Oh, so you kept him a secret for my benefit. I see. How considerate of you," I snap. "And how did you see that panning out long-term, exactly?"

He gives me a look, and it's like a slap across the face. This time, I do laugh.

"Oh, of course. You didn't see it as a long-term thing, did you?" I shake my head, feeling like the biggest bloody idiot. I sit back as he edges forward a little more.

"At first, no," he admits. "I wanted you. Fuck, you've no idea how much I wanted you, baby, but I never thought . . . I didn't think I could . . ." He curses under his breath. "It went too far too fast. And by that time, it was too fucking late to tell you. I don't know." He drops his head to look at his hands.

I can't blame him for thinking that, I suppose. Not when I thought the same. No, I don't blame him for thinking this might not go anywhere. What I blame him for is lying to me and fucking someone else. That part he hasn't even addressed yet. I'm about to ask him to when the realization slams into my chest with a loud screeching sound.

"Vicky," I whisper. "She's his mother." It's not a question, but his face confirms I'm right. "So, you're with her?" Oh my god. I'm the other woman.

"What? No." He shakes his head, eyes wide. He moves forward off the chair completely then and comes to sit across from me on the coffee table. Jake takes my hands in his and looks me in the eye. "I'm not with her. I haven't been with her for a long time." He shakes his head again. "I'm with you."

His words don't bring even a fraction of the relief I hoped for. Weren't those the exact words I wanted to hear earlier? Didn't I want him to tell me it wasn't what I thought? That she meant nothing to him. That it was me he wanted. Yet he has a child with her. That's not nothing. That's everything. She's the mother of his child; I'm a woman he's sleeping with. *I'm* nothing.

I stay silent and instead look down at our hands clasped together. He begins to stroke his thumbs over the tops of mine. It feels comforting and soothing. When he lifts his head, he has that same look on his face. Like he's asking me for something—pleading even—but I don't know what it is he wants. I feel oddly numb, all my earlier emotions blanketed now with something thick and heavy. Maybe I'm in shock.

He has a son.

"Why was she here last night and today, when I came here?" If they're not together, then what? They have sleepovers?

"Because she called me last night. She was a fucking mess. She's always a fucking mess," he growls.

"That was the call you took in my kitchen last night? That was her?"

Jake nods. "She was out of it. She turned up at the club with him—I mean, she brought my three-year-old son to my fucking nightclub on a Friday night." He shakes his head angrily, and his nostrils flare. "Paul let her into my office, and she called me from there. When I got there, he was crying and confused, and so I brought him home and put him to bed. I fell asleep with him," he explains. His tone is almost apologetic, and it makes me feel guilty. I don't want him to apologize for having to look after his son. That's not what he should apologize for and feel guilty about. He should apologize and feel guilty for not telling me he had a son he needed to look after.

I picture him cradling his son to sleep, and it does something to my chest.

"You said you'd call. I was worried about you," is what I say. Because that's what you do when you're in love with someone. "That's why I came here today."

He nods. "I know. I left my phone in the car last night, but I should have called you today. I just . . . Fuck, Alex, I didn't know what to tell you. The things I said last night . . . I wanted to explain. But not over the phone, Alex." He looks down at our hands again. "I didn't want to lie to you."

"How often do you lie to me, Jake?" I ask.

He lifts his head, and his eyes are unflinching. "Only when I have to." His voice is raw and regretful.

How is that any sort of answer? There is a question I do need the answer to though.

"Did you sleep with her last night? Do you and her—"

"No. Fuck no," he cuts me off, sounding angry again. "I don't know what she said to you today, but that never fucking happened, Alex." He shakes his head as he stares into my eyes. The sincerity in them is piercing. "Tell me you believe me. You need to fucking believe that, baby."

I hold his eyes for a long time before nodding finally. He looks relieved. I do believe him. But even then, his not sleeping with her last night doesn't bring the sort of relief I was hoping for. There's too much other stuff rolling about in my head for that to make much of a dent. Now, though, I desperately need to know more.

"How long ago were you together?"

He gives me a half-shrug and a shake of his head. "It was a long time ago. It was never serious—not really. Not for me."

"It couldn't have been that long ago. He's—Christ, I don't even know his name."

"Caleb," Jake fills in.

I nod, letting the name settle for a moment. "Caleb is how old—three? It wasn't that long ago, Jake."

He takes a deep breath and closes his eyes, looking uncomfortable again. No doubt trying to figure out a way of not talking about this. About himself.

"You know, I can go now. I mean if you'd rather not share your shit with me. If this is where we are again."

His mouth twitches, and he fixes me with a serious stare. Then he runs a hand over his mouth and licks his lips before his body language changes. He sits up straighter and seems to harden before my eyes.

"I met Vicky when I was eighteen. I started working for her uncle. He liked me, helped me out when I needed it. I met her at the same time. We were both young. She was the first relationship I ever had."

Small, short, economical snippets of fact that tell me what I need to know and no more.

"Oh, so she was your first love? How sweet." God, how I wish he had fucked her last night. That she was just a one-night stand. Instead of this. The mother of his son and his childhood sweetheart. I feel another bit of something break off.

"No, it wasn't like that. Not for me." He shakes his head again. "I was young. I respected Freddie. I felt . . . I don't know . . . obligated to give her what she wanted." He shifts as I frown. "And she wanted me. I might have thought it was love once, but it wasn't." He looks at me intently. "I know that now. It wasn't even close."

I feel something sad and heavy in my chest. "How long were you together?" Why I'm still asking him questions about this woman, I don't know.

"About six years, on and off. You know how it is when you're kids. Then it was over. I ended it," he says.

I do know how it is when you're kids. I was fourteen. I stopped eating for a week when my first boyfriend broke up with me for a girl who had bigger boobs.

So, he stayed with her for five years. Because she wanted him. Because he felt obligated.

"So, you're not together and haven't been for years, but something happened between the two of you recently. Something that resulted in that little boy through there. But you don't have a thing?" I raise an eyebrow, disbelieving.

He closes his eyes momentarily as though remembering something he'd rather not. "A drunken mistake happened," he says quietly.

I try to imagine him making a drunken mistake, but I can't. He's always so in control.

"Didn't it feel like old times?"

His eyes flare. "Don't do that, Alex. No. It wasn't like that. I was wasted and in a dark fucking place. She still had feelings for me, and she was just there." He shrugs morosely.

Oh, I hate her then. For being there for him.

"Well, it looks as if she still *has* feelings for you. That much was obvious this afternoon," I say.

He shakes his head. "She's twisted that way. Can't bear to see me with anyone else. See me happy."

"Because she's still in love with you."

"Well, that's her fucking problem, not mine." He flares. "It's never going to fucking happen, and she knows it."

So, he knows she still has feelings for him. That his happiness is such a threat to her. Why I'm such a threat to her. I've ruined her perfect vision of him and her and their son being together.

Who knows, maybe I have?

"Did you ever try and give it a go with her? As a family. For Caleb," I ask. Christ, I have lost the plot if I'm putting ideas like *this* in his head.

"No. Because she's not the life I want. She never was," he says as he takes my hands again. "Aside from some terrible fucking memories, Cale is the only thing there is. It's all there'll ever be. You're what I want."

"Last night, you wanted me to end it," I remind him.

He swallows, pain seeping into his eyes. "Because I'm a fucking coward, Alex. Because I'm not ready for you to see who I am. I'm still not," he says. "But I still wanted you. I still do," he adds, softer. With his hands on mine again, he pulls me forward so I can't do anything but meet his gaze. A gaze that seems to penetrate right through me, making me feel as if I might be transparent.

I look down, and my blood kindles at the proximity and closeness of his mouth. I wonder if he kissed me now, what it would feel like. Whether he would still taste the same. He still smells the same. I need to focus.

"She knew about me," I say to change the subject to one that makes me feel colder. "About us."

"I know, but I didn't tell her. She speaks to Kev now and again. He must have mentioned you." I can tell how he feels about that by the way his eyes darken.

"So, your 'doctor bitch' is his name for me then?"

"If it is, I'll kill him," he bites. He doesn't sound as if he's joking.

"Does she often stay here with you?" I ask, ignoring the dark tone in his voice. I can't quite believe I'm still asking questions about her. I want to forget she exists. Except I can't because he has a child with her.

"She doesn't." His eyes are hard. "Last night was a one-off. I have no idea where she is. I fucking hate him living with her." He drags his hand through his hair, and I see a measure of helplessness echo across his face. It makes me hurt for him.

I'm already hurt, but I don't want him to hurt too.

God, my bones feel so heavy. My heart and my head as well. Filled with things I don't even know I have room for.

He stares at me for the longest time then, pleading and willing me to say something—though what, I don't know. That it's okay he kept his son a secret from me? That I understand why he did it? I can't say those things because it's not okay, and I don't understand. How could he not tell me this? If he had feelings for me that were even close to the ones I was having for him, how and why would he keep this from me? None of his reasons so far come close to fixing what he's broken.

"Alex, baby, I'm sorry," he says, finally breaking the suffocating silence. "I know I should have told you. Right at the start. I mean, telling you about the one good thing in my fucking life should have been easy for me. And I *was* going to, at dinner, but then I gave you the shitty childhood detail and it got so dark, and I thought I'd ruined it already. I didn't want to freak you out even more. Then here, I could have shown you his room, told you all about him, easily done. Then later, when you were talking about bringing children up in the States, I thought, 'This is your fucking chance, Jay—do it,' but I chickened out. Because I'm a coward." His voice is filled with regret. "But, fuck, I never wanted you to find out like this. I always wanted to tell you myself. I'm sorry."

He's sorry. He *did* have so many chances to tell me. But he didn't. He demanded I open up every aspect of my life to him, and I did, yet he wasn't prepared to give me the same in return. Is this really why he thought he was bad for me? Because he has a son? It doesn't make any sense.

"What happened last night?" I ask.

He looks confused. "What do you mean? I told you, she called me from the club."

"No." I shake my head. "Before that. It started in the car. Something happened after we left Rob's, when you asked why I didn't report what happened to you. Then why I was with you. You said I didn't know what I was doing, that I should end things. Was it about this? About Vicky and Caleb?" I ask.

He presses his lips together, some conflict in his eyes now. "Partly. My life is a fucking mess, Alex. Always has been. I just think I never realized how different we were—how much I could really fuck up your life—until last night." It sounds so genuine, so utterly bare of any subterfuge, that I almost believe him. But he's avoiding my eyes. "I know I chased you. I wanted you . . . You've no fucking idea how much. But meeting your friends . . . Fuck, seeing you happy like that, safe like that. In your own life . . . I don't know. I felt as if I'd tricked you. I always figured you'd end things before it went too far. Once you realized who I really was." He looks guilty again as he rubs the back of his neck.

"And how could I know who you really are when you've kept things like this from me since the day I met you?"

"You don't understand," he says quietly. "This is just who I am, Alex . . ."

"And I'm someone who needs honesty, Jake," I tell him. "You say I'm what you want, that what we had was more than sex. I mean, I assume you wanted to have a relationship with me, but how was that ever going to be possible when I haven't the first clue who you are? What sort of relationship is that?"

He looks lost again. "I was going to tell you."

"Oh, really? When? Let's not kid ourselves here. I only know about Caleb now because you were backed against a wall, and it was preferable to me thinking you'd gone off and fucked someone else."

"I was going to tell you," he says again.

I sit back. "When?"

He bites his lip. Searches my face. Pleads with his eyes. Finally, he shakes his head and looks down, defeat creeping over him. "I don't know."

Well, at least he doesn't lie.

I look down at where our hands are joined—he took hold of them again at some point, though I don't remember when—and marvel at how steady and smooth and strong his feel in mine. Still. Like our mouths, our hands fit together so well. Our bodies have always fit together so well. But perhaps that's the only part of us that fits. Maybe he's right. Maybe we're too different. That doesn't feel true though. Yes, we're different, but what drew us together was always so strong, so powerful, it seemed to eclipse that. Maybe it's why his secrets and mystery always seemed surmountable to me. Nothing else mattered.

Even now, exhausted and drained, my body wants him closer. He lied to me and kept things from me—huge things—but it doesn't seem to matter because physically, the pull is still as strong. Stronger perhaps.

Somehow, my voice finds its way out of my body. "Is there more?" I ask.

He looks up, and a darkness flashes across his face. His lips press together as though he's trying to stop something from breaking out of them. I feel him grip my hands a little harder. Still, he hides.

When it's clear he isn't going to speak, I nod and drop my eyes to our hands again. "So, I still really don't have the first idea who you are."

"You do," he says. "You know who I am when I'm with you."

I smile sadly as the tears well up behind my eyes. With me, he's who he wants to be. That's what he said. That's not the same thing. That doesn't mean anything. It's just some romantic notion that sounds good and for a while excused his mysterious hidden side. I know that now at least.

I slip my hands out of his grip. "I think I should go."

He moves forward quickly. "Alex, please don't."

I shake my head, unable to meet his eye. "I need to, Jake. I need to go. I need to think." I sound clumsy.

As I go to stand, he grabs a hold of my hands again, pulling me back down to the couch. When I finally do look at him, it only confirms to me that I *definitely* need to go. I'm tired, drunk, and emotional, and he is still so tempting to every single part of me. So bloody beautiful. I still want him a frightening amount. The sheer intensity of which scares me half to death.

But everything else feels as if it needs time to settle.

With his hands still holding mine, I try to stand again. I don't pull my hands out of his because he releases them before I need to.

"Could you call me a taxi, please? I need to use the bathroom," I say, leaving him sitting there.

I sit down on the toilet lid feeling leaden and heavy from too much knowledge, yet at the same time, not enough knowledge. Twenty-four hours ago, I was in love with him—with some manageable reservations. Six hours ago, I was standing face-to-face with the woman I thought he'd cheated on me with. Half an hour ago, he told me she's a woman he has a child with. I try to rationalize it for a moment, to consider if he did have a right to keep this to himself until he was ready to tell me. Maybe. Yes. But with Jake, it's a pattern. He's never wanted to share any part of himself with me—nothing outside of the physical anyway. And there's more he isn't telling me, I'm certain of that, but I'm not sure I can handle knowing about it. So maybe this time, I'll let him keep his secrets.

At the sink, I run my hands under the cold water and pat my cheeks, my forehead, the back of my neck. Then I tilt down to drink a few cold, welcoming gulps. I suppose I could look a lot worse after the day I've had. I pinch my cheeks and flatten some of my eye shadow before licking my lips.

I wonder why I'm bothering, but deep down, I know why. When I walk out of here in the next ten minutes, I want him to feel as if he might have lost something.

When I come out of the bathroom, I stop dead in my tracks, traitorous body roaring at the sight of him. He's standing in front of one of the ceiling-height windows with his back to me. His T-shirt is tight around his upper body, the undeniable strength in his arms defined and pronounced. I want them wrapped around me. He's resting his head on the glass as he looks out at the enviable view of Tower Bridge from the east side of his living room. He doesn't seem to be looking at it though; he looks miles away. But if I asked him where he was in his mind, he probably wouldn't tell me.

"You called a taxi?" I ask quietly.

He turns around and stares wordlessly for a few seconds before nodding once. He has a beer bottle in his hand, and as he lifts it to his mouth, his T-shirt rises, and I see a flash of inked skin on his stomach.

"The tattoo. It's for Caleb," I say with a nod. The Roman numerals are his date of birth, presumably.

He nods. "Yeah. Had it done the day he was born."

"I always thought that tattoo was for a girl. It made me jealous of her." I smile, feeling as pathetic as I always knew I would if I ever told him that.

He walks toward me, depositing the beer on top of one of the shelves on his way past. As he walks, I look down at his feet, and my stomach somersaults at his hairless, tanned skin. It gives him a softer edge, making him vulnerable somehow.

When he stops in front of me, the heat from his body settles around me like a blanket. "And what if I told you no woman ever meant anything to me before you? Would you believe me?" His eyes are glittering and serious.

"I'd want to believe you," I say, my gaze dropping to his mouth. It's wet and bitten red, and I almost ache from how badly I need to feel it on mine.

He sighs, tilting his forehead down to rest it on top of mine, eyes closing over. His mouth is so close like this. The barest tilt of my head, and I could kiss him.

I need to go.

"I know I've made it harder for you to believe me now, baby, but I've never lied to you about how I feel. How you make me feel." His voice is scratched raw.

I feel the sting of tears rise behind my eyes, sad and angry. Of course, I'm still angry with him, but I know he's hurting too, and it's clear to me he *is* sorry.

I just don't know how to deal with it. I bring my hands up to gently push him away, but I can't bring myself to do that, so I just rest them flat on his chest. It's warm and hard, and his heart thunders quickly under my fingers.

"Please don't go," he says. "Stay. Stay the night. You can meet him in the morning. Fuck, I'd like for him to meet you." He moves his forehead from side to side in a rocking motion while he breathes deeply.

Stay. Stay with him and fall asleep with him and wake up with him. Stay and meet his little boy. His little boy I didn't know existed until half an hour ago.

It doesn't sound that bizarre anymore.

Stay. My body wills me to say yes, but that's always what my body has done where he's concerned. It's selfish and desperate. My mind though, my good-girl reasons—they're louder now.

"How would you introduce me to him?" I ask.

"What?"

"Who am I to you?"

He pulls back to stare into my eyes as he ponders my question. "I'd tell him your name and how you fixed me once when I was hurt. I'd tell him how special you are and that his dad cares about you so fucking much," he says.

I picture his little boy's face peering shyly up at me from behind Jake as he says this, and I feel myself smile a little.

Jake takes a deep breath and wraps his arms around me, so I'm pulled flat against his chest. Oh, the heat and comfort of being held by him again is immense. Today, when I left here, I thought I'd never get to have this again.

He moves his mouth to the side of my head to my temple, where he kisses me gently. Then he kisses softly down my cheek, my jaw, until he reaches my mouth. He holds the sides of my head as he slides his lips over mine, gentle and deliberate at first. When he pushes his tongue into my mouth, I can't help but sigh into the kiss. He still tastes the same. Of course he does. His hand on my hip, he pulls me into him, rocking his hips against me as he deepens the kiss.

"Alex . . . please," he whispers. "I need you. You have no fucking idea how much I need you. How much I need this. *Us.* Something good."

Between his mouth and the words, I feel turned inside out. My arms hang by my sides, but I want so much to wrap them around him, to slide them under his T-shirt and graze my fingernails across the dip of his spine. But that would be weak. And I don't want him to know how weak I am.

I want to be strong.

If I wrap my arms around him, it would be some kind of forgiveness. It would be me telling him that what he did is okay.

"Jake, please . . ." I protest, but he kisses the words from my mouth with his own.

Stronger than this, Alex. Much stronger.

Then, saving me, his phone rings. He ignores the noise entirely, but I twist my head and use my hands to push at his body until he releases me. A small growl of frustration leaves him as he steps back. He's breathing hard, and his eyes are dark and fiery as he stares at me, his phone continuing to ring. He needs to answer it before it wakes his son.

Finally, he takes the phone out of his pocket, glances at it, and shuts off the call.

"Your taxi's downstairs," he states.

As I nod, I realize I can't drag my eyes or my body any farther away from his. The idea of leaving him makes me feel nothing but dread, as if it's some insurmountable task I've no hope of completing. He looks as if he wants to say something but is holding his mouth shut tight to stop himself.

With some degree of effort, I manage to force myself to turn away from him, crossing to the breakfast bar to lift my jacket and bag. When I look back, he's staring at me, hands in his pockets, shoulders tense, and eyes sad.

"Let me walk you down," he says and moves toward me.

I shake my head. "No. You can't leave him."

He stops and begins to bite the inside of his mouth again in that way he does. The way I now know is his way of stopping himself from talking. Because he doesn't want to talk to me. Because he wants to keep things from me.

"Alex, I need you to know. Before you go, I need you to know that I'm . . ." He pauses, a tortured look on his face.

"You're sorry. I know." I nod.

His expression flickers with something before he drops his shoulders then his eyes and nods. Without his gaze on me, it feels far easier to move, and so I do. He follows behind.

When I get to the door, I stop to turn around, to say goodbye, but I don't get a chance. He moves so quickly, his mouth and body pressing me back against the door with a gentle force. He kisses me again, and this time, it's rough, dominant, bruising almost. He runs his hands through my hair, down my face, over my neck, as though trying to commit me to memory.

The gnawing heat begins to build between my legs, desperate to pull him inside me. Right there with the need and desire, though, is anger. I'm so bloody angry with him. It didn't have to be like this. He didn't have to do this. But it will always be like this with him, won't it? He'll never let me in—not fully. That much was clear tonight.

It doesn't matter. You'll never feel a fraction of this with anyone else. If you think you will, you're kidding yourself. He's everything you want. You're in love with him.

I need to get out of here.

I push at his chest, but he doesn't move and continues to lap at my mouth with his tongue as he slides his hand between my thighs, cupping me possessively with hot, greedy fingers.

"Don't leave me, baby, please," he breathes against my mouth.

I moan as his fingers slide up my thigh, grazing the seam of my underwear. My legs threaten to buckle with need. With one final push of my body, he moves back, and all at once, every last ounce of heat disappears from me. I don't look at him as I turn and reach for the handle.

"Tell me we aren't over," he says as he pushes his foot against the door. "Tell me you need some space. Tell me you fucking hate me but that it isn't over. Tell me you still want me, Alex. I need to hear you say it." It's a demand.

It makes me turn my head to look at him. The intensity in his eyes is a level I've never seen before. Dangerously dark, sad too, but the heat and desire in them is suffocating. I can't breathe.

"Jake, please don't . . ." I whisper, dropping my eyes again. My vision feels blurry. Am I crying? It feels like I am. "Let me go. I need to go."

"Tell me you still want me, baby. I need to hear you say it." It's softer now—not a command anymore; a plea. "I can let you walk out of here if I know you still want me."

"You need to let me go now, Jake," I whisper.

Immediately, regret seeps into his eyes. He looks down at his hand over mine and nods before I feel the pressure ease off.

Jake steps back from the door. As I walk away from him, I feel his eyes burn heavy into the back of my head.

"That's not a no, Alex," he says as I slip out into the hallway.

For the third time that day, I walk to the elevator on unstable legs and with a heart that feels heavy and ever so slightly broken. I don't look back.

TWENTY-EIGHT

THROW MYSELF INTO THE TAXI—WHICH *IS* A TAXI THIS TIME, AND NOT Jake's driver. As I give him my address, he sighs, and that's enough to cause the tears to break free.

"I'm sorry. I know it's a bit far out," I sniffle.

The driver looks stunned—a little horrified even—by my outburst. "Oh, it's okay, love. It's not a problem. You're my last fare of the night anyway," he says as he steals a look at me in the rearview mirror.

I nod, wiping the back of my hand across my face. How embarrassing. A minute later, I see his arm appear between the two front seats holding a box of tissues. I thank him, still sniffling.

"Don't tell me. Man trouble."

Oh, he has no bloody idea.

I laugh a small, sad laugh. "So predictable."

"Aw, I see the lot doing this job, sweetheart. You wouldn't believe. Once picked up a bride the night of her wedding—caught her husband and her bridesmaid at it, you know."

"God, really?" Yes, I'm sure finding out the deeply secretive man I've been sleeping with, who I've fallen in love with despite not knowing anything about, turns out to have a son he didn't think to mention isn't the wildest thing he's ever heard.

For the entirety of the journey, my temporary father figure offers me reams of assumed wisdom and advice with regard to my "man troubles," as he keeps referring to them. It doesn't come across as patronizing because he has such a nice manner about him. Not what I expected when I first got in. But listening to him chatter away in his warm Cockney accent stops the scene with Jake from playing over and over in my head.

"I'm sure it will work itself out," he says. "I'm sure if it's meant to be, it will be," he says. "He's likely not worth it anyway," he says. I tell him I'll be fine. I don't mention that I feel as if I've been run over by a truck. As if my bones and body are shattered and broken, my heart crushed to a pulp.

When he pulls up at my house, I pay and tip him generously, thanking him for the friendly ear. He tells me I'm a lovely young girl and he's sure I'll find the right man soon enough. I'm about to tell him I'm pretty sure I did, that despite his secrets and his lies I still want him. I want to ask if that's weak-willed and female, but I doubt he'd know. Instead, I give him my polite smile and wish him good night. I'm scared to say any of that out loud anyway in case someone does have the answers and none of them are what I want to hear. I never wanted to talk about Jake with anyone from the start because to me, he always felt like some treasure I'd stolen. Something that didn't belong with me. Sounds as if Jake saw it like that too.

After feeding Fred, I crawl into my freezing, empty bed. It matches how I feel inside, and the dark quiet of my bedroom magnifies everything times one hundred. Before I forget, I message my brother to tell him I'm home safe, it was lovely meeting Jin, and to thank him for dinner. It's a few minutes before he responds with a dozen smileys, saying Jin loved me too.

I shed some more tears into my pillow before finally passing out.

Sunday, I spend in a trance interspersed with fake normalcy because I have to speak to people. Nick calls to find out what I *really* thought about Jin and to tell me about the rest of the night. He sounds so giddy, if a little hungover, that I feel somewhat less dead inside when I hang up. Betty pops over to thank me for the wine and give me some of her homemade marmalade and takes forever to leave. I completely forget about Tash's Skype call until she messages me at 4:00 p.m., and so I try to rearrange for midweek, but she's having none of it. I manage to negotiate her down to a phone call though, because I look awful and won't be able to fake anything over a video call.

In the end, I'm glad we did it, because simply hearing her voice lifts some of the oppressive weight hanging over me. She's chirpier than ever, and I swear I hear an American twang in certain words as she babbles at me for close to an hour. After telling me about her house hunt in Malibu, we have a quick chat about France before she asks what my exciting news is. The news was supposed to be Jake. I brush her off, saying it's about the possible partnership spot at work, which, thankfully, she buys. Before hanging up, she asks when I'm moving over, and I ask if I can come tomorrow. At that moment, I wish I were going. That I were running far away from here and everything I have to make a decision about.

I need you, Alex . . . You have no idea how much I need you . . . Please don't leave me.

I feel sick again and wipe at the tears that well up in my eyes.

By some miracle of god, Mum doesn't call. She usually always calls on Sunday nights, but buried way in the back of my head somewhere is the memory that she and Dad are at a Sam Shepard play tonight. At least, I think it's tonight. I should listen to her more when she talks.

By 9:00 p.m., I'm in bed with the worst headache I've had in a long time, though I'm sure it's just my mind finally grinding to a halt from overuse, some great mechanical beast of a machine that has seen better days. He hasn't tried to get in touch, which I'm glad about. One day apart isn't nearly enough space or time anyway.

The following week goes by in a blur, with me practically sleepwalking through each day. I see my patients in a detached, robotic fashion, nodding and smiling and reassuring in alternating patterns, and by Wednesday, I've managed to perfect a smile so fake it makes my temples and jaw hurt. It works though.

By Thursday, he still hasn't contacted me, or I him. But then, four days isn't enough space or time either.

My mask of fake normalcy lasts until Thursday evening, when I sit down next to Dad at the dining table in my parents' kitchen. He knows immediately something's wrong, and though he doesn't ask, he does stare at me through slightly narrowed eyes during dinner. He's extra comforting though and steers the conversation to random topics, such as Bob from down the road's new classic sports car, the Sam Shepard play that was too *"theatrical"* but well done, and Nick and Tash and France.

When Mum does ask about the boy Ben saw me with, I tell her we went out a few times and we're simply trying to slow things down a little. This seems to satisfy her, though she definitely gives me one of her sad looks and lingers on my face too long. When we finally settle on some dates for going to France, I feel something like excitement start to build. In five weeks, I'll be relaxing under the shade in the south of France, and this will all be dealt with. One way or another, I'll be beyond it.

I often try to think of unwelcome things in this way, as transient points in time with very little shelf life. Interviews, speeches, exams, social events I'm dreading. I focus hard on the vision of me I have on the other side of it. Relieved. It normally works.

Where will Jake and I be in five weeks? Will there even be a Jake and me in five weeks? For once, he seems to have left the decision entirely up to me, and I resent him for it. If he bulldozed his way into my house now, demanding things of me, it would make this a whole lot easier.

One positive that emerges from my wallowing is that I spend most nights upstairs at the Steinway. I play more than I've played in months—depressing, melancholic pieces Rob doesn't want anywhere near her wedding. It occurs to me if Jake and I are truly over, I might not be able to play anything happy ever again. Then I almost smack myself for how pathetic that sounds. If we can't sort this out, my life will go on. I'll meet someone else. Someone who isn't him.

I feel sick.

I've only *just* about managed to scrape through the week like this—how the hell am I supposed to manage the rest of my life without him? Though that's probably because it's not over yet. Because neither of us have ended it. I'm lingering here, waiting for my heart—or, rather, my head—to make up its mind. At least if it were over, I could start to move on. But it's not. Right now, it feels like an open wound, and again, I need to decide whether to open the door and knit it back together or leave it to bleed out.

The two things seem to be this: Can I ever trust him to be honest with me about anything after keeping his son from me? And can I live without him?

I mean, I did. For a long time, I lived unperturbed by the existence of Jake Lawrence—a name I'd probably never have even heard or uttered had he not needed medical attention that night. Now, it lives under my skin and in my body, flowing through my veins.

God, I miss him. Almost a week apart, and I miss him so much it hurts. The smell of him, the warmth of him, the way he looked at me. The deep, scratchy growl of his voice. How I feel when I'm with him. I miss all of it so bloody much it aches. It feels like a great lead weight inside of me—one I've been carrying about all week, and which is only getting heavier. It's in my chest and my throat, and my whole body feels dragged down by it, harder to carry around.

I swear, if I went swimming, I would sink straight to the bottom.

Throughout the week, I make sure all my contact with Rob is brief and non-verbal. If we speak or meet up, she'll know immediately something's wrong and make me talk about it. By Saturday though, I can avoid it no longer. It's wedding dress fitting day. Rob's dress arrived on Wednesday and is waiting in La Fayette de Monde, a stylish wedding dress boutique in Mayfair.

I get there at 10:00 a.m. and open the door into a world of white, lace, and tulle. I'm really glad I'm wearing my sunglasses. Mainly because of the shade of the place, but also because I wasn't fully able to cover the dark circles under my eyes this morning despite my overpriced and falsely advertised concealer. I've learned this week that beauty sleep isn't a myth. I counted, and about twenty-two shitty hours of unconsciousness is all I've managed to clock up. It's more than evident on my face. Especially under this light.

I spot Robyn immediately, chatting animatedly to a sales assistant, happiness and exuberant positivity radiating from her whole body. Perhaps if I stand close, I can absorb some.

I try to will myself back into the body of someone who feels happy and excited. I mean, I can remember what it feels like to be happy. It was a thing I felt once, so I'm sure I can fake it. But then I feel angry at Jake again for making me need to fake it. My best friend is marrying the love of her life in eight weeks, and I should be happy and excited for her. I *am* happy and excited for her. My own misery can take a back seat for the day. Jake and his secrets can take a back seat for the day.

I'm hoping the excitement over the dress will impair her unsettlingly observant perception. When she turns around, I fix on my practiced smile—which, to be fair, is easier than it has been all week, because it's Rob, and it's her wedding dress, and I've waited my whole life to see her try on her wedding dress. She rushes toward me, wrapping her arms around me in her tight, fragrant, familiar hug.

"Hey. Sorry I'm a bit late. Parking was a bitch," I say as I squeeze her tightly. Having her arms around me is unexpectedly warm and comforting, so I hold onto her longer than necessary.

"Oh, you're not, babe, don't worry." She pulls back, smiling nervously.

"Your mum not here?" I ask as I look around. They don't get on, but I assumed Jane would be here.

"I told her I only wanted you to see it today." She shrugs, something cold coming over her eyes before they brighten again. "Okay, so, you go have a seat, and I'll go put *IT* on."

As I walk over toward a white silk chaise, a young sales assistant offers me coffee or champagne. Coffee has become my life force this week; it won't let me down now. Plus, I'm driving.

While I wait for Rob, I look around the huge, modern space, which is all hardwood floors, red brick, and gorgeous dresses on contemporary displays. Some of the dresses are incredibly beautiful, and if I were feeling even remotely human I might even try a couple on for fun. I've always imagined myself in something simple, maybe vintage, which I don't see here, but I never tried on a single wedding dress the entire time I was engaged to Ben. Maybe because deep down, I always knew I was never going to need one.

From literally nowhere, an image of Jake waiting at an altar for me flickers through my mind. He looks beautiful and strong in a dark suit, his body pulled up tall. Across his eyes comes a flicker of nerves before his mouth tilts up at the side to smile his cocky, canine-flashing smile. I rub a hand over my eyes in an attempt to banish the vision entirely. What the hell is wrong with me?

I hear rustling to my left. I turn my head, and my mouth drops open. I gasp aloud as Rob comes toward me in a vision of strapless, slim-fitting ivory silk. There's the faintest hint of delicate lace around the hem and bodice, but it's mainly soft, buttery silk. It's divine. The perfect silhouette for her elegant figure. Her shoulder-length blonde hair is down now in semi-waves about her face, and she has one side of it pinned up loosely with a diamond comb. For the first time in days, I want to cry with something other than despair. She looks utterly breathtaking.

"Oh my god, Rob," I say as I rise slowly from the couch.

"What do you think?" She sounds tentative and uncertain, and I try to scramble for the words she wants to hear. Except I'm practically speechless. She's picked a wedding dress that could only have been made for one person. Her.

"It's perfect. So you. It's so beautiful, babe. You look stunning . . . my god." I bend down to place my cup on the table by the chaise before going toward her. At her feet, I kneel, running my hand over the lace of the hem and under it, stopping to wipe a tear away from my cheek. "It's as if it were made for you."

She beams at me. "Oh, god, I love it too. I was so worried, you know. But yes . . ." She turns around to appraise herself in the floor-length mirror. Down the back and to the end of the short train is a stream of delicate lace buttons. It's classic but stylish at the same time. Dan is going to have a fit when he sees her in this. "Yes, I love it!" she exclaims as she swishes around. "Yes, I do. I'm so glad I love it! I remember why I loved it!" She jumps up and down a few times, making me smile.

The smidgen of excitement and happiness inside me grows and isn't even half-fake anymore. It's the only warm thing I've felt in days. Seven, to be exact.

"It's stunning, babe. I honestly couldn't have imagined you in anything more perfect. And I don't even think it needs altering either," I say as I run my hand along the top and kneel again to pull down the hem, which sits a few inches long. In heels, it will be a perfect length.

"I know, right? It is a perfect fit!" She squeals with delight as the assistant kneels beside me and confirms she doesn't think it needs altering either.

We discuss the shoes at length until she settles on an ivory peep toe with a lace design. She'll wear an off-white veil belonging to her grandmother, which she's having a flower crown sewn into.

We leave a short while later with the dress covered in a metallic, armor-like hanging bag and the shoes packed and wrapped neatly in silk tissue paper inside a gold and yellow box. She asks if I'll keep them safe at my house to stop Dan's prying eyes, and after laying them delicately in the boot of my Mini, the dress flat on the back seat, we walk to a nearby Japanese restaurant she finds on her phone for lunch.

"So, you're bringing Jake to the wedding, obviously," she says halfway through lunch.

I was counting myself lucky she hadn't mentioned him the entire afternoon and thought I might be able to get away without mentioning him too. No such luck.

"We booked an exec room for you anyway because you're my bridesmaid and pianist, and because you deserve it, so if he's coming, you can both have a magical night at Illeam Castle on us! It's the next best room to the bridal suite. And it has a hot tub, I think." She winks.

I can't hold her eyes and so look down into my half-eaten bowl of ramen soup instead.

"What? You have asked him, right? I mean, I was going to on Friday, but I didn't think it was my place. Wait—what? What is it, Alex? Oh no . . ." she says, and it's then I realize the tears are rolling pathetically down my face.

I wipe at them angrily with the back of my hand. Christ, I thought I was done crying. I *want* to be done crying. Isn't there supposed to be a next phase I should be at by now?

Rob comes to sit next to me on my side of the booth and turns me to face her. "What happened? What did that bugger do?"

I shake my head because I can't even think of where to start.

"Oh, I knew he'd be bloody trouble. The ones who are *that* good in bed always are." She puts an arm around me and pulls me into her.

At this point, the tears seem to dry up, so maybe that was the last of them.

"It's complicated." I sniff. *"He's* complicated."

"Really? They're normally so easy to figure out too," she says.

"He has a son, Rob," I blurt. I watch as her eyes go wide. "A little boy he didn't tell me about. Can you believe that?"

She looks speechless for a moment. "Why? Why didn't he tell you?"

"He thought it would complicate things. Then he said he wanted to, but he was a coward." I shake my head.

Her mouth is open and her eyes still wide. "Wow. And so how did you find out?"

"Because I went over to his place the day after your dinner party, and some woman answered the door. I thought he'd slept with her, but no, he just has a child with her. She was just the mother of his secret child." I laugh a little hysterically then, but it dies out immediately. When I look up, Rob looks confused, so I tell her about Vicky and how they don't have a thing, and about how she means nothing to him.

She goes from looking shocked to looking sad to saying nothing for a short while. Finally, she shakes her head. "God, Alex, that is . . . complicated."

I nod. "Oh, and that's not even the worst part. The worst of it is that I'm in love with him. Totally in love with him. I mean, that's crazy, isn't it? How can I be in love with him when I don't even know him? I've fallen in love with someone who keeps things like this from me. I'm an idiot."

She takes a deep breath before speaking. "Ugh, you're not an idiot, babe. Love is weird like that. You're an adult. A smart, intelligent woman who knows her own heart and her own mind. You knew Ben wasn't right for you. You bloody knew it. You knew it way before he started screwing around on you."

I frown. "This isn't about Ben, Rob," I tell her.

She raises an eyebrow, skeptical. "Right, but that prick hurt you. Then this sexy, exciting nightclub owner comes along, and you want to forget about how he made you feel."

I think about this. Was I easy prey to Jake because of Ben?

"It's not about Ben. It's about Jake."

She takes a deep breath. "If you love him—if you really love him—then you have to find a way to understand why he's done this. And forgive him for it." It sounds so easy when she says it like that. "Now, I don't advocate that approach for cheating pricks like Ben Cooke. But this isn't the same."

"You think secrets are fine then? As long as they don't involve cheating?'

She licks her tongue over her teeth as she thinks about it. "No, they're not fine. But you can't know everything about a person, babe. It's not realistic."

"You know everything about Dan," I point out.

"Well, I've known him for ten years, so, yes, I know a lot of his secrets. What I don't know, I ask him, and as for the rest . . . well, maybe we're all allowed to keep some stuff for ourselves, you know?" Somehow, I don't think Dan's secret habit of betting on the Grand National when he knows Rob hates horse racing is anywhere near the sort of secret Jake kept from me. I frown at her, but she goes on. "You knew Ben for years, and look what happened there. You never saw what he did coming. I mean, I never liked him a whole lot, as we know, but no one thought he was going to go and do what he did to you. Goes to show nobody ever really knows anyone like they think they do, Al." She reaches across and lifts her water to take a sip. "Also," she continues, clearly on a roll, "maybe the situation with the mother is complicated and messy and he didn't want to terrify you with it. She sounds like a right horror." She gives me a look of warning.

"If he doesn't trust me with things like this, doesn't it say I'm not important to him? I mean, didn't it occur to him how much it would hurt me to find out about it later? If I found out about it like this."

She nods. "He's messed up there, and for that, he's the bloody idiot. But maybe he thought you'd run at the thought of getting involved with someone with a kid. Some people would. I know you wouldn't, but he didn't know that." She shrugs. "This is one thing, yes. A major fuckup on his part. But what about everything else? How he makes you feel. Does he make you happy? These are important too."

"I wanted him to be honest with me, Rob. What other things will he keep from me because he thinks I can't handle them?"

She sighs. "Trust comes with time, Alex. And from both sides. Show him he can trust you, that you're not going to run a mile."

I look at her sadly because Jake said those same words, and what did I do? I ran.

"Listen, seeing you with him the other night . . ." She stops and changes direction, searching for new words before nodding when she finds them. "I've never seen you look like that before, ever. You looked . . . serene. The two of you may as well have been alone in that room for all the difference we made. His eyes followed you everywhere, Alex. He watched you while you spoke, hypnotized, as if he couldn't look away from you for a second in case he lost you or something. From what I saw, he cares about you, and he'll know he's fucked this up massively." She smiles, her voice wistful and soft. "I mean, Dan and I have been together for years, and you guys looked like the about-to-be-married couple. So, he has some secrets. Don't they all? Give him time to open up to you. You don't know much about his past relationships or his upbringing, but there will most likely be an explanation there. Mark hated him, of course, but then who doesn't Sherlock hate? He has an inherent distrust of every guy of a certain age who isn't Dan. And even then . . ." She rolls her eyes. Then her face is serious again. "But I think you will regret it for the rest of your life if you don't fight for this, babe." She nods a final time before picking up an edamame bean and popping it delicately into her mouth.

I stare at her, speechless. Did she seriously just figure Jake Lawrence out over a Japanese noodle salad when I've tried for weeks to do it? Everything she said makes it all seem simple and manageable. Give him time to open up to me. I do know some of his upbringing and past relationships, and there is some explanation there. I also know this kind of thing is new for him.

Suddenly and unexpectedly, a feeling of weightlessness overcomes me, washing away the heavy, oppressive anxiety that's filled my body all week. It's replaced a moment later by something else—something worse. Fear.

"What if I've ruined it?" I say.

She looks at me, frowning. "*You* haven't done anything wrong."

"You didn't see him that night, Rob. He begged me to stay with him. Pleaded. But I didn't—I left." I shake my head, the fear gripping hold of me tightly. "Walked out of there and never looked back once." I wasn't able to. The pain and torment in his eyes almost killed me.

She puts her hand on my arm again and squeezes. "Listen, you haven't ruined anything. You needed time to fucking think. *He* was the one who almost ruined it. And if he knows what's good for him, he'll have been sitting wherever sexy nightclub owners sit with everything crossed, waiting for you to give him another chance. He's crazy about you, babe. It was obvious to everyone. You *haven't* ruined it." The conviction in her eyes is life-affirming.

I nod as I twist my hands together. "I haven't spoken to him all week. I've not got a clue where his head is. It could be anywhere." Between Gemma or Dawn from the elevator's legs, for example.

Okay, that's not helping.

"He'll think he's lost you," she says. "Call him, Alex. Put him out of his misery. Put yourself out of your misery. No regrets. Remember?" She smiles, and I laugh out loud. We almost got matching tattoos on our first girls' trip to Marbella that said "no regrets" but then realized we'd probably regret them.

"I'll call him tonight."

"Good, and don't think about it anymore. I know what you're like—you'll overthink it, talk yourself out of it. But if you don't call him, you're going to regret it and overthink it for the rest of your life." Her voice is as serious as I've ever heard it.

She's right.

Because she knows me inside out. I *would* regret it for the rest of my life. If I don't at least try to work through the secrets, then I'll never know. He hurt me, yes, but he's been hurt too. His experiences have molded him into this hard-shelled, mistrusting person. I need to show him he can trust me.

Robyn pays for lunch as a "head bridesmaid with man troubles treat" and walks me back to my car. When I'm inside, she taps the window, and I press the button to open it.

"Call me later, okay? If you need me, call me. Anytime. Everything's going to be fine. I was witness to you two together." She fans her face. "HOT. Now, go get your bloody man!" she says dramatically, and I can't help but giggle.

Rob hugs me again through the window, and I promise to guard her dress with my life before pulling out of my tight parking space and driving off into the ridiculously busy London traffic. She waves at me from the pavement until I turn the corner.

I'll start by telling him I'm in love with him. That should make the rest of it easier.

TWENTY-NINE

TELL HIM I LOVE HIM. EVERYTHING ELSE SHOULD BE EASY.

Jake having a son isn't an issue. All it does is add another layer to him. I can be with a guy who has a child. It's different and unexpected, but it's not an insurmountable issue. The issue has always been him keeping things from me—himself, mainly. It's his not trusting me.

Of course, Rob is right. Trust is given and earned over time, but given how we met, how I've kept his secrets since the moment I knew him, maybe I feel as if he should have given me more credit in the trust department.

If we're going to do this—be together—then I need to be able to ask him questions and get proper answers back. I don't need to know about every single aspect of his life, but I need to know the important things. If he wants this to work, then he needs to be prepared to open up to me at some point.

After dinner, I pour myself a glass of wine to steady my nerves . . . and then a second because, well, two glasses are better than one. As I call up his name in my phone, my heart feels as if it might explode out of my chest. I stare at it for almost five whole minutes until the light goes out on the screen. I'm not afraid that calling him is a mistake, that being with him is a mistake, but I am scared the distance I've put between us this week has altered his thinking in some way. I'm scared I've left it too late, and he's decided it's over. I'm not sure I'm prepared for that.

I guess that's where the wine will come in handy.

As I hit the dial button on his name, I think I stop breathing entirely until, on the second ring, he answers.

"Hey," he says quietly. His voice is steady, but he sounds surprised, I think.

My breathing starts up again, and my heart staggers at the sound of his voice, so deep and close and still with the power to make goose bumps break out across my skin. God, I've missed the sound of his voice. It's warm and soft, and it seeps into my cold, lonely bones.

"Hi," I whisper.

There's a moment of heavy silence before I hear him let out a deep breath. "Been hoping all week that you were going to call," he says, his voice sounding uncertain and un-Jake-like.

"You could have called me."

He sighs. "I almost did. About a hundred fucking times. I just didn't want you to hang up on me. I figured if you wanted to talk to me, you'd call . . ."

I nod even though I know he can't see me. "I think we should talk, don't you?" I say tentatively.

"When?"

The speediness of his reply takes me by surprise. "Um, well, what are you doing now?" I look up at the clock on my wall. It's 8:10 p.m. on a Saturday night. "You'll be going to the club later, I assume. Or are you there now?"

"I'm at home. I was going to head down in a bit, but I don't have to. I can come and see you." Then, soft and uncertain: "I mean, if that's what you're saying. If that's what you want."

Of course it's what I want. It's all I've wanted all week. I take another sip of wine to cool down.

"I don't want to keep you from work, Jake. We can arrange to meet through the week, when—"

"Alex, I'd much rather see you tonight if it's an option," he cuts in. "I want to see you. I need to see you, baby," he adds, urgent now.

My body softens further at the nickname, and I close my eyes and chew my lip hard. I've had two glasses of wine, and I'm not entirely confident I won't throw myself at him if he comes here tonight. This was about arranging to meet and talk. I should have prepared for this. It's not sensible for him to come over now.

I take another sip of wine and swallow. His breaths are faint and shallow down the other end of the line while he waits.

"Okay. I'm at home. Come over," I hear myself say.

"Okay, I'll leave now," he says in a businesslike tone.

"Okay," I manage.

"See you soon," he whispers, and then he's gone.

Okay, now I'm nervous. Thrumming with anticipation, I sit there for a few seconds wondering whether to call Rob. In the end, I decide to text her instead.

Me: He's on his way over now. I've had wine. I'm afraid I'm going to drag him upstairs to bed the minute he walks through the door. Help me be serene please?

I sip my wine and inspect my nails until she responds a minute later.

Rob: Haha! As long as you talk before, during, or after then go for it, babe. Call me tomorrow! He's crazy about you. Go get your man! Xx

Smiling, I go upstairs to run a brush through my hair and wash my face. Then, as I'm coming out of the bedroom, I decide on a whim to change my underwear. It's pathetic, I know, but the set I put on this morning was not supposed to be seen by Jake—or anyone else for that matter. It's what I'd consider utility underwear; the kind you put on when you're mourning the loss of a guy, not for making up with a guy. He doesn't need to see unattractive utility underwear. Not when I have a whole drawer full of lingerie.

So then, clearly, I've *accepted* the fact I'll be taking off my clothes at some point.

Redressing in my cream button-down dress, I go back downstairs and walk through to the kitchen to rinse out my glass and drink some water. When I glance at the clock again, it's gone 8:40 p.m. He literally will be here any minute. I'm so bloody nervous. Prickles of heat ripple across my body at the idea of seeing him, of touching him, of having him close again.

For something to do, I check the fridge to see if there's anything to munch on to pass the time and grab the bowl of strawberries I picked from the garden earlier. Five strawberries in, I jump out of my skin when the sound of the doorbell echoes around the house.

For some reason, as I stand, I look around the room to make sure I haven't left anything embarrassing lying around. Utility underwear, for example. Before going to get the door, I take a deep, necessary, stabilizing breath and pull it open.

My stabilizing breath was utterly useless, because I feel as if I'm about to collapse when I get my first look at him in days. His mouth is reserved and the look on his face uncertain, as though he's not sure whether to smile or not. His hands are shoved deep into the pockets of his jeans, and he's wearing a light blue T-shirt that hugs his perfect body and teases me with glimpses of the art that decorates his arms. He looks painfully gorgeous. His hair is longer than I've ever seen it and mussed carelessly to the side, the hair on his face longer too. It's not exactly a beard, but it's far longer than his usual stubble. It suits him. It makes him look serious.

"Hey," he says, his eyes piercing and intense. He drops his gaze down my body before returning it to hold mine.

"Hi," I say as I step back into the hallway to let him inside. When I step forward to close the door, our bodies graze together, and I feel a thrum of electricity move through me. It ignites something inside, like a cold room that's been given the warmth and light of an open fire.

He steps into my body and leans his head down, his arm snaking around my waist. His touch is light, gentle, but then he takes a deep breath against my hair and wraps his other arm around me to pull me tighter. I don't stop him.

"I missed you . . ." he murmurs.

I move my head back and tilt it up to face him, staring deep into his eyes. That's when I know what I was nervous about before. I was scared that when I saw him again and felt him again, something might have changed between us, altering it irrevocably.

I was wrong.

Nothing's changed. I still want him. More than I've ever wanted anything, probably.

I know I should move back and not let him kiss me—not yet, not until we've talked about everything—but I can't move. The touch of his mouth on mine is all I want at this moment. I need to feel the taste of him spread across my tongue. I've been starved of him. When he bends his head to kiss me, his lips are rough and angry despite his gentle tone a moment ago.

He moans into the kiss as he pushes his tongue deep into my mouth, greedy and insistent. His hands come up to hold my head as he tastes me with every part of his mouth, licking along my teeth, curling his tongue around mine, sucking on my lips. With his hips, he forces me back against the wall.

"Jake . . . wait. We should talk . . ." I manage between his addictive, hypnotic kisses that make my body think differently. "We need to talk . . ." I insist.

He pushes into me harder, and I feel the erection punch through the front of his jeans. "I know, baby. We will. Anything you want. I'll do anything you want. I just need this right now. I need to just . . . be with you. Let me be with you right now." His voice is urgent and breathless as he drags his hot, wet lips down my neck. At the dip of my collarbone, he sucks a little too hard for a moment before his mouth begins to move again. At the same time, his hand slides under my dress and between my legs, past the seam of my knickers. As his fingers make contact, we both gasp, and then he's spreading me open, searching, teasing. Forceful, greedy fingers turning me inside out.

He pulls his head up then and meets my eye, kissing me hard again. "Tell me you missed me," he says as his fingers continue to stroke.

My thighs open a little of their own accord, my body turning pliant under his practiced touch. "I missed you," I whisper.

A look of satisfaction flashes over his face before his eyes flare and he leans forward to bury his face in my neck. "I thought I'd lost you. Do you have any fucking idea how that felt? How it felt being without you?" His voice is low and intense like his fingers. It rumbles against my skin.

I know how it felt.

"I'm sorry," I whisper, though I'm not entirely sure why.

His body stiffens, and he removes his fingers from me to place them flat against my stomach instead. He lifts his head to look at me. "You've nothing to be sorry for, Alex. *Fuck. I'm* sorry." His free hand comes up to my face, thumb stroking across my cheek. "I missed you so much . . . wanted to come over so many times. To see you, touch you." He kisses me again, softer this time. "Be with you. Fucking beg you to take me back if I had to."

"Why didn't you?" My voice is more accusatory than intended.

He sighs. "Because I'm a coward, Alex. When it comes to you, I'm a total fucking coward. I think we've established that." His eyes are filled with that same mix of pain and guilt from last week when he begged me not to leave him. It makes my stomach twist and my heart hurt.

"I wish you'd trusted me with it . . ."

He frowns, confused. "Baby, I do trust you. I do." He takes a small step back from me then, running a hand over his mouth. "I've just seen so much fucking shit—*too* much fucking shit—my whole life. Where I'm from . . . fuck, I don't know. I always wanted to keep you separate from it all."

"Even your son?" I blink.

He looks pained again. "No, not him. But everything else connected to him . . ."

"You mean Vicky?" This is what Rob was getting at.

Jake nods, but it's conflicted, as if he's keeping something back. Something it's hurting him to keep back. *Baby steps, Alex. Give him time to open up to you.*

"But I was afraid it would make you see me differently, yeah. Make you walk away, maybe, yeah." He shakes his head. "Even now, I still can't believe you want to be with me. You . . ." He sounds genuinely confused.

"That's ridiculous."

"Is it? Do you remember how we met? You must have thought I was a piece of shit. And there you were, just being . . . you." His eyes soften, and he moves toward me again. "The way you looked at me, spoke to me—even though you must've been shit scared—I felt . . . fuck, I don't know, safe." He laughs a little as if this might be ridiculous. "You've never once looked at me how other people do. And I'm always fucking scared that's going to change, you know? I never want you to see me like they do—to look at me any differently. I don't fucking know what I'm trying to say, Alex." He drops his eyes again, looking exasperated, as though his words aren't doing what he wants them to.

"I *was* shit scared," I say, smiling.

He huffs out a quiet laugh. "Well, you didn't fucking look it. You never do."

"But I didn't think you were a piece of shit," I say. "I thought you were the most beautiful man I'd ever seen."

His eyes widen again, and he pulls his shoulders up, a faint tint of rose pinking his cheeks. To prove my point, I step closer to him and gaze up into his eyes.

"I still do. I want you more now than I did then. I want to be with you, Jake. Whether you have a son or not. If you'd trusted me and been honest with me, you would have known that. It just feels as if I'm giving everything here but getting half of you in return."

"Baby, I trust you. I promise you, I do. But it doesn't mean I don't live in fear you're gonna run. That you're gonna realize you deserve someone better, and you're gonna run. But right now, by some fucked up twist of whatever, you want me. So, I'm trying. Trying to be better, trying to go against the way I've always done things, so I can try to deserve you." He takes a deep breath. "There are things I have to do, and I'm not sure how I'm going to do it all yet, but I'll do whatever I need to do to be better for you. And for Cale. You both deserve better."

I don't understand what he means by that, not fully, and I can't listen to him talk about himself like this either. I step forward and kiss him hard. When I pull back, he rests his forehead against mine and closes his eyes.

"Just being with you makes me better, Alex. You've no fucking idea what you do, what you mean for me. What you are. You're everything I need."

My heart cracks open then, Jake settling firmly inside of it. I feel the same. My life never felt lacking before him—not really. Yet he's now something I can't live without. I'm only really alive when he's with me. I'm about to tell him all of this when he kisses me again.

My hands slip under his T-shirt to caress the hard skin beneath. I feel a shudder move through him, beneath the skin, as he pushes me back against the wall again, his hands sliding my dress up my thighs. This time, his fingers hook into my knickers, and he pulls them down my thighs roughly. As I step out of them, he lifts one of my legs and wraps it around his body, and the pressure of his jeans against me is delicious. But it's not enough. My hands go to the buckle of his belt, and I undo it quickly, unbuttoning and unzipping him so I can take his length in my hands. When I feel how wet and hard he is already, I whimper desperately, wetness pooling between my legs. I need it inside me. I need him inside me.

His head drops back as he bites down on his lip. "Yes, baby, take it. Fuck. It's yours." He moves his hand back between my thighs and teases me open before sliding his finger inside, then another, to begin fucking me with them.

God, I've missed this. I've missed his taste and his body and his precise touch on my most sensitive places. I can never be without this again.

Without warning, he drops to his knees in front of me and nudges my legs apart to take me with his mouth. It's searing and deliciously needy, and Jake groans as he begins to work at me.

"Fuck, baby, I've missed this," he hums against my clitoris, sending the vibration through my whole body. With my hands tangled in his hair, I pull his mouth closer, leaning back against the wall as I move wantonly against his tongue.

Jake moves his hands to my hips and turns me toward the stairs, tugging on my waist to lower me down onto the carpeted step. Then his mouth is back, and the access is better, and he's giving me oral sex on my hall stairs. I gasp loudly as he slides his tongue in deep, twisting it before pulling out. I feel my body start to coil hotly, tummy tightening with that familiar pressure.

"Jake . . ." I pant, bringing a hand up to muffle my moans as he licks, sucks, and flicks his mouth over me in tight, perfect circles. The new longer facial hair makes it feel more intense too, scraping over the sensitive flesh and heightening every sensation. When he presses his hand flat on my tummy, tilting me up so he can go deeper with his mouth, the pressure snaps, and I let out a small scream, my legs trembling around his shoulder.

"That's it, Alex . . . that's it, baby," he breathes. "Let me feel you come for me again."

And I do. I come intensely hard. Great, rejuvenating, radiating outward from the point and through my whole body. He watches me intently while working me through it, his eyes glittering with arousal.

Once he's sucked me dry, Jake kisses his way up my body to my mouth and crashes his lips onto mine. I can taste myself on him, sweet and bitter at the same time, but I can also taste him—that familiar taste of him that feels too addictive now.

There's no warning before he slides inside me, and I can only whimper and let my legs fall open farther. He lets out a low, filthy noise as he thrusts all the way in, large and so bloody hot, and spreads my body wide open to him. He fills me so completely. It's breathtaking. My cheeks are burning, and every part of me throbs from him. He feels as good as I remember. No. *Better* than I remember. Because now, it feels as if a deep, lonely part of me has found something it lost.

"Did you miss this?" he asks as he rolls his hips, making me moan again.

I tilt my body up to take him deeper. "Yes. So much . . ."

He looks satisfied as he moves to unbutton the front of my dress, tugging it open to expose my nipple and take it into his mouth. He flicks his tongue over it first, wet mouth coaxing it to sensitivity before he sucks on it hard. When he lifts his head again, he looks so focused—so intense it takes my breath away a little. Then he begins to circle his hips even faster.

"I belong inside you," he says. "I belong here." He presses his hand flat over my heart before kissing me hard with his eyes wide open.

"He couldn't look away from you for a second in case he lost you or something . . ."

As I lean up to kiss him again, I wrap my legs around him to bring him even deeper inside.

"Jake . . ." There are no words I can say, so I stop trying to find them and just hold onto his mouth with my teeth as he begins to speed up. It's glorious. He mouths at my neck as he moves into me at an almost painful pace.

But then he stops, sliding out of me completely, leaving me cold and aching.

"Jake . . . w—what are you doing? Please . . . I need you," I whine.

He takes his cock in his hand and begins to rub it on the outside of my body, around my opening, teasing me. I feel like sobbing. His breathing is labored and deep, a thin sheen of sweat over his forehead. He looks as if he's trying to calm himself.

"Do you remember when I told you that one day, I'd get you to beg me to fuck you hard?" he says.

I nod and bite my lip.

"I need you to ask me to fuck you hard right now. I need you to know how fucking mental the thought of losing you made me. I need you to feel it."

The look in his eyes is strange, and I don't entirely understand, but I'm also sure I'd do anything he asked me to. So, I nod. He leans down and kisses me tenderly, the softest he's kissed me all night, before he slides inside me again, slowly. Too slowly. I want it rougher, harder. And tonight, I will beg him for it.

"Harder, Jake. Please," I beg. "I need you to fuck me harder. Show me what I mean to you."

His eyes flare, and he takes hold of my hips and slams into me in one hard, deep thrust. A guttural groan comes from his throat as he does. As I feel the scream of pure pleasure crawl up my throat, I bite down on my hand to stop it from escaping. I can't think. I don't need to think. All I need is to feel him. To feel how the space between our bodies ceases to exist.

"I can't lose you again, Alex. I can't ever lose you again, baby . . ." he murmurs as he buries his face in my neck and continues to thrust. It's almost painful, but the pleasure eclipses it, each slide of his body hitting a place inside me I didn't know existed before.

"You won't. You can't . . ." I manage.

He crashes his mouth onto mine again and kisses me roughly, biting at my lip as he takes me hard. Harder than I've ever been taken. As he fucks me.

"You feel so good, baby. I love being inside you. I love fucking you . . ." His words aren't stable—they're part-moan, part-growl, but they're forceful. "I can't lose you again," he repeats as he kisses his way down to my throat, my neck. My eyes close as I focus hard on every delicious movement he makes. "Alex . . . fuck, baby, I love you."

My heart skips, and my eyes snap open as I process the words.

He lifts my leg, and I lose my train of thought again because he's so deep, and it feels so good, and the noises he's making drown out every other sound. The feel of his breath on my neck and his tongue on my throat and his smell in my nose drives me insane. My orgasm is sudden and blinding, and as he slows his thrusts a fraction, my body grabs onto him from the inside, caressing him desperately.

This time, I don't put my hand in my mouth to muffle my screams. This time, I grip his shoulders and cry his name so loud it scrapes the back of my throat on the way out.

"That's it, come around my cock. I feel you. So good—fuck, yes . . ." he growls.

When his movement begins to speed up again, I'm helpless, boneless, and powerless beneath him. I like the feel of it though. The feel of his powerful body pounding into my own like this. I like the feel of him using his strength and power to take my body however he wants. I more than like it. I know then that it won't be the last time I beg him to fuck me hard.

"Fuck, Alex . . ." He thrusts once more, his body stilling for an instant before I feel his orgasm rock through his body. He lets out a depraved-sounding moan as he chases his pleasure, followed by smaller, quieter ones aided by the slow rocking of his hips.

He brings his head up to kiss me again, first on the mouth and then on each cheek, and then, lastly, on my forehead. He fucks the last of himself into me before his hips slow to a stop, his chest heaving with shallow, ragged breaths.

Then, with his mouth nuzzled against my ear so there is no mistake this time, he tells me he loves me again.

THIRTY

HE LOVES ME. HE MEANS IT. IT WASN'T SOMETHING THAT FELL OUT of his mouth in the middle of frenzied sex. He loves me.

Like I love him.

From nowhere, I feel tears well up behind my eyes, my heart swelling to bursting point. He loves me, and I love him. It's earth-shattering.

My next thought, which is cold and sobering: I just had unsafe sex.

His breathing slows, and he lifts his head from the crook of my neck to meet my eyes. The way his own shimmer with satisfaction and the way his mouth tilts up into a small but uncertain smile makes my chest thrum. He looks so beautiful after sex, I always think. Of course, he always looks beautiful, but after sex, he looks even more heart-stoppingly so. Flushed cheeks, mouth kissed wet and red, hair mussed, and a look in his eye so wicked it makes me want to beg him to do it all over again.

When he eases out of my body, he touches his lips to mine and kisses me softly. As he does, I feel the wet stickiness of him seeping out, evidence of our careless and illicit lovemaking. He sits up and buttons my dress then smooths it down around my thighs. When he moves to stand, I do the same, sitting up on the step and smoothing down my tousled sex-on-the-stairs hair. He pulls on his jeans and boxers, zips and buckles his belt, and runs a hand through his hair. My legs tremble as I watch him as well as his semen running down the inside of my leg.

We stare at each other for a long time, only the sound of our breathing and the loud ticking of my grandmother's old clock filling the sexed-up air of my hallway. The air also feels heavy with the weight of his words. Words I always thought would be mine to say first.

"You said you loved me," I whisper after what seems like hours of heavy wordlessness.

Something flickers across his eyes, and he nods. "Yeah, I did."

I feel my breath catch in my throat, my mouth dry and papery. I run my tongue along my lips to wet them.

"Why?"

"Why, what? Why do I love you, or why did I say it?" His eyes twinkle with sex and amusement.

"Why did you say it?" My voice is barely-there.

"I said it because I mean it. I love you. I'm in love with you. I wanted you to know that right then." He runs a hand through his perfect, just-fucked hair. "Maybe it wasn't the right time. But all week, I was thinking about how I should have said it last week before you left, and how if I had, then maybe you wouldn't have gone. But I didn't want it to be the reason you stayed either, you know?" His eyes are gravely serious now. "But the way I feel about you . . . Well, I told myself I'd tell you the next chance I got. If I got one." He reaches out and takes my hands in his. "Baby, I know I almost killed it. I know that. But I don't know what the fuck I'm doing here, and, fuck . . . nothing in my life has ever felt as good or as right as you do, and I'm trying to get used to that, I suppose." His voice is so sincere it takes my breath away. I can't think. Or move. I want to cry with happiness. I also desperately want to reach down and catch the warm droplet of his climax running down my leg before it lands on the carpet.

"What are you thinking, Alex? Tell me." He squeezes my hand.

"What am I thinking?" I repeat. Mainly, my head is loud with echoes of, "I love you. I'm in love with you," sounding through it. "I'm not sure I ever know what I'm thinking around you. I don't know who I am either." I give him an accusing glare, but it's playful.

"So, I'm a bad influence—that what you're saying?" he says as he steps closer to me.

I hook my arms up and around his neck. "Mmm. I haven't decided yet." When I kiss him, I hear him sigh into the kiss. It doesn't get heavy, but when he pulls back his eyes are serious, and the atmosphere feels intense again.

"Does this mean . . . you're gonna try this with me?" he asks quietly, sounding faintly shy. "That we're . . . you know, okay?"

I'm still not sure we've talked about everything we need to talk about, and I'm still not completely sure I understand his reasoning behind not telling me about Caleb. There's still so much I don't know, but there's no rush. He loves me.

I nod. "We're okay."

He beams before leaning in to kiss me again, a little deeper this time, a little needier. His hands slide around my body and under my dress, skimming along the backs of my thighs. I know when he feels it because he pulls back, a dark look flashing over his eyes. I look down between us, color flooding to my cheeks.

"That was careless, Jake. I'm on the pill, but it's not sensible."

"I'm clean, baby. I promise you," he asserts.

I wasn't even thinking about that. Why wasn't I thinking about that?

"I get checked often," he adds, but then he realizes how that might sound and so shakes his head. "What I mean is, I'm sensible that way. Always. Well, normally always. There's been no one except you since the last time I went."

I nod, but the feeling that I should have known better doesn't dissipate. He pushes his hips into me playfully, his hand slipping between my thighs.

"We both should have known better. Me especially . . ."

"Mm-hmm, maybe. But do you have any idea how fucking hot this is? Feeling my cum running out of you?"

My mouth drops open as heat knots in my tummy. I can only stare at him dumbstruck for a moment.

"You are a complete deviant—you are aware of that?"

"I know. And you fucking love it," he says. "But I love watching you act all shy and proper as if you don't."

I hit him lightly on the arm. "It's not an act. I *am* shy and proper. It's how my parents raised me." I smile shyly, properly.

He gives me a long look before his mouth curls up into a smile that makes my legs feel weak. "Yeah, you are. It's one of the things about you that drives me fucking insane."

"I drive you insane?"

"Fucking mental." He smiles wide before scrunching his nose up adorably. "Come on. Think it's high time we had that bath we always talk about, because you, baby, need to be cleaned. You're fucking filthy." He glances back over his shoulder and winks, and I let him lead me up the stairs.

"I remember a day when you wouldn't even entertain the idea of having a shower while I watched. Now, look at us." He pulls me closer, my back resting against his chest, and places a kiss to the back of my head. I feel him brush away a few loose strands of hair that have escaped before he peppers the back of my neck with warm, wet kisses, sucking at the perspiration that's begun to settle there.

"Can I ask you something?" My voice is quiet and small. Maybe because I don't want to scare him with the question.

There's a pause before he answers. "Okay."

"What happened the night we met? Why did someone try to kill you?" I ask in an even tone.

He has one arm stretched along the bath, and he lowers it into the water to find mine, linking our fingers together. He lets out a deep sigh.

"I don't think they wanted to kill me."

I frown. "Why else would someone stick a kitchen knife into your neck?"

He doesn't answer right away, and though I can't see his face, I can imagine his jaw is tense as he chews on the inside of his lip. When he speaks again, his voice is even and businesslike.

"I went to collect some money for someone. For a friend. Someone I used to work for. Money he was owed that had been stolen from him. When I got there, the guy decided that instead of returning it, he'd threaten me instead. Or, rather, someone close to me," he says.

Close to him? Who's close to him?

Oh my god.

I sit up and turn to face him. "Caleb? He didn't threaten Caleb."

He doesn't have to answer me because the confirmation is clear on his face. His eyes are hard and dark, nostrils slightly flared.

"So, he stole from your friend, threatened Caleb, and then pulled a knife on you?" I feel my fingers curling into fists at the thought of this man. As I picture him threatening a child and then plunging a knife into Jake's neck. My mind goes back to the night downstairs when I asked why he never went to the police. Why he let them get away with it.

What makes you think I let them get away with it?

I'm glad he didn't let them get away with it. I'm glad the man who threatened his son never got away with it. So, I condone violence in certain circumstances then? Where Jake and his son are concerned?

"No, not him," Jake says with a small shake of his head. "He wasn't the one who stabbed me."

I frown.

He drops his eyes for an instant. "His wife. She panicked, I guess. Thought I was going to kill her husband. Did what she had to do."

What she *had* to do? In what kind of world is that something someone *has* to do? Would I do it if I thought someone was going to kill Jake? A horrible chill sweeps down my spine. I push the thought out of my mind and shake my head.

"You wouldn't have killed hi—" I start, but he cuts me off.

"Alex, he's a piece of shit who threatened my son. He crossed the fucking line. If she hadn't stopped me, he'd be dead." He doesn't sound in the slightest bit sorry about it, I don't think, just uncomfortable with telling me.

"But he's not. And you didn't, so . . ."

He shakes his head, but when he speaks again, there's still more than a tremor of anger in his voice. He fixes me with a look, intensely direct.

"But I could have, easily. And I'd have felt justified. Do you understand what I'm saying?"

I understand the words—it's the implication that feels lodged in my throat. Thick and suffocating.

"There isn't a lot that I care about, Alex. But what I do care about, the things that are important to me, I protect. No one gets to threaten or hurt them and walk away from that. I need you to understand that."

It takes me a moment to find a voice. "I do understand."

When he looks satisfied I do, he nods and gestures for me to turn back around. As terrifying as it was to hear it, to understand it, there's so much strength in what he's saying. I don't think I've known anyone who talks with as much conviction about things as Jake does. Who is so certain about the things he wants, about how he feels. *These* things he's always been open with me about. It's everything else he keeps to himself. Maybe now I'm only beginning to understand why.

So, this is the man I love. A strong, fiercely protective man who does what he needs to do. Who protects the people he loves.

He slides his arms around and pulls me into his embrace. "Good. Because you're one of the things I care about, Alex," he whispers as he kisses the top of my head.

Sunday morning breakfast in bed with him is everything I always wanted it to be. The papers scattered across the duvet, the breakfast tray between us, both of us well-rested and half-naked. It's picture-bloody-perfect. He is anyway.

After I gave him directions to Ken's bakery, he went out for croissants and the papers while I brewed the coffee and prepared a tray with marmalade, butter, and the remainder of yesterday's strawberries. They need to be eaten today because I left them out of the fridge last night while he fucked me on the stairs.

He's examining the sports insert of *The Guardian* while I read through the rest of the paper. I say "read," but really, I'm watching him read while I absently flick through the pages *pretending* to read. Is this how our Sundays will look from now on? Him reading the sports pages looking gorgeous and sleepy like he does now? He's sitting up, resting back against the headboard, his legs crossed at the ankles while he blows gently on his black coffee without milk or sugar.

As I break a piece of croissant off and pop it into my mouth, a loud sigh of pure contentment leaves my chest. He lifts his head and smiles at me before dropping his eyes back to the paper and whatever it's telling him about the state of the Premiere League.

"Must be a really interesting article you're reading there," he says without looking around. The side of his mouth quirks up into a half-smile.

"Oh, it is." I nod.

"What's it about?" He turns his head to me and brings his coffee to his mouth as he places the paper down on his lap.

"Avocados."

"Sounds fucking riveting." He smiles.

"Mmm, it is. But not quite as riveting as you."

His eyes glow, and my tummy swoops because it knows what that look in his eye means. It reacts accordingly because it wants the same thing. He's always looked at me in that same intense way. As if he wants to consume me whole. And I've always been more than happy to let him, it seems.

I lean across the bed and kiss him on the side of the mouth, flicking my tongue across his plump bottom lip.

"You had marmalade on your face," I lie. Of course, he didn't—he's the neatest eater I've ever seen. I just want my mouth somewhere, anywhere on his skin.

He smiles and moves his mouth back to mine, grazing his lips over mine before sliding his tongue into my mouth and groaning softly. When he pulls back, he runs his tongue around the inside of his mouth and across his lips.

"Strawberries." He nods. "You tasted like strawberries last night too. Good memories." His tone is warm like the look in his eyes.

I sigh. "Yes . . . Our careless lovemaking on the stairs."

He slides the breakfast tray out of the way and places his coffee on the nightstand then moves across the bed. He climbs over my body and pins me partly beneath him.

"I told you not to worry about it. I'm squeaky-clean, and I know you are, and if you're on the pill then we're all good." He dips his head to kiss me.

My body stiffens slightly. It doesn't mean we're "all good" at all. It means I should get the morning-after pill to be on the safe side.

"Okay, I'm not worrying," I lie, fixing him with my shy, proper smile.

He nods and pushes his hips into me. "Good. So, how about we be careless again right now?" He lowers his head and begins to kiss a trail down my neck to my chest, causing the tops of my thighs to vibrate and tingle. "You know, since the damage is already done." He moans while he draws his tongue between my breasts, untying my silk robe with his free hand. When his hand skims over my belly and he slides it between my thighs, my body arches up off the bed. The fact I want to be careless with him again right now proves what I've always known: he is a bad influence on me.

"As tempting as you are," I pant, "I think that would be less careless and more . . . Christ . . ."—his finger teases my sensitive spot—"that would be more like completely idiotic . . . so, no . . ." I close my eyes and slide my hand into his hair as his mouth reaches my belly button, which he circles with his tongue.

"Mmm, are you sure? Fuck, it felt good . . ." He slides his finger inside me and moves his head lower until I feel his wet tongue against my slit. He opens me with his finger and slides his tongue inside while I gasp and buck against his mouth. "Your tight little cunt clenching against my cock when you came." He makes a low, filthy noise as my eyes fly open.

I lean up on my elbows to stare down at him speechless, cheeks burning. He peers up at me with that wicked look on his face as he presses his lips to the skin above my pubic bone.

"Seriously? How on earth do you get away with saying things like that?"

"Because I'm a sexual deviant?"

"Well, whoever said that was spot-on."

"She doesn't even know the half of it either, but she will soon enough . . ." He grins, and then his amazing sexually deviant mouth is on me again.

My head drops back down onto the pillow as I giggle, but the giggle is swallowed quickly by a whine as he sucks loudly on the crease of my thigh. He moves to pin open my thighs with his shoulders and grabs my hand, linking his fingers with mine. He holds me tight in place with the other as he shifts position, lowers his head, and slips his tongue inside. Oh my god.

"Mmm, so soft and tight and sweet. This also tastes like strawberries, by the way." He flicks his eyes up before lowering his head again to lick his tongue the entire length of me. I have to bite the side of my free hand to stop myself from screaming. "And stop doing that," he says, pulling his mouth away. I look down at him, puzzled. "When I fuck you, I want to hear you."

He makes no move to lower his head until I remove my hand from my mouth.

"That's my girl," he says as I slide my hand into his hair, pulling at it hard. He doesn't seem to mind. He hums in approval.

Shortly after, with one hand in his hair and the other in my mouth, I let him hear me.

I'm lying in his arms with my head on his chest as he strokes his hands softly across my naked back. His breathing is deep and even, and its movement coupled with his fingers on my skin is hypnotic. I feel sleepy again. Odd, since last night was the best night's sleep I've had in a week. It was long, deep, and unbroken, and when I awoke, I no longer had that heavy, oppressive weight of emptiness in my body that I had every day since last Friday.

"I love you too," I say quietly.

His body tenses as if it's been electric shocked.

"Fuck, that must have been a really good orgasm." His tone is light, but I still hear a tremor in it.

I turn my head up to smile at him. His eyes shine gorgeously, and my chest aches in the most beautiful way.

"It was. And I do. Have done for a while now."

He blinks. "A while, huh?"

I nod.

"Kept it fucking quiet then."

"I thought it was pretty obvious." I give him an innocent look.

He lets out a soft sigh. "Alex, nothing about how you feel about me is pretty obvious, trust me," he says and pulls me up his body so he can kiss me. He sucks deeply on my mouth, lips and tongue, almost as though he wants to taste the words for himself.

"We should stay in bed all day," I murmur against his mouth.

He pulls back and gives me an apologetic look. "Fuck, I'd love to, but I have Caleb today."

God, yes, of course. His son. An image of Jake playing football with him fills my mind, and my heart swells.

"What are you doing with him? Do you have plans?" I ask.

"Ah, I'm taking him to the zoo. He wants to see the lions. Been fucking mental about them since he saw the Lion King." His voice is warm and soft, and there's a long pause before he speaks again. "You could come too. If you wanted to."

Meet his son. Today? God, why am I terrified? I shouldn't be, but I am. "Oh, today . . .?"

Immediately, I worry the look on my face is horror and that I'll offend him with it, so I turn away and look around the room instead. "Today is . . ." What is today? What on earth do I say? *I'm terrified of meeting your son. I'm terrified you'll see how terrible I am with children and then you won't love me anymore.* I feel his hand on my arm.

He's smiling. "Alex, it's fine. It's okay, don't worry. It's soon, I know. There's plenty of time for you to meet him. It'll happen when it happens." He shrugs, looking utterly fine.

I nod slowly. "I do want to meet him, Jake. I just . . . I guess I hadn't prepared myself for it to be today. Christ, what if he hates me?"

Do three-year-olds even know how to hate someone? I don't know much about children outside of a professional capacity, so I don't know.

Jake laughs softly and shakes his head. "Baby, he won't hate you. Seriously? Is that what you're worried about?" He pulls me back into him and wraps his arms around me. "He's not going to hate you."

"How do you know? It could happen. I mean, won't he wonder who this strange woman is with his father? The one who *isn't* his mother?" I point out. "I mean, what's happened in the past when you've introduced women to him? How does he normally cope with them?"

He shakes his head, frowning. "I've never introduced any woman to him."

Oh. *No woman ever meant anything to me before you.*

"But I know for a fact he'll love you," he says.

"Oh, you do, do you? How is that?" I smile as I trace my finger over the large eye he has tattooed here.

"Because he takes after his dad." He gives me a bright, boxy smile, and I practically melt. How does he do that? Make me love him more than I thought possible? "You'll be amazing with him, I know you will," he says. "But we'll take it slow. For his sake as well as yours. I don't want to freak either of you out."

I nod and reach a hand up to brush my fingers across his jaw, enjoying the feel of the thick, wiry hair under my fingers. "Okay. Lay the groundwork for me then. Talk me up to him, okay?"

Jake laughs and leans in to kiss me. It's slow and deep, and it kindles my blood again. I want him again.

He groans as he peels his mouth away. "I should go shower. Said I'd get him at twelve. But can I come back for another sleepover later? Happy to spend the whole night on your stairs this time."

"I'd like that." I nod. "The sleepover, not the stairs. Bad for the spine."

He tuts. "Okay, bed it is then. I also think it might be about time you cooked for me. Have my dinner on the table when I get in, yeah?"

"Hammering home the gender roles already, are we?"

He gives me a light peck on the nose and pats my head in condescension before lifting me off him and climbing out of the bed. The sight of his perfect naked backside makes my mouth water.

"Damn right, baby. I'll bring some of my shirts over for you to iron too," he says, throwing a cheeky wink over his shoulder.

As I flop back down on the bed, I think about what I could cook for him. I'm not that great at anything in all honesty. First, I give him the impression I'm terrified of children, and tonight, I get to underwhelm him with my cooking skills. He'll probably leave me first thing in the morning.

From the en suite, I hear the sound of the shower being turned on.

"Oh, and I'll be expecting you to get in here with me and wash my back as well," he says as he comes strutting back into the bedroom.

My body prickles with heat, and I kick the covers off. Out of bed, I stop in front of him and lean up to nip softly at his mouth as I wrap my hand around his length. He groans, and his eyes close over.

"Let's go get you wet then," I whisper as I stroke him gently.

"Oh, I won't be the only one getting wet, Doctor. Trust me on that."

"Oh, you shouldn't have too much work to do. I might be about half-way there already."

After he leaves to go get Caleb, I strip and wash the bedsheets—because they have sex and marmalade on them—and hang them out on the line in the garden to dry. With some reluctance, I decide to use today to do the thing I've been putting off for what seems like forever: bloody grocery shopping.

Waitrose is always busy on a Sunday afternoon, and because of that—and because I'm a million miles away thinking about tattoos, Sunday break-fast in bed, and four-letter words—I bang the trolley more than once into the ankles of unsuspecting shoppers. I debate over what to make him for dinner and decide finally on homemade lasagna. Mum has a great recipe, and he likes Italian, so I know he'll eat it at least. How bad can it turn out? Except, what if he's allergic to dairy or something? He never puts milk in his coffee, and I've never seen him eat anything I'd class as dairy . . . Christ, maybe he is.

As I wander down the vegetable aisle, I text to ask how the zoo is and if he's allergic to anything, i.e. dairy.

Jake: Allergic to dairy? You're fucking filthy, doctor

I giggle. Then my phone vibrates again.

Jake: Nah, I'm not allergic to anything except bad cooking. He loves the zoo but was terrified of the lions. Wish you were here. See you tonight x

I'm smiling like a schoolgirl as I head toward the tomatoes, and the shopping cart stops dead in front of me. Or, more accurately, I ram it into the back of an older gentleman's ankles. Quite rightly, he turns around to glare at me.

"Oh my god, I'm so sorry! The wheel on this thing is completely buck-led. I've been fighting with it all the way around." I glare accusingly down at the innocent wheel. "I'm really sorry." I give him my sweetest smile, and he nods and turns back to inspect the cucumber basket.

Okay. I really have to focus.

When I get home, I realize I've bought three different kinds of pasta—thankfully, one of which is lasagna sheets—and I've picked up the wrong kind of cat food for Fred. He will not be happy with me. Apparently, shopping isn't something people in love do.

I'm putting away the groceries when the doorbell goes, and since I'm not expecting anyone, and since I have Jake on the brain, I'm worried I've forgotten about a lunch with Mum and Dad or something that's slipped my mind. Well, I have some food I can feed them now at least.

As I approach the door, I see a tall figure behind the glass, and my heart swells. He's back early. He doesn't need to knock—I need to tell him that. Maybe I should just give him a key.

My heart deflates when I open it to find Sherlock standing there. He gives me a tight smile and removes his sunglasses.

"Hey, Alex. How are you?" His smile seems to tighten even further.

I smile back politely, confused as to what on earth he's doing at my house.

"Um, I'm fine, Mark. You?"

"Yeah, not bad." He nods, but his mouth stays tight, his eyes serious. "Do you have some time to talk? You don't have company, do you?" He glances behind me into the house.

"No, I'm alone. Um, yes, I have some time."

"Ah, great. Do you mind if I come in?"

A strange feeling of foreboding seems to bubble up from nowhere, dark and unwelcome. "Sure, come in," I tell him, and then I'm standing back to let him inside.

THIRTY-ONE

GESTURE FOR MARK TO GO THROUGH TO THE KITCHEN.

"This place looks amazing now. You and Ben did all this yourselves?" he asks, looking around—glancing up the stairs, peering into the living room as he passes.

I try to remember when Mark was here last, realizing it was the house-warming party we had back when the house was still a time capsule of the 1930s.

"God, no, not all of it. For the big stuff, we hired the professionals." Ben, an orthopedic surgeon, was utterly useless at any sort of DIY. No dexterity whatsoever. Something that used to amuse me. "The rest was a labor of love."

"Looks great," he says, gazing around the kitchen.

"Can I get you something to drink? Tea, coffee? Something cold?" I ask, heading straight for the kettle.

"No, thanks, Alex. I'm good. You're probably wondering why I'm here."

I give him a weak smile. "Rob and Dan-related, I presume?"

"Ah, no. Rob and Dan have nothing to do with this. They don't know I'm here." He purses his lips before taking a deep breath. "I wanted to talk to you about Jake."

My stomach does a little flip-flop. "What do you mean? Oh, wait—is this to apologize for how you were at dinner?"

Mark huffs out a small laugh, more like a scoff. "No. No, that's not why I'm here."

"Okay . . . then what do you want to talk about?" Something begins to gnaw deep inside me—something small and quiet.

Mark stares at me for a long time before running a hand through his dark hair. When he speaks again, his voice is serious and concerned. "How much do you know about this guy, Alex? How well do you know him?"

I flinch. I'm not sure why the question is such a shock; it's one I've asked myself a lot since I met Jake. I'm used to asking it. Mark has no right to ask it though. I feel defensive.

"What on earth does that mean?" I ask sharply.

Mark doesn't offer any clarification.

"I know him as well as anyone knows someone they've been seeing for a few weeks." I cross my arms over my body, hating myself for the spin I've put on that. He's so much more than a guy I've known for a few weeks. I'm in love with him. He's in love with me. Why am I spinning this?

Mark nods and purses his lips. "So then, you don't know."

The gnawing sensation that a moment ago was deep and small begins to get larger, climb a little higher. "Know what?" I frown.

Mark leans up off the counter, and it's only then I notice he has an A4-size brown envelope in his hand. Why didn't I notice that before? My body backs away from it slightly as if it might be dangerous. It looks dangerous.

"Who he is. What he is," he says.

"I know who he is." I flare.

"Then you know he has a criminal record. That he's been inside. That if he wasn't so good at hiding what he does, then he'd be going back. And for a long bloody time too."

The bottom drops out of my stomach then, falling away, and some of the air disappears from my lungs. The words go in and zip around my head, knocking things over. When they stop, I feel defensive again—fiercely so. What on earth is Mark doing? How dare he waltz in here like this and tell me things like this?

I narrow my eyes at him. "Why are you telling me this?" My voice is high and accusatory as I move away from him to go stand by the sink.

"Because you're a friend. Because you're Dan and Rob's friend, and I'm concerned about you. I want to help you." His voice is soft, but I hate it. I hate his soft, almost pitying tone. I hate the words. They make me feel foolish and sick. Can I throw up in front of Mark?

I sense him coming toward me, and when I look around, he has his arm outstretched, envelope thrust toward me.

"You've no idea who this guy is, Alex. The kinds of things he's mixed up in. The kinds of *people* he's mixed up with."

I stare at the envelope, dumbstruck. "Is that what's in there?"

He nods. "Everything you need to know, yes."

I'm not even sure that's bloody legal, him bringing me this. Clearly, he thinks it worth the risk. My blood is cold. So cold.

"How is this helping me, exactly?" I ask.

Mark blinks and lowers the envelope.

"How is telling me things Jake should have the right to tell me himself helping me?"

"But he didn't tell you, did he? He never would. But you have a right to know. Someone had to tell you. *I* had to." He sounds sorry for me now.

Oh, Mark's pity is awful. I don't want his pity. I want him to leave.

I think about the words he's just said though. Are these things Jake would have told me eventually? He promised to tell me everything. As soon as he was sure I wouldn't run a mile, he was going to tell me everything. Is this one of the things he thinks will make me run? A criminal record? Prison?

I shake my head again and glance at the envelope.

Mark sighs loudly. "He's not the man you think he is, Alex. This is a violent criminal we're talking about here."

My mouth practically drops open. A violent criminal? What the hell does that even mean? It doesn't mean anything. It could be anything. I need to talk to Jake.

An image of him smiling at me over breakfast this morning swims to the front of my mind, and I shake my head and close my eyes, tears springing up hot behind them. There's a loud, crumbling noise inside my head, the sound of the walls of my delusion crashing down around me.

A violent criminal.

Is that who Jake is? The same person who strokes my hair as I fall asleep, who tells me how much he needs me, who sees me as his something good. That would mean I truly know nothing about this man. This man I'm in love with. He'd be a total stranger. He's not that. He *can't* be that.

Yet . . . someone cut him open with a knife. *I would have killed him, Alex. If she hadn't stopped me, he'd be dead.* No. He threatened his son. Jake was protecting his child. That's different.

I turn my head away from Mark to stare out the kitchen window. I should open it. It's so stuffy in here. I stretch forward and twist the handle to let some fresh air in. The breeze feels comforting over my face as I close my eyes.

"Don't you want to know what for?" I hear Mark say finally. His voice sounds like a memory, and I've honestly no idea how much time has passed since he told me Jake was a violent criminal.

As I turn my head around to face him, my eyes dip warily to the envelope in his hand. What could be in there? My mind runs through all sorts of possibilities. Horrible, vile things I know Jake isn't capable of. He just isn't.

Mark watches me carefully, and I wonder what he's thinking about me right now. Probably that I'm a naïve idiot who knows nothing about the man she's sleeping with.

"I think I'd like to hear that from him. If what you're saying is true."

Of course it's true. Mark is hardly likely to come here, risk his job like this, if he wasn't certain of it. God, I want him to leave now. So I can collapse to the floor and start ordering this into neat, manageable little piles.

"What about what he does for a living—is that something you guys spoke about?" He sounds a little condescending now, as though I'm the victim of some horrendous crime he needs to treat delicately. It flicks my defensive switch back on.

"He runs a nightclub for a living, Mark," I snap. "It's how we met."

Something glimmers behind Mark's eye, but it's no more than that. He sighs and takes a step toward me. "Everything you need to know about him is in here. Everything we have on him." He stretches his arm out, and I take another step back from the brown envelope. "This is who Jake is, Alex."

I laugh almost hysterically. I *feel* hysterical. "There is no way I'm reading that, Mark. I want to hear it from him. He can tell me whatever it is for himself." As I say this though, I wonder how true it is. I wonder if deep down, it's no longer what I want. Do I want to hear Jake tell me he's a violent criminal who's been in prison for some horrendous crime?

"Or he can lie through his teeth like he's been doing since he met you," Mark says. "You're not a stupid woman, Alex, so he'd have to have lied a great fucking deal to have you look at him the way I saw you look at him last week at that dinner table. Don't let him keep doing it."

"How often do you lie to me, Jake?"

"Only when I have to."

"Well then, I guess I'll have to take that chance, won't I, because I don't want to hear it from you or a piece of bloody paper." My voice trembles with rage and something else. It sounds weak.

He looks at me again before letting out another sigh. When he steps back, he takes the instrument of my torture with him.

"I didn't come here to upset you, Alex. That's not what this was about. I came to warn you because . . . I care about you. This is not a good guy we are talking about, and I'm trying to protect you the only way I know how."

I want to laugh again. Because didn't Jake say that to me too? How he wasn't a good guy and that he was only keeping things from me to protect me.

I believed him each time he told me those things. I believe Mark too.

I know Mark isn't doing any of this to upset me, but that doesn't make any of it any easier to hear.

When I say nothing, Mark nods then turns to place the envelope on the dining table. I can see it's unsealed, and the front is blank. He takes a deep breath before he speaks again.

"Does the name Fred or Freddie Ward mean anything to you? Did Jake ever talk about him with you or introduce you to him?" he asks.

I shake my head. Kevin, Vicky, and Caleb are the only people from Jake's life I've met. Then I remember the guy who was in Jake's flat when he took me there last week, and I scour my memory for the name.

Paul. Yes. Paul. Not Freddie.

"No," I confirm.

"Okay, good. That's good." He nods. But then his eyes are concerned again. "I know you say you want to hear it from him, and I know you don't want to believe what I'm telling you is true, Alex, but I strongly suggest you arm yourself with what's in there." He glances at the envelope again and looks to be debating something else. He scans me over quickly—my neck, my arms, and down to my legs—before bringing his eyes back to mine. "The most recent suspicion is the serious assault and battery of a woman. She was beaten pretty badly. Broken arm, broken ribs, and a fractured jaw."

I can tell he's holding something back. I can also tell that whatever it is isn't likely to help with what's happening to my chest as this new information sinks in.

Mark sucks in a quiet breath. "We suspect she was sexually assaulted too."

My legs almost buckle beneath me then, and I have to grab onto the rim of the sink to keep myself upright. Bile rises in my throat, and I have to swallow it back down. *No. No. No.* I'm shaking my head now. This is not who he is. I know him. I'd know if this was who he was. I'd know.

You know nothing . . .

"What are you talking about?"

Mark nods gravely. "The wife of a known associate of his was assaulted a couple of weeks ago. Jake was known to have had . . . relations with this woman. Her husband was badly beaten a week before, and we suspect it's related. We don't know how, and neither of them is talking to us. These are the kinds of people who don't talk. Certainly not where Freddie Ward or Jake Lawrence are concerned," Mark says.

Hearing Mark say Jake's full name like that almost makes him sound like a different person altogether. Someone I don't know. Maybe even someone who beats and rapes women.

No. I don't believe that. I can't seriously think he would do that. Jake would never do that.

"Alex, if I had any say in this, I'd tell you to pack a bag and go to Rob and Dan's or your parents' for a few days. Tell this guy by phone that it's over. I'd tell you to stay the hell away from him. You have no idea what he's capable of." His face has that same sad, concerned look it's had since I opened the door. "But you're not going to do that, are you?"

"Jake would never hurt me," I tell him in a hollow, robotic voice.

A woman. Serious assault and battery. Possible sexual assault. The words are loud and painful, and there's a sharp ringing noise in my head as though a bomb's gone off inside it.

Mark nods again. "Well, I sincerely hope for your sake that you know him better than we do." He looks around my kitchen then reaches into his pocket and brings out his wallet, pulling from it a small white business card. When he tries to hand it to me, I stare at it like I did the envelope, as though it's dangerous. "Please take it, Alex. Store it in your phone. I need you to know you can call me if you're ever afraid. If he ever does anything or says anything that makes you feel afraid."

With uncertain hands, I take Mark's card and stare at it hard. It has his full name, his rank, direct telephone number, and the address of New Scotland Yard in small, plain lettering. Will I need to use this because I'm afraid of Jake? It's almost unfathomable. Almost. If I were asked the same question a few hours ago, my answer would have been no with complete certainty. Now?

Now, I know nothing.

"You knew him, didn't you? You recognized him. At dinner." I lift my eyes from the card to him.

"I knew the name. We all know his name and what it means, but I'd never seen him in person before. The task force involved with Jake is a sep-arate division, so I had to check afterward that it was the same guy I was looking at."

They all know his name and what it means? Does he mean the entire Metropolitan police force? I feel sick.

Something horrible pricks at my chest. "Do Rob and Dan know? Did you tell them?" I don't know why I'm asking this or why it even matters, but them thinking badly about Jake makes me feel cold and ill. More ill.

"No." He shakes his head. "They think he owns a nightclub. There's no reason to tell them anything other than that." He reaches out slowly and puts his hand on my arm to squeeze it gently—a gesture of comfort, I assume. His touch is warm, but not as warm as Jake's.

"Alex, promise me you'll call me if you need to. Promise me that if he ever says or does a single thing that makes you feel in the slightest bit afraid, you'll call me. Promise me that." His tone is authoritative and forceful, and I find my head nodding in response. "Good. I'm only at the other end of the phone." He smiles reassuringly. It's the sort of smile I give my patients when I tell them not to worry about something until the results come back. The kind of smile I also use to tell them it's treatable.

Then, because I don't know what else to say to him, I nod and tell him thank you. *Thank you.* Thank you for coming in here and breaking my heart with some words and a brown envelope.

As soon as he leaves, I bend over the sink and throw up twice. I feel ill. Light-headed and weak as though I might have the flu coming on. I rinse my mouth out and drink two glasses of water, but the nausea doesn't pass. Neither does the light-headedness. With trembling legs, I move to take a seat at the dining table and stare hard at the envelope.

I'm scared to touch the thing. But I'm also scared to throw it away. Jake's secrets, which I kept telling myself I could wait to hear when he was ready, are right in front of me.

I realize something then with horrible clarity: I don't want to know what they are. Maybe I never did. Maybe deep down, I was always afraid of what he was hiding because it might mean the end of us.

The face of a woman, beaten to a pulp, flashes across my mind. *What makes you think I let them get away with it?*

God, I can't possibly be considering he would do that. A man I've allowed inside my heart, and my body, and my soul. A man I'm deeply in love with. I can't be considering he'd do that. I'm not. No. He wouldn't.

I've never sensed that in him—not once, not even the night he came to my house furious after my date with Sam. He has a temper, yes, but I've never once felt afraid he would hurt me.

I'd never hurt you, Alex. I'm different with you, Alex. I'm better with you, Alex.

My brain is circling and retreating and maneuvering at one hundred miles per hour, but my body is completely and utterly still. With my back straight and my hands flat out in front of me on the table, I keep staring at the godforsaken envelope.

I should be tearing it open, but I'm not ready to know whether I've been beguiled by a lying, violent criminal yet.

When I look up at the clock, I see I've been sitting here for over an hour. Over an hour of staring blankly into space and trying to hold down vomit. I can't think about this any more right now; Jake will be here shortly, and I haven't even started the lasagna.

I stand up from the table, my legs trembling.

I need to cook.

THIRTY-TWO

WHEN HE TEXTED TO SAY HE'D DROPPED CALEB OFF AND WAS on his way over, I replied saying only that the door was open. That was an hour ago. I'm terrified. Not of him. I've never been afraid of him, and I'm still not. The only thing I'm afraid of is that bloody envelope.

My hands didn't stop shaking the entire time I prepared dinner, trembling violently as I chopped tomatoes, peeled onions, stirred the pot, and layered the oven dish. Yet my mind was eerily calm. I somehow managed to forget everything else as I focused solely on that one task. The lasagna actually looks good. But then I've always been an impressive multitasker.

I'm at the sink and almost jump out of my skin when I feel him behind me, warm, strong arms sliding around me as his mouth nuzzles deep into my neck.

"Shit, sorry, baby. I thought you heard me come in. I knocked first. Didn't mean to scare you."

My heart constricts tightly as I take in the full sight of him. He looks the same as he did this morning, except now, his cheeks and nose are slightly red from the sun. He's smiling at me the same way he did this morning too, with eyes soft and warm and full of love. He's still so beautiful, and I'm still completely in love with him, and my delusions truly know no bounds if I thought I'd feel any differently upon seeing him now.

When he pulls me into his arms and kisses me deeply, my body responds like it always does, warm need settling under my skin and sending goose bumps down my spine. Though I'm unable to do anything but welcome his mouth on my own, it takes effort to keep my arms by my sides and not wrap them around him.

"Mmm, I missed you today," he murmurs before pulling back to smile at me.

I want to return his smile, but the lump in my throat is almost suffocating, and the tears are threatening to appear again. So, I turn my back on him and face the sink instead.

"How was the zoo?" I ask in a voice I don't even recognize. How was the zoo? Has there ever been a more banal question asked at such a moment?

"Busy, overpriced. But he loved it. Think penguins are his new favorite thing now. Spoke about them all the way home." I hear the note of concern in his voice.

With my back still turned, I nod, reaching my hands under the water to rinse them before squirting them with some more hand soap and repeating the process.

"Everything okay?" he asks.

I swallow and bite down hard on my lip to stop the tears from rolling down my face.

"Alex?"

Christ, I need to hold it together here. We can't have any kind of conversation if I'm an incoherent mess.

Suddenly, I feel his hands on me, and he spins me around to face him. "What's the matter? What's going on?" His eyes are narrowed with worry.

Oh, Jake, you should be worried. I have no clue how to start this conversation. "Tell me about the time you were in prison" isn't appropriate, and "Did you beat and rape the woman who stabbed you?" aren't words I will ever be able to say to him.

"Alex, answer me. What's wrong?" His voice is louder now, and it jolts me into myself.

Drying my hands on the dish towel first, I walk over slowly to the dining table and lift the envelope, turning to hold it out to him. He looks down at it with some confusion before taking it from me. Then, keeping his eyes on mine, he opens it and pulls out its contents.

For the first time, I see the file isn't overly large. There are maybe ten or so bits of paper, a few with a different shinier material that I can see are photos. My stomach turns as I consider what those photos might be of since I can only see the reverse of them.

I don't pay much attention to the bits of paper anyway as Jake leafs through them. Instead, I watch his face. Outside of sex and anger, his eyes have always been difficult for me to read, so adept at hiding his emotions from me, so I expect them to give nothing away here either.

How wrong I am.

They widen with shock and disbelief, the sun-kissed flush draining quickly from his face. Then his eyes darken, his nostrils flaring as a hard line settles over his mouth. When he looks up at me again, he's utterly furious.

"Where the fuck did you get this?" he asks. As always when he's angry, his rough East End accent peppers every single syllable.

I frown, deciding not to answer that question. "Is what's in there true? Is that you?"

His mouth twitches as his gaze deepens. He doesn't say anything for several long, torturous seconds. "What do you think?" he asks finally. "You read it. Is it me?"

How do I tell him I was too much of a coward to read it? I look down at my hands.

"Well, I'm gonna guess by the way you can barely fucking look at me, you think that it is."

"I never read it."

When I look up, he's smiling coldly. "You're a fucking liar. Why wouldn't you read it?"

I narrow my eyes on him. He has the nerve to call *me* a liar? "Believe what you want, Jake, but I never read it. I never read it because I wanted to hear it from you. I always wanted to hear it from you." Except, deep down, I wonder if I am indeed a liar, because I never wanted to hear *this* from him.

His eyes soften, and he blinks a few times before he begins to chew his lip hard from the inside. He's thinking. About how to do this, perhaps. About what to say. How best to present it to me. Which words to choose. How much to *share*. As he does, I say the same thing over and over in my head. A mantra. *Please tell me the truth. Please let the truth be something manageable. Please tell me the truth. Please let the truth be something manageable.*

"So, you know nothing about what's in here?" He holds the papers up.

"Mark told me you were in prison and that you had a criminal record. That's all I know," I lie. I can't mention the woman. I'm not ready to go there yet.

His eyes narrow and darken again. *"Mark?* Who the fuck's Mark?" He rolls the name around in his mouth for a moment until he remembers. I know the second he does because his eyes snap back to me. "Dan's brother? He gave you this?" He's nodding now, so I see no point in confirming what he just said. "Course he fucking did." He squeezes his eyes closed with his fingers then runs a hand over his mouth and licks his lips. "Fucking hell."

"Was he lying?" I ask after what feels like a long period of time.

He turns his head and looks at me, studying every inch of my face for what feels like hours before finally, he shakes his head. "No. He wasn't lying."

And there it is. It's not as much of a shock as I expected. There's no crashing down of hopes and dreams at his confirmation. I guess I've known since 3:00 p.m. this afternoon that Mark wasn't lying. Hearing Jake confirm it doesn't have any effect other than my finally being able to accept it as the truth.

"Why the fuck did he come here with this, Alex? Did you ask him to find out about me? Didn't you trust me to tell you?" His voice is still angry, but there's a measure of hurt there too. "You went behind my fucking back?"

"What? No! Of course I didn't go behind your back!" I feel upset he'd think I would. "I never asked him to find out about you. Of course I didn't. He came here with this of his own volition." I hesitate, not sure if I should say anymore. In the end, I decide Mark's motivations are important somehow. "He said he was worried about me. Worried I had no idea what I was getting myself involved with. That you weren't who I thought you were . . ."

Jake inclines his head slightly. "Oh, that's what he said, did he?" He sounds entirely unconvinced about Mark's motives. "And let's not kid ourselves here, baby, yeah? You had *some* fucking idea what you were getting involved with. You'd need to be a fucking idiot otherwise."

His snide tone makes a chill sweep over me. This person again. The one with the cold smirk who says things to hurt me. *This* is the Jake I have no idea about.

"Oh, really? You think I had an inkling you might be a violent criminal who beats and rapes women?" I hiss, cheeks burning with rage.

He flinches back, frowning.

"Yes, you're right, Jake. I knew that, and I let you into my bed anyway because I love a bad boy." My voice is laced with disgust, and he seems to shrink back from it. His face rearranges into something like abject confusion.

"What the fuck are you talking about?" he asks.

I say nothing and hug myself tighter.

"What did that fucking pig say to you? Alex, I've never hit a woman in my life. Did he tell you that? Seriously? Fucking hell." He sounds almost scared as he takes a step toward me. Instinctively, I move back from him as he does.

I can't let this man near me. Not until I know who he is and what he's capable of. Not until I'm clear which version of him I'm likely to get from one moment to the next.

"Baby, please tell me what he said to you." His voice is softer now, the Jake I know seemingly back.

"I presume it was the woman who hurt you. He said the wife of an associate. She was assaulted badly. They think she was raped too. I don't know any more than that," I tell him. I know I should keep looking at him, watching his eyes for the truth or lies that may be written in them, but I can't. It physically *hurts* to look at him, and so I look down again.

"Alex, I promise you, I never laid a finger on her. That didn't happen. I never hit her, and I certainly never . . ." He can't even say the word, and when I look up at him, he's shaking his head. "I never touched her. I never did that."

He looks and sounds so sincere, and *god,* I want to believe him. But something niggles and gnaws away at me.

"I asked you that night here why you would let the person who stabbed you get away with it. Do you remember what you told me?" I ask him. I do need to see his eyes for this, and so I watch them closely. The sad, lost look that comes into them tells me he remembers exactly what he told me that night.

He shakes his head, eyes and mouth hard. "That's not what I meant, Alex."

"Convenient, you saying that now, don't you think?"

"Oh, come on! Seriously?" he cries. "You think I'm capable of that? Of doing something like that! Baby, please, you know me. You know I would never do that. You know me." His eyes implore me.

I huff out a small, sad laugh. "Oh, I think it's abundantly clear that I do not know you, Jake. That I've never *known* you. Not really."

He looks hurt again as he shakes his head. "I never touched her, Alex. *Fuck,* you have to believe that."

"Then tell me what you meant," I snap. "That night, next door, you insinuated you'd meted out some justice of your own for what she did to you. What was it?"

He sighs deeply and squeezes his eyes shut with his fingers again. When he opens them, he looks resigned. Still, he meets my eye unflinchingly.

"What I meant was that she was going to have to look after her cunt of a husband for a very long time. Because I put her husband in a coma, Alex. That's what I meant."

I swallow, my anger dissolving on my tongue. He beat a man into a coma? Is that more or less acceptable than beating and raping a woman? My mind thinks it's more acceptable, but since I met him—or, more accurately, since 3:00 p.m. this afternoon—my mind hasn't been processing things like a normal person's would, so I don't know that I trust it.

"Were you sleeping with her?" I ask for some reason.

"Jake was known to have had . . . relations with this woman."

When his eyes flicker and blaze, it's all the confirmation I need. Oh, he fucked her all right.

"Well, they know you were, and they think it has something to do with all this. They don't know about your little debt-collecting visit to her husband," I tell him.

He nods, his mind ticking loudly.

"So, I assume you 'touched her' when you fucked her? So, you saying you never laid a finger on her wasn't technically true, was it?" I'm being petty, and I hate myself for making this about the fact he fucked this woman when it's about everything but that.

He sighs again, sounding tired now. "Yes, I fucked her once. Yes, I touched her then, but it was consensual, Alex. I never hit her before, *during,* or after. So, whatever that lying prick told you about it is bullshit, yeah?"

"And you have no idea what happened to her either, I assume? She stabs you with a knife, and then a week later, she's beaten half to death. That's purely a coincidence, I take it. I mean, seriously? You expect me to believe that?"

"I expect you to believe me, Alex. And trust me. Because you love me, remember?" he says, sad.

I glance away from him.

"Or do you only love me when I'm fucking you? When I've just made you come?"

I look back to find his eyes hard and mean again.

"Is it my cock that you love, baby? 'Cause in that case, we could have just done that bit—the fucking bit, you know—instead of all this love bullshit that, when it comes down to it, is apparently worth fuck all."

I narrow my eyes and stare him down. I won't even respond to that. To *him.* Mean, smirking Jake.

Finally, his eyes soften again as if he doesn't have enough energy or desire to hold onto the rage. His shoulders slump, and he sighs loudly.

"I don't know what happened to her, but I'll find out. Trust me."

Oh, that word again: Trust.

"Why were you in prison? When? And what for?" I ask, feeling bold all of a sudden.

"Oh, he didn't tell you that bit? He told you a pile of bullshit about me, but the truth he left out?" He snorts derisively. "Sounds about fucking right."

"Oh, he offered to tell me everything, but I told him I wanted to hear it from you."

He gives me a long look and then runs his hand through his hair before nodding once as if he's just made a difficult decision about something. When he moves toward me, I don't flinch this time. He walks past me to the dining table, where he pulls out a chair and indicates for me to sit down.

"I'm fine standing," I tell him.

"Please sit down, Alex," he says softly.

"Oh, so this is the part I should sit down for?"

He sighs. "Please."

Because my whole body feels weighted down, I walk toward him slowly and sit. Jake takes a seat to my right, leaning forward on his elbows with his hands together and steepled under his chin. At one point, he places his palms flat on the table and slides a hand toward me as though he might take mine in his, but he doesn't. He drops his hands onto his lap and leans back in the chair. When he finally opens his mouth to speak, his whole body deflates, shoulders dropping and the tension lifting off them before my eyes.

"I was sixteen and utterly out of control," he starts. "Jon had fucked off to the army by then, and I hadn't seen my mother for close to five years, so I was on my own. No one to answer to for whatever shit I did, and no one who gave a shit what I did. I started drinking when I was ten, I think. It was easier to get a hold of stuff than you'd believe. I mean, they call them care homes, but honestly, no one fucking cares. No one gives a shit." He laughs, but it's a sad, empty noise.

"Anyway, by the time I was fifteen, I was on something every day. Coke, speed, pills—prescription or not, didn't matter—anything I could get my hands on, really." He flicks his eyes up to check my reaction to this. As far as I'm aware, it's impassive. "None of this is an excuse for the things I did, it's . . ."—he shrugs—"context. Anyway, the guys I hung around with were always older and just as bad—worse even. Their hobbies were stealing cars, robbing houses, dealing. I used to tag along, happy to have something to do

322 | SCARLETT DRAKE

and people who didn't mind having me around. At one point, one of the older guys got a job at a security depot and told us about a safe in the office. Told us the duty guys had the codes. I wasn't told any details—I was only supposed to be the lookout." He runs a hand over the back of his neck and focuses on a point on the table. "Anyway, it went wrong. The guy on shift didn't know the code and somehow managed to press a panic button. It was a total fuckup. We got separated when we split. I got caught."

It's not what I was expecting. Not at all.

I shift forward in my seat. "You were fifteen?"

He nods.

"So, you were a child and a lookout? You couldn't have been given much of a sentence."

Some hope floods into his eyes for a moment, but then it's gone again. "I took part in the beating of the security guy. He was messed up pretty badly. Lost an eye. I hit him with a baseball bat a few times, and he identified me in court. What did me in though was that I wouldn't talk. I gave them nothing on the others. That was worse to them. I got four years."

Oh, god, that seems cruel. Too cruel for a damaged teenager from a broken home.

"Eighteen months in a young offenders, and then ten in Wandsworth after I hit eighteen. They let me out early for good behavior."

As I process this information, I think what I feel is relief. It's not a nice story, but it's also not unmanageable.

"Why didn't you talk? Give up the others?"

Another empty smile. "Four years is nothing compared to what would have happened had I grassed. It's not how it's done. You learn that shit pretty young where I'm from, Alex. I got caught. I paid the price."

"You were a child, Jake. And under the influence of older people. They should have taken that into account." I feel bloody angry now.

"They did." He nods. "I'd been in and out of Feltham since I was thirteen. I was a repeat offender. Judge said I needed to grow up. He thought a longer sentence would sort me out. He was right. Certainly helped me mature."

I picture a thirteen-year-old Jake, lost and lonely with no one who cared about him, and I feel my heart break some more. He must have been so afraid and so angry at everyone. He's still lost and lonely. He thinks I don't see it, but I do. I try to remember what I was doing at thirteen. Having piano lessons and vacationing in the south of France surrounded by a happy, loving family. I feel sick.

"It must have been awful," I say, tears welling behind my eyes again. I glance down, focusing hard on the wood of my dining table.

"It wasn't so bad. It got me off the street. And keeping my mouth shut and taking the fall for it got me respect. It was how I met the guy who pretty much changed my life." He says it in a way that makes it impossible to know if this man changed his life for good or bad. Though, looking at the person he is today, I suppose it can't have been all bad.

Maybe he's talking about Freddie Ward. The guy Mark was so interested in.

"Which guy?" I ask.

He's silent for a moment, his gaze inscrutable. "You really didn't read that file, did you?"

I shake my head.

"He isn't someone you need to know about, Alex. It's best you don't. It's best you're not involved when it comes to him."

We're both silent for a long time as Jake draws circles on the table with his finger, and I watch him. My stomach twists with dread and fear, but it's not over yet. I need to be brave now.

Sliding my chair back, I cross the kitchen to the fridge and inspect the wine chilling inside. I fill my glass far beyond halfway and take a long, welcome sip, then another, all the while feeling the weight of his stare on me. Lifting the glass and the bottle, I carry them back to the table and sit back down. My body needs wine for whatever might happen now. For whatever he might tell me now. He watches me intently as I take another sip of the cool, sweet white.

"How do you make a living?" I ask as I lower the glass from my mouth.

"What do you mean?" His eyes are suspicious, like he's trying to figure out what I'm keeping from him, or what else I know. Which is still exactly nothing since I didn't read what was in the envelope.

"I mean, is your nightclub your only source of income, or do you have other less legitimate streams?" My voice is steady, but my body feels as if it's about to shatter into pieces at any moment. I'm surprised my hands don't shake when I lift my glass again.

His mouth twitches slightly—so slightly I almost miss it. "There are a couple of others, but the club is my main concern now."

To be honest, I'm surprised at the speed and clarity of his reply, and so I don't have my next question ready. "Because it's where you launder money for your less legitimate streams?" I stare him down.

His nostrils flare. "No. The club is completely legitimate, and I plan on keeping it that way."

"But you do have other streams. What are they?" I press on, feeling oddly exhilarated—in control even.

"Alex . . . be careful," he warns.

"Is that a threat?" I narrow my eyes.

He blinks. "Of course not. I just mean, be careful about how much you think you need to know. Do you really need to—?"

I thump my glass down on the table with such force I'm surprised it doesn't break. "How much I *think* I need to know? Are you serious? I think I *need* to know the truth, don't you? Who the hell are you? *What* the hell are you?" My voice is loud, echoing around the quiet kitchen.

He says nothing, just watches me. Then, "You know exactly who I am, Alex. You've always known." His tone is so calm and soft it magnifies and intensifies the rage swirling inside me.

Well, I have to hand it to him: he has always managed to be the calm in the eye of my emotional storm.

"Excuse me?"

"I've never lied to you about who I am. I've withheld shit from you, yes, but I've never lied to you about who I am, Alex. There are things about who I am and what I've done that I can never tell you though."

Never. He was never going to tell me. I go to cut in, but he puts up his hand.

"And believe me, it's not because I'm afraid you'll run a mile. That shit is all pointless. It's far too late for that now anyway. The reason I can never tell you these things is that it's safer for you. Do you understand what I'm saying?" His tone is grave and his eyes resolute.

"No, I don't. I don't understand what you're saying. Safer? What does that even mean? How can it be *dangerous* to know who you are?"

Jake's eyes plead with me, tortured pools of green. *I knew the name. We all know his name and what it means.* Seriously, who is this person sitting in front of me?

"You know, I thought I could wait, let you keep your secrets. But I can't live like that. Not now." My voice fades as breathlessness overtakes me. How much more is there? How much more am I in denial about? Do I keep moving the limits of what I'm willing to accept so I can be with him?

"I need you. I love you," he says quietly. "Nothing else matters."

Oh, that's cruel. I give him a look that I hope conveys I think it's cruel before lifting my glass and downing the rest of it. No, it matters. He *knows* it matters. It's why he can never tell me about it.

We can't keep doing this. Over and over. I need him to tell me it all now so that when it's over and I'm alone, I can tell myself it's because he left me no other choice.

"What are your other streams of income?" I ask. "I want to know." I don't want to know—I *need* to know.

His nostrils flare, and his mouth presses into a hard, stubborn line. He says nothing though. He studies me. Warning me, evading me. There's heat and desire in his eyes too, and from nowhere, the image of him taking me rough and hard and angry across the table currently wedged between us teases the front of my mind.

That's when I know I'll always want him. No matter what he is or what he's done, my body is conditioned to want him. I refuse to let it take control of me right now. To try and wash away the illicit thoughts I can almost taste on my tongue, I reach forward and refill my glass. Jake's eyes observe me with interest, but he says nothing, of course. He's going to make me play the stupid game of questions again. Nothing has changed since that night in the restaurant. That night now seems like years ago.

I'm still playing the game.

"Less legitimate. *Dangerous* to know. What does that even mean?" I muse aloud, lifting my glass to my mouth. As I swallow this time, the wine feels sweeter and thicker, far more potent. I look him over: the small scar on his eyebrow, the reddish scar on his neck I helped put there, his knuckles that always seem to be bruised or angry, the expensive watch on his left wrist. I think of Mark's words at Rob's dinner table too: *"Someone brave, connected, or fucking stupid."*

"I mean, are you a drug dealer?" It's a stab in the dark, but when his eyes flicker slightly, I know I've struck something.

"I'm not a drug dealer," he says carefully. *Too* carefully. I need to press on another spot.

"Okay. Do you make money from the supply or manufacturing of illegal substances?"

His eyes flicker before he lets out a small breath. "It's complicated, Alex."

Oh my god.

I push the wine away and sit forward. "What's complicated about it? You either do or you don't. There isn't anything complicated about it. It certainly won't be when you're arrested."

"That's not going to happen, Alex." There's an easy confidence in his voice that makes my blood boil.

"Oh, it's not? You know that for a fact, do you?"

"Yes." Again, he looks staggeringly confident.

I can't breathe. I'm going to be sick again.

I push the chair back and stand, crossing the kitchen to the window to get some air into my lungs. I hear him stand and come toward me then stop. I don't know how close he is, and I don't want him near me. I feel him slipping farther and farther away though, becoming far less manageable.

"Alex," he says from close behind. Too close. "Say something."

I whip around to face him. "What about where these drugs of yours end up, Jake? Schoolchildren. Addicts. Families torn apart. Do you care about any of that? About the damage they do?"

He sighs, looking less sure of himself than he did a moment ago. "Alex, you need to try to understand that this shit happens all over the world. It'd be happening anyway—they'd be coming in from somewhere. It's how the world works. At least our stuff is clean." He sounds almost reasonable.

"Oh my god, you're serious?" I shake my head. "How dare you? *Our* stuff? I'm a bloody doctor—I see firsthand what *your stuff* does to people. I think what you mean is that it may as well be you profiting from other people's misery. That's really what you mean, isn't it? I mean, you have to pay for your duplex apartment in Central London and your fancy car somehow, right? Is that how you bought your nightclub too, Jake?" I'm shouting now, and I can't breathe properly. He moves toward me. "Don't you dare come near me. I don't want you near me. You disgust me."

He freezes, eyes wide and afraid. "Alex, please . . ."

"What else? There's more, I assume? With people like you, there's never just one thing, is there? Keep going. The safe stuff, of course—the stuff it's not dangerous for me to know about. Human trafficking, perhaps?"

"Don't be ridiculous."

"Oh, so that's a ridiculous income stream, is it? Sorry—my mistake. But drugs are fine? Selling people poison is fine?"

"You dish poison out too, baby. Only difference is yours comes on a piece of paper with your signature at the bottom." He flares.

Before another thought enters my head, I bring my hand up and slap him hard across the face. He barely flinches, but my hand stings, and so I know I've hit him hard.

Immediately, his eyes soften, remorse seeping into them, but I turn away from him. I can't look at that. I feel bone-tired, bodily exhausted, a deep, aching tiredness that makes my head feel too heavy for my neck. I don't want to hear anymore. I don't think I can stomach it.

In the garden, a sparrow sits on the bird feeder and stares back at me with what looks like pity. It looks stronger than I feel. Even its tiny little legs, which normally appear so fragile, look strong compared to how mine feel right now.

"Say something, Alex," he says.

I sigh and close my eyes. "What's left to say? I told you to tell me the rest."

"I don't want to hurt you anymore. I never wanted to hurt you."

As I press my eyes shut tighter, I feel the tears squeeze out and down my face.

"Then you should go. Your being here hurts me," I tell him in a dead voice. When he doesn't move, I turn to face him, watching as his face twists at the sight of me and my pathetic tears. I use the back of my hand to wipe them away. "I want you to leave now."

He shakes his head. "Please don't do this to us again, Alex."

I want to hiss and snarl at him then. How dare he? "I haven't done this—you have!" I cry. He doesn't argue with me as he drops his gaze to the floor. "You were right. You and I don't work. I can't be with a man like you—someone who does the things you do. I can't—"

He moves toward me quickly, his hands on my arms, pulling me into his body, the heat and smell smothering. "All of that was before. But if you give me time, baby, please. I'm working on it. I'll do whatever I need to do to change for you. To be who you need me to be. But I can't lose you, Alex. I'm done if I lose you. I told you that." He has my head in his hands now, eyes searing into mine. "I love you. You love me. We can sort this. Please let me sort this." His voice is scratched raw, and normally, it would stir my insides into a frenzy, breaking everything else down so I can't think straight. So all I can think of is him.

But I don't feel any of that now.

It feels as if there's nothing to break down. I feel empty. As if he's taken everything I feel for him and turned it into something else. Something that was never real. Something made of paper or air or nothing.

You know exactly who I am, Alex. You've always known.

"No." I shake my head and push at his body. "I can't. I can't love you. I can't be with you." I'm not saying it to him, I don't think; I'm saying it to myself. A warning or an alibi for the pain that will come later.

When he steps back from my body, I feel so bloody cold.

"You *can't* love me, or you *don't* love me?" he asks, eyes glittering and hard. "'Cause those are two completely different things, baby. One of them makes you a coward, and the other makes you a fucking liar."

Under the weight of his stare, I think about that. I suppose I'm a coward then. A coward like him.

"I don't know . . . it doesn't matter," I mutter, looking away from him again, back out the window. I need him to go now. The sooner he leaves, the sooner the pain can really start. The sooner it starts, the sooner it will be over.

"Course it fucking matters," he growls. "Alex, you're the woman I waited my whole fucking life for. You're everything I want."

Why does he say these things? How am I supposed to hold onto the strength I need to end this when he's saying things like this? I don't turn around to see his face because I'm not strong enough for that. I grip onto the sink hard and watch the sheets we made love on this morning blow gently in the wind. They're stark white with faint pink petals on them. The sparrow from the bird feeder is perched on top of them now and creeps across the top of the line, tentative.

"Please take the envelope with you when you go," I tell him.

He doesn't respond, but eventually, I hear the sound of his footsteps going across the slate floor. The sound of him lifting the godforsaken envelope. When I hear him come back toward me and stop, I hold my breath.

"So, this is it this time? You're gone."

I can't decide if it's a question or not. From somewhere, I find the strength to look at him. His face is ashen, eyes wide and unbarred. He's so bloody beautiful. Painfully so.

"Did you expect anything else? Once I knew everything. Isn't it what you said would happen—that I'd run a mile? This is what you meant, isn't it?"

A sad look crosses his face. "Yeah, I expected it. Just deluded myself, I guess. Thought maybe once I had you, once you loved me, all the dark shit wouldn't matter."

So then, I confirmed his worst fears. I was everything he expected. The thought depresses me, as though I've let him down.

"But I'm glad it matters to you. It should. It should matter to someone like you." He nods. He has that look on his face again, and I think maybe he's going to come toward me again, pull me into him again, not let me go this time. I can't decide if I want him to, because I don't think I'm strong enough to resist it.

But when he moves, it's not toward me. It's away, and instantly, my whole body begins to throb with the weight of a heavy, suffocating loss. Quiet and slow, with shock the past few hours, my brain explodes with a torrent of thoughts.

He's leaving. He needs to. He can't. I can't let him go. I need to let him go. I love him. I'm in love with him. I can't be without him. I know what that feels like, to be without him. It's walking, living, breathing death. I can't go through that again. What am I doing?

I stand there and watch as his tall, powerful form distances itself from me. When he stops at the kitchen door and turns back to me, my heart stops beating entirely—I'm certain of it. He stares at me for a long time before speaking, and the look in his eyes is so painful to see.

"You know, I wish I'd been born into a different life, Alex. I wish I'd been born into the kind of life where I could have met you and you could have been with me without any of the dark shit or the secrets and the things you can't ever forgive me for. When I was little, I used to daydream I'd been dropped into someone else's life, 'cause I've never felt as if I belong in this one." He stops and looks uncomfortable, embarrassed even, before his eyes are serious again. "I stopped dreaming about that, but I've never stopped wishing I were someone else, that I were living a different life. What I did, I did to survive. To make a life for myself that was in some way tolerable. Then it was to make my son's life better than what I had. I know you won't understand that, and I get it. I get why to you, I should have made differ-ent choices, and you know what? You're right. If faced with better options, I would have made different choices. But you know something? I wouldn't change any of it now. Not a single fucking thing. Know why?"

Strong. His words are always so strong. There's so much strength in what he just said. Since I don't know where my voice has gone, I shake my head. No, I don't know why he wouldn't change a thing.

"Because everything I've ever done, every bad choice I ever made, was worth it the night I met you. I'd never have been there that night if I hadn't made those choices, and I believe in things happening for a reason. It's one of the only things I believe in, actually." His eyes shine with conviction. "I don't judge you for not wanting to be with a guy like me. You deserve better, I know. I always told you that. But I guess I believed you when you told me I was wrong."

As I stare back at him, every single second of our relationship plays through my mind like a movie. A beautiful movie in which everything is given a sort of nostalgic romanticism: the night we met, the night in his office, the first time we made love. All of it plays quickly through my mind against a beautiful piano instrumental, and it looks perfect. Every single frame of it.

"You shouldn't have listened to me, Jake. I didn't know what I was doing." I shake my head. "I didn't know anything." I knew some things. But mainly, it was secrets and evasions and delusions.

He closes his eyes as though the very sight of me is causing him pain. When he opens them again, they're glittering green.

"I never wanted any of this," he tells me.

Of course he didn't. Why would anyone want *this*? I've no idea what he wants me to say in response to that, so I just nod and steady myself by turning back around to look out the window.

"Please go now. I need you to go now," I beg.

"Alex, please . . ."

"Please go." I'm pleading now. Why isn't he leaving? He needs to go. I need him to leave.

When I turn to face him, I almost shatter completely. His face is unbearably sad, filled with torment, and it twists everything up inside me tightly. Then, with a nod of finality, he turns and walks out of the kitchen, out of my house, and out of my life.

After I hear the door close, it's a full five minutes before the tears come again. I know this because I stare at the clock the entire time. It was 6:10 p.m. when he walked out, and I didn't feel the sharp sting of slow-moving tears roll down my face until 6:15 p.m. They seem to come from my throat or my lungs, and they burn on the way up, suffocating me. As my body finally gives in, I slide down to the floor and cry like a child. Great, heaving sobs that shake my entire body. A moment later, Fred comes padding up to me and curls up at my feet, nudging his head against my knee in what feels like solidarity.

He's actually gone. I *let* him go. I'm in love with him, and I let him go. I had to. I *had* to.

Except how do I live like this? Without him?

My heart feels as if it's been battered and tortured and left out to die. As the tears keep falling, Fred presses his warm little body tighter against me, purring softly.

I'll be fine. It's young, my heart. It will recover. It has to.

EPILOGUE

S O, THIS IS WHAT IT FEELS LIKE. LOSING SOMETHING PROPERLY. IT
feels as if my guts have been ripped out by a pack of hungry dogs.
I had a taste of it last week, of course, but this feels different. This
time, she knows.

I knew the pig wanted her. I saw how he looked at her that night. I saw,
and it made me want to fly across the table and rip his fucking throat out.
Except I couldn't because I wanted to impress her. Beating her friends to a
fucking pulp wouldn't have done that. In the end, he did it his way, and, I
have to hand it to him, it was seamless. Clean. There's a part of me that still
wants to rip his throat out, but there's another part of me—a deep, masoch-
istic part—that almost wants to thank him.

Because now she knows, and I didn't have the guts to tell her myself.
I'll only ever wonder how long I'd have been able to hide it all from her. I
mean, how do you tell your darkest, most horrendous shit to someone like
her? How do you tell someone who looks at you like you're something special that you're a piece of shit?

You don't.

I knew she'd walk away when she found out, and that I'd have to let her,
because a woman like her doesn't belong with someone like me.

For almost twenty minutes, I sit outside her house with the overwhelming urge to go back in. Crawling on my hands and knees like the piece of
shit I am. I should tell her I'm not letting her go and promise her the moon
on a fucking stick if she'll stay with me. I'll beg her if I have to. I'll tell her
I need her because my life before her was a cycle of shit, and I'm probably
going to drown in it without her.

But I don't crawl back in. Because I don't deserve something as perfect
as her. Alex was unconnected to everything else in my life. She was pure and
perfect, and I loved her for it. An idea pops into my head of taking Caleb and
her and running off someplace where no one knows me. I almost groan out

loud from how much I want that. Would she ever even agree to something like that? Maybe. Before. Before I disgusted her. Before she couldn't love me.

I glance down at the pieces of paper and photographs on the passenger seat: pictures of Kev and me, Freddie and me, even Eddie Cartwright and me before I put him in a coma. The others are random: me with the Russians, Freddie and me standing by the docks, me putting Cale in the car, Freddie with Steph. They've been watching us for months, by the looks of it. It's not a surprise. Freddie instilled in us the notion they could always be watching. It's why we never do anything in public. It's why I'm not worried. I'd have been arrested by now if they had anything concrete. What I don't get is how they knew about Sharon. That I fucked her. Only two people know about that, meaning either Kev or Sharon has a bigger mouth than I thought.

As I glance back at the house, something pulls at me, urging me again to go back. To give in to the gnawing feeling that's been eating me up inside since I walked out of there. Then I remember the utter disgust on her face as she looked at me. The face that only this morning looked at me like I'd always wanted it to. The look she gave me when she thought I was a fucking rapist is all I can see now.

As I realize I'll probably never see her look at me like that again, my entire body clenches with rage and loss. I can't go back in there—not right now. Not until I've sorted it. And I know exactly who to start with.

I pick up my phone and dial. Kev answers on the first ring.

"Where are you?" I ask him before he has a chance to say hello.

"Dropping shit off for Fred. Why? You need something?" he says. It sounds echoey, as if I'm on speakerphone in his car.

"Meet me at the club in half an hour, yeah?"

"Yeah, cool, soon as I'm done here. Everything cool?" he asks. Kev would only ask me that question if he thought things were not cool, so by that assumption, I guess my voice is the giveaway.

"Not really, Kev, no," I say as I shove the contents of the file back into the envelope.

He snickers. "See, Jay, chicks are not worth the fucking hassle long-term, mate, I've told you. Headaches, the fucking lot of them."

"Thirty minutes, Kev," I say and hang up.

Kevin's thoughts on my relationship with Alex have never been welcome. I don't like the way he talks about women in general, and since it's far safer if no one knows how serious she was for me, I had to bite my tongue a few times whenever the subject of my "hot doctor" came up. I never wanted her involved in any part of my life; I wanted her separate. Always separate from the dark parts that could taint her. Kev is most certainly a dark part. Ours is a friendship forged by mutually destructive experiences, debts owed, and secrets kept. He's not the darkest taint though. Fred's that. Freddie's a fucking blackout.

With a final look back at her house, I start the engine. The next time I see her will be after I've sorted this. Then I'll come back and do the begging bit. I'm not above begging her. She's the only person I'd beg for anything. I'll worship at her feet for the rest of my fucking life if I have to.

The drive back to London I do in complete silence. Normally, I like music while I drive, turned up so loud it blocks out every other thought. Since I met her, that need has lessened. Maybe because since I met her, she's the only thing I can think about. I'm not thinking about deals or drops or Freddie or what sort of mess Kev will get us all into next. Instead, I think about her. As if she's a drug I need every minute of every day. Years ago, when I was using, it was to forget the pile of shit my life was. Now, *she* does that. She is how I cope. The only thing that can make my mood change in an instant. Thinking about her, seeing her, being with her. She's the most addictive drug I've ever fucking tried, and I know she's the kind you don't ever get over the craving for. Except I'll need to find some way to get over the craving, and fast, because she's gone.

She can't love me. I disgust her.

Paul and some bar staff are the only ones inside when I arrive at the club. Kevin's white BMW isn't parked around the back either, and the fact he's late only darkens my mood further. I nod at Paul as I walk through the place, the sense of achievement I normally get from being here doing absolutely nothing for me now. I couldn't give a shit if the club burned to the ground. My head is full of her—the sound of her voice when she told me she loved me this morning, then when she asked me to leave her alone. The look on her face when she said I disgust her. She didn't say she *doesn't* love me. Only that she can't.

That still means *something*. It means she still loves me.

My mind settles back on this morning when she told me she was in love with me. Why the fuck didn't I do more? Say more? What the fuck did I say? It felt like fireworks going off in my head, I remember that much. But I remember feeling guilty too. Guilty for making her love me. For making her believe I was good enough for her love. For making her think I could make her happy. *Fuck,* I want to make her happy, but some things, no matter how much you want them, just aren't fucking possible. It was always going to end like this. Once she knew. She was always going to leave me when she knew.

My office is cold, but I don't feel it. I never really feel the cold. I've always had an abnormally warm body temperature—some sort of evolutionary process that came about during my formative years, maybe. The consequences of Susan choosing vodka over paying the electricity bill.

The fridge is fully stocked, and the first thing I do is pull out a beer. Then I realize beer's not gonna do it, so I grab a bottle of Jack from the low cupboard next to the fridge instead. The cupboard is also fully stocked with four bottles of Jack from what I can see. Yeah, that should do it. For an instant, I contemplate the tequila, but I haven't touched it in nearly four years, and it ended up with me fucking Vicky in a pub toilet last time, so it's probably safer to steer clear of that. Not that there's any chance of me making that particular fucking mistake again. But there are plenty of others I could make instead.

I pour three inches of Jack. It's gone in four gulps, and so I refill my glass quickly, grabbing a handful of ice from the fully stocked bucket to throw that in too. I need to find out who stocks my office and give them a pay rise. Probably Gemma. She spends far too much time hovering about the vicinity of my office. The Jack burns my insides but sends a jolt of warmth to the ice-cold pit of my stomach.

Ten minutes later, as I'm staring out the window onto my club and feeling the effects of a third of the bottle, I hear a knock on the door and the sound of the code being punched in. Kev shuffles through it, smirking. He always looks as though he's smirking. Laughing at something unseen.

"All right, mate? How's it going?" His eyes flick to the bottle on my desk, and he raises his eyebrows. "That bad? Smart ones are always the worst. High fucking maintenance." He shakes his head and goes to take a seat on the low leather couch by the window. He props his legs up on the table and rests his arms behind his head, looking relaxed like he always does.

Even when shit is crumbling down around his ears, Kev wears it like a guy without a care in the fucking world. It's something I've always admired about him. It's the only thing I admire about him. He's a complete fucking sociopath.

As I stare at him, I wonder who would care if I put a bullet in him right now. He has a sister I'm pretty sure despises him, and a father in prison. No one would care. Freddie might be slightly pissed off that his most eager lap-dog is dead, and that would mean I'd have to fill the Kevin-sized whole for a while, but other than that . . .

I keep staring at him while the idea takes root in my head and settles comfortably.

"Did Freddie ask you to pay Sharon a visit, or was it your idea?" I ask, lifting the glass to my mouth. As soon as Alex told me that little nugget this afternoon, I knew who was responsible. I'm not sure the details are exactly like Mark the copper says, but this piece of shit in front of me is the reason Alex thinks I'm a woman-beating rapist.

Kev doesn't look surprised by my question. Probably knew I'd find out eventually. In fairness, I've been pretty distracted lately, but he would have known I'd get around to it at some point. He doesn't move or change position; he just continues to sit there looking relaxed and conscience-free.

"Fred still wanted his money. I offered to get it," he says, shrugging.

"From Sharon? I fucking told him *I'd* give him the money. To make up for the mess I made."

The night Alex sorted me, I called Freddie in Greece when I got home to apologize for losing my temper. I offered to pay Eddie's share since he wasn't in a position to make withdrawals. Freddie told me I wasn't thinking straight and that he would talk to me when he got back. He never mentioned it again.

"It wasn't your debt to pay, mate. Fred was never going to go for that," he explains. "You seriously think he'd let Tony, Eddie, and that psychotic bitch get away with swiping him? Eddie Cartwright deserved what he got." He sniffs. "You know what Fred said when I told him what happened? Why you went off? He asked why you never finished him. The cunt deserved what he got. He deserved worse than what he got, and there was no way Fred was gonna let you clear his fucking debt for him." He shakes his head and sits up, looking irritated. Looking at me as if I should know better than to question Freddie's way of doing things. As if I haven't lived my whole life by Freddie's way of doing things.

"So, he condoned what you did? He sent you over there to beat up a woman. Or did you improvise?" I ask.

Freddie has dark parts too. He's the fucking king of dark parts, but it seems out of character for him to order something like this. It's beneath him. This has Kevin written all over it.

"A few days after, while you were indisposed, he asked me to go see if I could get anything new out of her—with Eddie out of the way. He thought she might give up something on Tony's place in Malaga. It got kinda ugly. Course, she would have opened her mouth and her legs a whole lot easier for you, but that is one violent fucking bitch, mate. Think I still have the scratches." He shudders as though reliving a painful memory.

"Is that 'cause you fucked her when she didn't want you to? I imagine women tend to scratch when that sort of thing happens." I scowl.

He looks mildly annoyed now, as though maybe I've touched on some nerve he didn't know he had. "Wasn't like that at all. We had a few drinks, I said Fred was sorry about what had happened to Eddie but that this still needed sorting. She practically begged me for it, mate," he says. He doesn't flinch. He never flinches.

"So'd you break her jaw before or after she begged you for it? Just so I have it straight."

"Why the fuck are you so bothered about this, Jay? That fucking bitch could have killed you. She stuck a knife in your neck, for fuck's sake. She's a fucking lunatic." He holds his finger to his temple as he jumps to his feet. "She got what she fucking deserved!" He grabs the bottle of Jack, unscrews the cap, and downs a few large gulps before slamming the bottle back down on the desk angrily.

I take a moment before I speak to give him time to calm down. Kevin angry isn't something I like having to deal with. He's fucking unmanageable when he's a ball of pent-up rage. People get hurt when Kevin's angry. It's not me I'm worried about though. No—he'd leave here and take it out on some poor, unsuspecting person. Sharon again, maybe.

"So, what—you saying you did this for me, mate? Revenge for what she did. You put her in the hospital out of some sort of twisted loyalty to me?"

He licks his tongue across his mouth and squeezes his nose, snorting loudly to swallow down whatever remnants of shit he shoved up there before he came here. "I'm saying I didn't do anything she didn't fucking deserve. The bitch stabbed you." He reaches out to lift the bottle again, which he carries over to the large window. As he stares out of it, I watch the huge expanse of his back flex as he lifts the bottle to his mouth and drinks. Kevin is a huge guy, bigger than me and terrifying to most people, but there are only two things he's scared of: Freddie and me.

"You know they think I did it?" I say, and he turns around.

"Who does?" He looks angry again, alert and ready to defend my honor. He's loyal like that, in his own fucked up way.

"The filth." I lift my glass to my mouth. "Alex has a friend in the Met. He paid her a visit today. Told her they've reason to believe I beat and raped Sharon Cartwright."

Now, he looks concerned. Guilty even. That's a fucking first.

"Fuck . . ." He exhales. "Shit."

I chew my lip and nod at him before sitting up to refill my glass. "You fucked up, Kev. You went too far."

The fourth glass of Jack goes down much easier than any of the others.

"They've been watching again too." I open my top drawer, pull out the file, and slide it across my desk to him. He stops it with his hand before it slides onto the floor.

"Well, we'll have a word with Sharon, and she can tell them you had fuck all to do with it. But if she's told them she was raped, she's a lying fucking bitch, Jay, 'cause that's not what happened."

Talk to Sharon? Him *talking* to Sharon is part of the reason Alex can barely fucking look at me.

He lifts the photos and walks back over to the couch. I suppose it's possible he's telling the truth about what happened. Would Sharon fuck Kev consensually? Sure, why not. Would Kev beat her up afterward for not giving him what he wanted? Most definitely.

He flicks through the photos absently as he drinks. "Well, it's not as if it's a surprise. Fred knows they're watching him. They're always fucking watching him. They still haven't got a fucking thing." He shrugs.

I laugh and raise my glass. "Well, no. Not on Fred, they haven't."

"Or you. They've got shit all on you either, mate. Don't worry about it." He flicks through a few more of the photos, eyebrows raised. "So, he gave this to her? He showed her photos of Fred and us and told her about you?"

"He gave her the file. She never looked at any of it."

"Just as well. Don't imagine your hot little doctor would be too excited to know how you spend your free time," he snickers.

I feel my fist curl around the glass. *She was all right, wasn't she? Did you see that fucking arse? Wouldn't mind a go on a bit of posh cunt like that, mate—know what I mean?* All things he said about her in the car on the way home the night she fixed me. I wanted to punch him right there and then. But I couldn't 'cause that would mean it bothered me, and that would mean she was important, and that would mean she wasn't safe. I still made a silent promise to myself that I'd kill him before I let him touch her.

"I told her some of it. She kicked me out," I say.

"Like what?" He raises his eyebrows.

"Only what she needed to know. And only about me. She knows nothing. Calm down," I tell him. I squeeze my eyes shut tight with my fingers.

I mean, you have to pay for your duplex apartment in Central London and your sports car somehow, right? Is that how you bought your nightclub too? You disgust me.

"Probably for the best, mate. You and her." He shakes his head and twists his mouth up. "I mean, don't get me wrong, she was worth a dip, but this thing long-term? Nah. Didn't work for me," he says conversationally, as if we're two friends talking about women over a drink. "You're better off out of it. Women are cunts, you know this, which is funny 'cause it's the only thing good about them." He chuckles at his own joke as he sips his drink.

How the fuck have I put up with his shit for fifteen fucking years?

I think about the gun in my top drawer again and plan out how quickly I could get it out and pull the trigger before he even realizes what's happened. I'm more than halfway pissed if I'm thinking about shooting my best friend in the head in my office. I'd never dream of doing it here. Who'd help me clean up if I did?

Paul probably would. He's never come out and said it, but I'm pretty sure he despises Kev. Yeah, he'd help.

I'm fucking drunk. Or insane.

I need a cleaner plan than that. Than shooting Kev in the fucking head. I need a plan that'll get rid of all the dark parts of my life in one fucking go. A plan that makes me worthy of her. A plan that gets rid of the bastard sitting in front of me and the bastard he takes orders from. The same bastard *I* take orders from. The same bastard who calls me the son he never had.

It's not as if the idea comes to me in a flash. It entered my mind briefly the night she told me the guy sitting across from us at dinner was some pig from the Met. Only for a second or two, but I thought about it. I thought about how I'd give up every single one of these pieces of shit if it meant I'd get to keep her. But I was a coward then.

I'm still a fucking coward. But when it creeps back into my mind now, it's brighter and louder, and it takes the breath right out of my fucking lungs. It's still the kind of thing reserved for the lowest of the low. For the scum and the bottom-feeders and the people without an ounce of self-respect. But that was before. *Before her.*

Now, getting the fuck out of the dark is all that matters. I've lived this life for far too long anyway. I want a different life. I always have. She offered me glimpses of it, of what my life could feel like with her in it. *She* is the life I want. And if I can pull this off, then taking her and Caleb and starting somewhere else might be possible.

My heart beats fast and loud, and whether it's with fear or anticipation, I honestly don't know. But my mind seems to be hurtling forward now, and there's no way of stopping it or changing its direction. Not now.

"Kev, I have to make some calls. Do you mind?" I say as I sit up in the chair, the back of my neck prickling.

He shrugs and grabs the bottle of Jack then stands up, his knees cracking as he does. "Just tell me you're not gonna phone her and grovel, Jay. You're better than that."

I shake my head. "Nah, fuck her. Plenty more where she came from," I lie.

Lying I'm good at. Always have been.

"Good man," he says, raising the bottle toward me. "That's my boy. Speaking of cunts, is that hot little Gemma still working here? She has got some set of tits on her. You've had them, right?" He smirks.

I nod and smile back. "Yeah, they're pretty tasty, mate. Think I saw her downstairs."

"You're not going back there, are you?" He leaves the question hanging, and I shrug.

"Plenty more where she came from too. Go for it. Do me a favor and try not to upset her, yeah? She's good at her job."

He holds his hands up as if to say, "Would I?" to which the answer is yes.

When Kev leaves, I pull out my mobile and search the number of the switchboard. Before I hit dial, I stand up and go to check both the doors to my office are locked tight, so that even someone with a code can't get in from the outside. Then I walk across the office to the large glass window and stop.

As I look at the place again, a small tingle of uncertainty creeps over me. I worked my fucking arse off for this place. The things I did to get it I'm not proud of, but everything past the front door is legit. I'm proud of that.

Though, what does any of that mean when I disgust her, and she can't love me? It's a building at the end of the day. A legitimate income stream, as she called it, not a life. This place doesn't make me smile or give me a single moment of satisfaction that comes close to what she does. She and my son are the only things that matter now. And I've always fucking said, if you want something, go get it. Do whatever you have to do to get it.

Guess this is where I see if I practice what I preach, huh?

The number rings through and is picked up by a bored-sounding woman who, by the sounds of it, has about ten minutes left until the end of her shift. She's mentally clocked out already.

"Detective Mark Holmes, please," I say.

"Who's calling?" she asks me, still bored.

"Dr. Alex Marlowe," I say for the record, and she tells me to wait a moment.

Some shitty hold music starts to play down the other end of the line. Below me, I watch as Kevin walks up to where Gemma is wiping down the glass bar, crowding into her. I roll my eyes as she startles, mouthing something smart I can't make out. He says something, and she hits him lightly, glancing briefly up at my window.

"Alex, are you okay? You should have called my direct line." He sounds concerned. As if he has the right to be.

"It's Jake Lawrence. Sorry to get you all excited for nothing," I say.

He's stunned, because he says nothing for a minute. "Yeah, I'd say surprised is more accurate," he replies.

"You must be pissed off then—you know, since surprises are your thing today." I take another sip from my glass and let the Jack rest on my tongue for a second before swallowing.

"So, to what do I owe the honor?"

"Well, first, cheers for the photos. I don't normally photograph that well, but I looked really fucking good in those. Had no idea you liked me so much." I try to smile, but I'm starting to doubt what I'm about to do now. I'm more than halfway pissed. I've decided to do this under the influence of alcohol, and nothing I've ever done under the influence has been a good fucking idea.

Then I think about her.

Smiling at me this morning over breakfast, hair tucked behind her ear, cheeks flushed. Pale, flawless skin screaming to be touched and kissed. The ache in my chest gets stronger and louder until it sounds like a drumbeat, want and need and loss rocking my entire body.

No, it's the right decision. It's the only fucking decision. I'm just a coward who needs to be half-pissed to make it.

"What do you want, Lawrence?" he sighs.

"You know I'm single now, right? So, if you wanted to fuck me in the arse, you could just come over and ask. I'll still break your jaw, but you could at least fucking ask."

"Threatening a police officer?" he says. "You're smarter than that. Come on."

"Oh, you know I am, mate. You fucking know I am. Enjoy yourself today, did you? Bet you felt like a real fucking hero today, didn't you? If you wanted me that much, you only had to ask, mate, it's all I'm saying."

Mark's chuckle down the phone makes me want to put my fist through the window. I remember quite clearly the way he looked at her across the dinner table last week. I'm certain ninety percent of his visit to her was about wanting to fuck her. Sure, he'd like to put Freddie or me or both of us away, but this was mainly about Alex. Seems we have at least one thing in common.

"You're not my type," he says.

"No, but Alex is, isn't she?" I say as I take another sip, circling my tongue around the Jack before I swallow it.

"Is this why you called, Jake? To talk about your *ex*-girlfriend?" He sighs again. The word "ex" is like a kick in the balls. "Okay then. Any tips or advice for me? Apart from not being a lying fucking lowlife, obviously. Any ticklish spots? What about how she likes it?" he says quietly, and my hand curls into a fist around the glass. An image of him with his arm draped over Alex's shoulder eating dinner in her friend's dining room flashes in front of my eyes, and I practically need to swallow down a roar.

Mine.

The word is strong and loud and clear.

Make it fucking happen then, coward.

"No, actually. I called to talk about Freddie Ward. You know the guy—the one from the photo you didn't wank over." My voice is clear, and my head is too, finally. I'm doing this.

His extended silence tells me he's as shocked as I expected he'd be. "I'm listening," he says eventually.

Yeah, I'll bet he's fucking listening.

"I'm guessing your buddies down there have been after him for a while. I'm also guessing you've made little to no progress on that." I swig back the last of the bitter liquid courage.

"Are you going to get to the point?" he asks, but I can practically hear the hard-on he has over the sheer thought of putting Freddie Ward away. At being the one to finally put him down.

"Yeah. So, I might be able to help you out with that. Providing you can offer me something worthwhile in exchange," I say in a calm, clear voice I barely even recognize. "I want to make a deal."

And with that, it's done. A police informant. The lowest of the low. The scum of the fucking earth.

But that means nothing now.

None of the shit I've lived my whole life by means anything now. She's what matters. Having her be able to love me is what matters. I just hope it's enough.

'Cause otherwise, I'm a fucking dead man.

ACKNOWLEDGMENTS

Firstly, thank you to anyone who read this book in its very earliest of versions. Your words of encouragement and love for it are the reason it is here in this form today.

Thank you to my little group of Jake trash who helped me through the huge editing process: Niccie, Gail, and Emma.

Thank you to my redheaded writing sister Lindsey, who is always telling me I'm a far better writer than I actually am—one of these days I'm going to believe you.

Thanks to Bryony Leah for the beautiful copy edit—you took this huge albatross of a book and helped make it into something I'm proud of. You're really a writer's dream.

And finally, thank you to Joel. Thanks for listening to my rambling, incoherent plot detail and helping me out of holes. Thanks for all the back massages and the glasses of wine.

ABOUT THE AUTHOR

Scarlett writes romance, fantasy, and fanfiction on Wattpad and this is her first self-published novel. She lives in a small village in Scotland but still dreams of emigrating to Canada. She's a self-proclaimed Cat lady and fangirl who writes in her spare time.

If you'd like to read more of her work, you can do so here:
www.wattpad.com/user/ScarletteDrake

Or you can follow her on social media

Twitter here: twitter.com/ScarletteDrake

Instagram here: www.instagram.com/scarlettedrake

Made in the USA
Las Vegas, NV
13 October 2021

32229337R00193